THE MOSLEY
RECEIPT

By the same author

THE MOSLEY RECEIPT

KENNETH ROYCE

STEIN AND DAY/Publishers/New York

First published in 1985
Copyright © 1985 by Kenneth Royce
All rights reserved, Stein and Day, Incorporated
Designed by Louis A. Ditizio
Printed in the United States of America
STEIN AND DAY/*Publishers*
Scarborough House
Briarcliff Manor, N.Y. 10510

Library of Congress Cataloging in Publication Data

Royce, Kenneth.
  The Mosley receipt.

  1. Mosley, Oswald, Sir, 1896–   —Fiction. I. Title.
PR6068.098M6 1985   823'.914   84-40729
ISBN 0-8128-3029-6

Corrupt influence, which is itself the perennial spring of all prodigality, and of all disorder; which loads us, more than millions of debt; which takes away the vigour from our arms, wisdom from our councils, and every shadow of authority and credit from the most venerable parts of our constitution.

Burke 1780

THE MOSLEY RECEIPT

1

*T*OM Moody was taking a bath when the two men let themselves into his small Fulham apartment. For a retired detective chief superintendent, his home security was far less than adequate. He had always maintained that he had nothing worth stealing, an attitude he would have scorned in others.

It was ten years now since Moody had retired from the force. He had been an exceptionally good policeman. Opportunities to take cash on the side had been many and some of the sums offered would have made him rich, but he had a fortunate attitude toward money; as long as he had enough to keep his family modestly comfortable he had been satisfied. His ambitions had never been financial. His present apartment reflected this clearly.

Retirement was relative. Too good and far too experienced a man to waste, he had been used in many ways by H.M. Government agencies.

He did not hear the outer door open for he was splashing about and deep in thought. He was not often troubled, his placid disposition coped with most problems, but now he was worried more than at any time in a long and distinguished career. The bathroom door was opened before he could move and the automatic pistol that pointed at his dripping chest ensured that he remained where he was. Moody recognized the hard face above the gun but hid the fact with his fear.

The man came farther into the bathroom and stood near the taps, looking down at Moody with a killer's indifference. The second man squeezed past his colleague and went to the end of the bath so that he was slightly behind Moody; he was apparently unarmed and a stranger to Moody.

"Stand up," the gunman ordered.

"Don't be stupid."

"Stand up."

Moody suffered the vulnerability of being naked. The feeling was psychological; a bullet would pierce him whether or not he was dressed. "If I stand and you shoot me, I'll only finish where I am."

"This is the last time. Up." The voice was coarse.

Moody eyed the gun, then the face above it. He was not sure what they really wanted of him. He placed his big hands on the side of the bath and his head came forward slightly as he levered himself up. He had risen no more than an inch or two when he realized what was to happen.

He was too late to react. As he took his weight on his arms and as his head dipped he was coshed savagely and expertly at the base of his skull. He fell back with a splash that sent water cascading over the floor. The man with the cosh quickly pocketed it, grasped Moody's gray hair with both hands, pulled the head clear of the water, then smashed it down viciously against the back edge of the bath. Blood began to trickle into the water, increasing as the body slid down and the head slowly submerged.

The man with the gun holstered it, leaned across to the bath rack, picked up the tablet of soap, and dropped it into the bath.

"Nasty slip," he commented dryly.

"Yeah. Nasty."

"Make sure he's dead."

"He's croaked all right."

"I said make sure."

The second man groped beneath the water for one of Moody's wrists. The head was fully under the water by now and there were no air bubbles, but a cagey man might hold his breath if conscious. "He's dead." The man let Moody's arm drop back into the bloodied water. He held his hands over the bath while he used his handkerchief to dry off.

"Okay, let's go over the place. And watch how you do it."

SCOTT READ THE short obituary. He sat back sadly, recalling all the good things about Tom Moody. The clatter of Lulu's typewriter

10

from the "cell" next to his office jarred him. He closed the communicating door as the currently redheaded Lulu gave him a bright, wide-eyed look of surprise. Back at his desk he abstractedly watched the dim moving shadows of Charlie Hewett, his office manager, and the young clerk beside him at the travel counter on the other side of the thick, translucent glass partition.

Tom Moody brought back many memories to Willie "Spider" Scott. Moody was the only policeman whom Scott had unconditionally liked from their first meeting. The combination of an ex-cat burglar and a detective chief superintendent had been strange, and they had hidden much from each other. Yet beneath the superficial suspicion had been a mutual respect. A deep trust had grown between them as circumstances had forced the issue.

Scott reached for the telephone to inform Maggie, then thought better of it. It was the wrong time for that. He read the short obituary again. There was no mention of how Moody had died; he couldn't have been that old. Sixty-five maybe? But Tom had always been fit and healthy. It was far too soon.

The telephone rang and Scott jerked from his reverie. But Moody's death left a deep impression on him.

DETECTIVE SUPERINTENDENT GEORGE Bulman did not read of Moody's death but heard of it on the police grapevine. Moody had been out of the force for some years so that Bulman knew of him more by reputation than actual association. They had worked together once, briefly, and long after Moody's retirement. It was then that George Bulman had learned that Moody's retirement was really a sideways shift to the same gray area where Bulman himself operated— an indistinct zone, carrying police rank and with their facilities, but operationally closer to Special Branch and MI5. Bulman saw himself as something of a liaison officer, but that designation hardly described his work.

So Tom Moody had slipped on a bar of soap and had cracked his head open on the bath. Baths had been dangerous since they stopped making them with a porcelain lining. As Bulman directed his chunky figure toward New Scotland Yard, apparently impervious to the traffic and to the crowds milling around him, he reflected that not everything about modern living was worthwhile. The stiff breeze cut over the almost-convict crop of his sparse, dark hair, and he reflected that it was time he bought a hat. He rubbed his roughcast face with gloved hands as he crossed the street toward the revolving sign outside the police block. It was midsummer and it felt like November.

Bulman's office had been partitioned off; two-thirds for himself and a third for Detective Sergeant Haldean. The partition was so thin that both men wondered why anyone had bothered, except that Bulman's rank demanded a separate office. But he was not in the police as the rest of them saw it, so the compromise over accommodation was a back-handed snub.

The desk was government issue but the captain's chair of studded leather was his own. He sat down and rifled through the messages on his desk. "Who's Mrs. Moorcroft?" he bawled through the open door.

The unseen Haldean's voice came back. "The daughter of Mr. Moody. She wants to talk to you."

"Tom Moody?"

"The legendary."

Bulman gazed at the note and put it aside. The office, small and lackluster as it was, boasted one unusual innovation. It possessed the most up-to-date combination wall safe, and the wall had been reinforced to support it. He crossed to the safe and unlocked it: not even Haldean knew its combination. He withdrew two folders and returned to his chair, leaving the safe door open as a challenge to anyone who might be foolish enough to go near it while he was there. When he had finished with the files, he removed his gloves and then rubbed his hands and loudly complained of the cold and lack of heating. In the next office Haldean heard but made no comment: George Bulman was looking for an argument.

By mid-morning Bulman had caught up with his telephone messages, including that from Mrs. Moorcroft. At midday he returned the files to the safe and locked it. He then left the office without telling the resigned, but frustrated, Haldean where he was going or when he would be back.

He met Mrs. Moorcroft at a basement bar in Northumberland Avenue off Trafalgar Square. He had tried to get there before she did, but he picked her out sitting alone in a far corner of the bar. As he weaved through the tables toward her, she glanced up uncertainly. She smiled slightly; Bulman's pointed and almost aggressive approach could not be a try-on.

12

"Mrs. Moorcroft?" He smiled, and his craggy face changed completely, the stone image splintering, the dark eyes softening.

"Mr. Bulman? How did you know me?"

"Years of practice." He asked what she was drinking and returned to the bar for a gin and tonic and a pint of ale. He sat opposite her. Betty Moorcroft was an attractive woman in her late thirties. There was an open freshness about her that Bulman liked on sight. She was dressed soberly in a neat suit and her hair was long and dark. "You have your father's eyes," Bulman observed. "And that can't be bad."

She smiled, toying with the stem of her glass. "It helps that you remember him."

"I worked with him only once and that was very briefly and some time ago, but he had the sort of face you remember. I'm sorry to hear about his accident. Very sorry. Would you rather I dropped the subject?"

"Does it upset me, you mean? Of course it does. I loved my father. You might think of him as an outstanding policeman, but I can only think of his sadness, particularly since Mum died."

"He had you," Bulman smiled, raising his pint. "That must be a plus."

She gave him a skeptical glance. "Are you married, Mr. Bulman?"

"Married? What's that?"

She laughed a little. "You have a way in spite of . . ." She floundered.

"My ugly mug?" He was teasing her now. "That's my secret weapon. Nobody rates me. Now, how can I help you?"

Betty Moorcroft considered her answer carefully. Her features straightened, and Bulman could now see that she was drawn and worried. She stared at her untouched drink. "Are they sure it was an accident? Absolutely sure?"

Bulman lowered his drink slowly. He had come with an open mind, but he had not expected this. "You mean you don't think it was?"

She was flustered by his bluntness, her gaze leaving his and her hands motioning helplessly. "Put like that I can't answer you. I can't imagine my father slipping on a bar of soap. Can you?"

"He might have slipped anyway, without the soap. Happens all the time. It's happened to me. He *was* getting on."

"Rubbish. He could have taken you on. He was young for his age, active and fit."

13

Bulman was seeing another side of her; determined, with strong beliefs. Just like her father. "He still could have slipped."

"You say you've done the same. What happened?"

He stared at her, took his time. "You're implying he would know how to fall? Even in a split second?"

"I've seen him do it. We had a dog once who ran straight across him as he was jogging. I remember yelling out in panic, and I can still see it in slow motion. Dad turned as he crashed, lifted his head, and took his weight on one shoulder."

"There's not much room in a bath to do that. He couldn't have avoided the sides." Bulman held up a placating hand as he saw her scathing doubt. "All right. You're suggesting he simply wouldn't have fallen that way. Have you passed this on to the police?"

"You *are* the police."

He glanced across at her wryly. "I sometimes forget. But I really mean the division who dealt with the accident."

"I prefer to tell *you*. You know that my father did work for—others."

"He told you that?"

"Be your age, Mr. Bulman. Father was a clam when he wanted to be. When he closed up on me I knew he was beavering at something or other."

"I wish you'd be straighter with me. You're all innuendo. Nothing you've said so far would warrant any kind of inquiry. What was he on at the time?"

"How can I answer that? How can I give you anything but innuendo? He did not discuss his cases. But over the last few weeks of his life he became morose and withdrawn. He was not ill, but there was something very much on his mind."

"He was worried?"

"There were times when he appeared to be very frightened."

Solid Tom Moody frightened? A man who had faced a gun more than once without turning a hair? Had the job finally got to him? Bulman took a longer look at Betty Moorcroft. Essentially feminine, there were still visible traces of her father about her. She did not appear to be a girl who would panic or have fanciful ideas. Bulman shook his head. "It's not enough, Betty. Fear might have erupted from his private life."

"*No.*"

He did not argue. He sat back and eyed what remained of his ale. The

14

room was crowding up, the noise level rising with the smoke. He shook his head again slowly. "I can now see why you singled me out. He must have talked about *me* sometime or you wouldn't be sitting here."

"Only that he respected you. As he was not in the force at the time, I concluded that you and he were on similar, non-police, capers. It was a long shot. I don't think I was wrong. You know very well that the Metropolitan Police Force won't act on what I have to say. They're dealing with black and white, evidence and villains. They'd listen and behind my back suggest that I was suffering an early menopause."

Bulman finished his drink thoughtfully. "If you weren't Tom Moody's daughter, I might think the same. You haven't touched your drink, and that offends my mean nature. How can you take away a drink in a doggie bag?"

She raised her glass, knowing that he wanted time to think. And then she said, "If I am only partly right about the work you do, you will be much nearer the source who would know if my father was working on a job."

"You're shrewd, Betty."

"Shrewdness is an attribute I could do without." She hesitated before adding, "I've wracked my brains for something to help you. I've been through his flat. There's nothing at all that might be useful. The only thing I know, which might not be connected in any way, is that he made a couple of visits to the Isle of Wight during the last two months."

"Maybe he needed a break. It's warmer down there."

"The first time he stayed the night. The second time he came back the same day. That's not a break."

"Did he tell you he was going there?"

"No. He always gave me the key when he went away. The second trip he expected to stay the night and surprised me when he returned that evening. I don't know who he went to see but I do know where he went. Albany Prison."

Bulman gazed at his empty glass. Before he could ask the obvious question, she gave him the answer.

"I had the briefest glimpse of a prison visitor's pass. The name Albany was rubber-stamped in big print at the top right-hand corner of the pass."

This was true, Bulman reflected. The passes were standard, Home Office issue, number 252. "Couldn't you see the prisoner's name?"

"No. There's a small rolltop desk. It was open, and the pass was lying

15

there among other things. I merely noticed it as I went past to sit down. It was a small piece of paper about four inches square. There was a printed number at the top right-hand corner above Albany. Would that be a prisoner's number?"

"No. That's the number of the pass. The prisoner's number is on the top left-hand corner, followed by his surname. Underneath that are the name and address of the visitor."

"I'm sorry I didn't notice more, but there was no time and I had no idea my father was about to die."

"Did you by chance notice the date of issue underneath Albany?"

"No."

"Can you recall when he went?"

She opened her handbag and passed an envelope across. "The dates are in there. April 16 and May 28."

Bulman held the envelope between thumb and finger. "Is there a woman's intuition in any of this?"

"I see. Doubtful already?"

"I've been doubtful all along, but I'll still see what I can dig up."

"There's no intuition that I'm aware of. I'm a copper's daughter. My feeling is based on my own observations and his uncharacteristic state. I couldn't get a thing from him, but whereas before he would stop me by telling me I should know better than to ask, this time he made some really puerile excuses and tried to cover up."

"I must get back," he said. "I've a sergeant who thinks I nip out to have drinks with attractive women."

"And do you?"

Bulman rose to pull back her chair. "He's right this time."

Betty Moorcroft smiled. "You have my phone number. My address is in the envelope."

"Whether I come up with something or nothing will you accept what I say?"

"I'll have to." She picked up her gin and passed it to him. "You've had your eye on it long enough, you'd better finish it." Bulman sank it in a single gulp.

16

2

*T*HE spirit seemed to have gone from Maggie ever since her baby had been stillborn. Maggie and Spider Scott had waited so many years before marrying that their few friends had been resigned to its never happening. The coming baby had decided the issue and they had married as planned and everything was fine until the birth. Maggie had taken it badly. She saw it as some form of retribution. Her parents had never liked the idea of the marriage or even of the couple being together. All the objections to Willie Scott came to mind, all the warnings, all the words down the years. It seemed to her that the very act of marriage had perversely severed the link with him. Nothing was the same.

Scott had helped in every way he could, but her depression was undefeatable. He knew what had caused it, but that did not help to lift her from it. He too had been shocked by the loss of the baby, but never in their whole association had he seen Maggie like this. They had been married only a few months, yet he was already thinking that to leave her for a while might help her. His presence was a constant reminder of what had happened.

Now, as he went home to their apartment in St. John's Wood, Scott had dread in his heart. It was worse each time. He was sure that she blamed him. Not because he had not cherished and looked after her, he had done all of that, but because he had become involved with an old

17

antagonist. Maggie had been kidnaped and had suffered, and nothing could convince her that that was not the cause of her losing the child. If Scott had not become involved, she would not have subsequently suffered.

Scott would never tire of her, but he was increasingly convinced that she resented him. At times it was all right. She would cling to him, terrified to let go. But that usually happened with tears, and they had become noticeably fewer. Maggie had become no more than a dutiful wife. She said little, she cooked his meals, she read or watched television with no visible sign of enjoyment from either, or from him.

When he left the elevator he summoned his courage, unlocked the door, and, sick at heart, called out as he always did, "Maggie, I'm home." He dreaded the silence that so often followed.

"I'm in the kitchen."

He closed the front door quietly and stood by it for a while, relieved but still anxious. Her reply had not been bright as it used to be, but it encouraged him. He left the small hall and passed into the living room. The television was on with the sound turned off. He could see her through the open kitchen door.

"There's a drink on the sideboard."

He could not believe his luck. For some time now he had been used to pouring his own. He crossed to the nineteenth-century mahogany sideboard. Two whiskies were poured. By their color he could see that one had ginger ale, the other, his own, had water in it. He raised it and called out, "Cheers!" still nervous of going into the kitchen.

"It's strong," she called again.

"I know!" She had not forgotten to use chilled and filtered water. It tasted good. He usually went to the bathroom to scrub up at this stage, but he did not want to destroy the moment.

She came into the living room then, wiping her hands on a Mickey Mouse apron. She had lost weight over the past few months, her face more elfin than before. Her makeup could not completely hide the stress smears under her eyes, but she had made an effort. She still looked pale. She would always look beautiful.

Maggie did not come up to kiss him, as if she knew that to do so would be to go over the top. He had always greeted her with a kiss and a hug, but that stopped some time ago when he could no longer take the sometimes-chilling response.

She lifted her glass. "Cheers, Willie. I've been a bitch, haven't I?"

18

He had to be careful with his reply. This could turn out to be a brief recession from the darkness. She was looking for understanding, a word he dare not use for fear it might sound condescending. "Yes," he said with a slowly spreading grin. "In your place I'd have wrecked the furniture."

"And would have got it out of your system. I can't do that."

"Are the pills any help?"

"Pills? Damn the pills. I won't touch them. Doctors don't understand depression; give her a pill and a pat on the head. They don't realize there's nothing to cling to."

"Not even me?"

"You've been there to take the kicks. Don't think I don't know what it's been like for you." She put down the glass and stared up at him. He was over six feet tall and well proportioned. His wide eyed innocence made it impossible to believe that he had a criminal record and an expertise that authority had subsequently found convenient to exploit.

"Will you give me a kiss? A real one?"

He fumbled as he put down his glass. "Oh, Maggie, Maggie. Come here, you chump."

AFTER DINNER HE did not know whether to mention Tom Moody or not. Maggie had known and liked Moody. He did not have to tell her but had always found it difficult to withhold anything from her, She had a knack of knowing when something was on his mind.

When they were cradled together on the settee, he decided to put Moody out of his mind. It was not the time to mention it. As he felt the responsive warmth of Maggie, he counted the blessings he had at that time. She was by no means back to normal. Even over dinner there had been brief, silent lapses followed by a brittle smile, as she realized what had happened. There was a long way to go. But tonight was the most wonderful he could recall for a very long time.

GEORGE BULMAN RANG Scott the next day, and they arranged to meet for a snack at the Crown off Trafalgar Square. They arrived at the pub just after midday, before the lunchtime crowds came in. They took sandwiches and drinks to a table by the bottle-glass windows, and, as Bulman had paid for large whiskies, Scott knew that the detective wanted something more than a reunion.

Once enemies, the two men had been thrown together a few months

19

ago and had learned not only to rely on, but actually to like one another. The years of antagonism had now bonded into something quite different, although it was doubtful if either would admit it.

Scott raised his glass. "What do you want, George?"

Bulman appeared shocked. "To see you, old son. How's Maggie?"

"I think she's coming out of it. It's too soon to say, though."

"Thank God for that," Bulman said, genuinely relieved. "Do you think the Kransouski caper was really responsible for her losing the baby?"

"The doctors don't think so. It was traumatic, but there was no deep physical damage."

"But she blames it all on that? And you?"

Scott smiled wryly. "Did you hear about Tom Moody?"

"You read my thoughts, Spider. I was about to ask you the same. You worked with him once, didn't you?"

"You know bloody well I did. Years ago. Most of the time I didn't realize he was on my side, though."

"As I recall you were both on the committee of a prison-reform panel."

Scott nodded. "I thought the authorities were interested in an old crook's viewpoint of survival in prison. They had planted me on the committee to sniff out the chairman, who was up to his eyeballs in treachery. Tom Moody was my unknown backup."

"It was a compliment just the same. How did you get on with him?"

"Tom? One of the few straight coppers I've met and that includes you. I had tremendous respect for him. I liked him a lot."

"Not the type to panic then?"

"Solid as a rock."

"Was he afraid of anything?"

"How do you mean?" Scott stared across the table.

"Well, did he ever show physical fear? Did anyone threaten him enough to frighten him?"

"Tom didn't take kindly to threats. Whether he was scared by them or not I wouldn't know because he was not the type to show it."

"So he wouldn't back off from a threat?"

"I couldn't see him backing off from anything. He wasn't foolhardy, but I don't think he'd have known how to back off. Is someone raising doubts about his character?"

20

"On the contrary. I had a visit from his daughter yesterday. I got the impression from her that she thinks he was murdered." As Scott stared silently, Bulman added, "Fetch a round and I'll fill you in."

"You're a crafty, mean bugger," Scott observed as he drained his glass.

"Be quick, the bar's filling up."

SCOTT SAT BACK and listened, shutting out the noise around them. The sandwiches remained uneaten as Bulman talked; when he had finished he asked, "What do you think?"

"I'm hearing it secondhand. How serious was she?"

"Very. Steady like her dad. No fanciful stuff."

"I just can't see Tom Moody showing fear like that. It sounds as though his nerve had cracked.

"So what would crack his nerve, Spider?" Bulman bit into a sandwich.

"How would I know? I haven't seen the man for years. He could face a gun, unarmed. He wasn't afraid to die if it came down to it. He had this very high sense of duty. Unlike you."

"That's how I read him," Bulman replied ignoring the barb. "So if a threat to his life didn't scare him what the bloody hell did? Somebody else's life? Something different altogether?"

"I just can't see him showing open fear. In any circumstances. If he knew it was to be the end, he'd have told a gunman to steady his aim to make it clean. He *must* have cracked up."

"I don't think Betty Moorcroft thought that. Edgy, yes, frightened, but still doing whatever it was he was doing."

"Can't you find out what he was on?"

"Nothing. Not for months."

"Officially?"

"Officially."

"Would they tell you?" Scott insisted.

Bulman hesitated. "*We are only vulnerable and ridiculous through our pretensions. Mme. de Girardin.*" Scott gazed expressionlessly. "I'm a nobody in the scheme of things, Spider, but I'm satisfied that I didn't receive a brush-off. Had he been on a caper they might have claimed no knowledge. I doubt that they'd have told me what he was on even if he had been doing a job. But I got a definite no."

21

"What about Albany?"

"That's different. They're used to my asking for details of prisoners in various jails. The information given me was not complete."

Scott studied Bulman's expression. "How do you know?"

"I know of three villains who are in Albany, and two of them weren't mentioned. There may be others I don't know about."

"Are they holding out?"

"More likely someone is simply incompetent. Happens all the time. I'll go to Albany and find out for myself."

The bar was emptying as rapidly as it had filled. Bulman was eyeing his empty glass in a way that Scott chose to ignore. Scott glanced at the bar clock. "I must get back. Why have you told me all this?"

"I wanted your reaction to Tom Moody."

Scott gave Bulman a warning. "Don't try dragging me into anything, George. I've a chance of saving my marriage right now. Leave me out of it; Maggie could be driven over the edge.

Bulman, seeing that he would have to buy his own drink, reluctantly rose with Scott. "I realize that. You've been helpful just the same. It's probably pie in the sky. Betty Moorcroft's got it wrong. Tom slipped on the soap."

"HOW'S GEORGE BULMAN?" Maggie shouted as Scott opened the front door.

He tried to detect accusation in her tone but could find none. "How did you know?" He closed the door. She was standing in the middle of the living room and smiling, thank God. She held her arms out to him, and they embraced like new lovers, rocking and swaying.

"How did you know?" he repeated.

"Charlie Hewett told me you were out with George."

It was a long, long time since Maggie had troubled to ring the office. He suddenly felt tearful. It was all going too well; he had got into the habit of expecting the worst. "He wanted to see me about Tom Moody." It was out before he realized it.

Maggie stood back from him. She was wearing a simple, sleeveless green dress and her hair had been cropped close to her head in a twenties style. She was trying so damned hard for him that Scott could not speak for a moment. "You look terrific," he managed at last.

22

"Why didn't you tell me about Tom Moody? It was in the paper you brought home last night."

He noticed the drinks were on the sideboard, and he handed hers over. "I thought it might upset you."

"Well it did. But it helped take my mind off myself. He was a nice man. And he protected you. Didn't he save your life?"

"Sort of. Certainly I might have lost it had he not been around."

"Well?" Maggie had a leg stretched out, hip protruding.

He eyed the leg. Everything was beginning to look different as the leg took on new meaning, but he did not want to spoil things, "Well what?"

"What did George have to say about Tom Moody?"

He told her, because she would have detected a lie.

She came over and put an arm loosely around his neck. They clinked glasses and drank. "If he needs help you'd better give it to him."

Scott stiffened. This was not how it should be nor how he could allow it to be. "He doesn't need any help. He's dead."

"Don't be obtuse, darling." She reached up and pecked his cheek. "I'm talking of George."

Scott lifted her arm from his neck. "No, Maggie. Don't try it that way. There's nothing to make up except lost time. You don't owe me anything."

She sat on the arm of the settee. She put down her glass on a side table and titivated her hair, an action that would have been provocative but for the seriousness of her expression. She said, "These last few months have been a nightmare. It's been like having a clamp over my mind. Yesterday, the cloud began to lift and the pressure in my head eased. I cried a lot before you came home. And then after you'd gone this morning I read about Tom Moody, and things began to get back into perspective." There was a slight catch in her voice.

"You can't help what you are, Willie. I've always known and accepted that. It hasn't stopped my being scared on occasion, but I've never attempted to change you. The loss of the baby had nothing to do with you. When I read about Tom Moody I realized how some people had gone out on a limb for us. Look how George got suspended over me. I would never have believed that he could become a friend, but he almost ruined his career for us."

Scott could not cope with the turnaround. "You don't have to prove anything, love. Forget it."

"But I do. If not to you then to myself. The only way I'll get rid of this bloody depression for good is to cut loose from traditional thinking. I *know* you won't let me down. If George needs you then help him."

"He doesn't and I won't."

"He will and so will you."

Scott could not understand why he felt so miserable when he should be overjoyed. Maggie was being too reckless to please him and that could go the other way.

"Stop trying to psychoanalyze me, Willie. When you come back from the dead life can be wonderful." Maggie started to laugh softly, but it was mixed with a suspicion of sobbing.

Scott did not approach her. He floundered while he considered the best thing to do. Maggie verged on the hysterical, controlled it, then calmed down. "Oh, hell," she burst out, "I would have loved that baby. He'd have been like you."

"An awkward bastard. One in the family's enough."

She laughed again through some tears. "Oh, damn the cooking, Willie. Take me out somewhere plush."

He grinned now. "You've got a lot of eating to catch up on. Welcome home, love."

VERNON HEALY, MBE, sat back in his chair as if he had not rested for weeks. He appeared tired and worn and in need of a break. Bulman, sitting opposite him across the desk, felt sorry for the prison governor. The staff of Albany prison had been under great strain.

There were three clustered prisons on the tiny Ile. of Wight, which was separated from southern mainland England by a narrow strip of sea in the English Channel. Albany was a top security prison for long-term prisoners. There had been rumors over the last few days that another riot was imminent. Apart from the obvious dangers to the staff, the actual damage to the prison itself could be considerable. Healy studied some notes on his desk. "I'm rather surprised by your query. You, of all people, know there's movement in and out of prisons. Problems crop up, prisoners are sent elsewhere. New ones come in. We're overcrowded anyway. Who exactly are you trying to track down?"

"The man ex-Chief Detective Superintendent Moody came to see."

"Tom Moody? Well, we all know that name. What was the prisoner's name?"

"If I knew that I wouldn't need your help, sir."

Healy frowned. "It's pretty vague, isn't it? How am I supposed to know who he saw? He made no official request."

Bulman was apologetic. "If Tom had not slipped on the soap when he did I wouldn't be here now. He would have told me. There must be records of the passes. One of your staff is bound to remember. The dates of his visit are on the note I gave you, the last one only a week or two ago." Bulman watched the man across the desk. Prison governors' offices always depressed him, no matter how bright they were. It was obvious to him that Healy had better things to do and that his mind was more than half on them.

Healy studied the note again, as if he was having difficulty in absorbing its content. "I'll see what I can do," he said. "I'll ask the chief guard and will let you know."

Bulman hesitated. "Would it not be possible to check now, sir?"

"Not unless you give me a damned good reason, Mr. Bulman. I have more urgent priorities just now. Leave it with me."

For a reason he could not then explain, Bulman decided against telling Healy what Moody's daughter had told him. It was not a question of trust. Healy deserved an explanation, but the governor had a good deal on his mind and at the moment Bulman's request, without substantial backing, must appear trivial.

"Then I'll take up no more of your time, sir." Bulman stood up. "If you can find out who Tom visited it would be a help."

"I'll do what I can. Where shall I drop you a line?"

"The Yard, sir."

"A long journey for an inquiry like this. You could have telephoned."

Bulman smiled and held out his hand. "You might not have accepted my credentials over the telephone, sir. I appreciate your help. Anyway, I'll stay a couple of nights and look around the island." But Bulman did not stay. He found a cab to take him to the ferry at West Cowes and afterward caught a train back to London from Southampton. He carried with him a sense of failure and wondered why he had been unwilling to impart more than he had. It had nothing to do with the governor, and he understood that his request was a bloody nuisance. But something had happened to him in the office that had pricked a warning. It was ridiculous, because, like Betty Moorcroft, he was not given to fancy. Yet something, somehow, had made him uneasy. And he still felt queasy. Scott would understand, he reflected, as the train headed north through the farmlands of Hampshire; Scott had carried these sorts of feelings through his life, but he had known how to deal with them. What Bulman now felt was alien to him and he did not care for it, as if he had eaten something oily to give him nightmares and a nasty sense of insecurity. He gazed out of the carriage window and through the ghost of his own reflection. He was seeing too many bars of soap lying around.

3

GEORGE Bulman was already at Tom Moody's apartment by the time Willie Scott called. Scott rang the bell and gave a two fingered salute to the spy-hole as he heard the door catch go back. Betty Moorcroft held the door open and Scott was flustered. "I'm sorry," he apologized. "I thought George was here alone."

"I've seen worse." She was rather surprised at his discomfort. "I'm Tom's daughter," she added as he stepped past her.

"Willie Scott," he replied. "Where's George?"

"In the bathroom."

Scott nodded briefly and followed her pointing finger. As he entered the bathroom Bulman said, "You're late."

"So next time give me more notice." Scott stared at the turquoise bath, now spotlessly clean, and at the matching tiling above it. The built-in soap recess was dry and empty. "Why do you need me?"

Bulman was gazing down at the bath, hands in his pockets, bullet head pushed forward. He did not answer at once.

Scott observed, "You look just like a copper trying to give an impression of shrewd and sharp observation when your head is either empty or full of bullshit."

Bulman did not stir. "Maggie must be better; you're back to your charming self."

Scott had closed the door behind him once Betty had made it clear that she had no wish to enter this small room. "Found anything?"

"No. That's why I wanted your cat-burglar's mind on the job. Where would Tom hide something he did not want to be found?"

Scott sat on the edge of the bath, then rose again as he remembered what had happened in it. "*We* did the hiding, *you* did the finding. What's wrong with your copper's mind?"

"You were particularly good at it, Spider." Bulman still had not moved.

"You're going back to the jewelry stuffed into a loaf of bread, and rings-along-the-curtain-rod days. I don't even know what you're looking for."

"Nor do I. If Betty is right about how he died then he had to be hiding something."

"He wasn't the paperwork type. It would have been in his head."

"Maybe." Bulman stepped back.

"Who cleaned up here?" Scott asked.

Bulman glanced at the door. "Betty. Couldn't have been pleasant, but she refused to get a cleaner in. We'd better join her."

The two men went into the living room, where Betty Moorcroft was smoking a cigarette and gazing out of the net curtained windows. She glanced over her shoulder as they entered. With the daylight on her face Scott could see the resemblance to her father.

As if from habit, Scott and Bulman stood in the center of the room and simply gazed around it noncommitally. "Is this exactly as you left it?" Scott asked, gazing at Betty who was still looking over her shoulder.

"Yes, I think so." She caught Scott's laconic expression and turned away from the window. "You want me to think like my father? Is that it?"

"A 'think so' is no good to us, Betty," Bulman said critically. "If you want us to back your judgment, we want it right."

"I'm sorry." She scanned the room slowly, noting the position of the easy chairs, the bookcase, the television set, the long low table with some books on it, and the small rolltop desk. Bulman moved over to the bedroom door so as not to obstruct her, and Scott went into the small hall where the telephone table was set against a wall behind the door. He checked the telephone number index right through the alphabet.

28

There were one or two names that vaguely registered with him but none that flashed a warning. Right at the back, under Z, but with no names against them, were two London numbers. He made a note of them, then went back to H in the index. Dr. A. Habise. An unusual name with a central London number. Scott picked up the E to K directory. Habise was in Harley Street. Scott made a note. He went back into the living room to find that Betty and Bulman had moved into the bedroom. He joined them. "Who was your father's doctor?"

Betty groped for the answer. "I don't know. I can't remember the last time he went to a doctor."

"He's likely to be registered with someone."

"I suppose so." She turned to Bulman. "It all looks the same to me."

Scott signaled Bulman and they went into the hall. Scott told him about the two unnamed numbers and of the doctor. "This is one for you, George."

"Okay. I don't think anyone's been here since Tom died. If someone has, he is a top pro. If there was anything to find it would most likely have been taken when he was topped."

"You sound convinced that he *was* murdered. This could all be rubbish."

Bulman shrugged. "I was always a chump for a sob story. Deep down I'm very compassionate. I believe in people."

"Jesus Christ." Scott stared at the ceiling.

"And I believe in *Him* too. I'm a lay preacher these days, Spider. We all change; a few of us for the better."

"We've got to go through the place when Betty's finished," said Scott. "Will she leave the keys?"

"It's arranged. I appreciate your giving the time, but you might remember hidey-holes I've forgotten about." When they went back into the living room Betty was just closing the rolltop desk. "It's impossible to say," she said. "At the time I tidied up I hadn't this in mind." She spread her arms to encompass the flat. "It looks the same as when I left it."

Scott had moved over to a small magazine rack at one side of the fireplace. Beside it was an armchair and a side table, on top of which were a copy of the *Police Review* and the *Daily Telegraph*. Scott leaned over to check the date of the newspaper; it was dated the day Tom Moody died.

"Everything here?" he asked, pointing to the rack.

"I didn't check the magazines. I don't know what's there. I only tidied up."

"Was the *Telegraph* there? And the Copper's Comic?"

"Yes." Betty caught Scott's unspoken question. "I didn't want to touch them. That was Dad's favorite chair."

Scott thought that she could still see her father sitting there.

"Okay," Bulman said. "Leave Spider and me to go over the place. I'll drop the keys off later."

Betty went to the door. "Did I tell you it was I who found him?"

Neither man replied. It was the first time she had really shown her feelings.

"Bloody good job I didn't have the kids with me." She was choking on a sob, then she closed the door quietly behind her.

The two men gazed at one another; Betty must have suffered a terrible shock.

Scott went back to the side table. He picked up the *Police Review* and went through it page by page. Then he unfolded the *Daily Telegraph* and laid it flat on the floor to open it page by page. "Here's something," he said, on reaching the city news. In the left hand margin of the right hand page, three newspaper clippings were fastened by tiny strips of adhesive paper. Very carefully he detached them while Bulman came to stand behind him.

Scott stood up, holding the clippings. They were the accounts of three deaths. "Who's Michael Rassi?" he asked as he passed a clipping to Bulman.

Bulman stared at it. "He rated more space than these few lines. Clever devil. Quiet, unassuming, undemonstrative, ostensibly passive, but actually the power behind the many thrones scattered throughout the country."

"What are you on about? I've never heard of him."

"You and the rest of the hoi polloi. Masterminded most of the industrial unrest. A great strategist. A veritable brain bank for militant unionists." Bulman waved the clipping. "Died last year, I remember. Heart attack."

Scott handed over another. "Bit longer. Red Jock McLaren. I remember him, though. Everyone would. Miserable sod. Had more men out on strike than any other union leader. Should have been in the *Guinness Book of Records.* Didn't he hang himself? Woman trouble?"

"Man trouble. His case was due to come up, but he couldn't take the strain of being a gay and an out-and-out militant. Must be eighteen months ago. Who's the other one?"

Scott gazed at the few lines in the report. "Character called John Selbie. Never heard of him, either. Fell under a tube train. Here."

Bulman took the clipping. "I remember the inquest on this. Subject to dizzy fits, it was reported. Cock-and-bull. There is no harm now in saying that he was with MI5."

Scott looked interested. "Dizzy fits with MI5?"

"Exactly. Strange business. Why would clippings like these be hidden like that?"

"Hidden? Or planted?" Scott questioned.

"You think we were intended to find them?"

Scott gazed down at the *Telegraph* at his feet. "I dunno. These are old clips. If Tom hid them then he must have done it on a daily basis. The paper is dated the day he died. If the place was searched they'd have shaken out the magazines and papers, but these were stuck in. Why would Tom want to hide old clips like that? Everyone's seen them already."

"Makes you think," said Bulman, still gazing at them. "I'll hang onto them."

BULMAN WAS SHOWN into the lush waiting room. The brocaded chairs were enough to furnish the place; it was not the sort of doctor's office to have more than one patient waiting at a time. It was late afternoon, the only time Bulman had been able to fix. He browsed through the *Tatler* and *Country Life* from the magazine table. They were recent, as were the issues of *Punch.* There was a separate section of comics for children. He waited about ten minutes before the nurse entered to tell him that Dr. Habise would see him.

The office-cum-examining room was no bigger than Bulman expected, but still at least four times bigger than his own.

"Detective Superintendent, do sit down." Habise was tall and spindly with glasses, but there was a twinkle in his eye. He wore a sober, well-cut suit and the familiarity of a close friend. "I rarely get a visit from the police. Sorry you had to wait."

"Waiting is the main part of the game, sir." Bulman could see nothing to connect the name with the man; the accent was public school, the approach essentially English upper class. He could see Habise's gaze taking in his own stocky frame and could almost read his thoughts; thin doctors invariably flashed the overweight message to those who were not thin.

"Thomas Alan Moody was a patient of yours, doctor." Bulman could feel no real comfort in the hard seat.

"Are you asking or telling me, Mr. Bulman?" Bony hands clasped each other on the desk. The eyes still smiled.

"Asking, sir, and for your cooperation."

"May I see your warrant card?"

"Of course. I should have shown it." Bulman handed it over, by now convinced that Habise would want more than a glance.

"Good." Habise handed it back. "Have to be careful. So many people make false claims these days for so many reasons."

"Usually to make money, doctor. Was Tom Moody a patient of yours?"

"Yes, he was." Habise was checking an index and pulled out a card. "The reason I remember so spontaneously was because his visits were fairly recent."

"What was wrong with him?"

"Why do you want to know?" Habise slowly stiffened and he held up a hand. "Perhaps you've already answered. You said, 'was.'"

"He died a day or two ago. I'm merely checking to see if there was any medical reason for what happened." Bulman explained how Moody had died.

"I'm so sorry. I have not been notified. Who issued the death certificate?"

"He was found by his daughter. She called the police and an ambulance. The police doctor arranged the certificate. There was nothing complicated about what killed him."

"What made her call the police? Was there something . . ."

"She's a policeman's daughter, doctor. It wasn't a pleasant sight to find—her own father. She had no idea then how it had happened."

"Is there some query over the cause of death?"

32

"Not that I know of."

"Then why are you here, Mr. Bulman?"

Bulman had created his own trap to see if Habise would snare him into it. Habise's attitude surprised him in spite of the doctor/patient confidence. Moody was dead; what the hell could it matter? "Your name was on his telephone pad. It's fairly routine inquiry to discover if there was something wrong with him that might have caused his accident."

"Quite so." Habise held the card in front of him. He stared seriously at Bulman. "I'm afraid there was every reason why he might have fallen. He was suffering from dizzy spells. That need not be significant. He was a big man, heavy shouldered, and the muscles can sometimes trap a nerve or make it difficult for blood to get through. Usually this is brief. But I was also treating him for blood pressure. I warned him to reduce his weight."

"Ah! That puts some light on it. Tell me, did he come from his local GP? That's usually the procedure, isn't it?"

"Usually. But with private patients there is nothing to stop them ringing for an appointment. All my patients here are private. My National Health work is at hospitals and clinics."

"A patient would have to hear of you first, of course."

Habise smiled tolerantly. "You seem to be having difficulty in accepting that Mr. Moody *was* a private patient. There are a number of ways he could have heard of me. Usually it's by recommendation. Is there anything else, Mr. Bulman?"

"No, sir. You've been most helpful.

IT WAS THE first time Bulman had seen her since before her child had been stillborn, and he was cautious in his greeting. Maggie pecked his cheek. "It's all right, George. I've come out of the forest."

"You look fine, Maggie." He thought she looked too thin; the loss of the baby had taken its toll on her. "You sure it's okay for me to talk shop with Spi– Willie?"

"Sit down and stop fussing. Willie told me about Tom Moody and his daughter."

"Did he give any opinions?"

Maggie opened the sideboard for the whisky while Bulman reflected that her loss of weight had not reached her shapely legs. He removed his gaze quickly as she straightened.

33

"About whether Tom died naturally or not? I don't think he has an opinion. There was one thing. He thought the writing of the doctor's name in the phone index might not have been Tom's."

"He didn't say anything to me."

"He would have done. It was something of an afterthought. If that's too much for safe driving I'll tip some back."

Bulman grabbed the glass. "Thanks, Mag. I'm always hoofing or taxiing these days. Your health."

Maggie smiled sweetly. "Did you come before Willie's due home to make sure it's safe?"

"Safe?"

"With me, George? That I'm not quite a loony?"

"Perish the thought. I came early because you're more generous with the Scotch." And then with feeling. "But I'm glad, Maggie. Really glad you've come through."

"I know you are, George."

Maggie sat opposite Bulman, and he could see that she was about to change tack. "I've told Willie that he must help you if you need him. I won't throw a tantrum or stand in his way. But don't throw him to the lions, George. So many have done that. I've lost our baby. If I lose him I lose everything."

"It's not like that, Maggie. Not this one." Bulman shifted his gaze from her; he had not even convinced himself but he could not explain why.

BULMAN WORKED LATE at his office that night. He had given a good deal of time to Betty Moorcroft's misgivings and other issues had been neglected. Detective Sergeant Haldean had covered for him, but there was a lot to catch up on. At nine P.M. he had a coffee and went back to his office with a sandwich. With his jacket and tie off he sat munching while studying reports. There was a polite knock on his door, and a well-weathered face peered around it.

Bulman scrambled to his feet, his jaws champing like mad at a mouthful of sandwich. "Sir Lewis!"

"Sit down, George. I didn't mean to disturb you."

Bulman sat down again, swallowing fast. "Didn't expect you, sir."

"Of course not." Sir Lewis Hope sat on one of the government-issue chairs and crossed his long legs. He was well built but very tall, which

34

gave the illusion of thinness. His face was lined, not by age but by earlier years at sea. His eyes were creased and screwed as if still facing biting winds and stinging spray on the bridge of a ship. His hair was black and brushed back, and Bulman suspected that the sides were occasionally touched up for there was no gray. He was head of the Security Service and once, for a long spell, head of Naval Intelligence. He appeared to be in his early fifties but was older.

"I was in the building," Hope said smoothly, "so wondered if you were still up and about."

Balls, Bulman thought. "Nice of you to call, sir. I suppose you were with Special Branch?"

"Routine. I can see that you are frightfully busy so I mustn't stay. Sad about Tom Moody, don't you think? He once did the job you are doing. Great pity."

"We all have to go," Bulman ventured, wondering what Hope was leading up to.

"Yes, George, but not in that way. Not nice. Perhaps for the best, though."

"For the best?"

"Did I say that? Must have come out the wrong way." And then at an apparent tangent, "You know Tuomo?"

"I've seen him. Never actually spoken to him."

"We're sending him back home, George. He was getting a bit too naughty. No announcement. Nice and quiet. He'll just slip off behind the curtain with that gorgeous Finnish wife of his. Pity about her." Hope cocked his head, gazing seriously at Bulman but uttering an apparent throwaway: "Moody knew him quite well."

"If he held my job, I suppose he would have."

"Oh, Tuomo hasn't been over here that long."

Bulman refused the bait. He was becoming annoyed. He would rather face direct lies than prevarication. Hope was a cunning prevaricator. Bulman supposed it went with the job. Sir Stuart Halliman, who both Scott and Bulman had known as Fairfax, had been Hope's predecessor, and he had been cunning, too, but in a different way. Hope never varied his image, and Bulman found it hard to imagine him in a real storm. Perhaps it was part of his deceit, that on occasion he could be almost foppish.

"Am I missing something, sir?" Bulman asked with icy politeness.

35

Hope smiled. "That would be difficult to believe, George."

Bulman rubbed his eyes wearily. "Perhaps it's too late for me. I could have sworn you were having a dig at Tom Moody."

"My word, that wouldn't do. That's one reputation we must protect. He was often a guest lecturer on police courses, y'know. And when he wasn't he was quoted or held up as an example of all that was good in a high ranking police officer. Oh dear me, no. What would happen to police morale if his name was sullied?"

"As that's hardly possible, I can't grasp why it was mentioned."

"These things are always possible, George. The yellow press and all that. He can't answer back now, and I'm sure his daughter knows too little about his work to answer for him. Let's leave him alone. Let him rest in peace, poor devil."

"Even if he was murdered?"

"Murdered? I understood he slipped in the bath."

Bulman was not convinced that the surprise was genuine. "His daughter isn't happy about it."

"Well she wouldn't be, would she? Poor girl. She found him, I believe? Terrible shock. She wouldn't want to accept the possibility of any infirmity. Strong, vigorous man. That's how any daughter would want to remember her father. Presumably she's mentioned this to you? How unfortunate."

"For her or for me, sir?"

Hope's eyes were piercing through the puckered lids. "For you both. You won't want to upset the daughter of an old colleague by dismissing her fears too easily. Have you done anything for her?"

"A little."

"Enough to humor her?"

"I can't answer for her."

"Well, have you done enough to convince her that poor old Moody really did slip in the bath?"

"No. Nor enough to convince myself."

"My dear George, you're not saying you've turned something up?"

"No. But I'm encouraged to continue."

"Forget it, dear boy. You've done enough. Pander to the lady, by all means, but waste no more time on it. Look at you." Hope indicated the cluttered desk. "My people are waiting for much of that. Some is well overdue. Drop it, George. Get on with the official business. We have no time for futile favors. Say the right words to her and drop quietly out of it."

"Is that an instruction, sir? An order?"

Hope rose and straightened his back. "When have I ever ordered you to do anything, George?" He smiled pleasantly. "But I can't stand back and see you overwork, or you yourself will be slipping in the bath from fatigue. Good night, old chap."

LONDON SPREAD OUT below them, fogged here and there by a sudden change of temperature that had created a heat mist. The sun-washed upper stones of tall buildings rose from low-lying, swirling shrouds. It was late evening, the midsummer sky still pastel blue, pierced in the near distance by the reflecting dome of St. Paul's Cathedral in the City and by Big Ben near the Houses of Parliament.

The two men walked around the observation platform of the General Post Office Tower, stopping now and then to obtain a different view of the wide mosaic split by the gray coiling serpent of the Thames.

Scott tapped a telescope. "Cased the Chinese legation through one of these," he said. "Broke in through the lead roof."

Bulman stopped by the parapet. "I know. That was our first big clash."

"A lot of casing is done from up here," Scott explained. "Can't get a better view. All the approach and escape routes."

"You don't say," commented Bulman dryly. "The Chinese legation moved, by the way."

Scott laughed. "And we all know bloody why. So you've been warned off Tom Moody?"

"Looks like it. I didn't care for the innuendoes. Something's up."

"But you'll have to do what you're told?"

Bulman shrugged and peered over the edge of the parapet. "Good view down there. Buses look like lozenges. It restricts me. I can't drop it because I'm now sure there's something to hide. But I can't give the time to it without its being noticed. Why don't you break in to Dr. Habise's pad? I've nothing to raise a warrant on, so we can't go in legally."

"Why don't you break in?"

"Come on, Spider. I'll have a word with the divisional super. Keep the area clear. You could do it in your sleep."

"Why?"

"I want to find out if Tom Moody actually was a patient there."

"A West End consultant isn't going to lie about a thing like that."

"Be your age. It's strange. You mentioned a possible difference in writing in the telephone index. But if Tom had high blood pressure he'd have had pills, wouldn't he? Something to reduce the pressure?"

"I suppose so. Yes, I think that's right. The only pills I found at his flat were Panadeine. For headaches mostly. But the bottle seemed full."

"So what happened to the pills Habise prescribed? He distinctly said he was treating Tom for high blood pressure."

"Tom was the right size for high blood pressure."

"Balls. There is no right size. I've seen thin ones go. Betty Moorcroft knew nothing about it and was close to her father."

"Okay, if it's simple I'll break in, provided I have your word that you'll get me off the hook if I'm caught."

"You've never been caught."

"What was I doing in stir, then?"

"That was *after* the event. Got bloody careless."

"I'll take a look. No more. Cheers." Scott left Bulman gazing at the great city while he took the elevator down.

THE GEORGIAN TERRACE house had only one consultant's brass plate. Scott stood under the portico with his back to the huge door. The street was quite busy, the odd Rolls Royce or Bentley flanking its sides. As he took in the general background he wondered if Habise lived on the premises. He turned around to examine the solid pine door, the lintel of which he would have difficulty in reaching, and was not surprised to find it had two locks. He examined them, without stooping.

When the door opened behind him, he stepped sideways so that he could not immediately be seen. A middle-aged, expensively dressed woman emerged. Scott had a whiff of Guerlain. As she stood there someone behind her said, "Goodbye, Mrs. Wilton-Smith," and closed the door. A uniformed chauffeur appeared from the line of cars and mounted the steps to help the lady down. When she had gone, Scott turned to the letter boxes. The upper floors seemed to be let out as offices judging from the slotted cards.

He stepped to the front of the portico to examine the lace-covered windows on either side, then went down the steps to view from there. He went back up the steps. When Mrs. Wilton-Smith had left he had heard only one door catch engage, which, during daytime, would be fairly normal. Taking another look at the locks he believed that Bulman was right; it should not be too difficult for him to get in. But there was probably an easier way, one that would not keep Maggie up biting her nails with worry.

Scott ran down the steps with his hands in his pockets and sought the nearest phone booth. He phoned Dr. Habise's office to ask the closing time and then made two more calls.

AT FIVE-FIFTEEN P.M. Scott went back to Harley Street and waited opposite the doctor's office with a small parcel under his arm. A taxi pulled up and a man, stooped and elderly, alighted and started to climb the steps. Scott skipped through the traffic and joined the man before he reached the top step. "May I help you?" he asked politely.

"No, thank you." The face under the homburg was lined with pain. "Used to it. Anyway you appear to be loaded up."

They reached the door together. "The doctor?" queried Scott, his hand over the bell.

"Do I look that bad?" And with a faint smile, "If you would."

When the receptionist opened the door, Scott stood back to allow the elderly patient through, then he followed before the receptionist could close the door. "Lanix Press," he explained, pointing to his parcel.

"I believe they've gone. They close at five."

"I'll leave it outside their door. What time do the cleaners come?"

"Eight. In the morning." The receptionist was helping the patient into the waiting room.

Scott smiled. "I'll slip a note on it to make sure they don't throw it away." But by then the girl had gone and Scott was alone in the arched hall. He mounted the stairs slowly. There was no hurry. Lanix Press was on the top floor and he had already established that it closed at five and the doctor's office at six-thirty.

When he reached the top floor he found four offices off the landing and a washroom. Two doors were marked private, the other two had Lanix Press printed across frosted-glass windows, and one held a notice: "Reception. Please enter." He tried all the doors to make sure everyone had gone. Then he laid down his parcel and inserted a prepared note that read: "Cleaner, please throw away." With the note was £1. He sat on the carpeted stair and waited.

39

At five-thirty some of the offices below began to empty. Mixed voices floated up the stairwell. Going home time. The house grew quiet around him as he continued to wait.

By six-thirty there was no movement at all. He crept down one flight and sat again. Voices floated up. The front door opened and closed. He could hear no footsteps from the hall, but the carpet was so thick on the ground floor that sound would be muted. At six-forty-five he moved down another flight, which left one more to the ground floor.

He heard a man's voice, subdued but authoritative, and a woman answering. Bulman had told Scott that the nurse also acted as reception-ist. Then he heard, "Good night, doctor," and the front door opened and closed again. Scott waited. Someone was still there.

Dr. Habise left just before seven. The door slammed, engaging the Yale, and then a key was turned from the outside to lock the mortise. Scott continued to sit.

At seven-twenty, he went quietly down the old staircase, keeping to its edges. He stood in the hall, the house deadly quiet around him. He wandered over to the door, crouched, and could now see the wiring tucked in along the edge of the carpet and running from a hole bored into the lintel. So the house was wired.

Scott found the control box at chest level under the stairs. The alarm had not been set. Someone had carelessly left the key in the box. He went back into the main hall. Light streamed in through the magnificent glass shellhood above the door. There was a lot of daylight left.

Scott felt that something was wrong. The empty silence did not unnerve him, but something else did. He delicately turned the waiting room doorknob, and he gently pushed the door open. The chairs stood in line, like green-jacketed soldiers. Magazines had been tidied by the same caring hands. Nobody was there. He went back into the hall, closing the door behind him, and feeling that his back needed watching.

He examined the nurse/receptionist's office. The nurse had tidied all around, the small desk clear of papers, filing cabinets all neatly aligned, all drawers closed. A portable television sat on a stand at the side of the desk. The room was bright, the large lace-curtained windows letting in plenty of light. When he tried the cabinets, they were locked.

Scott crossed the hall again to find the consulting room door locked. He screwed a skeleton key onto a shank he had designed himself and moved the tumblers. He pushed open the door slowly, until it was against the wall. He stepped in, taking a very long stride to avoid pressure pads; not satisfied about the alarm control box.

The room was as Bulman had described it. In the furthest corner was an elaborate, brass-mounted, opaque, engraved-glass folding screen, concealing the changing area and the examination couch. Satisfied that the large room was quite empty he went to the desk, pulled out the drawer of the index box, and extracted the card for Tom Moody.

He sat and read the card. Medicines had been prescribed, although the writing was so atrocious that he could not read what. But he could just decipher the dates Moody had called. He made a few notes, copying the entries in the same style as written. He then examined some of the other cards, for color and wear. He closed the tray.

Before leaving the room, he examined the alarm contact points on the door edge and the inside lintel, then he locked the door and returned to the nurse's room. He sat behind her desk on a less comfortable seat than the doctor's and tried the central drawer. It was quite easy for him to pick the simple lock. He found a loose-leaf appointments book and went through the more recent entries. Moody's appointments were entered up, but Scott detected a slight difference in the paper on which the entries were made. The dates and times followed quite consecutively. The writing carried the hallmark of the nurse: clear, very neat. He put the book back exactly as he found it, the nurse would know exactly how she had placed everything. He rose and made sure that the chair legs fitted into the carpet indentations.

He checked the alarm contacts before closing the door and took a long stride over the possible pressure pad area. Then he took another look at the waiting room door, which did not rate contact points, but he guessed the windows would be wired. He could not effectively examine them without moving the net curtains.

Scott reentered the hall with the same feeling of being setup. The house was quite empty, he was sure of that. There were no television scanners, no infrared. Why had he thought of scanners? How could a place like this warrant them? That led him to considering audio bugs, but unless they were finely tuned he knew he moved too quietly, even in a vacated house. He went back to the control panel for a final check and did not care for his reaction to it.

Finding the right key head he unlocked the front door mortise, released the Yale, and let himself out. He relocked the mortise from the outside, then skipped down the steps, taking in a wide range of doors and windows opposite before he reached the street. He had seldom felt so unhappy about a job. All he now wanted to do was to get home. Before he reached the end of Harley Street he had the sensation of being followed, but did not check until after he had taken the necessary evasive action. The whole episode left a nasty taste in his mouth.

Maggie detected Scott's mood as soon as he reached home, even though he tried to conceal it. She had seen him like this so often before. It worried her but it also took her mind off herself. For this reason alone she was glad that she had told him to help George Bulman.

"Didn't it go well?" she asked, giving him a peck.

He gave her a hug. "I must get this lacquer off my fingertips."

She followed him into the bedroom and stood by him while he sat in front of her dressing table. As he cleaned his fingers he said, "All straightforward. Nothing easier."

"Is that what's wrong?" With soft fingers she gently massaged the back of his neck. "Too easy?"

"It was a simple job George knew he couldn't get a search warrant for. Funny, bloody copper when you think about it. Bent and yet as straight as a die. God, he's changed."

"For the better, Willie."

He wiped his fingers on cotton wool. "If going bent means better, I agree. He used to go absolutely by the book. Never understood what changed him." He put an arm around her thighs.

"So what will you do?"

"I'm going back," he said. "Tomorrow night. When it's dark."

Her hand froze on his neck, fingers digging in. "You're mad, Willie." She stifled the frantic plea just in time, but was aware that he had seen her panic through the dressing-table mirror.

4

"IT stinks," Scott said. He had refused to meet Bulman at Scotland Yard. Even now he found it impossible to enter any police station voluntarily. As his own office was anything but soundproof, they met in the Crown. The day was hot, one door had been jammed back, and a wall fan spread the heat around, while they drank chilled lager.

"Because Tom Moody's card was there?"

"Because the card was there, looking too new, because the alarm was off when there are pads and points all over the place, because the appointment book is dodgy. And I might have been followed."

"Aren't you sure?"

"It might have been a mistake to show my hand by checking it out. If they were there I lost them."

"If they took a mug shot of you they'll know by now who you are. You're on file."

"You sound as if you're talking about the bloody police, George."

Bulman shook his head thoughtfully. "Not the police. Funny though, that's how it sounded. Why would my boss try to smear Tom Moody?"

"Maybe he knows something."

"And maybe he's just trying to put me off. Would you believe something like a connection with an iron curtain diplomat and Tom Moody?"

"No. But I'd lost touch with him. He wouldn't cross over but perhaps they had something on him. How about those clippings. You sure he wasn't on a job?"

Bulman gazed in disgust at his lager; it was already tepid so he drank it quickly. "That's about the only thing I am sure about. It's no use," he said, putting down his glass, "I've got to have a Scotch."

Scott grabbed the empty glass. "Marvelous how you time the change to my call."

"Don't get mean like me, Spider. It would destroy my faith."

When Scott scrambled back with the drinks, Bulman asked, "Tell me about the appointment book."

"A big loose-leaf job. All the dates are printed on, a page for each day. But where Tom's appointments were entered up the paper color was very slightly different. I would guess that the entries concerning him were put in later. Had they been squeezed in on the old pages it would probably have been noticeable. So those pages were taken out and new replacements were completely rewritten to include Tom's appointments. These pages must have been taken from a spare diary; they did not quite match the others."

"So the girl is in on it?"

"To some extent anyway. Doctors sometimes make appointments themselves; he might have spun her a yarn."

"If I go for her it would warn him. I'll gamble she won't know why it was done. For the moment we simply assume the entries are false."

"Can you check on Habise?"

"I'll check his medical background. You think that with my boss interceding he might belong to the 'Firm'?"

"Don't you?"

"There's no way I can find out all doctors who are used by the 'Firm.' If I started that sort of ripple I'd be back on the beat or inside on a trumped-up charge."

"Then maybe we should drop it. We could be soiling our own backyard."

"Even the whisky doesn't taste right," Bulman complained. He wiped sweat from his forehead. "I sometimes think that's an impression we are supposed to adopt."

"Can you speak to your friend and get the fuzz looking the other way about eleven tonight?"

"Jesus! You're pushing my luck, Spider."

"So it's okay when it suits you but not when I want it?"

"You're not going back in?"

"Why not, it's easy enough? Don't sweat, you've nothing to worry about."

"Eleven, you say? I'll do what I can. Don't bank on it."

"I wouldn't mind so much if I had a clue about just who the hell we are taking on and whether it's worth it."

Bulman watched the passing shadows on the street side of the windows; he always found them therapeutic, like fish in a tank. "I reckon Tom Moody found out," he observed soberly. "The other day I had the faintest taste of the fear Betty described in him. And I was only sitting in a train."

"I had a whiff of it last night," Scott admitted. "Maybe we're just getting old. They say it gets to you sometime."

"You could be right." Bulman straightened. "I must get back." And then with a crooked smile, "But we're not kidding ourselves, are we?"

MAGGIE PUT THE phone down. "That was mother. They're going on a cruise."

"Didn't they ask you to go?"

"Is that what you want? To get rid of me?"

"Of course it's what I want." Scott was changing into a track suit. "Because you need it. It would set you up."

"And you could go on breaking the law."

"Ah, Maggie. It's not like the old days. I don't take a thing. Anyway, I've got George to protect me."

"And who's protecting George, Willie?"

He was about to say it was her idea but it would not have been fair. Maggie noticed the fleeting expression. "Mother did ask me. I said I'd ask you."

"No need. You'd be crazy not to go. Where?"

"Greek Islands."

"Bloody marvelous. When?"

"Two weeks time. They've been booked since last year and had applied for an extra single on the basis that you always taught me: it's easier to cancel a booking than to try to book too late. Anyway there

45

were no singles then; a cancellation has just cropped up. I'd be deserting you, Willie."

"You would never do that, love. Never. Ring her back."

Maggie hesitated, torn between love of Scott and what might be best for that love. "We need a break from each other, don't we?"

He crossed over to her, picked up the receiver, and placed it in her hand. "No, we don't. But you need to get away from bad memories. I'll be here when you get back. It'll be good, Maggie." He held his hand over her tummy as he had when the baby had been there. "And you'll regain a few pounds. Ring her."

SCOTT WAS GETTING used to riding the cycle again, his muscles had eased and he was enjoying it. He had changed the old dynamo driven lamp to a powerful battery job, but the beam was swallowed by car lights. When well-clear of his own patch, he cut down alleys and took shortcuts where a car could not follow. He did not look back but made good use of the mirror.

He reached Harley Street. Night brought out the air of history. Everything slowed down, the hurrying had ceased, and people and traffic had thinned considerably. It was a time and an area where the sound of horse drawn carriages would not have come as a surprise.

He cycled past Habise's office on the opposite side of the street without looking across. At the end he stopped, dismounted, and pushed his cycle behind the row of parked cars. He looked back. It was dog-walking time, but otherwise there were few people about. He spotted the dull reflection of a policeman's helmet coming toward him. Damn Bulman.

Scott wheeled his cycle across the street and remounted. Unzipping a pocket he produced a fifty-pence piece. He rose off, past the policeman on the other side, and continued down, pedaling slowly. As he reached the doctor's office he pulled back his arm as if signaling a right-hand turn, then sent the coin spinning hard toward the waiting-room window. There was a crack of metal on glass, and an alarm siren howled, as its light flashed above the interior buzzer. He rode on without looking back, pedaling steadily.

The coin had set off the window vibration alarms, and probably every night, except last night, the alarm was switched on. Scott now knew that he had been set up. The surgery had been left open for him.

They would know he had called and had wanted him to. Now they would know that he knew.

THEY WENT INTO St. James's Park and found a spare patch of grass to sit on in the midday sun. The spot they had chosen was the wrong side of the path for a good view of the water and the ducks and birds searching for food, but it was less crowded.

"Why here?" Scott asked as they tried to get comfortable.

"I'm trying to give up drink," Bulman replied easily. "Whisky is too heavy in this weather and beer too bloody warm. And I like to watch the birds."

Scott smiled; he knew the kind Bulman meant. "You let me down. There was a copper there last night."

"I can't control the whole Met. Anyway, you're here."

They gazed at the back of a slatted bench some yards in front of them. Two summer-clad couples sat on it, surrounded by pigeons.

"Doors and windows with contact breaking points, vibration alarms, and pressure pads. No infrared."

"Beams can play up sometimes," Bulman observed dryly.

"It's a bloody lot for a doctor's office, isn't it? He wouldn't keep money there. No valuables."

"Except information."

"It would have to be pretty important stuff to justify that."

"What about upstairs. They may have something."

"They're small-time operators. Exclusive maybe, but I'd guess mainly check business, not cash. A pro wouldn't break in there, and vandals are more localized. What did you find out about Habise?"

"Nothing, except that he's a good doctor. But I turned up a few other things." Bulman leaned back on his elbows, clearly uncomfortable. "I dunno how people do this for pleasure," he complained. "I looked up the reports on the deaths of Jock McLaren, Michael Rassi, and John Selbie. The former caused a big stir at the time, but there is really nothing to add to the clippings you found. Funny business. I've had no call from Vernon Healy at Albany. When I phoned him, I couldn't raise him. The fact is, Spider, of the three blokes I know to be missing from the list of prison inmates, I've discovered on the grapevine that one is definitely there. My feeling is that there are two. The other one was transferred to Nottingham at his own request. Someone is blocking me."

Scott held out a hand to an approaching pigeon, which waddled off once it realized the hand was empty. "Is that it?"

"The two telephone numbers at the back of Tom Moody's index belong to Fairfax and a person high up in the Secret Intelligence Service —M16. The first and last digits were transposed in each case."

"The numbers may have been there for years. They don't mean he was on a job."

"The MI6 number for that particular person has only been around for six months. It's true that Fairfax is retired."

The two men were silent for a while. They watched the seated crowds basking in the sun, men shirt sleeved, women in flimsy dresses. Some students were stripped to the waist. Eventually Bulman changed his position and again complained of discomfort. Then he said, "We really need someone in Albany who can find out who Moody visited. Nobody will tell us otherwise."

"You want me to go down there?"

"In view of the brush-off I received, you wouldn't get past the car park."

"It was fixed before."

Bulman shook his head and then his gaze followed a pair of shapely legs. "This is different, Spider. We need someone *inside* to ferret around."

"Who are these two you think are there?"

"One is Horseface Harper. A heavy. The other is Wally Cooper."

"*Wally Cooper?*" Scott was suddenly attentive. "Wally the Creep?"

"I thought you'd know him, being in the same line of business."

"I know of him. He's some years younger than me. New generation. A bloody idiot, too. Got tied up with lifting secret documents. Didn't he get thirty years?"

"Surprised that you remember. They kept a very low profile on that trial. It was in camera. Some defense papers were found in his flat and large spasmodic payments in his bank account. Should have stuck to lifting jewelry."

Scott thought back. "About nine, ten months ago. I heard he was a good creeper. Must have been to land stuff like that. You think Tom Moody went to see him?"

Bulman's craggy face was screwed against a sun that partially escaped behind a tree. "Can't see why. I wasn't involved with it. I think MI6 was the first to know. They tipped off the Security Service.

"MI5?"

"It hasn't been that for donkey's years but people still use it. But when these guys are caught, Security wrings them dry. Wally wasn't a spy. He was used as you were once. But he was paid by the wrong people. There'll be no effort to get that poor sod out. I can't see Tom getting any more from him than had already been extracted. He'd know damn little anyway, beyond the mug of the guy who contacted him. He was very well paid. Our friends must be running short of moles to use old fashioned methods like that, although they apparently did quite well out of him."

"Not like Wally, from what I heard about him."

"What about you going inside to find out who Tom actually saw? And why."

In the excessive heat Scott went very cold. So far the exchange had been light and speculative and Bulman's tone had not changed throughout. In a way it made it worse for Scott because the suggestion had been so casual he almost missed it. "You've gone off your rocker." His chest was suddenly tight; Bulman knew what prison meant to him and what it might do to Maggie if he went inside.

"It's the only way we'll find out."

"For Christ's sake, it's not important enough."

"Not even if Tom was murdered?"

"That's the whole bloody point," Scott protested. "We don't know. His prison visit may have nothing to do with any of it."

Bulman abstractedly plucked at the grass. He turned his face somberly to Scott. "I think it's important enough, Spider. I can't tell you why. But it is. It's a feeling I thought you'd understand."

"It's your feeling not mine. Do you realize what you're asking me?"

"Yes, I do. For God's sake, we're being blocked. You know that. My own boss warned me off. Jesus, I feel like a pariah. I'm at the Yard but the police don't consider me one of them, in spite of my rank. I've been farmed out. Security Service considers me a useful outside link with the police. Special Branch doesn't even rate me as one thing or the other. I'm in the gray zone, and right now I'm being given the polite elbow."

"So it's your pride you need to save?"

"Balls. Something is wrong. It's not just Tom Moody, although that sticks in my throat. We're being given the runaround by our own people and that frightens me."

"I'm frightened, too. Of going back to jail. It scares the pants off me." Scott sat up, arms around his knees. What they were discussing seemed crazy in this, so normal, summer scene. "Spell it out," he said slowly.

"We have to rig a charge. There'll be no trial. We get you inside, you find out who Moody saw and why, and you let me know, and you are then released. A few days should do it. Routine."

"You're over simplifying."

"Trust me."

For a terrible moment Scott thought that this was what Bulman had been waiting for all these years; to get him back inside. He rubbed his face and then studied the one next to him.

Bulman gazed back, brown eyes reflective, features rather sad. "You think I'd do that to you?" he asked gruffly.

"No." Scott shook his head. "No. But how can you protect me when your own boss is against you? He could kick your legs from under you."

"I'll work out the details. I don't intend that he should know. I'll work through police channels. People I know. A prison plant is nothing new."

"The Home Office would have to know."

"They wouldn't know why. There are plenty of other reasons why we might need somebody in Albany. They've had a great deal of trouble there. There's rumor of more riots to come. I'll get the request to come from someone in the Met. Someone high enough not to be questioned. If I can't do that we forget it."

"My name would be a giveaway."

"You won't go under your own name. It's been years since you've been inside. We can change your appearance a bit. Dye your hair."

"Dye grows out."

"For Christ's sake, stop talking like I'm throwing away the key. It's an in-and-out job. There won't be time for your part to change color."

Scott sat there, chin on arms over his drawn-up knees. It had been a very long time since he had felt like this. He had forgotten the emotional agony of it and had sworn he would never again return to prison.

"It would destroy Maggie," he observed quietly. "Just as she is recovering. One shock to another."

"You think I don't know that? You think I don't reflect on how a luscious dish like your Maggie could fall for a villain like you? She has to be protected. If she's going on a cruise in less than a fortnight, that will give me time to set it up. You won't go in until she's left the country and you'll be out before she's reached the Med."

"You really think it's worth it?"

"I don't know whether it will prove to be. That depends on what you find out. But I do know we have to try. Something stinks, Spider, and you think so too."

"I suppose if you do your job okay I'll be all right."

"Is that yes?"

"No. We see Fairfax first. If his number is in Tom's index we have to check it out."

Bulman struggled to his feet, hands brushing grass from his stocky frame, bullet head bent down. "That was on the agenda anyway. Although if he knows anything he'd have contacted me or someone. He liked Tom, too."

"Everyone liked Tom. Except the bastards who killed him."

SIR STUART HALLIMAN had aged since Scott had last seen him, which was not many months ago. He appeared drawn, his skin had yellowed, and he was strangely subdued. Maybe he's just getting old, Scott reflected.

All three men had met at Halliman's club off Pall Mall. These days he used the club as an office on occasion. He could not shake off the old routine of not doing business at home.

Halliman was pleased to see them both but some of his sparkle had gone, as if they had just roused him from sleep. He was still straight-backed, though, hair just as thick and gray, and he carried the appearance of an ex-soldier, which in fact he had never been.

They closeted themselves by one of the large windows, and Scott could smell the dust on the huge, velvet drapes. As the drinks were set on the low round table, Scott noticed Halliman running a finger around his collar. The recent heat wave was still on but the high-ceilinged room was comparatively cool. It was then that Scott realized the real difference in Halliman. It had eluded him because it was not blatantly obvious, and Scott had never seen it in him before. Halliman was troubled. Those lined but handsome features usually covered emotions. Perhaps he felt little need to hide his feelings anymore.

The retired intelligence chief raised his glass and, with it, a brief smile. "I think it's the first time I've seen you two together like this. It takes some getting used to."

"Considering you connived to get us together, so does that remark."

"But I've not actually seen you together, Spider. It does my old heart good."

"And is your old heart out to pasture or are you still conniving?"

"You must forgive him, Sir Stuart," Bulman chipped in. "He has no respect."

"You've not too much yourself, George."

"For you I have." Bulman had not yet touched his drink, which was unusual. "It's strange, the three of us sitting here together. I must admit it's unique. We can trust each other implicitly when the chips are down, but perhaps not otherwise."

"And *are* the chips down, George? Is that why we're all here like some latter day musketeers?"

"I think the chips might be down. Sometimes it all looks stupidly trivial, but Spider and I have this telepathic link and we reckon it stinks more than Billingsgate."

Scott studied Halliman while Bulman related the story. Bulman left nothing out. If the man Scott still thought of as Fairfax could not be trusted in a matter like this, then nobody could. While he listened, Halliman gently rubbed his eyes as if he was immensely weary. At times he appeared to be asleep, but Scott knew that he was not.

After Bulman had finished he swallowed his drink. Without seemingly noticing, Halliman raised a hand for the waiter; his eyes were introspective, the nearest Scott had ever seen them to being weak. It startled Scott that someone so fundamentally strong as Halliman should tail off in this way. It could not possibly be age. It was almost as if Halliman was facing ultimate defeat; the possibility upset Scott considerably, and he wondered if Bulman was feeling the same.

Part of the reason for Halliman's apparent resignation, now came out. "The death of Tom Moody upset me considerably. I'm still not over it."

Scott and Bulman waited for Halliman to continue, but he seemed to be too grieved to carry on. After a while, when the silence had become almost unbearably uncomfortable, Halliman showed a flash of steel and brushed his military mustache. There was a glimpse of the old light in his blue eyes. "Sorry about that. I was very fond of Tom. He worked for me perhaps more than you realized."

"Do *you* think he was killed?" pressed Bulman.

Halliman waited for the waiter to put down a new round of drinks. "I simply don't know. And neither do you."

"Fairfax, it's not like you to hedge. You always were a crafty bugger, but in this I thought we were all on the same side."

"Perhaps that's why I'm hedging. I would hate to lose you two as well as Tom."

Scott and Bulman exchanged glances. "Do you mean there's a possibility?" Bulman's voice was rougher than usual.

"If I knew for certain I would also know what to do about it. I'm out of touch. I cannot get near to the heart of the matter. So I'm left with surmise and that could be hopelessly wrong and, in any event, no longer carries reference. I'm not sure of my contacts. I've been out of the game too long." Halliman smiled apologetically. "Perhaps it's as simple as an old dog being unable to learn new tricks."

"I'm not sure that I follow you."

"You should, Spider, of all people. I've lived so long in the world of shadows, so long with so many suspicions that I've carried them into retirement. Successful counterespionage can only be carried out at the expense of reversing the law. A suspect is guilty before being proved innocent, and everyone is a suspect."

Halliman crossed his long legs and hitched up his trousers. "It's difficult to retire, impossible to close the mind to matters with which one had had lifelong association. I'm no good at retirement. Being with you two raises old ghosts and memories. But I must not let my interests and memories intrude into your world of today. Perhaps my whole outlook has become one of growing fantasy."

"He's become a bloody poet," Scott goaded, deliberately crudely. "You've gone soft, old cocker."

Halliman showed something of his old self, as Scott had hoped he would. "I really don't see what Maggie ever saw in you, Willie. She's so gentle a person."

Scott grinned. "So am I. Was Tom murdered or not?"

"There might have been reason for him to be."

"He was doing a job for you, Sir Stuart?"

"No, George, he was not. Nor did he tell me he was engaged in any job, officially."

"But he came to you?" Bulman insisted.

"Yes. He wanted the use of a burglar. As an ex-policeman he would know of many, of course, but he wanted one who might have worked for the firm, one I could personally recommend. He had been out of the force for some time, remember. I pointed out that he already knew one. Spider, here. But he said that he'd heard that Maggie was having a baby and it would not be a good time to ask. The consideration was typical of the man."

"Not like some coppers I know," Scott said pointedly looking straight at Bulman. But Bulman had his eyes on Halliman. "Did you give him a name? Wally Cooper, for instance?"

"No. Spider was the only one I gave. Some of our own people are trained in ingression and irruption but it happens far less than you might think. When it does happen it's vitally important and has to be to justify the risk. I couldn't pass on any of the 'Firm's' personnel and, anyway, Tom made it clear that he preferred to use a villain." Halliman smiled wryly. "Probably trusted them more."

"And that was it? He said no more?"

"Spider, he was reluctant to talk."

"Like you are now, guv?"

"If I had anything that would help you, I would pass it on. I have nothing."

"Except suspicions?" Bulman suggested.

Halliman peered over tented hands. "Suspicion suggests a direction and of someone. I have nothing like that."

"Fears old mate?"

"You were always accurate with your throws, Spider. Fears might describe it. Enough to suggest to the two of you to forget it. Perhaps it's not worth pursuing. My fears, and they are far too vague to point you in any particular direction, might be groundless for reasons I've explained. If they are not then matters will sort themselves out eventually. Don't involve yourselves. Certainly not voluntarily. It could be a mistake."

"Balls," Scott said pleasantly. He indicated Bulman. "He thinks so too, but he's still in the service so he can't be so blunt. Fairfax, if there's something around to put fear into *you* then it's got to be worth following."

"I'm touched. The only advice I can then give you is to trust no one at all. And to watch your backs."

5

COMMANDER Richard Collins was in his early fifties and a big man. In spite of his name he was a Scot who could find no trace of an Irish connection in his family tree. At one time it had worried him when he had believed that somewhere along the line an ancestor had done a cover up, in which case there was a skeleton in the family cupboard. His search for an answer had first got him interested in police work. Glasgow born, he had pounded the beat in the Gorbals and had always sworn that his granite structure was a direct result of his fight for survival in those early policing days.

"Sometimes, George," he said shrewdly as he faced Bulman across his desk, "I get the feeling that you're crossing the line without telling me. You're a canny bugger."

"It's the groove I'm in. Nobody really wants me until there's a stink and then they use me."

Collins's gray eyes twinkled. He liked Bulman because the Englishman would not tolerate bullshit, a sentiment Collins himself nurtured. He had often wondered if that was why Bulman had been given a sideways shift, but he accepted that he was a fine detective.

"So you want a plant in Albany," recapped Collins. "I need to know why."

"I don't need to tell you about the recent riots there and the immense danger that was done. One wing virtually destroyed. Very ugly. There's a whisper that it could happen again."

"It hasn't reached *me*, George."

"It has now. Anyway you're not likely to hear are you? Not really in your line. This is clandestine information."

"If I'm not likely to know, why would I be interested in putting a man in?"

"Because ostensibly he won't be put in for that purpose. You'll have to inform the prison department of the Home Office, right?"

"You mean there's a leak there?"

"Hell, Dick, there are leaks everywhere. Ask the Prime Minister. I just don't want to risk my man. Make it a case of stolen bullion or deposit box stuff you're trying to track down. I can give you a list of prisoners so that you can pick out the right one."

"Who are you putting in?"

"Do I have to tell you?"

"Jesus, you're asking me to fix it. I have to have a name."

"He can't go in under his real name anyway. Say, Anthony Sims."

Collins clasped his huge hands on the desk and leaned toward Bulman. "You're asking me a favor yet you don't trust me?"

"Willie 'Spider' Scott. And I don't want the prison governor to know either."

Collins sat back and ran his hands over his hair. "What's your game, George? The governor *has* to know."

"There might be a weak link on his staff. The boys who started the riots could turn very nasty. Scott must have maximum protection."

"For God's sake, the rioters were split up. The IRA who were part of it and might well have started it, have been removed from Albany." Collins's accent grew broader with exasperation.

"Okay, I'm a liar. Trying to keep you sharp. Will you help me?"

"You've got a bloody nerve. You're asking me to put my job on the line."

"There's nothing new in this. I'll take the can if it comes to it. What the hell; you put a bloke in and you take him out. The last thing he's going to do is to cause trouble."

"You can't take the can," Collins' tone had hardened. "The responsibility will be mine. And you're asking me to fly blind with a notable ex-con."

Bulman felt he had lost. He knew that he was asking a very great deal without giving a valid reason. "Would you do it as a personal favor?"

Collins stared hard. "I like you, George. But for a copper you bend the rules too much. There's also a little matter of my family. You haven't got one."

Bulman inclined his head. "I'd take the same view, I suppose." He rose and went over to the window. Far below was the revolving Scotland Yard sign. "This is my family." He spread his arms. "It's all I've got."

Observing Bulman's melancholy, Collins said, "Why don't you clear it with the Security Service? They'd smooth all paths."

Bulman turned back toward the desk, hands in pockets, shoulders hunched. "They wouldn't help. It's too trivial for them. Something they don't believe in."

"Your last chance is to tell me what it's really about."

"I don't know and that's the truth. I believe that part of the answer lies in Albany. I might be wrong, but whatever it is it won't sprout from official channels. I've already tried."

"You're merely confirming that I was right to refuse."

"I know." Bulman moved toward the desk. He had one more card; one he had not wanted to play for it had so far achieved nothing but obstruction, and the fewer who knew the better. "Basically, it's about Tom Moody. I think he was murdered and I'm trying to find out why and who."

"Tom? Murdered?" Collins pushed back his chair as he rose to his feet. "George, if this is another . . ." He tailed off, his face taut with anger.

"It's what I believe," Bulman said simply. "It's what Scott believes, which is why he's willing to go back inside."

Collins was towering above his desk, and Bulman suddenly thought the Commander was coming around to manhandle him.

"For God's sake," Collins burst out. *"Tom was godfather to my kids."*

SCOTT KEPT A low profile at the docks. He had already made up his mind not to go on board. Time had not erased the dislike Maggie's parents had for him. Even marriage had not softened their attitude, and he was sure that they blamed him for the loss of the baby. How someone as warmhearted and as classless as Maggie could spring from what Scott saw as utter snobs, he did not know. Maggie was schooled at Cheltenham Ladies; so she had all the prerequisites of her family background.

She was so different from her parents, yet she loved them, and, in their way, he supposed that they loved her too.

He said goodbye to Maggie in the car, a deep, passionate moment. He helped her with her luggage and left her near the embarkation bay; it was best that she got on board quickly to team up with her parents and to lose herself in the pleasures ahead. He heard her call out behind him, "Be careful, Willie, *please*," but he chose not to hear. There were passengers and their friends milling all around him so he lost himself in their sound and movement.

He climbed into the old Jaguar, left the dock area, and skirted along the coast road to turn right at the roundabout that would take him through Southampton and back onto the Winchester-London road. He had not told Maggie what was about to happen to him; had he done so she would not have gone on the cruise. Already he was missing her. Right now he needed her more than ever, but he had been right to make her go. The trip would probably solve her problems. It would not solve his, and his mood was dark as he threaded through the traffic on this hot, humid day.

THE FORD TRANSIT van brought back terrible memories but at least he was the only prisoner in it; it was better than being with other cons in the traditional green-colored bus. Scott had expected to feel low, but he had forgotten some of his earlier recollections of prison, and of gate fever and the promise he had made to kill himself rather than go back. He glanced at the policeman sitting beside him, and to whom he was handcuffed, and suddenly felt silently sick.

With a deepening of gloom he could not, for the moment, acknowledge the intrigue that had brought him here. He was a prisoner. That was all he could assimilate. He sat morosely on the journey down to the south coast, and he was silent all the way. The fact that the good weather was holding only made matters worse. On the ferry to the Isle of Wight the sea was so smooth that there was no movement at all, the only sound the thud of the engines, which was like a bass drum beat in Scott's head.

The yachts would be out at Cowes, multicolored sails ballooning, hulls creaming the placid water. And Maggie would have seen something of such a scene as the cruise ship eased out from the estuary.

Commander Collins, Bulman, and Scott himself had agreed that it was best to act the moment Maggie had gone. That would give time in hand in the event of snags. What snags, for God's sake? It was too late to think about them now.

By the time the van reached Newport, where Albany Prison rubbed shoulders with Parkhurst, a unique combination particularly as both were top-security prisons, Scott had fallen into deep melancholy.

When he climbed from the van he could smell the prison all around him. The walls towered, and above them the arc lamp pylons and the television scanners. They rekindled terrible memories.

The routine of stripping and searching and of being allocated the blue prison clothes took place as though it were only yesterday that he had last done the same. But the layout was different and so were the guards, one of whom was trying to put him at ease.

He was in. All had single cells, the doors at present open. That routine had not changed; he doubted that much had. The cell doors were electronically opened at eight in the morning and closed after lunch had been collected and taken to the cell, at midday. They opened again at one-thirty and finally closed for the night at eight-thirty P.M.

Scott sat on the bed. There was movement all around him, but it was the wrong kind of sound, too leisured, too echoing. Laughter, calls, coarse humor, and someone was trying to play a flute, a beautiful instrument being tortured.

"It could be worse," someone said.

Scott peered up. A well-built con was leaning against the doorjamb, hands in pockets, shirt open. He had a solid face, and the angled head and the look-up-from-under gaze of a boxer measuring his opponent. The eyes were stone gray, the mouth and jaw straight lined; the nose had been broken. "I'm Joe Gregory. Three doors along. You've taken over from the Brigadier." The accent was London East End.

"Brigadier? The con man?"

"You know him?"

"Heard of him. I thought he was dead." Scott thought it best not to admit to knowing anyone.

"No. The Brig will go on forever. He'll be back. Can I come in?"

"Feel free." Scott's irony was intentional. He was not sure of Gregory, who wandered over to the high-placed second floor window and turned to lean against the wall, gazing down at Scott speculatively.

"What're you in for?"

"What are you?" It was usual to find out on the grapevine, not to ask a direct question.

Gregory's eyes were brittle. "I was trying to be friendly. Don't try that on some of the jokers here. This place is full of heavies."

"And now there's another one." Scott stood up and he could see that Gregory had not realized his full height and size, but he did not underrate the fellow Londoner. "Look," he said, "I'm just in. I'm not in the best of moods. Okay? Armed robbery. Caught bang to rights on the job before firing a bloody shot. Didn't make any difference with the magistrate. Category A. Twenty years. What's your excuse?"

"I croaked my old woman. Throttled the bitch. She didn't stop nagging for fifteen years."

"Couldn't you leave her?"

Gregory gave a sickly grin. "Funny thing but I couldn't. So I'd go out and get pissed and try to shut out the bloody awful sound of her. *Should* have left her." He grinned again. "In the end she left me for the great voice contest in the sky. Some poor bastard will be suffering somewhere wherever she is."

Scott had heard it all before. Strangely, he was feeling a little better. The macabre dialogue at least broke the monotony.

"Is Horseface Harper in here?"

"Horseface? I think he got transferred. Didn't he have some relatives up in Nottingham? I think he went up there."

"What about Wally Cooper?"

"Wally's here. You won't see much of him, though."

"How do you mean?"

Gregory stepped away from the wall. "I'd better fill you in. What's your name?"

"Tony Sims."

"There were four wings. One was wrecked during the riots so we're down to three, with eighty of us in each. They intend to increase to a hundred later on. They really smashed the place up *and* the roof. The inquiry that followed reckoned the whole scheme was hatched during exercise time in the yard. It was the one time when everyone was together. So the bastard guards decided that must not happen again. Each wing now exercises separately. They reckon it cuts down the chance to conspire. The bloody riots were a waste of time anyway."

"What's this got to do with Wally Cooper?"

"'E's in another bloody wing. Transferred the other day."

Scott's spirits sank. Was this a monumental mess? Had Bullman really thought it through? Very carefully, he said. "A pity. I believe he's a good creeper. Used to do a bit myself."

Gregory laughed, but it was an ugly sound. "You want to go back to college? No better place, Tony. But your only chance is maybe in the wood mills or library or somewhere like that. You won't be able to walk in on him as I've done on you." And then more thoughtfully, "How long you been at it?"

"Longer than I care to remember."

"First time inside?"

"No. I've done the Moor, Hull, Scrubs. Anyone ever break out?"

"Jesus. You can give up that idea. I believe two made it. Just two. But I don't now how long for or how far they got. Since the riots the security is even worse." Gregory crossed to the door. "Before the riots you could wedge a book in the crack by the hinges and then smash the door shut. The bloody hinges would fly off with the strain. No problem. But since the riots they've changed all the hinges. See those?" Gregory pointed. "Cantilever. The book dodge doesn't work anymore. We're the poor bastards who suffer. The sods who started it are no longer here. Forget it," he said again. "It's easier to kill someone in here than to break out."

Scott was not sure why he felt that was a warning for him. His depression might have gone over the top, and he was accepting that anything said was aimed at him.

They talked on for another few minutes and Gregory then left. Scott sat thinking. The security of Category A prisons is largely on the outside. There are, of course, internal safeguards, but it is considered that long-term prisoners are less likely to lose their heads in sudden fits of gate fever if they have more freedom in the prison itself. They could come and go from their cells and each had a key to lock the door when they left, but the key worked only from the outside.

Scott knew all this. His main danger was that someone here would recognize him, but it had been a long time since he had been inside and Bulman had arranged for Scott's dark hair to be dyed a straw color and his eyebrows had suffered the same treatment. As the stay was expected to be short the risk was acceptable and quick access to the governor had been arranged should a crisis occur.

When the cell door closed that night at eight-thirty he belatedly realized that he had nothing with which to occupy himself. He should

63

have taken a book from the library. Radios were allowed in the cells, but he had felt that he would not be in long enough. His personal preparation had been bad. He, of all people, well knew the soul-destroying monotony of prison, yet he had allowed himself to be too influenced by the need to get out.

He had already established one thing though. Wally Cooper was in Albany, and Wally's name had been omitted from the list of prisoners given to George Bulman. All Scott now had to do was to devise some way to meet Cooper and then get out fast. He slept restlessly that night, aware all the time of where he was and the devastating effect it would have on Maggie if she knew. Bulman was on another planet.

COMMANDER RICHARD COLLINS was in his office early in spite of a late-night fracas that had involved lending some of his men to the bomb squad. He felt tired, having got to bed at three in the morning.

At eleven A.M. while he was trying to focus his eyes on some debatable charge sheets, his intercom rang. His secretary's voice came over the box.

"A Mr. Ashton would like to see you, sir. Home Office."

Collins did not know anyone called Ashton at the Home Office. "What's he want?"

"He says it's for your ears only."

"Has he an ID?"

"Yes, sir."

Collins disliked Ashton the moment he walked through the door. The man smacked of establishment and that alone was sufficient to make Collins' hackles rise. Average height, neat dark mohair suit, spotless shirt, and Etonian tie, which was faultlessly knotted. Ashton had arrogant features but good bearing. Collins accepted the bearing as part of the superior image of the man. No bowler hat and no umbrella. Bloody miracle, reflected Collins, but he detected that the neat hair had been lacquered. There must be a breeze-up outside.

Ashton appeared to be in his early forties. He crossed the room to Collins and held out a hand. "Commander. So good of you to see me." He indicated a chair. "May I?"

"Of course." Collins was aware that he was wearing his feelings on his face. He had not intended to ask Ashton to sit down. "What can I do for you?"

Ashton sat, adjusted his trouser crease, and gazed indifferently across

64

the desk. His face was pale, with little character. But the eyes were bright, very steady, and very cold.

"I believe you've placed someone in Albany prison."

"The prison department of the Home Office is well aware of that. What's your problem?"

"What's the name of this man?"

"The Home Office is well aware of that too, Mr. Ashton. As you seem to be so badly informed do you mind if I see your ID, sir?"

"Your secretary has...." Ashton noted Collins's rock features. "Oh, all right." He produced the ID from a leather wallet and opened it for Collins to see. Collins leaned forward and took the folding card from the manicured hand. Ashton made a belated grab for it, but Collins had already placed it on the desk edge in front of him.

Ashton said, "That was totally unnecessary, Commander."

"Was it? You come in here as a total stranger, claiming to have come from the Home Office when your card mentions only Board of Trade Security, and you make demands."

"You know the form only too well."

Collins smiled as he spoke into his intercom. "Cathy, get on to the Home Office and check out F. Ashton, Board of Trade ID." He read out the remaining details and put down the phone. He flipped the card across the desk, and Ashton left his seat to retrieve it. As he picked it up he gave Collins a scathing glance. "It won't make any difference, Commander."

"It will to me. I like to know whom I'm dealing with. Now, please carry on with what you were saying." Collins was pleased because Ashton was ruffled, and he loved to ruffle establishment types. When Ashton made no further comment, Collins added, "Come on, Mr. Ashton, you should approve my security check."

"It's difficult to argue against it. It was simply unnecessary."

"One rule for you and another for the rest of us? If our positions were reversed, you'd have turned me inside out by now."

"Commander, we are simply getting nowhere. All I want to know is the name of your Albany plant."

"Refer back to the Home Office."

"Oh, I have the name of Anthony Sims. I mean his real name."

"He did not go in under an alias. So far as I am aware that *is* his real name."

"Was that the name Detective Superintendent Bulman gave you?"

"What's he got to do with it? George Bulman is nearer to your lot than mine."

"I didn't expect to find you so obstructive. We're both on the same side."

"I'm beginning to wonder. I don't like being questioned about the men I plant with Home Office approval. I say again, refer to them, Mr. Ashton."

"But they don't know that the man sent to Albany is not the man they think he is."

"Then you'd better tell them."

The internal telephone rang, and Collins put the receiver close to his ear. He watched Ashton's face as he listened. "Thanks, Cathy." He put down the phone, pleased that Cathy had used the phone and not the squawk box. He sat back and stared thoughtfully at Ashton. "You've lied to me, Mr. Ashton. You're not Home Office at all."

"I never said I was." Ashton was not put out. "I told your secretary I was here with the *approval* of the Home Office. Ring Toby Russell—he will vouch for me."

"Toby Russell, eh!" The most junior of junior ministers. "I feel no need to ring him, Mr. Ashton. If you need my help, you come for it openly and with the proper credentials. I'm sick and tired of people like you who think they can sneak in on some flimsy pretext and con an old copper like me into giving information that exists only in their own minds." Collins had risen and so had his temper. "I would suggest that you're nearer to the Foreign than the Home Office so what the hell are you doing here anyway?"

Ashton was still unabashed. "You're reacting well below your rank, Commander. I was hoping that if Anthony Sims is who I think he is, he might be of some use to us while he's in Albany. That's all."

"I don't know who you think he is but so far as I'm concerned Sims has enough on his plate sniffing out a great deal of missing valuables."

"As you explained to the prison department of the Home Office," said Ashton rising with a slight smile.

"As you say, Mr. Ashton. Get someone else to do your dirty work."

"It looks as if I will have to unless I go over your head, Commander."

"You haven't the muscle to go over my head, and don't threaten me in my own office. Tell them to send someone of authority next time. Good day to you."

"The degree of cooperation from the Metropolitan Police has been duly noted," Ashton said as he opened the door.

Collins sat down as the door closed. He looked like an angry bull, but his sharp mind was racing in every direction. He rang George Bulman.

"Someone's been nosing after Scott," he said bitterly. "Why the hell do I have to react like you when I'm doing your job. You'd better come and see me. Now."

SCOTT WORKED IN the carpenter's shop, or wood mill. During this time he tried to find out which wing Wally Cooper was in, but his chances were limited and he also ran up against some reticence. Wally was not popular with some. He had been jailed as a traitor, and a sprinkling of prisoners carried a strange kind of patriotism. Others were all for the Reds, someone who could destroy the present social structure. Scott collected his lunch from the landing hotplate and returned to his cell to be locked in; he had little appetite.

In the afternoon he did another spell in the wood mill. All the time he kept an eye open for Wally Cooper, whose photograph Bulman had dug out for him. The separating of the wings for exercise was proving to be devastating. Exercise time had always been a misnomer for a get-together and particularly to meet old friends from other wings. Scott decided that if he could not locate Cooper in three days he would ask to see the governor for a transfer. This was the arranged procedure for his release. The governor knew why he was here, or at least the reason that Commander Collins had contrived.

Ernie Porter was a bank robber of some considerable experience. His last job had been a deposit box vault. Officially, this was the man Scott had to contact for the sake of appearance. Only Bulman, Commander Collins, and he knew his real target.

Scott found Porter in his cell during the early evening. Porter was sitting on his bed reading a book. He looked up as Scott stood in the doorway, his gaze noncommittal.

"I'm from along the landing," Scott explained. "New boy. Tony Sims."

"Oh, yeah. You didn't knock."

There were too many hard stares about. Scott was not worried by them, he could cope, but he wanted information and he really needed

67

time he was not prepared to give. He weighed up Porter carefully. "Knock? Why don't you get a bell on your door?"

Porter glowered above his book. "Piss off. Learn the house rules and the pecking order."

"Don't try bullshitting me. You're an unfriendly bastard, aren't you? A pity. I had a lot of respect for what you pulled off."

Porter lowered his book onto his chest. "Well, you've interrupted, you may just as well come in." He did not move from the bed as Scott entered; nor did he ask how Scott had learned of the job he had pulled off; the newspapers had been full of it. It had been estimated that valuables worth millions were still missing, but it would be a long time before Porter would enjoy the benefit.

Scott pulled the chair out from under the small table and straddled it, arms along the back. Porter's eyes were suspicious and probing. "Your face rings a bell," he said bluntly.

Scott nodded, "It's possible. But I'm sure we haven't met. I don't forget faces." He was being as direct as Porter, refusing to be intimidated.

They talked for a while, but it was an uneasy exchange, with Porter giving the impression that he knew Scott was after something more than idle chat. While they talked other prisoners went past on occasion and one popped his head around the door to tell Porter that the two cigarettes he owed would be returned the next day.

At last Scott said, "I heard Wally Cooper was in here, but in one of the other wings."

"Wally? Yeah. He was here until a couple of days ago. When did you come?"

"Yesterday."

"It would be the day before then. You know him?"

"No. I was once in his line of business. Still do it on occasion but the heavy stuff brings better money."

"On the creep? Yeah, Wally was good at that. He swears he was fixed up but who can you believe?"

"Why did they move him? He's no troublemaker from what I hear."

Porter picked up his book. "Who knows? I know he didn't request it. Speak to Archie Shaw; he was close to Wally, if you know what I mean."

Scott hesitated as he moved to the door. Porter glanced over the top of the book. "One floor down." And then pointedly, "'E might be there now."

But as Scott left Porter's cell he was reflecting on the strange coincidence of Wally Cooper's being transferred just before his own arrival. He felt that someone was not only anticipating any moves that he and Bulman made but actually had foreknowledge of them. First Habise's office and now this. He no longer felt secure and had the sensation of being deliberately cut off.

6

*A*RCHIE Shaw was crouched on his bed with his knees clasped under his chin. The blue-clad figure had a defenseless, pathetic air, and the lean, hollowed face had furrows almost down to the elfin chin. Moist brown eyes stared fixedly into space. Shaw was so engrossed in his own misery that Scott felt compelled to give a gentle knock before entering. The large, dog-like eyes switched to Scott.

"Can I come in?"

"If you like. I've nothing to say to anyone."

The timbre of the voice, the half-whining style, confirmed Porter's hint of the possible relationship between Wally Cooper and Archie Shaw. "You miss him?"

The eyes switched again. "I don't know you. What would you know about it?"

Scott thought Shaw was about to weep. "Grapevine. I arrived yesterday. I particularly wanted a word with Wally. Maybe you can help."

"They shifted him. Now why would they do that? We were model prisoners. Took no part in the riots and have always cooperated with the guards. Why did they have to take him away? He was such a lovely man."

"Maybe you'll get him back. A little later." After I've gone, thought Scott.

Shaw showed more interest. Scott had not uttered the usual crude observations, the sneers, and the cruel jokes; he seemed concerned. "You know Wally?"

"No," replied Scott, stepping inside. "Heard of him. Sounded like the sort of bloke I'd like to meet."

Shaw's gaze sharpened. He clung to his legs as if cold. Suddenly he realized that Scott was not competition; there was no danger from that direction. He wiped his eyes, then moved his legs so that they dangled just clear of the floor. Scott could now see how small he was; a frail, vulnerable figure, the quick movements indicating a sensitive, perhaps volatile nature.

"You won't be able to meet him now," Shaw said.

"Maybe when things quiet down they'll allow the wings to exercise together again."

"That's no use." Shaw did not care how much he gave away. There were no more barbs that could hurt him.

"Why did they move him?"

Shaw gestured angrily. "Nobody knows. I've spoken to the guards and they don't know. The Governor will know but he's not likely to tell anyone. Everything was happy and then bang-wallop and Walter had gone. God, I miss him."

"Why didn't they let you go with him?" The staff turned a blind eye to illicit affairs, it helped keep the peace.

"I asked if I could go with him. They said there was no room."

"Maybe you didn't go because they know he's coming back."

Shaw's eyes brightened. "Do you think so?" And then, "How the hell would you know. You haven't been here five minutes."

"It's possible, though. Maybe they're punishing him for something." Scott took a chance. "Maybe someone doesn't like traitors."

Scott thought Shaw was about to jump at him. The small figure hunched up as if coiling, then his head went back and he laughed. It was a vicious grating sound, full of derision and disbelief. When he stopped, Shaw said, "My God, you don't know much. Walter was never a traitor; he wouldn't know how to set about it."

"But that was what he went down for; wasn't it?"

"The poor love was set up. Oh, he broke in all right. There was none better at it. He fashioned himself on an old creeper called Spider Scott. Ever heard of him?"

"Doesn't ring a bell," Scott replied uneasily.

"Then you couldn't have been at the game long." Shaw laughed bitterly again. "Government papers! They were planted on him."

"What did he lift then?"

Shaw pulled himself together. "What's it to you?"

"Christ, if I'd been set up, I'd be bloody mad. He must have pinched something that annoyed somebody to do that to him. I mean, thirty years?"

"Have you any cigarettes?"

"Sorry, mate. I don't smoke."

"And I suppose you only go with women?"

"I'm the old-fashioned type. But live and let live, I say."

"Well, that's something. Walter never knew what he pinched."

"Oh, come on . . ."

"No, it's true. It wasn't a normal job. He was doing a favor for someone. He was paid, of course. A simple job. All he took was something in a sealed envelope. It was so small the envelope could have been empty. That's what he told me, and he wouldn't lie to *me*."

"If it was sealed, it could easily have contained government secrets. How would he know?"

"If they were government secrets they must have been on microdots. But what he was pulled in for was a pile of stuff found in his pad that he'd never seen before in his life."

"Rotten bastards," Scott said. "Why do that to him? I suppose they could have come from the flat he broke into."

"That's what they said in court. It was all hush-hush. The name of the bloke whose pad he broke into wasn't even announced in court. But he was willing to swear that the documents had been taken the night Walter broke in."

"What happened to the envelope he did take?"

Shaw suddenly clutched at the bedside. His eyes became furtive as he realized how much he had said. "Mind your own business. You're asking too many questions."

"I'd be asking Wally if he was here. And he'd be giving me answers."

"Well you won't get any more from me. I've said too much."

"You haven't said enough, Archie." Scott thought it over. "What does Wally mean to you."

"I won't say. You're too bloody nosey."

73

"Do you love the man?"

Shaw stared at Scott. The question had been serious.

"Yes, I do."

"Enough to help him? Maybe get him out?"

"Nobody gets out from here."

"I don't mean break out. If he didn't really do it, then it needs exposing."

"You think he's the only innocent man inside?"

"He's not innocent. He broke into someone's flat. But if you're right then the caper has been distorted. Would you help him if you could?"

"Of course. But that's not possible."

"It might be. A lot depends on how much you care for him. You would have to keep your mouth closed from now on."

"You mean I haven't done with you? Well, I'm upset. And anyway you can't have it both ways. If it's important to Walter they can pull out my toenails and I won't talk. And that includes you."

Scott knew he was on a knife-edge. If he couldn't get to Wally Cooper, Shaw was the best substitute. "Supposing I can help Wally?"

Shaw's gaze swept toward the door. Prisoners were frequently passing, some making the odd bawdy remark. Both men had lowered their voices, aware that the dialogue was now on another plane. "That's impossible. Don't con me. Jesus, I don't even know your name."

"Tony Sims. I'm not conning you. If I knew what it was Wally took, who he took it from, and who he gave it to, I might be able to help him."

"You came to see me just to find all this out, didn't you?"

"Absolutely. I heard you were pals."

"Well, you can eff off. You're trying to find out what he wouldn't tell the court. You're a bloody copper."

"Keep your voice down for Christ's sake." Scott glanced anxiously toward the door. "How can I be a copper? *They* put Wally here. And if I was a copper I'd have been put in the same bloody wing. Use your loaf."

"Who are you then?"

"Don't be daft. But I'm here to help him. Believe me. If you love the man you'll never get a better chance to prove it."

"I need to think."

"Well, don't think with your mouth open. Keep it closed or we're both in trouble."

"I'll sleep on it. Ask me again tomorrow. But I don't like it."

"Whether you like it or not, don't seek advice on it. Not from anyone. Tell me one thing, though; did Wally have any visitors?"

"He wasn't married, although he had been once. He has two brothers who are both in South Africa."

"You haven't answered me."

When Shaw did not reply Scott added, "If I was the fuzz I'd bloody-well know, wouldn't I? I'm not asking much."

"He did have one. Not so very long ago."

"Who?"

"He didn't say."

"You mean he didn't say a thing?"

"Only that it was a man. He didn't say who. It upset me at the time. I thought it might have been an old boyfriend."

Scott turned his back to the door. He had been standing throughout realizing the risk of the rumors that could circulate throughout the prison wing. "I can put your mind at rest. I think I know who it was. But he gave you no hint at all?"

"Only that it was tied up with his trial. He seemed a bit hopeful for a few days. And then suddenly, quite recently, he became morbid and depressed. It worried me. He was still depressed when he was transferred to the other wing. They shouldn't have separated us; I could have helped him."

"Maybe they didn't want you to," Scott said bitterly. "I'll see you tomorrow then. But bear in mind I'm about the only bloke who can help Wally. Think carefully and dig out all you can."

On his way back to his own cell Scott was thinking that Wally Cooper's depression was probably a result of Tom Moody's death. Moody had most likely been trying to help him. Scott hoped that the pattern would not continue. But someone seemed to have overlooked Cooper's liaison with Shaw, unless it had not been noticed, or had been well covered up, but that was difficult to do in prison. It was possible that Shaw really had little to offer.

When the doors closed for the night Scott lay on his bed thinking. If Wally Cooper had been transferred because Scott was arriving, it was clear that someone in the prison already knew that Tony Sims was Scott. Equally, there must be something to hide. And the moves were being made very high up.

75

As Scott thought it through, the main possibility turned him cold. Wally Cooper had obviously been moved away from him in case he talked. The affair between Cooper and Shaw must be known. Which meant that someone had wanted Scott to approach Shaw, who might have only very limited knowledge; he did not know, for instance, who Cooper's visitor had been. But contact with Shaw would inevitably make Scott show his hand. Scott sat up. That could mean only one thing. And that, in turn, revealed the size of the opposition.

He slept restlessly. This was only his second night in the cell, yet already there was a feeling of permanency about it, as if he had been given a life sentence like Cooper. At slopping-out next morning he felt as if he had not slept at all.

He did not see Shaw again until exercise time. Shaw was across the yard, but Scott made no attempt to go near him. Shaw was talking to a small group of prisoners and seemed to be in no hurry to make any form of contact. Scott kept to himself, avoiding conversation with any of the other prisoners.

The guards served lunch on each landing, a job they detested, but it prevented recrimination against prisoners were they to be served by their own. Scott took his meal back to his cell, and all doors were closed at midday. He ate slowly, thinking all the time. At half past one the doors were opened again, and he cleaned his plate at the landing sink. He returned to the wood-mill and there was no sign of Shaw. He had no idea where Shaw worked. As the day progressed, it became clear that Shaw was making no effort to contact him.

In the evening Scott made his move. There were two television rooms, one with a black-and-white set supplied by the prison, the other, with a colored set paid for by the prisoners themselves. Scott took up a position without making it too obvious. He had selected a spot near the room with the black-and-white set. He was right. A little later Shaw approached with another prisoner whose arm was around Shaw's shoulders. They went into the TV room, and the sound of music briefly escaped.

Scott did not hesitate. He casually made his way to Shaw's cell. He knew that he was playing a dangerous game. If the other cons believed he was stealing from another prisoner there would be big trouble. The door was closed but unlocked. He stood with his back to the wall at the side of the door listening to the movement around him.

He searched the cell during the gaps between approaching footsteps. There were places he could leave until last, unlikely places like the wash area. But first of all he just stood there, scanning the cell section by section. He did not expect what he was searching for to be easily discovered, but it was, although hidden well out of sight.

Scott was aware of the increasing sounds from the landings. He would have to be quick. He stepped forward, stooped, and rolled on his back beside the bed. He located the bug almost at once. It was fixed to the framework near the foot of the bed. He rose quickly, just as someone scurried past the door.

He returned to his own cell while the fear built up in him. On the way his response to the odd greeting was dull and automatic, and he was relieved to sit at his small table.

Everything was stark and blank. He had nothing with him to remind him of the outside world; not even a picture of Maggie. He had never felt so cut off. He left the cell and walked the landing to the nearest warder. "I'd like an appointment with the Governor, please. It's urgent."

"It's always urgent, Tony, isn't it? Don't let it get to you." The guard was sandy-haired and tall and his tone was friendly. "You'll get used to it."

"It's not gate fever. I have an arrange . . . look, could you just tell the Governor I must see him."

"I'd have to give him an idea why."

"I want a transfer." God, it sounded pathetic. "Would you please let him know."

The guard smiled. "You've only just arrived here."

"Just tell him. He'll see me when he knows."

"Okay, I'll tell him. Now go and calm down. You'll just catch the early film on telly, if you hurry."

"Aren't you going to tell him now?"

"I'm on duty. When I'm off, I'll put in a report. Okay?" When the warder saw Scott's expression he felt compassion. "You must face it. You're in here without privileges. You've lost your freedom. That's what it's about. Now don't worry. I'll tell him as soon as I can."

Scott nodded hopelessly. He turned and walked slowly back to his cell. He sat on the bed and faced the door. The governor was his only line of communication. Bulman and Maggie were in another world. Someone had placed a bug in Archie Shaw's cell, with or without his

77

knowledge. If Shaw knew, then he had been primed, but Scott somehow felt that Shaw did not know. What was certain was that Scott had shown his hand. But to whom? Cells were periodically searched during spot checks. The placing of the bug must have come from the highest authority or someone had taken a grave risk of its being discovered. He recalled the case at Wakefield prison when a prisoner had bugged the governor's office and picked it up on his UHF radio in his cell. It meant one more uneasy night.

The morning could not come quickly enough for Scott, and he was dressed well before he needed to be. His impatience was not eased when he discovered that the warder he had spoken to was now off duty. After breakfast he tackled another warder and was told that the governor was away for the day. A request could be made to the deputy governor. But Scott wanted to see the governor himself. When would he be back? Perhaps tonight, perhaps tomorrow; he was in London.

The last piece of information was gratuitous. But it did not help Scott's mounting frustration. It was all going wrong, and he felt there was a sinister reason.

That morning he was approached by Archie Shaw in the exercise yard and was surprised but resigned. What difference could it make now; his cover was already blown.

"You were supposed to contact me," whined Shaw. "I've decided to help you."

"And I've decided I can do without it. Push off, we'll get talked about."

"After pleading with me? After claiming that all you want to do is to help Walter? What's happened?"

Scott was gazing around the yard to see who might be watching them. Nobody in particular seemed to be, not even the guards. Scott looked down at the whippetlike Shaw.

"Unless you can tell me what was in the envelope Wally lifted, or where he pinched it from, you can't help me."

"Well, that's a turnaround, I must say."

"I've had more time to think."

"I know he was worried about something."

"But he never told you what."

"Well, he hinted at things . . ."

"Archie, you'd better look under your bed. And in future keep your door locked."

"*What?*"

"Just have a look. And don't talk in your sleep."

"Have you been in . . ."

Scott walked away before Shaw could finish; he had noticed a guard taking an interest in them. Shaw was about to follow when he saw the unmistakable warning in Scott's eyes.

After lunch Scott did another spell in the wood mill and afterward went back to his cell. Someone's radio was on, not loud but enough to send out disjointed dialogue, and the flute was being tortured again.

"You're taking it badly, mate. You should snap out of it."

Scott looked up at Joe Gregory's solid frame. "I must admit I'm down."

"Why don't you ask someone to bring in a radio; you're allowed two letters out a month."

"Yes, I know."

"There's a bloke along the corridor who has a budgie. The bloody bird stands in his mouth. Or can't you afford one?"

Scott shrugged, hoping that Gregory would leave. "I can afford one. And a radio. I'll see to it." Suddenly his gloom was overridden by another feeling. Gregory was right; he should snap out of it. He was allowing depression to get on top.

Now something was warning him, an old instinct overriding his gloom. Gregory was standing just outside the door. Scott saw him glance along the landing in each direction. It was a casual movement but following it Gregory stepped into the cell, hands in pockets. "If you want to borrow my radio you can until you're fixed up with your own. I don't use it a lot. I read."

Coming from Gregory the offer was too generous. Scott was sitting at his table. As Gregory came in he replied, "That's good of you, Joe. Appreciate it." He took the chair with him as he rolled back when Gregory lunged with something that looked like a meat skewer.

Gregory, aware that he had hashed it, decided to go all the way. He skirted the chair as Scott rolled and used a "scissors" on Gregory's legs. Gregory crashed down, half on top of Scott, who was finding the narrow space far too restricting and besides, he had one arm trapped under Gregory's weight. Scott tried to pull his arm free, pushing at Gregory with the other, but Gregory was regaining his balance. From an awkward angle he lunged at Scott again.

Scott managed to squirm and the skewer slashed his shirt sleeve. He pushed with all his power and managed to move Gregory against the bed. He half-rose, and tried to steady himself. Gregory hooked the chair through Scott's legs, Scott lost balance, and Gregory reached up to pierce Scott through the stomach.

Scott fell to his knees holding his stomach, and Gregory scrambled away from him before finding his feet. Gregory still held the skewer by a rough wooden handle. He lunged again but Scott rolled away and kicked out at Gregory's shin. From along the landing came abuse as two cons started to argue; that would attract the guards. In panic, Gregory wiped the handle of the skewer on his jacket, then threw the bloodied weapon down and fled. He took one last look as he went; Scott was lying coiled on his side, quite still.

7

"I T'S time we heard from Spider," commented Bulman. Commander Collins tapped his desk. "It's only three days. Not that."

"He works fast. If there's anything to dig out, he'll get it."

Collins smiled. "It's funny that you should be so worried about an old lag like Scott."

"I owe him."

"I thought you'd settled that debt. Can't be that you've actually grown to like him?"

Bulman shrugged. He was sitting on the corner of Collins's desk, probably the only police officer below the rank of commander who could get away with it. "There's a lot going for him. His honesty, for one thing."

"You mean loyalty. How can an old thief like that be honest?"

"No. I mean honesty. *And* loyalty. I owe him for what he's doing now. I know what it meant to him to go back inside." Bulman wagged a finger. "And don't forget he's also doing it to sniff out any monkey business connected with the godfather to your kids."

Collins inclined his head. "Even so, it's early days. If he's to be like one of the cons he can't phone or have extra privileges. Contact has to be made through the Governor."

Bulman stood up and hunched his shoulders. His craggy face was

81

solemn. "That seems a weak arrangement now. I know it's what we agreed, but it's put the onus on him."

"Dammit, he's the only one who will know when he's ready. Stop worrying, George."

"I'm not happy about it. It's funny, isn't it? All three of us are doing this for an old friend. Sometimes it seems crazy."

"Not if it turns out that Tom *was* murdered. And knowing you, there's more to it than that."

"If there is, I'll let you know. Look, can't you ring the governor? See if anything's happened?"

"It's too soon. Even if Wally Cooper is our man, he's not going to blab until Scott has gained his confidence. If you're really worried, why don't you go down there?"

"I don't want to go officially because I'm not supposed to be involved. But even if I did show my hand, it would mean a private interview with him and that can get around. I don't want to frighten Wally Cooper off."

Bulman gazed miserably around the office. "I don't get anything this size."

Shrewdly, Collins observed, "You really are worried, aren't you? Is it because of the visit I had from Ashton?"

"Partly. What would a Foreign Office jerk be doing snooping after a prison plant who happened to be Spider Scott?" Bulman could not tell Collins that Scott had broken into a Harley Street practice that was wired up to the hilt.

Collins flattened his big hands on the desk. "Look George. Give it another couple of days, then I'll ring through. If nothing's happened or if Scott is not happy, I'll lift him out. Okay?"

Bulman said it was but was not convincing.

SCOTT CAME AROUND from the anesthetic feeling slightly sick. A hot poker was sticking in his stomach. When he put his hand down he felt a pad over the wound. He moved his head slowly. A blood drip was suspended by the bed, the needle taped to his arm. On the other side of the bed was a drip feed, but it was not connected.

Other beds were occupied by men reading or listening to the radio.

Hospitals have their own smell, even in the absence of the pervading redolence of ether and disinfectant. There was a guard by the door and

a male nurse passed by. Scott suddenly realized that he had been transferred to Parkhurst Prison Hospital; Albany had only a small sick bay
with one bed.

Nobody came near him, and when the lights went out he guessed that
nobody would. He assumed from that that his condition was satisfac-
tory. No one was expecting him to die.

Scott turned his head to the ghostly form of the drip. Already
someone was snoring heavily. He could hear men breathing and moving, yet he had never felt so alone in his life. Worse than that, he felt
abandoned. He was isolated and had nobody to discuss his problems
with. Gregory had tried to kill him for a reason he did not understand
but was somehow connected with Tom Moody and Wally Cooper.

THE DOCTOR CAME mid-morning. He studied Scott's chart, and
then came up the side of the bed. "How do you feel?"

"Fine." It was the right answer. The doctor was used to malingerers.

"Good. It's not much of a wound. Not very deep. And it's narrow.
You were lucky that more damage was not done."

"It feels deep."

The doctor smiled. For a man who dealt with tough villains on a daily
basis his manner was mild, but Scott could see that he would not be easy
to fool. "You have a thick muscle layer and a band of subcutaneous fat.
The weapon went in straight, fortunately. Had it gone between the ribs
for your heart, you'd have a sheet over your head and you wouldn't be
in here."

"Thanks very much."

"When you are questioned, it's something for you to bear in mind.
Whoever did this to you had the right tool but struck the wrong place.
But you're healthy, you'll heal quickly enough. You lost a fair amount
of blood, by the way."

"Can I eat normally?"

"A light diet only."

"Is the Governor back, doctor? I must see him."

"You mean the Albany governor? I've no doubt at all that he will
want to see you."

"When can I get up?"

The doctor was surprised. "Most of you hang on here as long as you
can."

"Not me. I'm feeling better already."

"Give your wound a chance. A few days. If you take it easy."

Scott sank back; he couldn't wait a few days. The doctor looked at him curiously. He could tell that prison was not new to Scott, but somehow he did not fit into one.

Vernon Healy, the Albany Prison governor, visited Scott just before lunch. He had with him the principal officer, who was in charge of the male nurses.

"Pull the screens around. And then leave us."

Vernon Healy still managed to hold on to compassion even though he sometimes had been trapped by it over the years. He was a good governor performing a very difficult job. He showed compassion now as he gazed steadily at Scott. "I'm sorry this happened. The story is that you tried to commit suicide."

Scott laughed and the pain of his wound made him stop sharply. "I didn't make too good a job of it then. I think I'd have done better."

"So do I, Sims. Just the same my officers tell me you were rather depressed."

"I had cause. It was a mistake coming here."

"You want to elaborate?"

It was difficult to report a bug under Archie Shaw's bed when, so far as the governor was concerned, Scott had come to make contact with Ernie Porter, the deposit box robber.

"I won't get anywhere with Porter. I'm going to pull out."

"Is that what you wanted to see me about?"

"Yes. Had I been able to yesterday, I might have missed this lot."

"That's doubtful, I'm afraid. My instructions are to keep you here for the moment."

"*What?*" The fear was like ice in his guts. He wanted to be sick. "You mean until I'm better?"

"That too, but until I receive instructions to the contrary."

Scott struggled up. The pressure on his stomach made him grunt in pain. "Whose instructions?"

"Well, now, you would hardly expect me to answer that."

Scott gazed at the governor, who appeared to be embarrassed by what he was saying. "Let's get this straight. I'm a plant here." Scott kept his voice very low. "You know it. I know it. And Commander Collins of the Yard knows it. When I wanted out I was to approach you. I'm doing that now."

"I understand that, Sims. What you say is true. What might not be is your real reason for being here. I, as governor, would not take kindly to being deliberately misled. But I have no power to change the arrangement. Someone else has, and that power has been exercised."

"There's no way I can be held here without committing a crime and being tried and found guilty of it. There will be one big stink over this. Governor, I suggest you contact Commander Collins straight away."

"But you *are* here, Sims. Perhaps someone thinks the crime has been committed here. My orders are clear. I've no doubt the whole business will be cleared up."

"Are you refusing to ring Commander Collins?"

"Don't speak to me as if our roles were reversed. Of course I'll ring the commander. But I have to tell you that my authority to detain you comes from a higher source than his."

"He can straighten it out, though."

"Unless he himself has been deceived. That could change things."

"He knows all there is to know." Scott was not sure of the truth of that or what Bulman had actually told Collins. Bulman would only tell him what was necessary.

"Well, then, there should be no trouble. In any event you must stay in the hospital until you're fit. Perhaps by then everything will be settled."

Scott's despair rose. "You realize that by keeping me here he'll have another go at me."

"Not in this hospital. Who stabbed you?"

"I don't know."

"You struggled with the man, your sleeve was ripped, and yet you don't know. You're not helping yourself, Sims."

"I was sitting at the table. He must have crept in behind me and brought his arm over. I don't recall the sleeve being ripped."

"I'm expected to believe that?"

"That's how it was."

"I had hoped you would know better. This is not informing. We're talking of attempted murder."

"I'm sorry. If I think of anything I'll pass it on."

The chair creaked as Healy moved. "Well, perhaps those on high know what they're doing by detaining you. There is the possibility that Porter, did it. After all, he was the man you were supposed to cultivate."

"I'd made contact. But it was too early to get anywhere. It wasn't him."

"How remarkable of you to be so sure, considering you did not see the man. I'll have him up just the same."

"If you do that, you blow my cover."

"Why should it worry you? You've already told me that you want out."

"Yes, but I'm not bloodywell getting out, am I? I'll still be here. He could open up a new danger."

"All right, if you don't know who, have you any idea why?"

Scott shook his head. "None. I don't know anyone here."

"Someone obviously knows you. Don't you think it strange, Sims?"

"I've been wracking my brain. Have you any idea at all why I'm being illegally detained?"

"That it's against your will does not make it illegal. Everyone here is staying against his will. I don't know what you've done or even if you've done anything. But if I find out that your reason for being here is other than stated, then I myself will demand some action against you. I will not have my prison used as a convenience for outsiders."

"I take it I can have visitors?"

"You can apply in the usual way."

"That sounds like a backhanded refusal."

"Visitors are a privilege. Right now you are not cooperating. I don't believe you don't know who attacked you. I have the strong feeling that there is quite a lot you are not telling me."

Scott weighed his answer carefully. He needed Healy's help but the governor would not ignore Home Office instructions, whatever his sympathies. In the present circumstances, Healy alone could not release him so Scott had little to lose; he was literally a prisoner. "I thought you'd know all about me by now. What there is, anyway. Nothing dramatic. It must have been you who authorized the listening-bug under Archie Shaw's bed. You must have picked up bits and pieces."

Healy had his hand on top of the screen, preparatory to pushing it back. He stiffened, looked down at Scott with a mixture of anger and surprise. It was difficult for Scott to determine whether the reaction was one of dismay at being found out or the sudden surprise of not knowing.

For some seconds he gazed at Scott and neither man gave way. In the end, Healy swung the screen back and disappeared.

Within seconds the screen was wheeled away, and Scott found himself being eyed speculatively by the other patients. He lay back. He had faith in Bulman and Collins, but he was beginning to wonder if they would be in any stronger position than the governor. He thought of Maggie. My God, he had better be out before she returned. Step by step he saw something of the fix he was really in. Somebody with a good deal of power did not want him to get out—ever.

While his wound was being dressed he noticed it was swollen and red, but the nurse told him it was clean and going well. The skewer must have bruised, as well as torn, his muscle.

The governor returned that evening and Scott did not like his uncompromising attitude. The screens were put around the bed, and Scott could see that Healy was having some difficulty in containing himself. He did not sit and no chair was brought for him. He kept his voice down with difficulty.

"I've had Shaw's cell turned inside out, Sims. There is no bug, nor was there ever one."

"Then it's been removed. It had served its purpose."

"Just what game are you trying to play?"

Scott accepted that he had gambled and lost. "It was there. Why the hell should I invent a story like that?"

"I think you are all-around trouble, Sims. I'm beginning to have some sympathy for those who obviously know you better. What were you doing in Shaw's cell anyway? Or is that rather a silly question?"

Scott glanced up. "You don't tell me why I'm being illegally held here, and I won't tell you why I was in Shaw's cell. But somebody knows."

"You're in no position to be insolent. You deliberately misled me. That was a monstrous suggestion; a bug in a cell. Why on earth did you say it?"

"Because it's true, as much as you can't swallow it. It's happened before. Someone put it there and someone took it out. The only thing I'm certain about is that it wasn't Shaw who . . ." Scott trailed off. He had warned Shaw. Had Shaw found and destroyed it?

"You were about to say?"

"Have you spoken to Shaw, Governor?"

"Naturally. He knows nothing about it because it was never there."

So Shaw *could* hold his tongue. It did not matter now; Shaw might have considered it prudent to keep quiet, whether or not he had found it.

Wearily Scott said, "There is no advantage to me in lying to you. That can only annoy you, and that's the last thing I want to happen. The bug was there, believe me."

Healy saw Scott's point of view. "I'll agree to a hypothetical premise. I ask again. Why Shaw? Porter would have made more sense."

"I can't tell you." That would mean explaining Tom Moody and Wally Cooper. "I'm sorry. I made a mistake in telling you about the bug. Had you found it, it would at least have given me credibility."

"Perhaps that's what you're after. You're very plausible, Sims."

Scott shrugged. There was no point in answering.

"By the way, there were no fingerprints on the skewer handle."

Scott was not surprised. "Well, that should stop the suicide talk."

Healy eyed Scott critically. "You're a strange man, Sims. There is nothing standard about you."

HE LAY STARING at the night light, wishing he were back in his own cell. As much as he detested prison, he preferred to be alone. He did not want to be drawn into the crude bandinage that went on between the prisoners during the day. In other circumstances he might have joined in, but basically he was a loner.

Darkness brought with it a kind of terror. He would never leave this place. Not alive, anyway. Had it not been for his own quick reflexes and Gregory's clumsiness, he would by now have been a cold statistic on a coroner's slab.

At about two in the morning, still wide awake, feeling everything closing in as the darkness had done, he threw back the blanket. It was hot anyway. He pulled himself upright and, when the pain had eased, swung his legs over the side of the bed. His feet touched the floor, and he gradually put more weight on them. Finally he stood up.

His legs were weak. He did not understand that; he'd been in bed for less than two days. Keeping one hand on the bed he started to walk alongside it. His wound pulled much more than he expected, but he kept going until his confidence returned and the degree of pain was tolerable. The sensation of burning in his stomach was spreading, but he was determined to go on.

He came around the bed and, feeling pleased with himself, headed toward the door. He had no idea whether or not it was locked and he had no intention of trying to leave the ward. The soft sound of hurrying footsteps came from behind him, and Scott swung around quickly. The movement made him gasp with pain.

A male nurse grabbed his arm and whispered viciously, "What the hell do you think you're doing?"

"I'm trying to walk. It's only a piddling wound."

"Get back to bed. You'll bust your stitches."

Scott climbed back into bed. The pain was intense.

When satisfied that Scott had settled down, the nurse said, "Don't try it again. That was really stupid."

Scott did not reply. He felt helpless and frustrated and without hope. He might as well be in an isolation cell, shut off from everything

COMMANDER COLLINS PUT down the telephone, his face grim. He flicked his intercom and asked Cathy to check whether or not George Bulman was in. When Cathy came back with an affirmative, Collins left his office and walked the stairs to Bulman's room.

Bulman was surprised to see the commander. In his recollection it was the first time Collins had traveled the corridors of Scotland Yard to this small office. He rose in surprise.

"Have a seat, sir," Bulman came around the desk to dust a chair with a handkerchief.

"Cut the crap, George. I've got bad news." Collins looked pointedly at the open communicating door to Haldean's office.

"Sergeant," Bulman called out. "Have another lunch break."

Haldean shuffled off, giving Collins a curious look on the way. When the main door was closed, Collins sat down.

"They're holding Scott at Albany. The governor has orders to detain him."

Bulman froze. Nothing had felt right about the Moody business from the beginning. But holding Scott was a very serious matter. "Whose orders?"

"Home Office." Before Bulman could answer Collins explained, "Take it for granted that I'll get to the bottom of who gave the order. Whoever it is is walking on very thin ice. But I thought you should know meanwhile."

"Shit," Bulman said angrily. "We've got to get him out."

"Of course. Right now he's in the Parkhurst Hospital. Someone tried to do him in with a makeshift skewer." As Bulman's expression changed, Collins held up a placating hand. "Keep your shirt on. He's okay. The wound was more than superficial, but it missed the parts that matter."

"He's a sitting duck," Bulman observed. "I suppose he won't cough who did it?"

"That's right. It's a bad business, George. You sure you've told me everything?"

"Everything that matters in connection with Spider going in as a plant. It's all about Tom Moody. It's typical of Spider not to inform, but I can see why this time. If he points the finger the thing will snowball and the real reason for his going in is likely to come out. The governor wouldn't like that. It's a bloody wonder these days that we're not made to ask all the cons if they mind us putting a plant in among them. I'd like to see some of these people in Civil Liberty in a tight situation where they needed our help the way we do things and not the way they want us to. Give every villain a free pardon and a pox on the poor old girl who's had her head bashed in."

"That make you feel better?"

Bulman gave a wry smile. "We're not saints but we're not twisted-minded bastards either. Do you know what it cost Spider to go back in? He dreads prison. Swore he'd never go back and never has until now. And the irony is that he's done it for one dead copper and a live one who should have known better than to ask him. But why would they try to kill him?"

"You'd better show your hand and go down there to sort it out. Meanwhile I'll find out who's playing silly games."

"What did the governor say?"

"Little more than I told you. Scott was attacked in his cell. Best and easiest place in top security."

"Yeah. Did Spider ask to be released by any chance?"

Collins appeared uneasy. "I was hoping you wouldn't mention it. He asked and he was refused."

Bulman stared. "He's been trussed for the kill."

COLLINS WASTED NO time in contacting the prison department of the Home Office. He had more than enough ground for complaint. Scott had been planted under his auspices, and he would not have heard of the detention had he not telephoned the prison governor. Nobody from the Home Office had given him the courtesy of an explanation. He was quietly furious as he set a chain of inquiry going.

It took the best part of the day to find someone who knew anything about it. Inquiries stopped at a minister named Martin Holmes, and he refused to discuss it over the telephone. When Collins pressed for an appointment he was smoothly sidestepped by the politician who claimed, perhaps accurately, that his presence was required in the House of Commons and his future schedule was tight. Sensing that Holmes was about to terminate the exchange, Collins growled into the phone, "If you hang up, Minister, I shall make official application to have your phone tapped."

"*What did you say?*"

"You heard what I said, sir. I am not a junior policeman. I am a very senior one, as you well know. I want to know why a man planted in Albany Prison by me is being illegally detained there by you."

"Illegally detained, Commander? Doesn't your seniority extend to the knowledge of the powers of detention under the Prevention of Terrorism Act?"

"Are you trying to say he's a suspected terrorist or something?"

"I'm not saying anything, Commander. I simply asked you a question."

"Why then, is he being held in a top security prison and not in a police cell?"

"Oh, he just happened to be there. It was convenient. Look, I said before that I'm not willing to discuss this over the telephone. Can you meet me at the House at, say five? I should have a few minutes then."

THEY MET IN the central lobby, beyond the security check. Collins announced himself at the desk and took a seat on one of the curved, padded benches from where he could survey the whole area. The mad rush of visitors and parties had died down, and the echoes around the arches were more pronounced.

Martin Holmes kept Collins waiting for twenty minutes. When he did come bustling forward, directed by the white-gloved badge messenger, he was apologetic, offering his hand and smiling in quite a friendly way. He was a stocky man in his late forties; dark, thick hair and heavy brows, and below them, placid brown eyes.

"This is as good a place as any, Commander. Let's sit here. Now, what do you want to know precisely?"

"Why my man is being held in Albany."

"Well, I think you recognize that I'm under no obligation to answer that. I'm not answerable to you."

"But I'm answerable to my plant."

"Was it entirely your idea, Commander?" The brown eyes were fleeting around the huge lobby.

"That has absolutely no bearing. I made an arrangement that when he wanted to leave he could. He wants to and he's being prevented from doing so."

"Yes, well the instructions were mine."

"Then I'd still like to know why, sir."

"I dare say, but I really can't tell you."

"You're forcing me to go to the commissioner to ask him to make a direct approach to the Home Secretary, sir."

"Well, that's your prerogative, Commander. Perhaps it's best that you do that."

While Collins reflected on this development, Holmes added,

"I really do understand your position. You think a trust has been broken. Well, perhaps it's been broken in other ways, too. What do you really know about this man?"

"Not a lot. But he's known to us. And to the SIS, too, I understand. He comes highly recommended."

"But he's a burglar, wouldn't you say?"

Collins accepted that Holmes knew Scott's real identity. "He was once. He's had no form for years."

"It's possible that there are things about him that you do not know."

"Quite possible. All I'm asking is what they are if they have bearing on his detention."

"Ah! Well, we are now stepping beyond the boundaries of police work."

Collins mulled this over. "Unless Scott is a threat to national security, I doubt that can be the case, and you are, therefore, holding back information I need to know."

"I might not be the only one holding back information, Commander. Why was Scott planted in Albany in the first place?"

"That's a matter of record, sir. I gave a reason and it was accepted."

"And suppose that reason was not the real one?"

"Have you grounds for saying that, sir?"

Holmes chuckled. "Perhaps you should have been the politician, Commander."

Collins was now convinced that he would get nowhere with this man. "Whatever it is you are obliquely accusing me of, my interest lies with Scott. He was given an assurance by me and it is important that my word is kept. If this got out we'd lose every stool pigeon and outside assistance we have. If you want him, then he must first be released. What happens after that is up to you."

"Dear me, Commander, you are showing a singular lack of understanding. There's a limit to how long we can hold him without making a charge. You know that better than I. What's all the fuss? One way or the other justice will be done."

"It's not being done right now. Meanwhile Scott's life is at risk. There's been one attack on him, there could easily be another."

"That was an unfortunate business, but frankly I don't see a connection between holding him and his being attacked. Do you?"

It was a loaded question. Collins said warily, "I have to assume that there might be. Scott remains my immediate responsibility."

"Well, give it a day or two and I'll see what I can come up with."

Holmes rose after glancing at his watch but Collins was not yet ready for a brush off. As he stood up he moved to make it difficult for Holmes to go around him.

"There's just one thing, sir. Obviously you have your reasons for holding Scott. Are you fully aware of them?"

Holmes hesitated, frowning.

"I'm not asking you to state those reasons, but I do want to know if they are actually yours."

"As the instructions to detain Scott came from me you must assume that they are."

"Does the Home Secretary know about it, sir?"

"Good lord, man, the Home Secretary can't deal with every trifling issue."

"It's not a trifling issue to me, sir. Nor to Scott. Perhaps it's time the Home Secretary did know. Thank you for your time, Minister." Collins turned to make his way toward the exit.

Holmes watched the big frame skip lightly down the stone steps, and

93

he frowned thoughtfully. Then, with a shrug, he turned toward the chamber.

BULMAN RANG ALBANY Prison and was put through to the governor. "Good morning, sir. This is Detective Superintendent Bulman; I called on you some days ago. I believe you have a prisoner there by the name of Anthony Sims? Would it be possible for me to pop down to interview him? Say tomorrow?"

"He's in the Parkhurst Hospital, Mr. Bulman. Can't you leave it for a bit?"

"Not seriously ill, I hope?"

"He has a wound. Not too serious. Is it so important that you see him so soon? A few days might make a difference."

"If he's capable of talking I'd rather see him sooner than later."

"All right. But you'll have to see him in the ward."

COLLINS THREW SOME bread to the ducks who made water arrowheads toward it. "Effortless," he observed. "Just gliding across the water, until you realize that under the surface their legs are going like the clappers."

It was a good time to go to the park. It was mid-afternoon and baking hot, but the lunchtime crowds had gone, leaving only the tourists. Both men were standing by the lake, outwardly soothed by the tranquility around them but inwardly angry at events. They had felt compelled to leave the Yard, to hurry through petrol fumes held down by high pressure in order to reach the fresh air of open parkland.

"That's what Scott needs," Collins continued. "Wings and flippers."

"You're not suggesting a breakout?"

"God forbid." Collins gave Bulman a hard stare. "You frighten me when you talk like that. How did you ever become a copper?"

"Hunger. It had to go one way or the other."

"Balls. Your old man was a sergeant major in the King's African Rifles. They paid 'em well out there." Collins pointed. "Look at the colors on that one. But his eyes are beady. Bit like yours."

"Well, I hope the beautiful little buggers give some inspiration. We're getting nowhere."

Collins threw his last crumbs. He stuck his hands in his pockets and gazed around the park, chin out, eyes narrowed.

"Right now there's nowhere to get, is there? The faceless ones are neatly tying our hands."

"Faceless? You know that Martin Holmes sanctioned the detention."

"I don't know on whose behalf."

Bulman raised a brow as he stepped around a pigeon.

"You think someone instructed him? That would have to be the Home Secretary."

"Not necessarily." Collins did not enlarge but added, "I am not convinced that Martin Holmes initiated it."

"Doing it for a friend?"

"I don't know. I think he believes that what he is doing is right. He's not afraid of it being raised over his head."

"And has it?"

"So far as I know. I saw Deputy Commissioner Cruickshank. Explained it all. He said he'd get it raised with the Home Secretary. But our position is weak, George."

"Ours? Yours and mine?"

Collins started to walk away from the lake, and Bulman fell in beside him. "There are times when you appear to be thick, George. But you're not, are you? You're just bloody devious. We'd better not forget that I put Scott in as a favor to you."

"No you didn't. You wouldn't do me that favor. You put Scott in because Tom Moody was godfather to your kids."

"It's the same thing," Collins said without explanation. "The fact is we contrived a cock-and-bull for the Home Office in order to get him in."

"The reasons were honorable."

"They won't sound it if they come out. Holmes seemed to know that I'd put Scott in for another reason. And that worries me." Collins turned his head. "Stinks, doesn't it?"

"Always has. But the smell's getting stronger. And we're no nearer to knowing who murdered Tom."

They walked along slowly, not speaking for a while. The grass was already drying up after the continuing heat wave. At last Bulman said, "He must be worried sick down there without contact. I'm going down tomorrow. We've got to get him out before it's too late."

8

SCOTT'S face brightened as Bulman walked into the sick ward. He could not recall being so pleased to see anyone, other than Maggie, and the miracle of it was that his visitor was once his bitterest enemy. Bulman was deadpan until the screens were up, and even then he poked his head around to make sure nobody was too near. "Hello, cocker," he said warmly as he shook Scott's hand. "Couldn't bring you grapes; it would have looked strange for a copper to bring a villain anything. There'll be talk as it is. How are you?"

"I'm okay. Not as bad as they make out. Have you fixed it for me to get out?"

"No." It was no use prevaricating. "They've shoved a chair in front of every step we've tried to take."

Scott sank back against the pillows. "Who's doing it?"

"Home Office. Jock Collins is raising it with the Home Secretary. They won't say why you're being sat on. Not yet anyway."

"What's it all about?"

"It's about us being right about Tom Moody."

"But the *Home Office*? I'll *never* get out."

"Look, there's a limit to how long they can hold you officially. Five days at most. But it's no use bullshitting you. They could drag it out if they want."

97

"Jesus Christ. What are you saying?"

"I'm trying to show you what we're up against. Grasp the worst of it first."

"You think I haven't? They want me in no longer than it takes to murder me."

"Maybe they just want to frighten you. A warning; when you're out, lay off or else."

"The attack was to fix me for good."

"Who was it?"

"I don't want him touched."

"That's a promise."

"A bloke called Joe Gregory. A wife-killer. As there's no reason why he should have tried it, it has to be for money. They'll be planning the next attempt now, probably have already." Scott eyed Bulman's sad face. "How can it possibly be the Home Office? I don't even know where it is."

Bulman tried to smile but it was not the time for humor. "I wonder if they have your breaking into Dr. Habise's office up their sleeve?"

"It's crossed my mind. It still doesn't justify this kind of detention."

"We don't know what Habise is into. Did you notice cameras or scanners when you were there?"

"No. Did you?"

"No. But I'll gamble that they have a shot or two of you inside, just the same. It could give them a lot of muscle."

"You're frightening the life out of me. Talking like that makes it sound as if the Home Office had Tom Moody done."

"I don't think it's ever crossed their minds that he might have been murdered. Martin Holmes is a Home Office minister, right? Okay, he's holding back something but he still made no attempt to persuade Dick Collins not to raise the issue at the top. He might not like the idea, but he put no obstacles in the way."

There was a silence between them during which Bulman took another look around the screen. He came back to his chair. "Why hasn't Wally Cooper been killed?"

"I don't think he knows anything. Certainly he didn't know what it was he lifted." Scott explained what had happened with Archie Shaw.

"Yet they moved Cooper away from you," insisted Bulman. "My backdoor check showed he was in the same wing as Ernie Porter. That's why we picked Porter as an excuse for your going in."

98

"They probably moved Cooper as a precaution. There was one piece of news he might have given me that he had not given Shaw. Whose flat did he break into? Can you raise that from the court records?"

"Difficult. The case was held in camera."

"When has that sort of thing stopped you?"

"It's just not easy to do. But I'll try. Who do you think planted the bug under Shaw's bed?"

"I've no idea. You've got to get me out, George."

Bulman did not reply. He ran his hands slowly over his thinning hair, and for the first time Scott detected his despair. Scott's feeling of dread returned; Bulman had no immediate solution.

At last Bulman said, "It's all in motion. I'll see the governor again before leaving. I was hoping that you might have something for me to use. Something I could exploit."

"I've told you all I know. Have you any paper on you? And an envelope?"

"I'll get some." Bulman pushed back the screen and went down the ward. He returned with paper, envelope, and a book for Scott to use as a rest. He handed over his own pen.

Scott wrote carefully with the book tilted so that Bulman could not see. He paused now and again but finally he slipped the paper into the envelope, which he sealed. He then wrote on the envelope, Hashimi Ross, and passed it to Bulman.

"George, they're supposed to see our letters before they go out. For Christ sake, don't let them see that."

"Don't worry." Bulman was staring at the name as he held the envelope in front of him. Bulman's tone changed. "You know what you're doing?" He was clearly worried.

"You want me to sit back and wait to be executed?"

Bulman could not reply to that. He said, "But *the Arab?* Libyan father and Irish mother. He's been tied up with the IRA, Spider."

"Is that a fact? I don't know where he hangs out. It used to be Kilburn. Can you track him down for me?"

Bulman flapped the envelope thoughtfully before reluctantly pocketing it. "*Every* police force has been looking for him. I can't work a miracle."

"That's what it will need. For God's sake, George."

"It won't work, Spider."

"You don't know what I've written."

99

"I don't need to. It'll make things worse. Don't try it."

"They can't be worse. The finger is on me."

"Jesus." Bulman stood up and gazed around desperately. "I don't know what to say to that. But you're dragging me into something I dare not be connected with."

"You got me in here. You get me out. Just find him and deliver."

Bulman had a hand over the pocket in which he had placed the envelope. "I'll try." Ill at ease, he added, "I'll talk to my boss to see if he can pull some strings to get you out faster."

"The only strings that have been pulled so far have tightened the net around me. Don't lose that letter. And don't let me down, George."

"I'll find him. If he's in the country. I'd better go. We are trying, you know."

"I know that, George. But I know, as you do, that it might not be enough. You're hamstrung by your own establishment. So is Dick Collins. In the end you both have to do what you're told. I don't. Be lucky and stop worrying."

But on the way back to London, Bulman was deeply worried. The letter was like a bomb in his pocket. It would be a simple matter to open it, but that was the last thing he wanted to do. Ignorance of its contents was the only defense he had and that would be too flimsy when it came down to it. And yet how could he seriously condemn Scott?

AS THE TRAIN gathered speed and started to sway, Bulman looked back down the years to when he had first met Willie Scott. It was so very long ago, and their association was then one of mutual hatred. He had not trusted Scott nor anything he said in those days. He could see his own unpleasant picture as a young detective. Young and brash and, where Scott was concerned, cynical. He supposed the first chip in his armor was made after the Chinese legation affair when Scott had been ruthlessly set up by Fairfax. Reluctantly then, and certainly without Scott's knowledge, he had admitted to himself that Scott had emerged more honorably than the ostensibly honest.

It had made no real difference to his attitude toward Scott at that time; he would still happily have put him behind bars. But time and evidence pointing to Scott's basic honesty and unquestionable loyalty had expanded the emotional corrosion that had already started. As the years

100

went by and as he mellowed and his attitude became more tolerant, a deeper belief gradually took root.

Now they had become friends and a mutual trust had developed between them. More than that, a mutual respect and liking had blossomed. That trust and friendship were now under their severest strain as Bulman considered what the envelope might contain. It was crazy and against everything he had ever been taught about law and order. He was torn between his duty as a police officer and his friendship for a man in peril.

Bulman touched the envelope. He could not convince himself that he would not do the same as Scott in a similar situation. The lines of deceit went very deep on this, perhaps the strangest case he had met. When he thought like this, Scott appeared less reckless; but if Bulman was right about it, it could destroy everyone involved. It was here that he needed complete faith in Scott, and that faith was about to be tested to the limit.

SIR LEWIS HOPE had an office in the Security Service off Northumberland Avenue, south of Trafalgar Square. Before going there Bulman called in at Scott's travel agency, just north of the Square, and had a few words with young Charlie Hewett and Lulu, Scott's faithfuls. He knew that Scott had made adequate arrangements during his absence but felt that the gesture would be appreciated.

At the Security Service offices, Bulman was checked and passed, and he took the ancient elevator to the sixth floor. The building reminded him of the old, Gothic-style Scotland Yard, before it was moved to its present site. He knocked on the unmarked door; his approach would already have been communicated. The electric release buzzed and he turned the knob.

Sir Lewis's office had large, old fashioned sash windows that faced the Thames: on such a clear day, it was the first thing Bulman noticed.

"Wish you had such a view, George?"

Bulman nodded appreciatively. A riverboat was cruising, white canopy like a flattened sail, trippers lining the rails.

"You wanted to see me?" Hope pointed to a chair. He was leaning back but somehow contrived to arch hawklike over his green leather topped desk.

Bulman sat down. "The Moody business has taken a strange turn. I thought you should know."

Hope appeared puzzled. "I thought you'd dropped that."

"I didn't and I'm glad that I didn't because there's a hell of a stink in the state of Denmark."

"Why didn't you do as I suggested? This really isn't your pigeon."

"Whose pigeon is it, then?"

"George, don't step out of line. Just let it go, there's a good chap."

"With respect, sir, I can't let it go. One of our plants in Albany prison is in danger. He's already been attacked. Another try could be fatal."

"What the devil has this got to do with Moody? And what do you mean by 'one of *our* plants'?"

Bulman had no alternative but to give the full story. He gave credit to Hope for listening without interrupting, and he noted that the long, intertwined fingers remained absolutely still while he spoke.

At the end of it, Hope said, "I grant you it is a curious story, but some of what you relate is not connected."

"I think it is, Sir Lewis."

"George, give me credit for doing my homework. Your man inside is Scott, isn't he?"

"How do you know that?"

"Oh, come, everyone knows. I should be very angry with you, but I'll grant that you've acted for the best of motives. You should have kept out of it. Scott is a friend of yours, isn't he? Isn't that why you're so het up?"

"Scott has been invaluable to the SIS on occasion. And particularly to the Security Service. He's a proven loyalist."

"You're going back too far. People can change."

"Often for the better."

"Yes, well, perhaps Scott has only himself to blame for the fix he's in."

"How can that be? He's in Albany because of me. He didn't want to go. He did it as a favor, to help me, Sir Lewis. And he gets a knife in his guts for his trouble."

"Don't exaggerate, George. He was a friend of Moody's, wasn't he?"

"A long time ago. He hadn't seen Moody for years."

"How can you be so sure?"

"Because he told me. Look, he's involved because I asked him to be. All I'm now asking is for you to use your influence with the Home Office to get him released at once."

"I can't do that." The two men stared at each other across the desk. Hope's eyes were steady and uncompromising. "I can't go interfering with the way the Home Office handles its affairs just because you gave a personal assurance to an old villain. Is this to help Scott or save your own pride?"

Bulman held down his temper. He hung on tight to the chair arms and prayed for a miracle that might bring back Sir Stuart Halliman. He had never liked Hope and did not rate him in intelligence matters. He said very evenly, "Scott will be killed if we don't do something very quickly."

"Don't be absurd. Physical attacks like that are not unusual in prison. It's unlikely to happen to him again."

"Because you refuse to see a connection between what happened to Moody and what almost happened to Scott."

"Perhaps there is a connection, but it is not what you think it is."

Bulman felt like throwing the heavy glass paperweight that was on the desk straight at the weathered, supercilious face opposite him. He started again. "Is the Security Service in any way linked to what happened to Moody and to what is now happening to Scott?"

"Moody slipped on a bar of soap, and we have done nothing to endanger Scott."

"With respect, that's no answer, sir. Do you know why this is happening to Scott? And why are you so unwilling to help?"

"None of this is your business, George. I've said so. You put Scott in but that's the end of it so far as you're concerned. *We are not directly involved.*"

"I am."

"From this moment you are most certainly not. You should have listened to me before."

"I won't leave him like that. If you want my resignation, you can have it right now."

"Calm down. I am listening to you, at least."

"No, sir, you are not. You hear me, but my words bounce straight back. There's something bloody queer going on, and I intend to find out what it is."

"In that case, I had better accept your resignation."

"I find that interesting. I'll type it out, of course, and will let you have it. But I now know for certain that you are covering up something that affects Scott."

103

"Good lord, you talk as if you've just joined the service. What's new about a cover-up? Provided the reason is sound, there is nothing wrong with that; particularly in our game. I believe it was you who said that in matters of national security a suspect is guilty until proved innocent. You've gone back on that premise, I see."

"I can personally vouch for Scott. So what is it he is suspected of?"

"We're drifting in circles, George. I don't want you involved in this at all. You're too close to Scott, too emotionally tied up."

Bulman rose. "If I knew what the bloody hell is going on, perhaps I wouldn't be. I've been badly set down, if not deliberately betrayed. And so has Commander Collins."

"What's a few more days in prison to an old crook? He won't be short of friends."

"I'll go type my resignation."

"YOU'VE RESIGNED?" COLLINS was startled.

"What else could I do? The old vulture was picking my bones. He should never have left the navy; should have been put out to sea on a paddle steamer." Bulman turned from the window and kicked out at the air. His face was tight and brooding, his eyes sharp with anger.

"Was this verbal?"

"I typed it out and delivered it in person."

"That was too hasty, George. You can only help Willie Scott by staying on the inside, beavering away."

"There's no more beavering I can do. Anyway, screw Hope. I can't bloodywell stand him. It's never been the same since Halliman left."

"George, you are not thinking, for once. That damned temper of yours has forced you into a mistake. When you came back from seeing Scott you were talking of finding the transcript of Wally Cooper's file. You can only try that from the inside."

Bulman stood still. Suddenly he burst out laughing. "I had to resign. I had the feeling that I was pushing him too far into a corner and that he would either fire me or place me on suspension. Either way it would have been immediately effective. Of course, at a later date suitable to him, he might have offered reinstatement but only when it would have been too late. By resigning I've left myself three months in which to work out my notice. That's the arrangement I have with Security."

Collins threw his pen down on the desk and laughed aloud. "You crafty bastard."

"How did your bloke get on with the Home Secretary?"

"It's being looked into." Collins shrugged. "I suppose we've stalled enough ourselves when it's suited us."

"Not when a man's life is at stake."

O'CONNOLLY'S BAR WAS in Kilburn. The evening was warm, and the bar doors were wide open. A few tables and chairs had been erected on the wide pavement and were overshadowed by striped umbrellas to shade the customers from a sun now below the building line.

As Bulman walked between the tables toward the door, he attracted an unusual amount of attention. When he entered the overheated interior the noise level was high, and the ceiling fan was spreading the smoke around. The sound died in stages as Bulman approached the bar and became the focus of attention. The muttered expletives were not missed by him, nor the variety of Irish accents.

The pub was used by IRA sympathizers. The Special Branch had infiltrated a very long time ago. The customers well knew it and had effectively discouraged most of them. Like London villains who frequent certain pubs, the Irish Republicans in O'Connolly's could smell a copper before he crossed the Kilburn High Road.

The noise had subsided. There was now whispered dialogue, or deliberately outspoken reference to "pigs." Backs were pointedly turned as Bulman reached the bar, and one man spat at his feet while another deliberately nudged him. The barman suddenly found custom at one end of the bar, and the barmaid at the opposite end. Bulman felt immediate sympathy for the undercover Special Branch boys whose job it was to lift useful information in this currently hostile environment.

He waited patiently and found himself isolated in a crowd. As it seemed that he was not going to be served in the immediate future, if at all, he turned around to place his back against the bar and to openly face the hostility.

The conversation was slowly picking up again. Having recovered from the original shock of Bulman's effrontery, the customers did not intend that he should spoil their fun. Some strong anti-British remarks were deliberately aimed for his ears. Bulman smiled benignly and looked as if he was enjoying himself.

Before the noise level rose too high again, he took out his warrant card and bawled at the top of his voice, "Ladies and gentlemen, may I please have your attention." He held his warrant card aloft. "I am a police officer." He waited good humoredly for the boos and the abuse to die down. Then with a grin he added, "I thought I'd better tell you that because I don't want to surprise anyone." There were more boos but some laughter, too. Someone slowly hand-clapped.

Bulman had their attention. They were curious. "I'm not here to arrest, detain, or otherwise molest any of you. This is my warrant card. And this," he fumbled in his pocket and then held up a penknife, "is to cut the atmosphere in here." He was grinning widely now.

Only the really hardliners were still abusive. There were more laughs and more clapping of hands. Someone bawled out, "Well, it's not the black velvet you've come for, now."

"No." Bulman lowered his arms and rested easily against the bar. "I'm looking for the Arab."

There was complete silence. Those he had won over were wary again. Somehow Bulman kept the smile on his face. He raised his voice. "I don't intend to arrest the Arab, warn him, or in any way harm him. I'm not even here as a copper, but I knew I couldn't fool you bunch of pirates. All I want to do is pass a message to the Arab from a very good friend of his who has lost contact. And that's the truth."

Someone nearby bawled out, "Bullshit."

Bulman turned. "Accuse me of that if you like, son." His features hardened. "But don't ever overstep the line and call me a liar. If I say it's the truth, then that's what it is." He smiled again. "With the landlord's permission I intend to have a Smethwicks if he's got one and a Guinness if he hasn't. My copper's pay does not extend to drinks all around. Meanwhile, if anyone can point me in the right direction, I'll be grateful. Cheers."

He received a few "cheers" back; he'd broken the ice. A surreptitious questioning would have achieved nothing. As Bulman turned to face the bar he knew the risks he was taking. If Special Branch had someone in here now it would be reported. What he had done he had done openly and off duty. He had not gone through official channels for the Arab's whereabouts.

The barman came up, a quizzical expression on his face. "Are you really a copper, so?" He was drawing a pint for Bulman.

"You were bloody sure when I walked in."

"Well, you're not like any bloody copper I've met. Here, have this on the house."

"Thanks. I'll give you a Republican song for a couple more."

"Mary! Mother of God." Smiling, and shaking his head in disbelief, the barman walked away to serve elsewhere.

Bulman stood at the bar sipping his Guinness for some time. The men on either side of him were no longer showing their backs and even had the odd word with him. He had walked into the lions' den and bearded some of them, but would he get what he wanted? At times customers came to the bar for replenishment. One or two winked and nodded to him. He was hustled but it was now good-natured. The bar was very full, many of the men in shirt-sleeves in the oppressive heat.

Bulman had a second drink. He went to the gents' toilet and returned for a third. Nobody had approached him about the Arab and he was toying with the idea of openly asking the barman. The problem was clear; while some might believe him they would be reluctant to pass on an address in front of friends.

A woman came up to the bar holding an empty sherry glass. She smiled at Bulman in a cheeky way and at once he saw that she was slightly drunk. Dark-haired, in her early forties, she was attractive. He made space for her and she said, "The Arab is wanted by you lot, y'know."

"I only want to pass a message. It's off-duty stuff. I've no warrant for his arrest. Nothing like that. Can I get you another sherry?"

"Sure. Just give the glass to Mick, he knows which one."

Bulman passed the glass over. Turning back to the woman he said, "What's your name?"

"Mary. But they call me Molly. Do you really mean him no harm?"

"Hand on heart. Do you know where he is?"

"Would you look around this place now. There are some hard cases. If I told you, they'd make my life a misery."

"How would they know you're not telling me now?"

Molly laughed. "You poor innocent soul. There are long ears here. *They* would know. Talking to a copper is one thing; trusting is surely another. Most of them here know I have form anyway."

"Form? *You*, Molly?" The drink arrived, and as Bulman paid, he thought he'd been overcharged.

"I used to be a dip. But I'm reformed now."

There was something in the way she said it that alerted Bulman. She winked at him but it was in her character, a meaningless, good-natured gesture.

"I used to be good at it but I was caught too often," said Molly illogically. "Cheers, copper."

"Cheers, Molly. They know how to charge for sherry in this place, don't they?"

"Sherry? Didn't I tell you? This is Middleton." Molly glanced over to the far corner of the bar. "My old man thinks I drink too much Irish so I use a sherry glass. Mick knows the form." Molly raised her glass and threaded her way through the tightening crowd, leaving Bulman smiling. When he had finished his drink he gave Mick the barman a nod and said softly, "Well, I didn't strike lucky but that's the way it goes. Thanks for the drink."

The sky was clouding up and the night was close. He skipped between the double-deckers and the cabs and cars and walked toward Marble Arch. After a few minutes he hailed a cab and, once seated, searched his pockets. Molly *was* a good dip, he thought. She had lifted his change from a five-pound note and had left him a legacy instead. On a slip of paper was scrawled the address of Hashimi Ross.

Bulman tapped the glass panel behind the driver and issued new instructions. He sat back smiling. Molly had charged for her information, but she had taken a risk and had therefore earned it. He thought about the Arab. Ross was his mother's name; in an unexpected show of loyalty to both his parents, Hashimi had used a name from each side of the family.

9

*V*ERNON Healy was an experienced and compassionate man, bearing in mind that top security prisons house long-termers, among whom, inevitably, were violent and hardened criminals. He was not happy about having Sims in his prison. And he was convinced that Sims was not his real name. Logically, if a man was undercover, he would not use his own name. Even allowing for this there was something about Sims that set him apart from the others.

Sims was obviously familiar with prison life. He had effortlessly fallen into the routine. Yet there was a strange authority about him. Most prisoners gave the governor some form of deference, but Scott could talk man to man, without giving offense. When Healy considered it, he came to the conclusion that Sims was not afraid of any form of officialdom and would never succumb to it.

Some prisoners would mercilessly exploit the weak, lie plausibly to them, and get their support. This happened with some of the prison social workers, whether or not they would admit to it. Psychologically, a person leaning toward an understanding of a section of society *wants* to believe and is therefore more easily fooled. But on reflection Healy had not found Sims like that at all. Sims had been almost aggressively blunt with a take-it-or-leave-it attitude that left the feeling that he was, in fact, telling the truth.

The mention of the listening bug was outrageous; so much so that Healy had come around to the view that Sims had meant precisely what he had said. As a consequence he had questioned his officers without getting anywhere. He did not want to institute a search of their persons or of their quarters. After the riots, staff morale was already low. In any event, he was quite satisfied that a search would be valueless, but he wanted whoever was guilty to know that he was aware of the bugging.

He informed the police. Shaw's cell was closed for a day while they examined it forensically. They found evidence of a small object having been stuck to the underside of the bed frame. He had also reported the attack on Sims to the police. It was not something he could sit on, nor did he want the responsibility of covering it up. But in cooperation with them, further inquiry was postponed.

Healy did not believe the police would get anywhere; the code of silence where the police were concerned was well known. This was a view the police shared. The wound was not serious and Sims was a fit man, so would come to no harm as a result of it. As Healy had already interviewed Sims, he did not consider the police would get any further than he had, particularly as there was a special relationship between himself and Sims. Or at least there should have been.

This was the second reason that Vernon Healy did not want the police too involved. Sims was, after all, a police plant, sanctioned by the Home Office. And now that same ministry wanted Sims detained in a clear contravention of the original agreement.

Healy did not like this at all. He felt that he and his prison were being used, and, personally, he would much rather let Sims go free. He was also worried about the attack on Sims. There had to be a reason even though he had played it down, and he did not want it happening again. Nor did he want Sims seeking revenge.

Healy, deeply concerned about these various issues, contacted the Home Office and requested permission to release Sims. He was turned down but advised that the matter would soon be resolved. He had been given a lump of sugar and a pat on the head. Healy was not a happy man. All he could do was to go through the staff files to find any possible pointers there.

THE PORTOBELLO ROAD was transformed to comparative tranquility at night. With the stalls absent, so too were the crowds that gathered around them. Tomorrow was Saturday, and from early morning antique stalls would line the street interspersed with fruit carts. Jewelry, silver, clocks, and furniture would be on display.

As Bulman's taxi crawled down the famous old street, it was difficult for him to believe how well known it was; how alive and vital and fascinating. This was really Spider Scott's territory, he reflected, as the dark empty street failed to impress him. Spider knew a thing or two about antique silver and jewelry; he had stolen enough in the old days, and he had learned quickly. If crime did not pay, it had at least provided Spider with a degree of knowledge while he had been engaged in it.

The taxi turned right and right again into Powis Square, Rachman's old territory. The landlord had exploited the unwary and the unwilling. But Rachman was dead and the Edwardian dwellings lived on.

"Stop here," Bulman said, tapping the glass. He climbed out and paid off the cabbie before checking the run of street numbers. The square had once been illustrious, now it was ragged at the edges and cosmopolitan, and in some ways perhaps, better for it.

It was dark, the dull street lights somehow adding to the gloom. Parked cars surrounded the square like a double necklace of beads. Because of the oppressive heat, one or two tenants were seated on top of the railinged steps.

Bulman mounted the steps slowly. When he pushed the heavy front door, it swung open to a darkened hall. He guessed that the light bulb had failed or new ones never survived long before the kids broke them. He climbed the stairs to the first landing.

It was very dark and he had to feel for the door. When he found it, he was not entirely surprised to find it was covered by sheet metal; it was probably the same the other side. He could find no doorknob, but he located a bell button and pressed it. There was no response from inside, but he knew that some of these apartments were huge. Nothing happened so he hammered on the door.

"Who's there?" A woman's voice, possibly West Indian.

"I'm a friend of a friend of Hashimi." Bulman spoke close to the door; the Arab could be operating under any name.

"There's nobody called that here."

"Can I speak to you then? I'm harmless."

The door opened as far as the chain would let it. Two wide eyes peered out, and the interior light from behind reached Bulman's face.

111

"I'm sorry about this," Bulman apologized "but your landing light has gone." He produced the envelope. "It's for Hashimi. News from an old friend of his."

The eyes surveyed him from a black and beautifully structured face.

"Do I look like a mugger?" Bulman asked helpfully.

"You could be."

Bulman sighed. "I can explain if you'll let me in."

"Let him in, love," said a quiet voice behind Bulman, who kept still as he felt the gun in his back.

"I come in peace," Bulman said feebly.

"And you'll leave in effing pieces if you put one foot wrong. In you go."

The chain was taken off, and Bulman entered a long hall.

"Straight down, second on left, follow Sophie."

As Bulman followed the slender, straight-backed figure of Sophie, he knew that the Arab had given nothing away. Names came and went in Hashimi's world. Sophie walked like a model and was expensively dressed.

They entered a high ceilinged drawing room, comfortably furnished with chintzy armchairs. The window drapes at the far end were floor to ceiling and the door that closed behind Bulman was solid pine.

"Hands on head."

"I'm not armed," Bulman protested.

"Search him."

Sophie ran long, red-nailed fingers over Bulman's body, giving him the impression that she had done it before. Her dark eyes were suspicious. She tossed Bulman's warrant card to Hashimi, who caught it one-handed and flipped it open.

"Sit over there."

The chair was farthest from the door and had its back to the windows. Bulman sat to face the Arab.

"Hands on lap."

"You're going too far. What the hell do you think I can do from here? Even if I wanted to, which I don't."

The Arab stood with his back to the door. He reached behind him and turned the key before pocketing it. He was a short man in his middle thirties, sparse black hair brought forward, not unlike Bulman's. Good looks were spoiled by a continuous fervor in dark, over-bright eyes that were seldom still. Bulman saw a trace of madness in them. In spite of his Irish mother, Hashimi appeared wholly Arab, but he was dressed in jeans and jacket with an unbuttoned white shirt beneath. "You didn't tell Sophie you are a copper." There was a trace of the midlands in the accent; Hashimi had been born in Birmingham and had graduated at Warwick University. His wealthy father was back in Libya, but had always applauded his son's revolutionary ideas.

"I'm not here as a copper. I'm here simply to give you the envelope that Sophie is holding. I am not on duty."

"Coppers are always on duty. You must know there's a warrant out for me."

"I'm not involved in this one. Antiterrorist squad after you, are they? Well, if you're guilty I hope they get you. But I'm here from a mutual friend and on a mission of trust."

"Once a copper, always a copper. What's your game?"

"Why don't you read the bloody letter. Give it to him, Sophie."

"Stay there, Sophie, it might be wired."

"Oh, my God. If it is, I'm in the firing line. And Sophie doesn't look too happy, now. Look what you've done to her."

"Cut the crap. You're on borrowed time. I can't let you go. Who's the letter from?"

"Spider Scott."

"*Spider?*" Hashimi frowned, his gaze reflective. "Spider? I haven't seen him in years. Where is he?"

"Albany."

"I understood he was going straight. What's going on? Did you put him there?"

Bulman felt real fear then. Hashimi had a reputation for recklessness; he would help any terrorist group that was going, wherever it was, provided it was not Israeli. And he had shot his way out of trouble more than once. The irony of the question was that Bulman *had* put Scott there, but there was no way he could explain that. He was forced to lie.

"Would I be here if I had? If you're afraid of the letter, let me open it for you. I don't want to see its contents."

The gun waved. "Give it to him, Sophie."

Sophie passed the letter over and then stood well back. She was not sure what was going on but she had seen Hashimi like this before, and it scared her.

Bulman pulled open the flap and partially pulled the folded letter out. He held it forward for Hashimi, but the ever cautious Arab gave a nod to Sophie, who took it over to him.

"Don't try moving. There's too big a gap."

"I couldn't get out of the bloody chair, anyway."

The Arab leaned against the door and, with gun still in hand, read the letter held in the other. Occasionally he glanced up to make sure Bulman had not moved.

"Have you read this?" he asked as he folded the letter one-handed.

"I've only just opened it for you."

"You might have seen it before. It was written in prison, so how come you've got it?"

"You trying to tell me that Spider hasn't mentioned I'd be bringing it?"

"I can't understand how Spider can be friendly with someone like you."

"Nor can I. Can I go now?"

"You're a copper. You'll bring the others."

"I should. But I won't. Not for your sake but because I owe Spider. To turn you in would be to betray his trust in me. And I couldn't do that. It's your lucky day, Hashimi."

"It's not yours." Hashimi seemed to have made up his mind.

"I could have slipped the damned thing through the letter box, but I wanted to be sure you got it. I could have had the place raided as soon as Molly told me. Oh, yes. I've no doubt she phoned you to hedge her bets, which is why you were waiting for me. I don't blame her. I'm getting up." Bulman rose from the chair.

Sophie said, "Let him go. It's true what he says."

"I don't trust him."

"Spider does. And he's a better bloody judge of human nature than you'll ever be. Now move aside or shoot me but don't prevaricate. Shooting me will put you and Sophie in one hellava mess. And you know it."

Hashimi had not moved by the time that Bulman reached him.

"Don't do it, Hash." Sophie pleaded.

"If we let him go we can't stay here." Hashimi spoke very quietly.

"Then I'll pack."

"No one will know from me where you are," Bulman interrupted.

"But that doesn't mean that someone else won't be as smart in finding you. Sophie's right, you've got to pack whatever you do. How did you meet Spider?"

Whenever Scott's name was mentioned, Hashimi seemed to change. "Dartmoor."

"That's a long time ago. He helped you, did he?"

"It's none of your business."

"Well, if you owe him, Hashimi, he won't thank you for knocking me off. Unlock the door, you're scaring the daylights out of Sophie and me. Think of the mess. Getting rid of me. You'll have to chop me up, you'd never get me down those stairs in one piece. Blood all over the place. Copper's blood. No self-respecting villain would ever live here again."

Sophie cried out, *"Let him go."* The aftermath of a possible shooting was getting through to her.

"Open the door for Spider's sake."

"You're too clever, copper." But Hashimi took the key from his pocket.

"Can I have my warrant card back? You wouldn't want that found around."

When Hashimi handed over the warrant card, Bulman began to think he was off the hook, but it was not until he reached the street that he really believed it. He leaned against the railings and almost gagged. It would always be touch and go with fanatics like Hashimi. Because this was true, it illustrated to Bulman more than anything else Scott's desperation to have made contact with such a man after so long. Even with all his experience it was difficult for Bulman to believe what was happening.

HASHIMI HELPED SOPHIE to pack. He was a man who always had alternative accommodation lined up through the terrorists' brotherhood, who was not short of safe houses.

Sophie was weeping quietly while she folded her clothes.

"Why don't you give it up? You'll always be hounded."

"If I give it up I'll still be hounded for what I've already done." He threw some shirts into a suitcase. "Anyway, I don't want to give it up. I should have killed him."

"No. He's a good copper."

"There's no such thing."

115

"What did this Spider Scott do for you? And what does he want now?"

"What he wants now is none of your business. He helped me when I was in Dartmoor. I was still in my twenties, and it was my first and last jail sentence. I was young and brash and cocky and nearly got killed in jail. Scott stopped what would have been a fatal beating up. Afterward he put it about that I was his friend. I was left alone then. He was a much-respected man, a cat-burglar of distinction, but he could also take care of himself. I was still inside when he was released, and he went and saw my mother for me. It made a difference to her, and he kept in touch with her until I was out."

Sophie snapped the locks of a case. It was difficult to believe that Hashimi was once worse than he was now. She loved him, as had many women before her; his beliefs made no difference. "So you feel you owe him? After so long?"

Hashimi was still cramming clothes into a case without folding them first. "I'm obligated to no one."

There was an unusual reservation in his voice, which Sophie noticed. "Will you help him?"

Hashimi flashed a warning. "Did I say he needed help?"

"I'm sorry. I was out of order. But I worry for you."

Hashimi shrugged. He suddenly looked weary. "It's too late to worry. I've no regrets about anything." He smiled at her and his whole face changed to an animated series of emotion. "Especially about you."

Sophie was pleased. She knew about the other women, and it made no difference to her. She was seeing a new facet of him. Hashimi's loyalties had always been with one cause or another; all had centered on a revolutionary theme. But now he was hiding concern for a person. His usual friends were all in the business of revolution and remained close only while their views were unwavering. This friendship was something different. As he continued to pack he was reflective, and she knew that his mind was on the man Scott. Perhaps Scott had shown him loyalty in a way that had got through. But who could know with Hashimi?

THE DOCTOR STRAIGHTENED, then signaled to a nurse to re-dress the wound. "So you think you're fit enough to leave?"

"I reckon so," Scott said carefully; he did not want to antagonize the doctor. "I'm going barmy in here. I might just as well be back in my cell."

"Home away from home is it? Or is there another reason you want to get back?"

"It's private. When that door is shut at night I'm on my own."

"A loner, then?"

"Always have been, doctor. I can heal there just as easily as here."

"It needs to be dressed daily. You'd have to report to the Albany sick bay. You'll have to stay for one more night."

Scott's nerves were screaming; he had to get to where the information was. He was transferred back to his cell in the late afternoon of the following day.

The cons in his wing knew what had happened, and they knew that Anthony Sims had not pointed a finger at anybody. They had an idea who had done it, but this they kept among themselves. For them, though, it was an interesting situation; they knew what Joe Gregory was like; most of them kept well clear of him, but the man known as Sims was an unknown quantity.

Scott finished the day quietly, taking a book from the library and sitting in his cell to read it. He was exercising great self-discipline. Time was passing, a week now since he had entered prison, and that was a week nearer to Maggie's coming home. The very thought of her return in present circumstances sickened him. Yet it was not the moment to make his move.

Nor was the following day. He rested almost all the time. At mealtimes he took the food back to the cell, and at slopping-out, he caught odd glimpses of Gregory. In the exercise yard Scott propped himself up in one corner and did nothing except to give the impression that he was in pain.

On the third day he was ready, but he waited until the evening. He moved quietly. Gregory was in his cell doing push-ups, facing the door.

Gregory saw a pair of feet and followed the body line up to take in a quietly smiling Scott, who was leaning easily against the jamb.

"Hello, Joe. Building up your strength?"

117

10

MARTIN Holmes met Freddie Ashton in the Kremlin bar of the House of Commons. It was not easy to conduct a private conversation there; the press was freely allowed in Annie's bar opposite, but although the Kremlin bar was restricted to members and their guests, the latter could come in many forms. They had a drink together and then wandered out onto the terrace facing St. Thomas's Hospital across the Thames. On such a fine day the terrace was crowded. The two members finally found a place of reasonable seclusion by the parapet.

The river traffic was as lethargic as the weather was enervating. Nobody wanted to move at great pace in the heat. Laughter and talk was subdued.

"I'm a little worried about this man Scott," Holmes said gazing across the river, arms folded on the parapet.

"Oh? I thought Toby Russell was handling your side of it. Not important enough for you, I should have thought."

Holmes tightened his lips. "It's gone beyond Russell and is now in my lap. The commissioner of police has been in touch with the Home Secretary who referred back to me."

"Well, would you prefer a meeting with Norman Murison?"

"Are you saying you can't answer?"

"I can answer so far as it goes." Ashton quickly gazed around to ensure they were not within earshot. "MI6 advised us that Scott is a danger to security. Apparently there's a lot involved that, understandably, they prefer not to pass on to me at this stage; it's all tied up with the ex-policeman Moody who died in his bath and an eastern bloc diplomat called Tuomo. And, of course, Scott. There's an intriguing triad there."

"We sent Tuomo home on the advice of the Security Service."

"There you are, you see. It's all linked."

"But we can't hold Scott forever. The police want answers."

"Well they would, wouldn't they? They put Scott into Albany prison as a plant. They renamed him Sims. Makes you wonder what they're hiding."

"They could hardly put him in under his own name," Holmes said icily. "Any plant deserves protection."

"Yes, but they were less than honest with your department about *why* they wanted him in. It makes you wonder."

Holmes watched a launch cream its way past. A girl waved from the cockpit. Visitors on the terrace waved back. What Ashton had said about police motive was true; it was one more aspect that worried Holmes. The police wanted to protect their man; that was understandable. What wasn't was why they had considered it necessary to lie to the Home Office. "Is there any point in seeing Norman Murison? I mean, will MI6 release any more to me than they have done to you? After all, you are in the Foreign Office, which is supposed to keep an eye on the day-to-day affairs of the SIS."

"I don't know," Ashton replied. "I shouldn't think they are too pleased with the way the police are acting. I can't see Norman Murison telling anyone anything that was not necessary. After all, all that's happening is that Scott is being detained for a few days while the department gets it together."

"Scott's been in a week," Holmes said emphatically. "And he's been viciously attacked during that time. I don't want a damned big scandal on my hands."

"Oh, the attack has no bearing. That's something that just happened; not unique in a prison. Scott is an old crook; he might have been recognized. He probably has enemies all over the place. If he had considered the attack to be tied in with his detention he would have pointed the finger, but he didn't. He's also done work for SIS in the past. So who knows why he was attacked?"

"A few more days, Freddie," Holmes said. "After that you either produce some hard evidence or I let Scott go. I'll have to. Tell Murison that."

"Of course. I'm quite sure he won't complain. Meanwhile he's grateful for your help. He has the country's interests very much at heart."

"No doubt. Just the same I should have thought this sort of nonsense was much nearer Lewis Hope's bunch at Security Service than Roland Powell's team at MI6. Where does Murison stand now?"

"In the hierarchy? At Sir Roland's right shoulder."

"ARE YOU WEARING our shoes, Rolly?"

Sir Roland Powell burst out laughing. Over average height, he was as muscular as Lewis Hope was lean, as broad-shouldered as his host was narrow. He had once been stroke for Oxford, but his athleticism had gone well beyond the bounds of rowing. All brawn and no muscle certainly did not apply to him; he had both. The brawn could not be hidden, but he was adept at giving quite the wrong impression about his brain.

He concealed a lot behind a natural good humor, a willingness for fun and laughter at the drop of a hat. In his younger days he had been a great practical joker. Blue eyes invariably smiled out at the world, but could switch to a piercing iciness when he chose. Powell enjoyed life. He had enormous vitality and when this was channeled into work that came his way, things began to happen. Like everyone else, he made mistakes, and his were usually bigger than anybody else's, but then so were his successes.

Because of his vacillating fortunes he was perhaps a surprising choice for the head of MI6, the overseas intelligence organization of the Secret Intelligence Service. He was not always a cautious man, but as he spoke to Sir Lewis Hope he showed that he could be. "We've always overlapped at some point, Lewis. Can't be helped. You're domestic, we're overseas; but I've known some of your inquiries to go well beyond these shores." Then, more in character, "Are you complaining?"

Hope switched off the television with his remote control. Both men had been watching the one o'clock news. Hope stretched his long legs and joined Powell by the empty fireplace. He sipped his sherry. "Not complaining. Curious. I'm only too happy to help, as you well know, but I'd like a little more information."

121

"Of course." Powell put his whisky down on the wide mantlepiece above the fireplace. "Strange, isn't it, that even on a blazing hot day like this we still stand with our backs to the grate, even when it's empty." He gazed quietly over the room, not liking Hope's contemporary taste in furniture and pictures. "I take it we're talking about Scott."

"My staff isn't happy about it. Nor, particularly, am I."

"I understand that. Are you referring to your general staff or a certain gentleman who is a more arcane part of your setup? Often wondered about him. How did he get to be there at all?"

"Stu Halliman used him a few times. George Bulman was trained as a policeman and without doubt is a fine detective. Halliman once had a problem with Special Branch that involved the IRA. There was a case of split loyalty, but it was difficult to pin down so Halliman used Bulman to winkle out the renegade, and it grew from there. Bulman was so awkward at times that I think the Met were glad to see the sideways shift. On the other hand Special Branch did not want him; they didn't see him fitting in and they were probably right. In truth they never forgave him for exposing one of their number. So he remained in limbo. There are sometimes advantages in presenting to would-be witnesses someone who does not carry the mystique of Special Branch or the Security Service. Ostensibly he is a policeman and some people understand and accept that much better than cloak-and-dagger."

Powell reached for his drink again. "That very much bears out how Stu Halliman once described him to me. 'A loose head' he called him. Of course, Stu was an old Rugby blue. So we *are* talking about George Bulman."

"I'm having trouble with him. He's difficult to keep in rein." Hope did not mention that Bulman had handed in his resignation.

Powell chuckled. "What's new? Men like Bulman will always be difficult. That's part of his strength."

"At the moment it's his weakness. He thinks I don't know what I'm doing." He turned to his visitor with a wintry smile. "And in truth I don't, except that I'm doing you a favor in trying to keep him away."

"Not me. My department. What's Bulman's reaction?"

"What you'd expect. He thinks Moody was murdered. Now there I don't agree with him. He's allowed himself to be influenced by the emotions of Moody's daughter."

"So he got carried away and had Scott planted in Albany to find out what he could?"

122

Hope stared in surprise. "How do you arrive at that?"

"Well, Scott wasn't put in for the puerile reason Commander Collins gave to Home Office. From what I've heard of Scott he would not operate against another villain. Not unless the country's welfare was at stake. I wouldn't consider the recovery of deposit box contents to come under that heading. Would you?"

"That's not what I mean. How do you know that Bulman had anything to do with Scott's being in Albany?"

Powell backed down. "Now *I am* wearing your shoes. I'm sorry, Lewis. Of course, I don't know. I do know from Stu Halliman that Scott and Bulman, as unlikely as it seems, have become close. I know from Scott's past history that he's far too independent to operate for anyone. He's extremely selective friendship being the key. I merely assume that Bulman asked Scott to do it. Am I wrong?"

Hope did not reply at once. He stared across the room to an unsigned Russell Flint print as if it gave him inspiration. Powell followed his gaze and was not keen on what he saw.

"Am I?" repeated Powell.

"No." Hope moved pensively away from the fireplace. He turned slowly and said, "You're not using us by any chance, Rolly?"

Powell seemed appalled at the idea. "How can I be? You're not involved. The Home Office have helped us, so far as I know, but the only favor I've asked of you is to keep your men out of it. For the time being, of course. A matter of too many feet trampling the same ground. As soon as we have something for you I'll pass it on at once."

"Why not let Scott go now? When all is said and done, he has been attacked."

"I doubt that's got anything to do with it."

"What about this Moody, Tuomo, Scott business?"

"Murison believes he has some very sound evidence. At the moment Moody would appear to have been far more connected than Scott. Murison is well aware that his time is limited. He needs a few more days and Home Office is quite amenable." And then hesitantly, "I have helped you too, on occasion, Lewis. If Bulman does crash madly on, then really, I am under no further obligation to you. That was all I asked of you which wasn't much."

Hope finished his sherry reflectively. "I've no objection to helping even if you have crossed the line into the domestic. These things happen. It's just that I prefer to be less in the dark. As you do."

Powell raised his glass. "You keep a good malt."

"Only for friends. I can't stand the stuff myself."

Powell made no comment, but he emptied his glass appreciatively.

GREGORY KEPT HIS head. He knew that Scott would not be so at ease if there was a "guard" nearby. But he was prone and at a disadvantage. To show that he did not care he continued with his push-ups. Scott's foot crashed onto the back of Gregory's head, whose face smashed into the floor.

As he stepped farther into the cell, Scott moved his foot to the nape of Gregory's neck. He used almost the whole of his weight to keep Gregory's now bloodied face on the floor. Gregory tried to push himself up, but Scott applied more pressure.

"You lined yourself up for me," Scott said pleasantly. "That was nice of you, Joe."

"I'll kill you for this, you bastard." The words gurgled out through blood from a broken nose and split lips.

"You didn't do too well before. I'll be ready next time."

"Let me up. I can't breathe."

"That's no loss, Joe." Scott applied more pressure. As Gregory tried to roll away Scott almost stood on his neck. He said, "You can put yourself out of your misery by telling me who paid you to kill me."

"Get stuffed." The words bubbled out.

"Sorry, Joe. I didn't get that." Scott stamped hard on the neck, and for a dreadful moment thought he had gone too far as Gregory convulsed. But he could still hear the labored breathing.

"You nearly broke my neck, you stupid bastard." Gregory could barely get the words out.

"I'm not asking you much," Scott responded reasonably. As Gregory made an effort to move, Scott almost lost balance but he quickly recovered. This had to be resolved quickly, before someone came.

"No one paid me. I can't stand the sight of you."

Gregory's hand was moving toward Scott's left foot. Scott stamped on it with his heel, and the foot on Gregory's neck momentarily took his full weight, effectively reducing Gregory's scream to a stifled gurgle. Scott realized that he might go too far. Equally he knew that with men like Gregory it was the only way to get what he wanted.

With an enormous effort Gregory rolled from under Scott's foot and onto his back. He made a grab for the foot but Scott moved. As Gregory tried to rise, Scott kicked Gregory's legs from under him and his head crashed against the bed.

Gregory pushed himself up using the bed as support, his face covered with blood. He was mad with rage and pain, eyes glaring and bloodshot, mouth emitting a stream of expletives, one curled hand extended to grapple with Scott. When he was halfway up, and while he was still levering himself, Scott hit him crisply on the jaw.

The sharp movement sent a stabbing pain through Scott's wound so he hit Gregory with his other fist as the man was falling. Gregory was on his knees, barely half-conscious. Scott came around the back of him, grabbed an arm, and forced it up Gregory's back. He grasped the little finger and levered it down.

Gregory arched in agony and Scott applied more pressure on the finger, which brought Gregory onto his toes.

"I'm going to break your fingers, one by one," Scott whispered into his ear. "Who paid you?"

Gregory kicked backward, but Scott had his legs well clear. Time was running out. He reached around, stuffed his handkerchief in Gregory's mouth, and snapped the little finger at the lower joint.

Gregory's scream was muted, but the sound was still too loud. Scott now had hold of the second finger and was bending it to breaking point when Gregory tore the handkerchief from his mouth. "For *Chrissake.* The Reverend. It was the Reverend. Let go. Jesus, let go."

Scott held on but eased the pressure. "The Reverend? Phil Deacon? He's not in here."

"He got word through the day you arrived. He was the one who paid."

"How?"

"Into a bank. I've had word."

"Which bank?"

"National Westminster in Kennington."

"You'd better be right."

"I'm gonna finish the job on you, Sims. I'll get you one way or another. You've busted my hand. I won't slip up again."

"I'll see that word gets back to Deacon, Joe. He'll be pleased to know you cocked it up. Watch your back. He'll have someone get you. I mean, you've had his money, haven't you?"

125

Scott released the grip and pushed Gregory forward. Gregory fell against the bed and slowly lowered himself onto it. He held the wrist of his injured hand. With his little finger bent back unnaturally, its joint already badly swollen, Gregory glared through a mist of blood. "I'll earn my money, Sims. Bank on it."

"You'll have to use your left hand, Joe. You'd better get that finger splinted up." Scott gazed down at Gregory. "You can keep the handkerchief. I wouldn't want your blood around me. Be lucky." He moved out to return to his own cell.

He sat on his bed, shaken now that it was over. Gregory would go flat out for revenge but meanwhile would have to explain his injuries away.

Scott propped his legs up to ease his stomach. The name Gregory had given him had shaken him considerably. The Reverend was a gangland rival to Rex Reisen, who had helped Scott on occasion. Reisen had run the London underworld scene for well over a decade, during which time he had been imprisoned only once and that had been a fairly short sentence.

Reisen ruled by fear and had the strange quirk of being a patriot. He had commissioned an oil painting of the queen for his office, and the Union Jack was carried on his desk on an eighteen-karat gold stand and mast. After the war he had served in the catering corps. But he had long spread the word, backed by badly faded snapshots in which none of the groups could be identified, that he had served with Montgomery in the desert. It was doubtful if he had been old enough to have done so.

Phil Deacon, the Reverend, had been trying to rock Reisen's boat for a long time. But although Reisen could be unstable at times, verging on the schizophrenic, he could be spasmodically brilliant. His outlook was crude, but his timing could be crucially sound. If anyone was born to be a criminal, it was Reisen. In his field, Reisen attracted respect and a good deal of fear.

Phil Deacon, on the other hand, was merely a thug who had reached the top of his particular heap by the crudest and most basic of methods. It was true that Reisen was also basic, but Deacon had none of his flair or precipience. Deacon was a protection man. That was easy; make demands and kill or maim if they were not met. So far as Scott knew, Deacon had no legitimate businesses; he would not know how to run one, and if he put someone else in, it was doubtful he would know whether it was being properly managed. Extracting money was different. Removing the opposition was something he understood. Until he tried to remove Reisen.

The net result of trying to pierce that formidable armor was a removal of Deacon's operations to south of the Thames, where, so far as Scott knew, he still operated.

The Reverend was an obvious sobriquet that sprung from Deacon, a man who would hardly recognize a Bible if he saw one. Deacon's only obvious talent was an ability to kill. Not simply a crude shooting or knifing or car accident, but a capacity to apply a surprising refinement. The underworld knew this, and so did the police. Nobody yet had been able to lay anything at his door. It was the one area where he could apply a measure of artistry. One of the problems of directly connecting him with a murder was that these days he did not commit them himself. The cynical claimed that he kept down the police list of wanted men and that they therefore closed their eyes to that part of his operations.

So why was the Reverend trying to kill him, Scott pondered? There was absolutely no sense to it. Unless Gregory was lying. But Gregory had not lied; he would not have dared to pull a name like the Reverend out of the hat. There were easier ways to commit suicide.

The massive frustration of being imprisoned struck Scott once again. He could not pass this information on to Bulman without risk of other eyes seeing it. If he told the governor it would be passed on to the police and the Home Office and neither was desirable. He would have to wait until Bulman called again or until he was released. But he was convinced that he would not be released. Meanwhile he would only be safe while he was in his locked cell.

GEORGE BULMAN CALLED on Chief Inspector Gerrard Sullivan of Special Branch. The office door was open, but Bulman politely knocked and waited for Sullivan to glance up at him. It was a small office, about the size of Bulman's own, but it did boast a window, which was open.

When Sullivan looked up, his expression was impassive, his pen poised in hand above the desk as if anxious to press on. Sullivan, not surprisingly, had very Irish features, clear gray eyes, and an open face with a thin lip line. "Can I do something for you, Mr. Bulman?" He spoke with a Cork accent.

Sullivan's politeness was no more than that; there was no friendliness in his tone.

"May I come in?" Bulman tried to raise a smile.

"It's a free country." Sullivan put down his pen.

"I need your help, Gerry," Bulman said, as he pulled up a police issue chair and sat down.

"Oh, yes." Sullivan was not encouraging.

"Are you going to hold it against me forever?" Bulman asked reasonably.

"Hold what against you, Mr. Bulman?"

"Cut out the blarney, Gerry. I nailed one of your countrymen, and colleague to boot, who was passing information to the IRA. He had taken the oath and betrayed a loyalty. Okay. I'd do the same to an Englishman or a Scot or a Welshman. I don't think he was really bent, but he let his heart rule his head and that placed certain people in danger. You should be grateful to me for sniffing him out. It took the pressure off every good Irishman in the force. And that includes you. So don't be so bloody touchy because he was Irish."

Sullivan's eyes adopted the suspicion of a smile. He pulled a desk drawer out and put a foot on it. His chair creaked as he leaned back. "Can I be blunt, sir? Man-to-man?"

"What's wrong with you? When were you ever anything else? What am I, a pariah or something? What do you want me to say? My father came from Ireland? He came from Shoreditch. And my mother came from Streatham. I was born just outside the sound of Bow Bells. You're bloody lucky, son, you're talking to someone with an impeccable pedigree. So come out with it. I need a favor."

Sullivan was forced to smile. "I didn't trust him either. He was a bad selection for the Branch. But it was *you* who winkled him out and you are not in the Branch. We all hate you. Officially. So we do."

"Well, that settles that."

"I can't promise to help but I'll listen."

"You remember the Wally Cooper case?"

"The guy who got thirty for lifting State secrets?"

"You were involved in it, weren't you?"

"I was the arresting officer. Four o'clock in the morning in the middle of a cloudburst."

128

"Well, the shamrock has to be watered sometime. Is that all you did? Arrest him?"

"Yes. A search team went in afterward and lifted some documents from his pad."

"You couldn't tell me what?"

"Even if I knew, I wouldn't go that far. All I did was to take the man to jail."

"Where were these documents supposed to have been lifted from?"

"Can't tell you."

"You mean you don't know, or you won't tell me?"

"I don't know. I wasn't at the trial."

"Oh! I thought you were. Who *was* at the trial?"

"Why don't you get the transcript of the trial?"

"Because as you well know, the bloody trial was held in camera. The transcript is under lock and key in the archives, and by the time I get permission it will be too late. I want some quick answers."

"On the old boy network?"

"Well, I am in the club."

Sullivan laughed. "Special Branch would dispute that. I'm sorry, I can't help you."

"You haven't answered my question. Who, in your lot, was at the trial?"

"Detective Superintendent Budd. Plus a character from Security Service. Why don't you ask him?"

"I don't know who he is. And Sir Lewis Hope won't tell me because it's his mission in life to make things difficult for me."

"I thought that was *your* mission to the rest of us."

"Don't take this man-to-man stuff too far, Gerry. It's a pity. I thought you could help."

"Ask Mr. Budd."

"I won't get anywhere. You're the only bloke in Special Branch who'll talk to me. It's a lonely life. Sometimes I feel I can't take much more."

Sullivan was grinning. "Is that your way of asking me to speak to him?"

"It's decent of you to offer."

"What do you want to know?"

Bulman wanted to know several things, but he had to cut down if he was to get anything. To ask for the contents of the documents would cause too many ripples. "Whose flat Wally broke into."

"And what's your interest?"

Bulman had to give an answer. "Justice. That old-fashioned word. Something reached me that might suggest Wally was a patsy. I have to follow it up even if it wastes my time, which it probably will."

"I'll see what I can do."

MARIA WOLFSTHOLME ARRIVED home late and very tired. She was a trendy girl in her mid-twenties. Her sallow, rather gaunt face with its high cheekbones and her long dark hair belied the Scandinavian origins of her parents, who had come to live in Britain in the mid-sixties. Her parents were well-to-do, her father a successful businessman, head of the United Kingdom division of his Swedish-based company.

But Maria, to the deep sorrow of her parents, had left home a long time ago; once she had graduated from the London School of Economics, she had drifted away from them in virtually every way. For a while she was a squatter, then a demonstration buff; whatever the protest, Maria could be relied upon to hold a placard for some cause or other, provided it was antiauthoritarian. In the early days of the Greenham Common antinuclear protests, she was well to the fore. There was no halfway with Maria, no compromise that she could make. She was a Trotskyist, and she clung fervently to the tunnel vision of her views. There was nothing either side, no argument, no debate, no doubts.

Maria was one of a crowd, but different in the sense that she had a reasonable amount of money to support her. When she had finally made the break from home, her parents, unable to see where they had gone wrong but unable to accept that they had not, had provided her with a bank account to draw upon.

Those on the extreme left of trade unions quickly saw the advantages that Maria could provide for them. She was a brilliant researcher and instinctively knew what to look for and what to ignore. And she was quick to grasp what was needed at a particular time of crisis. So she was put to work and became totally absorbed in what she was doing. Her hard-line image extended to her private life, which was almost non-existent. Her friends were as political as she, and an already narrow

130

viewpoint became an increasingly solitary focus. Political work was her life.

Maria remained very much in the background. It was how she preferred it to be, which suited those who saw the advantages. Certain men, when arguing their point on television or radio or in the press, liked to be thought of as the fountain of knowledge; an image that they owed to her. It was plausible stuff.

Maria worked solidly, sometimes day and night, in order to provide ammunition for the orators to project their own image, preen their egos, and support their cause. She became invaluable to them, better than a top-grade publicity agent; they were able to floor their interviewers with facts and figures that simply rolled off their practiced tongues. When later these figures were challenged it was invariably too late. The bland impression had been made.

It was eight o'clock when Maria reached her apartment that night. And, for her, that was early. But she needed little sleep, and her idea of relaxation was to scan the newspapers and get ready for the next battle.

She lived alone in Islington. When not working she preferred not to have company, and her parents' funds fortunately gave her the kind of independence she required. This night, though, she was unusually tired. It was hot in the basement flat. The large windows overlooked the gully below street level, and if she peered up she could see the hurrying legs of people passing. She kept the windows closed in spite of the heat; the garbage cans were further along the gully, but in any event, she was far from a fresh-air fiend.

She left the heavy drapes open and stared around an incredibly untidy drawing room. The furniture was old, some of it stained, and somehow there was too much of it. Piles of paper and magazines were everywhere.

Maria dodged around a raised ironing board, clothes heaped upon it, and found a gap between piles of books to view herself in a huge mirror suspended above the fireplace. She did not see herself as pretty or plain, but for once she noticed the wear and tear. She *looked* tired, and she almost despised herself for it. Her hair needed a wash, not because she was unclean but because she rarely found the time for personal necessities.

She flicked on the answering machine and listened to the messages. When they had finished, she reflected that they had all been from men not

131

ringing her up because she was a woman, but all making intellectual demands of her.

She turned from the mirror as the doorbell rang. Usually she could hear anyone coming down the stone steps, but this time she had missed them. She went to the front door. A salesman type raised his hat and gave her a smile. He was holding a suitcase, which appeared to be heavy.

"Yes?"

"I'm here to fill your head with knowledge, miss. *Encyclopedia Britannica*. New edition. May I show you?"

"Britannica?" Maria flapped her arms in disbelief. "At this time of night? You've got to be kidding."

"Everyone's out during the day—just let me leave a brochure or two." He moved his case to one side as Maria shook her head and was about to close the door on him. An arm came around the blind side of the door in the gap the salesman had created, and a second man, whom Maria had not seen, sprayed gas into her face from a small canister. Maria fell back, choking, with her hands to her face. The two men entered, bringing the case with them, and closed the front door behind them.

Maria was rasping. The men grabbed her as she retched, immediately stuffing a gag into her mouth. She struggled as they pulled her hands behind her back, but it was difficult for her to breathe while she was straining.

They dragged her into the living room, pushed her into a chair, and then tied her ankles. One of them taped her lips so that she could not eject the gag. Her breathing grew a little easier as her nose unclogged, but her lungs still burned. As she steadied down, coughing against the gag now and then, through smarting eyes, she watched them work with a horrible fascination.

One man heaved the suitcase onto a chair, knocking over a pile of magazines that had been on the seat. He unlatched the lid and ferreted inside. The second man pulled the drapes across the windows, then came back to watch Maria. The telephone rang but both men ignored it.

Gradually the cold-blooded purpose of their visit unfolded before Maria's widening, bloodshot, eyes. The cord of her iron was being removed. The man took his time, working carefully but quickly. The second man, seeing Maria's horror, said,

"Sorry, love. We'll be as quick as we can. Should have done the job days ago, but you're a late bird mostly and you dodge about a bit."

132

The bile of stark fear rose in Maria's throat. Incredibly she was receiving an apology for the delay to her imminent murder. At first her thoughts did not go quite so far; the men were trying to frighten her. But the fright turned to terror as it gradually sank in that they had made no attempt to hide their features, and their London accents were clearly natural. They even started calling each other by name.

"Pass the small screwdriver, Charlie. The green handled one."

Charlie passed it over, glanced at Maria, noticed the terrified eyes and said again, "Sorry, love. Some of these old screws are a bit rotten. Ted's doing his best."

She thought she was going mad; perhaps it would be better if she did, it was all so matter of fact. Ted coiled the cord that had been on the iron and dropped it into the suitcase. He took another coil out; as soon as Maria saw it, she knew how it was to be. The cord Ted was now fixing on was worn in a couple of places; she caught a brief glimpse of bare copper wire. Oh, my God, no. She retched against the gag, her stomach heaving.

Charlie watched her with concern. "Don't be sick, love. We'll have to clear up afterward." Maria heaved and then in a wild panic tried to get to her feet. She would have fallen face downward, but Charlie caught her and lowered her quite gently back into the chair. "You could have hurt yourself then," he said with some concern.

Maria gazed up at him. He was smiling quite politely. He was a psychopath. The knowledge removed the last dregs of hope she might have held. Her fear was quelled for a while, taken over by a numbness. She was about to die, and she belatedly realized that she had not even begun to live.

"Plug in," Ted instructed.

Charlie gazed around for the socket, found it, and put the plug in. Both men went to the suitcase and withdrew heavy rubber gloves, which they put on.

Maria screamed behind her gag and tried to throw herself from the chair. For the first time she noticed the unusually thick soles the men were wearing. What had she done to deserve this? Followed a belief? Or systematically set out by any means to destroy another?

Ted switched on the iron. Both men then grasped Maria by her arms and dragged her to her feet. They undid her wrists; she put new strength into her struggles, but they had expected it and held on tight while she expended her energy. Then, inexorably, Ted brought her right hand forward to the area of cord where it met the socket of the iron. The gloves made him clumsy, but he did not relax his grip. As though speaking to Maria he said, "I want to get the forefinger along that section there." She made her last frantic struggle before Ted managed to get her hand as he wanted it.

Maria convulsed madly, her bound legs kicking unnaturally, her flesh twitching.

"I want to be sure," Ted said and held her there as the current raced through her body again and again. At last he took her hand away. "Hold her while I undo her legs, and keep her there."

Charlie held Maria in place with difficulty. He said to the whitened corpse, "I said it wouldn't take long. You're okay now, love."

Ted undid the ankles, then straightened to help Charlie hold up Maria. "Right," he said. "Throw her slightly backward. Not too hard." They pushed the dead girl away, and she collapsed in an awkward position, her head hitting a chair.

Ted knelt down to examine her wrists and ankles for bruising and then removed the gag. He carefully wiped her lips. He then placed everything they had used into the suitcase. He knelt once more to ensure that Maria was dead. He examined the ankles and wrists again and once more wiped her mouth to remove any residue of adhesive from the tape that had held the gag.

Charlie, who was watching, grinned as he said, "Poor girl burned herself out."

Ted ignored him. He very carefully switched off the iron and pulled out the plug, then wiped the iron plug and socket before pressing Maria's hand over the handle of the iron several times. Next he laid the iron on the floor and plugged it in. The cheap cotton carpet began to singe as the iron heated up.

"Won't that cause a fire?" Charlie asked.

"It might. Pull the curtains back and let's go."

11

S IR Roland Powell sent for Norman Murison so that they could talk over morning coffee. They discussed various problems as they often did as a matter of routine. Committees were fine and had their place, but the real issues were more quickly tackled during moments like these.

Murison was what some would consider a typical Foreign Office figure. He had the right background—Eton and Oxford—he was very knowledgeable, knew his job and, would protect the Foreign Office at all times.

Of late the Foreign Office had come more under the public gaze, and its image had somewhat cracked here and there. At a time of national stress, the public took a poor view of the anachronistic size and splendor of some of the British embassies abroad. Spheres of influence had changed dramatically over the years, but the Foreign Office had clung to edifices suitable for a modern king in places where diplomatic influence had long lost its importance. Behind the scenes Murison had given full support to the old image.

Why change an image that had maintained respect throughout the world for centuries? He did not believe in change for the sake of it. So far as he was concerned, public money was well spent in supporting Britain's image abroad. Murison was of the old school in more than one sense. But none could deny his dedication. He was a highly experienced and efficient intelligence officer in his mid-fifties.

Powell knew that he could rely on Murison for any project he gave him to do. In terms of patriotism, an old-fashioned concept to many these days, Murison could not be faulted. Furthermore, and very important, Murison got on exceedingly well with his American counterparts. They, too, knew that he could be relied upon, and patriotism there was not yet a dirty word.

He was a handsome man, kept himself fit and carried no surplus weight on his six foot plus frame. Dark hair, gray eyes, Saville Row tailor; he deplored sloppiness of dress. He took life seriously.

He accepted the cigar that Powell offered him when the coffee arrived. Cigars usually meant a delicate situation and perhaps an extended session. He sat in his usual position in front of Powell's massive desk in the large, oak-paneled office. Murison approved of the paneling. Oak was part of old England like roast beef and good ale. Britain had grown great on them. Now the beer was chemical, the beef hormone fed, and the oak veneered.

"Scott," Powell said, tapping the note on his desk. "Willie 'Spider' Scott. Do you think you might be wrong about him, Norman?"

Murison gazed at his cigar, then he drew on it and exhaled slowly. He was seated sideways to Powell so that he could be close to the desk without his long legs knocking it. "Of course I might." But the words were uttered with an authority that suggested it improbable.

"You can't hold him much longer. The Home Secretary isn't happy about it, nor his minister Martin Holmes, nor Sir Lewis Hope. Nor, for that matter, am I."

"I'm not either. Actually I never have been. But the opportunity was too good to miss. My information still stands. There is a Tuomo, Moody, Scott link. I agree that the Scott angle is obscure and I agree that if it's not resolved in the next day or two he must be released. I would hate to see him leave the country, though."

Powell pushed his coffee cup away. "Who's your source?"

"Maria Wolfstholme."

"What? She's doubling?"

"I doubt it. The information comes from her via a 'friend.' In quotes."

"Has she a grudge against Scott?"

"It's possible. But he did once work with Moody, and it's doubtful if she knew that. I am keeping a close eye on it."

"Why don't you hand the whole damned lot over to Lewis Hope's crowd or Special Branch? It's their pigeon, not ours."

"It's simply the way it happened. I had no intention of encroaching. And indeed, if I do come up with a positive, I'll pass it straight over with the greatest pleasure. If it's negative then I won't have wasted their time."

Both men smoked silently for a few moments with their minds on the problem. Suddenly Murison said, "Look, Sir Roland, I know I'm apt to hold on. I think in my position anyone would have. But I don't want to embarrass anybody. If you feel that Scott should be freed now then I'll see to it."

"You find your line of inquiry is easier with him tucked away?"

"Oh, undoubtedly. He's no fool. He would certainly know how to block us if there is something to hide."

"Then keep him there for a day or two more. But no longer. Keep me in touch."

MURISON MET ASHTON at the squash courts of the Lansdown Club. They played three carefully paced games before Murison called a halt. He wiped the streaming sweat from his face and neck as they went to the changing room. "I'm really past it," he gasped.

"Nonsense. You had me going there." The younger Ashton threw his towel over his shoulder. He was shorter and slighter than his chief. The two men changed into bathing trunks and cooled off in the club's pool, after which they dressed and climbed the stairs to the bar above the pool and sat at a table at one end of the balcony, looking down at the water and the few swimmers who could take time out during the late afternoon.

Murison made sure that nobody else was within earshot. Even then he kept his voice down to little more than a whisper. "They certainly made a hash of it in Albany."

"Perhaps Scott is a natural survivor. There's still time."

"There has to be, Freddie. But it's tight. And there are complications." Murison gazed thoughtfully at the clear water below; male voices echoed around the pool. "The case I've built up around Scott and Moody, showing a link with Tuomo, can only hold up if Scott is dead. As you know the tenuous link is Maria Wolfstholme, as the messenger who collects information from a double agent who works as a female clerk in the London Aeroflot office. That can only hold up as truth for as long as Sir Roland is willing to believe me. The moment he has suspicions, pressure will be brought on you as the supposed contact with

137

Maria. Sir Roland will want to see you. He will probably put someone else on to contacting Maria. And that is when our whole case against Scott and Moody dissolves into the tissue of lies it is. There's no point in mincing words."

"Christ!" Ashton began to sweat.

"You knew the possibilities." Murison smiled thinly. "If you react to Sir Roland as you've just reacted to me, we could be in trouble."

"Well, dammit. I'm in the firing line."

"I thought you were made of sterner stuff, Freddie. Anyway, forget it." Murison glanced around, then leaned nearer to Ashton. "I've taken care of Maria. That leaves the fictitious link of the Aeroflot girl. I've made a discreet leak about one of the Aeroflot staff that will reach the KGB resident here. He may not believe it, but he cannot afford to ignore it. One of their airline staff will be repatriated. I'm sorry for the girl, for she might fair worse than Maria. But it was essential to cut off any possible inquiry Sir Roland might make. There is simply nobody left for him to contact."

"Won't it make him suspicious?"

"He leans heavily on me and with very good reason. He won't suspect my loyalty to the Crown. Nor should he. But you're missing the point. It will simply look as if 'our friends' have caught up on some doubling in their own ranks and have attended to it in their usual ruthless way."

"Neat." Ashton was relieved. "You'll have to tell him, of course. It will weaken your case against Scott."

"I'll tell him once I'm sure the Russian girl has gone back. If we get Scott next time, the weakness of the case won't matter. It will all look good."

Neither man was drinking; they simply sat at the small table by the balcony rail. Ashton glanced at his watch. "I must get back." But he made no attempt to rise and added, "I wish we knew why Moody started all this. It's caused us to sidetrack too much; too many people to silence instead of getting on with the real work."

Murison was unworried. "These things happen, Freddie. Keeps us on our toes. We've had a very long untroubled spell. We've veen lucky. It can lead to complacency." Murison grasped the rail. "We can never be sure of how Moody started on us. I would guess that Hudnell pointed him in the right direction."

"Paul Hudnell? Good Lord, he was one of us. Sound."

"He was a sixty-cigarette-a-day man and he was dying. In the end it went through him like an electric current. He lasted five weeks from the moment he knew. He was drugged up to the eyeballs and had to be kept isolated in case he talked during his fantasies. While I was there visiting, he thought the nurse was a police spy. You wouldn't have recognized him, Freddie. Poor Paul. But I believe Moody picked up something from him."

Ashton showed surprise. "You haven't mentioned this before."

"I couldn't be sure. But I've given it a lot of thought. I've had to, should there be some other source of leaks. I discovered that Moody visited him in hospital. A lot of people did, and Moody had a lot of contacts in the departments. We'll never know whether Hudnell sent for him because encroaching death triggered an unstable conscience, or whether he just babbled in delirium. If I'm right, it would explain why Moody kept it to himself and used an outsider. He wouldn't have known who to trust in the establishment. I think we grasped the danger very quickly and tidied up extremely well."

Ashton nodded thoughtfully. "Indeed. And it looks as if you've done it again," he said with some relief. "But we still haven't found the receipt Moody got Cooper to steal, and we still have to get Scott. We don't know what he knows, and even if it's nothing, I gather he's the type who soldiers on."

"The receipt is a nuisance, but you can forget Scott. I have a red alert out on him."

WILLIE SCOTT RECEIVED a letter from a Frank Obuti, who had just come over from South Africa and who had been trying to trace his old friend Tony Sims, only to hear on the grapevine that he was in prison. What could Tony possibly have done to deserve that? Was it a mistake? Send a visit order as soon as possible.

Scott read the letter again and guessed it was from the Arab. The address was a hotel in Paddington. Scott considered the implications. He had written to the Arab in desperation. And his desperation grew by the day. Yet it would be dangerous for the Arab to call here. Every police force in the country was looking for him. In truth, Scott had not expected the Arab to respond; the letter had not been written hopefully but out of immense frustration and fear.

The Arab had not remained free by being careless, but even so the risks were enormous. The strange thing was that Scott strongly opposed everything the Arab stood for, and yet, in prison all those years ago, there had been a peculiar rapport between them. Hashimi had well known what Scott thought of him, yet Scott had helped him. Scott understood that with men like the Arab it was too late to turn back after the first killing. In the long run they were as doomed as their victims, if not from authority then from their own kind as demands and policies perpetually changed. Hashimi was set on a course of inevitable self destruction.

Scott held the letter and considered what best to do. He gazed around the cell. He was trapped here and had committed no crime. Even Bulman and Collins couldn't help him, and that was both sinister and ominous. He left the cell and located the landing officer to make application for a visit order. He had to give the name and address the Arab had given him and the application was filled in.

Scott knew what would happen next. Unless the potential visitor was already known to the prison authority the details would be passed on to the police who would run it through the Criminal Records Office to see if the applicant had a criminal record. If he had, a visit could be refused.

The following day produced an incident that removed his hesitation. The alarm went off, and all prisoners were returned to their cells and locked in. A paper knife was missing from the library. Paper knives are invariably blunt and certainly the library one had been. But Scott knew, as they all did, that by now it would be a sharp as a rapier. A massive search was started from cell to cell. It was a long, annoying, uncomfortable affair, as beds were stripped, clothes and bodies searched. The fact that the search went on all day was indication of how well the knife had been hidden. The prisoners would be locked up until the knife was found. At least that was the theory. Who had taken it was a problem; who it was intended for was on everyone's mind, particularly Scott's. He sat down to write a letter.

SIR LEWIS HOPE called on Bulman the same day that he had met Sir Roland Powell. Bulman was in a bad mood, trying to attend to old jobs with his mind firmly fixed on the conspiracy that surrounded Scott. He had no doubt that there was a conspiracy, but he could not determine its form or purpose. It could well be a Home Office cock-up; it would not be the first, but he considered that too simple a solution. This was virtually confirmed when Hope walked in.

Hope rarely sat on the few occasions he visited Bulman. He stood in front of Bulman's inadequate desk, fingers in jacket pockets with his thumbs sticking out, and he offered his subordinate a passable smile. He glanced toward the open door of Haldean's boxlike room, as he usually did.

"He's out," Bulman said. "The door's open for ventilation." He did not stand up and pointedly looked back at some papers he had been studying.

"I have some good news for you about Scott."

Bulman looked up at once. "He's been released?"

"Not quite. But I've had a word with the Home Office, and they say that he'll be kept only for a day or two more, unless he's guilty, of course."

"Guilty of what, Sir Lewis?"

"Well, that's the point, old boy. If it was known for certain what, then we'd have all the answers. You must accept that there are certain pointers that appear to incriminate Scott. If the presumption is wrong, he will be released. There is now a time limit. I know you are concerned for him and about your own involvement. I thought you would like to know."

"Thank you, sir. I suppose it now depends on the Home Office definition of a 'day or two.'"

"I'm sure it will finish to your satisfaction. Just passing."

When the lanky figure had gone, Bulman picked up the internal phone. "Dick? I'm on my way down."

He came straight to the point when he entered Commander Collins's office. "Has Deputy Commissioner Cruickshank got anywhere with the Home Office?"

"Nowhere. He never got past the first hurdle. He has virtually told me to lay off."

"Well, Sir Lewis has just seen me. Seems to be backing down. Reckons that if nothing is pinned on Spider within a day or two, he'll be sprung."

"Nothing like that was said to me."

"That's why I'm checking. I don't think Lewis Hope was bullshitting. I think he's been told that. But if it was by the Home Office why

141

haven't they told Deputy Commissioner Cruickshank? If they wanted me to know they'd want you to know first. You put him there."

"Are you saying it's not the Home Office?"

"That's what it looks like. Someone there is doing someone somewhere else a favor."

"It happens."

"That's not what I don't like about it. You had a visit from the Foreign Office bloke Ashton. If they are really involved, then it's something again. I've never liked any of this, and I like it a damn sight less now."

Collins looked doubtful. "You're not saying the Foreign Office is trying to kill Spider?"

Bulman paced in front of the desk. "Sounds bloody crazy, doesn't it? I can't think of any reason why they should want to."

"You're going too far, George. They might have seen to it that he was kept in for some reason, but to top him? Or maybe you don't know Scott as well as you think you do."

"Maybe. And maybe that's not the only issue we don't know. The Foreign Office is in there somewhere. I have this terrible feeling that the 'day or two' Sir Lewis talks of is what's left for Scott on this planet. I hope to God I'm wrong. I'd better get down there again."

Bulman went by train to Southampton, caught the hourly hydrofoil to West Cowes, and hired a taxi outside the ferry terminal after the twenty-minute sea crossing. He paid off the cab before entering the prison grounds. As he walked up the broad concrete path, he reflected that the entrance to Albany had more of the appearance of a motorway restaurant than a prison; all wood and sheet glass. Until he raised his sight to the walls behind and the television scanners and arc lamps.

He had telephoned his E.T.A. and met the governor in the administrative block; noticing, as he went, the dog patrols on the outer perimeter. The two men shook hands warily.

"Sit down, Mr. Bulman." Vernon Healy tried to get some warmth into his greeting. "I would like to say how nice it is to see you, but as it's about Sims, that makes it difficult for me."

"I understand." Bulman appeared awkward and uncomfortably hot in the chair. "I don't think any of us like the situation. I only want to see him briefly. Can it be arranged for me to do that without the other cons seeing me? I don't want to add to his obvious problems."

142

"I'll get him brought across. You can use an office."

"Wouldn't that mean a guard or two present? I'd rather be alone with him."

"I can't risk that. I've already gone some way to meet you. What about the visitors' room? It will be closed to visitors at four. There'll be officers on duty, but it's big enough for a private dialogue. Join me in some tea until then."

"That's very kind of you, sir. Has something happened to change your original attitude?"

"I don't like being used. I don't mind helping out, either the police or the Home Office, but I don't like being entirely in the dark."

"I don't think the Home Office people are directly involved." Bulman did not get the reaction he expected.

"Oh, yes they are. My instructions are from them."

"They might be helping colleagues in another ministry."

Healy's expression tightened. "Are you sure of that?"

"I'm satisfied. I can't prove it, of course."

"If you could, I'd demand an explanation at once."

"So would I, sir. What extent is the involvement I've no idea. Is Sims all right?"

"Of course. There is the added complication of a paper knife being missing. It's caused a good deal of work, and we've had to confine the prisoners to their cells."

"A paper knife? It'll be a stiletto by now, if you haven't found it. Are they still locked up?"

"Yes. But I can't keep them confined forever. Just one more problem for a prison governor, Mr. Bulman."

"Do you think it's anything aimed at Sims? Whoever took it must have someone in mind."

"Sims and two hundred and forty others. Why should it be Sims?"

"Because they've already had a go."

"Yes, but these sorts of problems are invariably with us. Whoever took it might have nobody in mind at all. That could come later. Meanwhile, someone is armed."

Bulman thought it best not to pursue the matter. The governor had problems; running a prison was full of them.

BULMAN WAS ALLOWED into the visitors' room before Scott

arrived, a reversal of normal procedure. He was sitting at a central table when the end door was released to slide back and allow Scott through. Two guards came with him but sat at the nearest table to the door. Bulman did not rise, and Scott adopted a surly attitude. It was best that word did not get back that they were on friendly terms.

"What do you want?" Scott growled, pulling out a chair. He glanced over to the tea bar; it was closed. "You were always a mean bastard," he said, just loud enough for the guards to hear. "Timed it so that you don't have to put your hand in your pocket."

"Cut the crap, Sims. There is still some unfinished business and I want some answers."

Scott leaned forward, arms along the plastic-topped table. "Joe Gregory reckons the Reverend paid him to kill me."

"Who the hell's the Reverend?" a puzzled Bulman asked.

"You've been off the crime beat too long. His name is Phil Deacon. He's a hood with a very nasty reputation. Took on Rex Reisen and got a flea in his ear. Extortion and general violence are the main ingredients. Reisen will tell you where he hangs out."

"So will police records. I can do without Reisen. Are you sure?"

"Check Gregory's account at the National Westminster in Kennington. I don't know how many branches they have there, but you'll sort that out. You look disappointed."

Bulman swore for the sake of the guards, then lowered his voice again. "Confused. It makes no sense."

"I know. I've never crossed Deacon in my life. At least not knowingly."

"On occasion you have been close to Reisen."

"Yes, but not really associated. I've never worked for his organization. It's not strong enough for Deacon to get at me."

"Unless Gregory is lying through his teeth."

"His bank account should answer that."

Bulman agreed. "Every time I think I have a lead something sends me in the opposite direction. You'll be out in a few days."

"Oh." Scott appeared strangely concerned.

"I've had it on good authority. It looks like the Foreign Office is tied up in this. Perhaps they've had a bum lead from someone who doesn't like you. Anyway, they've gone over the top on this one. Have you been up to anything I don't know about?"

"Sure. I've been running a bloody spy ring from my travel agency."

"I'm serious."

"Look, if I were doing something dodgy on the security front, that's MI5's concern isn't it? Where does the Foreign Office come in?"

"The Security Service; yes, it would be their job, but these things do overlap. Sometimes it's unavoidable. Like Special Branch and the Met, and the FBI and the CIA. Can't be helped. Liaison is the answer, but the hostility between departments sometimes outweighs the goodwill." Bulman added thoughtfully, "If someone's had a bum steer, it could be for all sorts of reasons. A deliberate red herring to keep a department occupied, or sheer incompetence; and when that happens they'll fight to the death to prove themselves right, and there'll be no apology if they're wrong. Bureaucracy is never wrong; the establishment knows best at all times."

"It's beyond me. The Reverend might have some answers."

"Maybe." Bulman followed up shrewdly, "You didn't seem exactly pleased when I said you'd be out in a few days."

"It'll be feet first."

"Is that what you think?"

"That's what I feel. You heard about us being locked up over a paper knife?"

"Yes. You think it's for you?"

"If I say yes it'll sound like paranoia."

"Have you got anywhere near Wally Cooper yet?"

"They're keeping us apart. We can't visit from wing to wing. The only chance of a meet is somewhere like the wood mill if we're both working there, and we're obviously not. The library is for all wings but at different times. There's the gym, of course. A fine gym as it happens, but I've been forbidden entry until my wound has really healed. Anyway, I don't know if Wally attends gym classes."

"Do you think someone is simply trying to put the frighteners on you? So when you're out you'll drop whatever you were on?"

"If that's the case, they've succeeded. I am frightened, mainly because I don't know what's going on or why. But that brings us back to Tom Moody again. Meanwhile, I believe they'll try again." Scott paused. "Obviously within the next few days."

BULMAN, NOT WANTING to use any staff who worked under Sir

Lewis Hope, went back to his friend Commander Collins, who agreed to look into Joe Gregory's bank account with the National Westminster in Kennington. He had the answer within the hour. Gregory's account had received a cash payment of ten thousand pounds a day after Scott arrived in Albany.

"What do you make of it?" Collins asked.

"Spider was right and Gregory told the truth. What's more interesting is that it would seem that Scott's arrival at Albany was known before it happened. Deacon couldn't have negotiated in a day. It's too tight."

"Only the Home Office knew. We had to arrange it with them. And, of course, that little fart Ashton from the Foreign Office seems to have known from them. That means they were pretty sure it was Scott we were planting from the outset, and Ashton tried to verify it through me."

"The smell gets stronger, Dick."

"Scott *must* have done something we don't know about. It can't be because he's trying to get lined up on who killed Tom Moody; if he *was* killed. The Foreign Office would be just as interested to know. Wouldn't they?"

The two men looked uneasily at each other. Bulman said vehemently, "We've made no bloody progress at all. None. It's like walking backward and losing sight of where you're supposed to be going."

"You want me to look into Phil Deacon's finances?"

Bulman shook his head slowly. "It would take too long. Blokes like that have money tucked away in all sorts of dark corners, and they deal too much in cash. But I'll drop in on him and see if I can shake the tree a bit."

PHIL DEACON LIVED south of the Thames in Wandsworth in a huge terraced house. In a mixed area of gradual decay, his was one of the few houses that looked cared for, well decorated and renovated. It was like a burning fagot in a long line of unlit bundles. Everyone knew Deacon's house; everyone was intended to. Nobody sat on *his* scrubbed steps, nor tried to reach the wide exterior ledges of the big bay windows. There was always parking space for two cars outside the house, and the cars themselves, a new Jaguar 5.3 liters and a Mercedes Benz, were among the few cars in the district that had never been scratched. Nor were they ever stolen or used for joyrides. Phil Deacon ruled supreme.

Bulman was observed as soon as he turned the corner into the long, fairly narrow, shabby street. Children playing stopped to look. Some called him names. He was recognized as a copper quite quickly; identification of this kind was the result of an in-built education. As he walked briskly, he smiled benignly at all the kids, immediately making them suspicious. It was sad, he thought. There was not a lot going for them. He climbed the steps to the freshly painted ocher door and hammered the brightly polished horse-head brass knocker.

The door was opened by a hard faced blonde, expensively, but badly, dressed in a too-tight skirt and blouse. Very blue eyes scanned Bulman like radar. Over-made-up lips parted to eject, "Yes?"

"Madam, I would like to have a few friendly words with Mr. Deacon."

"Which Mr. Deacon? Ted, Tommy, or Phil?"

"Phil would be the one."

"Are you a copper?"

"How observant you are, ma'am."

"Piss off. If you're a copper, make an appointment. Anyway, he's not here."

Bulman tried his sweetest smile. "There's a Jag and a Merc by the curb, guarded, it would seem, by half the child population of Wandsworth. If Mr. Deacon walked to wherever he is then perhaps he did not go too far. I'll wait."

"Not on our steps you won't; they've just been cleaned." About to slam the door on him, the blonde suddenly hesitated. "You're not local, are you? Haven't seen you before." Her voice was as brittle as her face.

"I've traveled far. From Scotland Yard, in fact. You couldn't spare a cup of tea, could you?"

The unexpected request perplexed her. His whole approach was different from the usual. He had even sounded friendly, and he had a sort of roughened, humorous face. "You don't sound like a bleeding copper. Where's your card?"

He produced his ID and held it steadily while she read it.

"Are you Vi?" he asked.

"Yes. How did you know?"

"I heard that the fortunate Phil was married to a luscious dish called Vi. It had to be you."

Vi patted her hair and stuck out a hip. But Bulman was still a copper. "What do you want him for?"

147

"A chat. No more."

"Let 'im in, for Christ's sake. We don't want the bloody fuzz standing on the steps." The voice had bawled out from the rear of the house.

"Oh, he's back." Vi said, as if Deacon had just walked in. She opened the door, and Bulman entered a scented hall.

"He's Detective Superintendent Bulman," Vi shouted out to a shadow down the hall. She then hived off into another room.

"In here."

Bulman followed the shadow and the voice and entered a room to find himself surrounded by electrical apparatus. A stereo speaker stood in each corner. A converted oak chest with its doors open revealed a tuner, amp and preamp, and cassette player, and under the raised lid sat a turntable and reel-to-reel deck.

"That's the old gear," Deacon said in a voice coarser than his wife's. "Over there is the new laser-beam player. Bloody marvelous. This is my music room. Whadyer think?"

Bulman glanced around. Armchairs were placed in the center of the room. Walls were lined with records and cassettes. "Harold Lloyd had a room like this. Probably bigger, though. Devoted to music."

"'Arold Lloyd? The comic with the glasses?"

"Ah, you've heard of him."

"Before my time, mate. Whadyer want? I'm busy."

"I know you are. I ran across part of your schedule."

Deacon scowled. He was not particularly big, but he appeared to be powerful and had the features of a bully; piggy eyes and jutting lips set in a concreted orange peel. He had big restless hands. His lightweight suit was beautifully cut, but he had not let the tailor do his job. Deacon's interference in how the suit should be was evident in the too-broad shoulders and the waspish waist.

"You're off your beat, copper, aren't you? Scotland Yard. You 'aven't come to arrest me or you'd have someone with you." Deacon laughed like a cold motorbike engine trying to start. "You'd certainly bloodywell need somebody else if you tried that lark here."

Bulman said calmly, "Nothing like that, Phil. I simply wanted to know why you paid Joe Gregory ten grand to knock off Tony Sims in Albany."

The shock treatment almost worked. Deacon was left with his mouth open and an odd look in his eyes. He recovered quickly. "Say that again."

"You heard."

"Give me the names again."

Bulman rode along. "Joe Gregory and Tony Sims. Gregory made a mess of it, by the way. If I were you I'd get my money back. And if you've paid anyone else to finish the job meanwhile, I'd call him off quickly. As you can see, we've means of tracking contract payments."

"You're off your bleeding rocker." Deacon had gained the time he needed. "I don't even know the names. What are you trying to pull?"

Bulman knew that he had a weak hand, but that Deacon could not be so sure. "Gregory talked. Why do you think I'm here? As Vi said, I'm not local. Gregory failed. If he hadn't, it would be murder. As it happened, not too much damage was done. I'm willing to close an eye, but in return I want information. *That's* why I'm alone. No witnesses. You're safe."

"I know I'm bloody safe. I've got a lot of legal muscle so don't go pulling this kind of stunt on me. Maybe I should phone the locals; they'd love to hear that the Yard is crawling all over their patch. I'll gamble they don't know you're here."

"If they are to know, then they've got to be told that it's attempted murder. Ring them and tell them."

Deacon dropped his sneer. "Don't try it, copper. I don't know a Gregory and I don't know a Sims."

"That's strange because one of your boys visited Gregory shortly before Sims was locked away."

A slow smile spread over Deacon's coarse face, to show perfect dentures. "Bugger off, you silly sod. None of my boys have been down there."

Bulman realized his bluff had failed. It crossed his mind that it might have been a woman, unless there was some sort of written code. "All I want to know is *why* you tried it? Why Sims?"

"I'm asking myself the same question. I don't know him, but you can't grasp it. Is that all? Would you like some music before you go?"

Bulman glared around the room. "Ten thousand is not a lot for you. Call it off, Phil. For if it goes through now, we'll have our confirmation." He took out a miniature tape recorder and held it up. "It's all on there, Phil. You've been warned."

Deacon stood there, apparently wondering whether to grab the recorder or not. He finally decided not to assault a police officer. "All you have on that are my denials and your claims. You're talking absolute cock. That's really a wild one you tried to pull. Can you find your own way out?"

"There's also my warning on it, Phil. Don't try again."

ON HIS WAY back to Scotland Yard Bulman was feeling disappointed by his performance with Deacon. Perhaps he was too emotionally involved; he owed a duty to Scott, and he had been stonewalled in his efforts to help. He was convinced that Deacon had paid Gregory, but was no nearer to knowing why. Deacon had obviously taken sound precautions. The money paid into Gregory's account had been in cash. Anyone could have paid it in. Bulman accepted that without Sir Lewis Hope's support he could not put a watch on Deacon; even if he did, he did not believe it would help.

As he sat in the cab he took out the small recorder. He opened it up; there was no tape and no batteries. Even if there had been, the small microphone would not have been capable of picking up a conversation through his pocket. I'm losing my touch, he thought. None of his bluff had worked, and he had gained no more than a confirmed impression. He arrived back at his office in a depressed frame of mind.

WHEN SCOTT RETURNED to his cell after seeing Bulman, he was more depressed than ever. He did not expect the information he had passed on to achieve anything of real significance and the promised release in a few days' time scared him. Why not now? Why delay? He knew why.

As he sat on the end of the bed he saw a piece of paper protruding from under it. He curled his foot back and hooked it out. It was a piece of folded toilet paper. He had locked his cell door on leaving and there was no fracture in the observation slit. The paper had been flicked under the door. He knelt down and opened it carefully, corner by corner.

At first he saw little. There was some gray dust in the middle of the paper. When he touched it, it felt gritty. He lifted the paper up and held it in the palm of his hand. The grit now looked like iron filings. It was a near guess. He screwed the paper up and crushed it in a clenched fist as he glared around the cell in frustration. He held the filings from the sharpened paper knife. The knife was now clearly meant for him, and somebody wanted him to know.

12

"MARIA Wolkstholme is dead, Sir Roland. Apparently electrocuted herself. Faulty wire on an iron."

Powell stopped searching his drawer for a lost lighter. "That's awkward." His gaze dropped to the open drawer again, and then he looked up slowly. "Where does that place Scott?"

"It's annoying that she should die at this time." Murison was thoughtful.

"I don't suppose she enjoyed it either. Inconsiderate of her."

"I'm sorry, I didn't mean to be so callous. These things happen."

"Scott," Powell said acidly.

"Yes, of course. I'll have a word with Maria's contact. We might strike lucky. If we don't, we'll have to let Scott go."

"You're still hanging on," Powell remonstrated. "Is it all worth it?"

"I believe so. But if I'm wrong I'll get Scott out fast."

"But not immediately?"

"It won't do any harm to keep him there a day or two longer."

BULMAN WENT BACK to his studio apartment and tried to put himself in Willie Scott's shoes. The room was large and shabby and tonight it was particularly depressing. The bed was neat; he always made it up before leaving in the morning. There were three old armchairs, worn but comfortable, but the slip covers looked somewhat dull tonight. A plywood screen in one corner concealed a small stove but mostly he ate out, usually at the King's Arms pub nearby. The blank screen of a television set stared soulessly at him, and he felt like kicking it in.

He had rarely felt so low, and as he threw himself into a chair he wished he had married. There had been opportunities but he was the first to admit that he was not the easiest man to live with. Affairs had usually started off strong, only to fade as his job inevitably intervened. He loved his work, but one day he would be retired and then he would have nothing.

He felt lonely and unusually inadequate. Tough cases were nothing new; he thrived on them. He was also used to being warned off or toned down by his own department, particularly when carefully nurtured diplomacy was in danger of collapsing under the weight of his bull-headedness. Government departments were always conspiring; there was nothing new in that. And most times he disagreed with what they were doing. But he believed in the oath of allegiance; if you don't like what you're signing, then don't damn well sign it, and don't squeal afterward if you do. He had a contempt of civil servants who set themselves up as judge and jury and ignored their sworn commitments for political reasons. He would jail them every time, for Bulman was solid in his loyalties; a common denominator with Scott.

Bulman climbed awkwardly out of the chair and half-filled a tumbler with Scotch from an array of bottles on a small Victorian table in one corner of the room. He stared through the windows. All he could see was a row of drab houses opposite. London was flaking off around him; huge chunks of it needed a face-lift.

"I'm a detective," he said aloud to the glass in his hand, "and so far on this job I haven't detected a bloody thing." As he tilted the glass the spirit changed color as if in answer.

He stood there for some time, gazing out and sipping his whisky and wondering whether Scott would do anything really stupid. He hoped not. On the other hand how could he blame him if he did. How the hell had he got Scott in this position? His mind went back to the root of it. Tom Moody. And then the meeting with Fairfax.

Bulman stiffened very gradually until even the whisky in the glass did not move. A great fear surged through him but it was painfully slow,

154

taking over his body part by part. He wanted to be sick and put down the glass to go to the bathroom. He retched over the wash basin, holding on to it, then finally looked at himself in the mirror above the basin. He appeared old, his eyes bloodshot. He hoped to God that the thought that had crossed his mind was hopelessly wrong; wild, as Deacon had said.

His stomach felt empty and heaved again. If he was anywhere near right, then Scott was in greater danger than Bulman himself had realized. And so was he. Not yet, perhaps, because he was restricted by the harness of his profession; there were certain lines he could not cross. But Scott could. If he ever got out. Scott could look after himself, but for the first time Bulman had a whiff of what Scott was really up against. He prayed to God that he was wrong.

He shook off his gloom and his sickness, finished his whisky, and rang Betty Moorcroft.

SINCE LEAVING THE prison hospital, Scott had locked his door every time he left the cell. Once in the cell it was impossible to lock it from the inside. The doors opened inward, but there were two ways of insuring reasonable privacy. Each door had a vertical observation slit that could be smeared with any fat mealtimes might provide and that prevented anyone from looking in. The door could also be jammed not too obviously by slipping any form of wedge under the linoleum by the hinge side. It was by no means foolproof, but it was a deterrent to any con trying to enter someone else's cell.

Scott's position was unnerving. He did not think that Joe Gregory would be used again; the influence of men like Phil Deacon was far-reaching. Scott felt safe only at night when his cell was locked. For the rest of the time he remained rigidly on guard, but a blow could be struck at almost any time. And whoever did it would be protected by the others.

BULMAN CALLED AT Betty Moorcroft's suburban house at nine o'clock that evening. Her husband let Bulman in with bad grace. A tall, executive type with a nervousness probably due to business pressures, he made it clear from the start that he disagreed with Bulman's presence.

"About Betty's father, is it?" he asked as he crossed the small bright hall. "Waste of time. I've told her. She can't accept the simple solution."

155

He opened a door. "You'd better speak to her in here. I'm missing my program."

Bulman found himself alone in a study; small desk, two chairs, bookcase, and three country prints on the wall. Betty Moorcroft came in before he had a chance to sit down.

"I'm sorry if Bob gave you a bad time. He thinks I'm obsessed by Dad's death. I suppose I am. Have you found out anything?" She indicated one of the chairs, and Bulman sat down with his back to the desk.

"I'm no nearer to solving Tom's murder. I use the word deliberately; I think you are right. I believe he *was* murdered."

Betty lowered herself onto the other chair but was sitting on the edge, as if she should not be comfortable.

"I have a half-baked theory, which I'm sorry I ever thought of and which I hope will go away. Willie Scott and I went over Tom's flat again after you'd left. All we found were three newspaper reports of people who had died. One was a character called Michael Rossi, another was James McLaren. And the third was Bertrand Hill. Have you heard of them?"

"Everyone's heard of James McLaren. I should think he was about the most hated union leader in Britain. Nasty bit of work. Committed suicide. Wasn't it about little boys?"

"Something like that. But did Tom ever talk about any of them?"

Betty cocked her head as her husband turned up the volume of the television in the other room. "I'm sure that he didn't." She considered the question again. "No. I'm certain."

"Did he ever mention a cat-burglar called Wally Cooper?"

"Oh, yes. He was very upset for some reason when Cooper was convicted. Wasn't it an espionage charge? All very hush-hush."

Bulman inclined his head. "Would it surprise you to know that Tom employed Wally Cooper to do a breaking and entering?"

"Yes, it would." Betty was startled. "Dad was as straight as a die. He wouldn't use a thief."

"Well, he did, but not to steal money or valuables. I would guess that Tom wanted some kind of document. I doubt that Wally Cooper knew the content of what he stole. But Tom knew what he wanted. What we can't find out is whether or not he obtained it. Did he ever leave anything with you?"

"No. He wouldn't involve me, anyway."

"Think. He might have done it in a way you wouldn't know about. So as not to embarrass you."

Betty considered the question. "He rarely called here. He never got on with Bob, although he was very fond of the kids."

"Nevertheless he did sometimes call?"

"Yes. Maybe two or three times in a year."

"And he never left a thing?"

"He gave me a letter to post once. That's about all."

"Can you remember who it was to?"

"You must be joking." Betty flapped her arms. "It must have been a couple of months ago."

"So he brought the letter here and asked you to post it? From his place to this place you'd think there was a mailbox or two, wouldn't you?"

Betty frowned. "He didn't bring it. He wrote it here at that desk."

Bulman turned to gaze at the desk. It was a small reproduction piece with a gold leather inset and veneered borders.

"Anything of his in here?" he asked.

"I'd have to look."

"I mean, he could have slipped something in one of the drawers while he wrote the letter."

"He could have. But I told you, he wouldn't have. He wouldn't bring me and the kids into anything he was doing. If he had wanted to leave something, he would have asked." Betty was getting irritated by Bulman's persistence.

"Straight Tom," Bulman commented.

"Is that meant as a slur?"

"God, no. He was just that. When we first met you said there were changes in him, but what you're now saying is that there were not."

"We're at cross-purposes. He *was* afraid of something. He still wouldn't have dragged us into it. He wouldn't talk about it."

"Have you ever been burgled?"

Betty was startled. "Funny you should ask that. I came back one day to find the back door unlocked. Well, not quite; the key was only partially turned because the lock is stiff. I'm very careful about locking doors when I go out."

"You're not careful about leaving a key in a lock, though. A copper's daughter should know better. They can turn an inside key from the outside."

"I know. I was careless and I haven't done it since. But it made me
157

wary at the time, and I went over the house. There was nothing missing that I could see."

"You don't seem all that sure."

"I had an *impression* that someone might have been in." Betty shivered slightly. "It was a nasty feeling. This will sound daft . . . but everything looked so neat, and I don't think I'm as tidy as that. I don't know. It could have been fanciful thinking." She gazed apologetically at Bulman. "I mean, if someone came in searching for something specific, wouldn't he have torn the place apart?"

"Not if it was important enough to keep the search a secret. Only amateurs vandalize a place. A good pro knows where to look, and how to spot signs of concealment."

"You make it sound creepy."

"Come on, Betty," Bulman said, "have a search through this desk and tell me what might have been Tom's."

Betty seemed surprised that the desk contained so much, even a screwdriver and a long-lost pair of pliers. She worked systematically, laying the contents on the desk top, going through them and then putting them back before starting on the next drawer. There were two old passports, the top right-hand corners cut off. Bulman went through them page by page and felt along the edges of the covers.

"You're wasting your time," Betty said.

"The story of my life. What are those?"

"A bunch of old keys. Why?" The keys were on a ring. They were small, the usual collection of suitcase and vanity box keys that somehow never fit anything anymore. The cases wear out but the keys remain.

"Go through them. One by one."

Betty did as instructed. "This is an odd man out."

It was a small, flat key that might have fitted a suitcase but was really little different from the rest. "Why do you say that?" Bulman asked.

"Well, I can vaguely remember the others and the cases they fitted. This one doesn't come to mind."

"Describe what the others fitted."

"You're a bastard," she said without offense. But she was able to place the old cases from memory. "It's not a deposit box key, is it?" she suddenly asked.

Bulman smiled. "Whatever that locked could have been opened with a hairpin."

"Then why the fuss?"

He ignored the question. "You produced some old airline ticket covers just now. Let's have another look."

She produced them from one of the drawers. "I keep them as a souvenir. Tickets to Malaga. It was the only holiday I had with Dad since I got married. Bob was away for six weeks, and his mother offered to look after the kids. She liked Dad. I often thought she would rather have gone on holiday with him."

"So you wouldn't throw them away?"

"No." Betty held them fondly, as memory came back. "We both needed a break. Bob and I were having problems; the break helped heal them, and so did Dad in spite of the fact that he didn't like Bob."

"And Tom knew you kept them?"

"I suppose so."

"Let's have another look." Bulman took them from her. "Do you mind if I unstaple the baggage tickets? We can pin them up again." He sat at the desk and went over the covers and the baggage tickets. "Have you got a magnifying glass?"

"Bottom drawer, right. We haven't started on that yet."

Bulman took the glass out and produced pen and paper. He studied the back of a ticket and made careful notes. He rubbed his eyes. "An address has been written in pencil, but it's so faint I can hardly see it. Can you switch that desk light on, Betty."

Bulman held the ticket this way and that and at last he said, "D. Avery, 6, Cheniston Terrace, W2."

"Dick Avery. I've met him. An old colleague of Dad's. I don't think they'd seen each other for years."

"Tom must have written this. Who else?"

She could not answer. It had to be her father.

They went through the rest and it took time, but at the end of it Bulman said, "May I have the key you're not sure about? I'll return it. That's as far as we can go at the moment."

IT WAS DIFFICULT for Scott to determine when the change of attitude in the prisoners first took place because it was fragmented. Open hostility to him came piecemeal, odd cons casting a vicious glance, or mouthing an obscenity at him. At first he was confused, wondering

159

what had happened, but by mid-morning the hostility had consolidated and he knew. Someone had spread the word that he was a plant.

The loathing directed at him was almost physical, something he could reach out and touch. It was not a case of ignoring him but a definite attempt by everyone to show contempt and hatred of him. When two or more walked past him he was almost certain to be nudged or pushed or sometimes blocked and sworn at.

He was glad to be locked in his cell at lunchtime. He ate little as he considered the odds. Who had spread the word and what had actually been said? Whereas before he suspected one man had been hired to kill him, there were now eighty potential killers in the one wing. Some had nothing to lose, another conviction would be meaningless to those serving twenty or thirty years. But nobody would be caught because whoever took the action would have up to seventy-nine alibis. Whoever wanted him killed had virtually made sure that it would happen with everyone turned against him. He could not fight it. They would nail him, but they wanted him to know and to run scared first. The death sentence had been passed on him. It was on all their faces. He had no hope now.

Scott stared at his uneaten lunch. Bulman, Collins, and most of all Maggie faded in memory as if somewhere he had read about them but they were difficult to recollect. He was going mad and was not really in a cell at all. How could he be, for he had committed no crime? All he was doing was trying to help an old friend who had probably felt as bemused and helpless just before he was killed. It was a terrible numbing sensation from which there was no escape.

"MR. AVERY?"

"Yes." Avery was in his late fifties and had run to seed a little. It showed more because he possessed a slight frame and the belly protruded obviously from it. Virtually bald, his thin face was weary.

"Detective Superintendent Bulman. Could I have a word with you?"

Avery glanced at his watch. "It's a bit late, isn't it? Half-past ten."

"It won't take a minute. It's about Tom Moody."

"Tom? Show me your card."

Bulman did and was let into the apartment hall. A television blared from behind one of the doors.

Avery said, "Half a mo'." He opened a door and poked his head

160

around to say, "Won't be long, love. Friend of Tom's." Music faded as he closed the door again.

"*Are* you a friend of Tom's?" The weary eyes were suddenly sharp.

"More than you might think."

Avery opened another door and they went into a very comfortable living room, expensively furnished and modern.

Bulman gazed around. "Not bad for an ex-copper," he said without offense.

"Drink? Whisky?" Avery moved behind a sizable bar. "I didn't get this while I was in the force, nor by writing my memoirs." He placed a liberal drink on the bar, and Bulman hooked up a stool.

"Security and insurance companies," Avery continued. "There's always good scope for a retired copper if he was far enough up the tree. I was lucky."

"So they're not all wasted years," Bulman observed, taking a good swig at his drink.

"Not for me." Avery had stayed behind the bar and leaned on it to face Bulman. "Never heard of you, though."

"Never heard of you, either. Until tonight."

"Tom could have had something like this," Avery said. "Over and over. But he preferred to play cloak-and-dagger. Look where it got him."

"Where did it get him?"

Avery's features reddened. "You playing silly buggers?"

"No."

"You must know he slipped on a bar of soap."

"But that could happen to anyone. Nothing to do with cloak-and-dagger. Was it?"

"Jesus." Avery held his glass down on the bar. "Stop being a copper to an ex-copper. What's on your mind?"

"I found your address scribbled on the back of an old airline baggage ticket at Tom's daughter's place. Betty, you probably know her. Either it was an innocent inscription or it was important. Betty swore that Tom would never have dragged her and the kids into anything he was handling. So why did he scribble down your name and address?"

"How do I know? People scribble on all sorts of things. He might have done that before she hid the ticket away."

"How did you know she hid it away?"

Very deliberately, Avery swallowed some of his drink. "You need a refresher course, Bulman. She didn't rake it out of the dustbin for you, did she?"

Bulman shook his head sadly. "I should resign," he said wearily. "At the moment everything I touch is a cock-up."

"Poor feller. You haven't come for a handout?"

When Bulman looked up, Avery was grinning; he began to warm to the man. And he would get nowhere with this line of questioning. He drank quietly for a bit, and when he had finished Avery replenished his glass.

Bulman placed the key Betty had given him on top of the bar and pushed it toward Avery. "Recognize it?"

Avery stared at it. "Yes," he said seriously. "It's the key to Barclays Bank vault in Jermyn Street."

Bulman burst out laughing. The frustration and fears of the last few days flowed out with the laughter. He looked at the key; he could have bent it between his fingers. When he simmered down he said, "You're either a very crafty devil, or you really know nothing. But I like your whisky." He picked up the key and held it in his palm. "So it means nothing?"

Avery shook his head. "You're in trouble, aren't you? That laugh did you good."

Bulman slipped the key back into his pocket. "I'll have to take a chance on you," he said at last. "I don't suppose it could make it any worse; I don't think much could. I believe Tom was murdered."

"That doesn't surprise me."

The laughter, the leg pulling, the fencing was behind them. "To save you asking, Tom was in a state I'd never seen him in before," Avery said. "We'd drifted apart yet he took the trouble to look me up, and he was clearly more than worried."

"What did he want?"

"Just a chat. He wanted to off-load, talk of old times, as if by so doing he could get his feet back on the ground. But he wasn't the Tom I knew. He was scared, but he wouldn't talk about it."

"Did he leave anything with you?"

"No." Avery gave the question a second thought. "No," he repeated. "Why?"

"Has anyone broken in here?"

"You've got eyes. I'm wired up to the hilt. Every door and window

162

has contact points. Hall, living room, television room, dining room all have passive infrared. Pressure mats by every window and door. I didn't trust most people when I was a copper, but since I've been looking into insurance claims I've even taken fingerprints of my wife."

Bulman smiled. "You didn't mention the kitchen."

"Sonic. Heat and reflection can affect infrared. What the hell would he want to give me?"

Bulman thought back to Betty Moorcroft. "I don't know. But it's bloody strange he wrote down your name and address like that. Why not in his address book?"

"Not important enough. Haven't seen him since. Just the one call."

"In here?"

Avery did not move. And then he started to drum his fingers on the bar, his head lowered.

"You've thought of something," Bulman suggested.

"Odd thing. He was drinking gin. I keep bottled lemon slices in the fridge under the bar, and I'd placed it on top of the bar when he asked if he could have *fresh* lemon. Said he was allergic to the preservative in the bottled stuff."

"So you went to the kitchen to slice a lemon?"

"Sure. How big is the thing you're looking for."

"The last I heard it should be envelope size. Did he know you were wired up?"

"He had a copper's eyes too. But now you mention it, he did sound me out." Avery reflected again. "And that was before the lemon. I'm sure it was."

Bulman eased down from the stool. "You want a hand?"

"Yes. I suppose a liqueur bottle is least used."

They searched the mass of bottles in vain and then put them back. They finally found an envelope taped to the bottom door rack of the refrigerator. The fridge was low down and set into the bar. The envelope would not have been seen, even by someone on hands and knees; it was located by touch, and it had taken a long time to find it.

Avery laid it on the bar with the same respect he would give to a letter bomb. The envelope was thin and torn, now that the tapes had been removed, and it was blank.

"He must have been desperate to pull a dodge like that," Avery said. "Who's going to open it?"

"I will."

163

"Well, I want to know what's in it. If this is what Tom was killed for I want to know why, in case someone tries it on me."

Bulman shrugged and produced a penknife. "He borrowed your security. I suppose he'd have taken it back with the same stealth had he lived. Not like Tom at all." Bulman slid the blade under the envelope flap.

13

H E shook out a single flimsy sheet and laid it clear of the envelope. The piece of paper measured about three inches by two and was discolored with age. One edge was perforated. The single printed word at the top was RECEIPT in large capitals. The two men stood side by side, neither touching it.

The handwriting was poor and was faded but the pale ink was just about decipherable. "It's fifty years old," Bulman said in awe.

"Slightly more." Avery craned his neck. "Twenty-fourth of June, nineteen thirty four. Thirty thousand pounds. That was a fortune in those days. I can't read the name properly."

"Neither can I, but the signature at the bottom is clear enough. Oswald Mosley."

"*Sir* Oswald Mosley. What skeleton is this we've raised?"

Their voices had dropped to low key, as if they both knew that this simple receipt for a large sum of money would open a closet of ghosts they would rather not see. They stared at the receipt, a common printed one that had obviously been torn from an ordinary receipt book.

"His wife is still alive. Living outside Paris. One of the Mitford girls. Still fine looking; they all were."

They did not move, aware that they were gazing at a piece of history.

"Leader of the British Fascist movement," Avery murmured. "We need another drink." He poured the drinks, handed Bulman's over, but could not take his gaze from the receipt. "That name looks like Robert Langley, don't you think?"

"As near as dammit. You'll have noticed that the receipt itself differs in writing from Mosley's signature. There are similarities but there are differences too, as though someone else made it out for Mosley to sign. So Mosley received, from what looks like Robert Langley, a sum of thirty thousand pounds on the twenty fourth of June nineteen thirty four. Now just what the hell does this mean?"

Avery supplied no answer. "Do you think you'll get fingerprints from it?"

"Probably. But they'll be useless. I wonder how many people have handled it over fifty-odd years." Bulman turned to Avery. "I'll have to take this with me."

"I don't want it. Look what happened to Tom. I'll get you a plastic bag."

Avery went off while Bulman continued to study the receipt. Nothing was solved. On the contrary, until the significance of the receipt became clear, it was all the more puzzling. But it would seem that Tom Moody had died for it, and it was probable that Wally Cooper was serving a thirty-year sentence because he had unknowingly stolen it.

Avery returned with a kitchen bag and a pair of eyebrow tweezers. "Dot wants to know what's going on. Told her we're talking over old times. She doesn't know I took her tweezers." He delicately lifted the receipt while Bulman held the transparent bag open. The envelope was dropped in after. Bulman folded the bag over and carefully placed it in a pocket.

"Is there a back way out?"

"There's the fire escape. You think you've been tailed?"

"I dunno." Bulman tapped his pocket. "There might be a curse on this thing. Make sure you put your alarm on."

"I'm sorry I met you, Bulman. I was having a quiet evening."

"Well, thanks, anyway. If you'll show me the way out."

The fire escape led off a small balcony from the kitchen. Avery put the kitchen light out, and Bulman opened the door. The platform creaked under his weight. He shook hands with Avery, who closed the door. Bulman went down the iron staircase as softly as he could. Policemen don't expect to be followed, but he was beginning to think that he might have been almost from the outset. The receipt was like a death warrant.

166

How many, other than Tom Moody, had been killed for it?

He stepped off the escape and found himself in a narrow back street; he could hear footsteps at either end. Someone nearby swore, and he realized that he had disturbed a courting couple. He got his bearings and strode off, hesitating at the corner before crossing the main street in search of a taxi.

For once he knew how Scott must have felt when he was being hunted, and he did not care for the sensation. He wished Scott was with him now; Spider would know if he had a tail. But Spider was locked up and had grave problems of his own.

Bulman strode out, his back prickling, his ears alert, his footsteps as silent as he could make them. It was dark, too dark suddenly, and he quickened his pace.

WHAT HAD HAPPENED during Mosley's day was now a matter of public record. Bulman had no problem in obtaining copies of the declassified papers. He also got Sergeant Haldean to dig up all the press clippings on the man who might well have been prime minister of Great Britain if he had acted a little differently. Mosley had been brilliant; not even his enemies argued against that.

By early afternoon Bulman had acquired a mass of information, some of it contradictory. In the mid- and late-thirties, Mosley was one of the best-known names in Britain. Everyone knew of him and his blackshirts. Bulman went through the old Special Branch and MI5 reports of the day to find that, in the early days of his movement, Mosley had a good deal of backing in high places and the youth recruitment was widespread.

Groups were set up in English public schools such as Stowe, Beaumont, and Winchester. Exchange visits were arranged between young British Fascists and the *Hitlerjugend,* the Nazi Youth movement. And there was a section for women.

Well-known names were displayed as contributors to Mosley's funds, although he himself was a wealthy man. Lord Rothermere, who owned the *Daily Mail* and other newspapers, contributed, and so did other wealthy industrialists. Names like William Joyce, to be hanged later as the traitor Lord Haw-Haw, were mentioned with others less known now, but well known at the time. Lord Nuffield paid into the funds, so did Sir A. V. Roe, the pioneer in aviation; and the shipping magnate Lord Inchcape. Some of these contributions were paid in cash. Lord Rothermere enjoyed handing over bundles of notes.

Later, of course, as Hitler's purpose became clearer, many of these people withdrew support from Mosley's British Union of Fascists. Some had always preferred to be in the shadows, others now regretted their public support. Perhaps the full story would never be available, but the government's released records were comprehensive, and Mosley's Fascist movement had clearly been under surveillance from a very early time.

Had Robert Langley been one of those who preferred to be in the shadows? Evidently so. There was no mention of him in the MI5 or Special Branch files, nor in the many press clippings Bulman had obtained. At nine o'clock that night Bulman was still working, having read through everything that was laid before him on his cluttered desk. He carefully packed reports and clippings together, tied them, and crammed them into his safe. But still he did not go home.

Haldean had left some hours before, the communicating door was still open, and now only the dark shadow of Haldean's desk could be seen beyond it. Bulman sat down with the receipt before him. He did not take it out of its plastic bag; he had learned little from it. Nowhere at all had there been mention of Robert Langley. He had no doubt that there would have been others like him; anonymous donors whose only connection was a receipt. Perhaps some had not even wanted that.

Bulman had got Haldean to trace the name, and it turned out that the donor to Mosley's funds had been *Lord* Robert Langley, dead for twenty years. Langley had run a light machinery conglomerate, increased his already considerable fortune during World War II, and had then dissipated it over the ten years following the end of the war. The huge company had gradually lost its trading position and had shrunk until it was finally wound up in 1957. Lord Langley would have died destitute but for the success of his younger son in finance.

Raymond Langley, unlike his two elder brothers, both now dead, had refused to enter his father's business right from the outset. At no time had he worked for his father. His ability had not lain in engineering. To him, a safety pin was a major feat of science. His head had always been full of figures, and the irony was that, at the time his father's empire was collapsing, Raymond had the financial expertise to save it. But he was far too busy building up his own business empire. Whether his father had ever asked for Raymond's help was as yet unknown to Bulman, who could not really see how it would help him to know.

The only thing Bulman was sure of was that the receipt, with its obvious suggestion that Lord Langley subscribed to Fascist funds, was no longer a threat as a slur to the family. Sons did not always follow in their father's political footsteps; some were even almost violently opposed to them. In this day and age, whatever Lord Robert Langley had done back in the thirties was of no consequence to Raymond, who was still extremely active at sixty-eight years of age.

Bulman rubbed his face, desperately tired by now. He had no idea of what menace the receipt held, nor to whom. Not to Lord *Raymond* Langley, surely? Not unless there was some other message in the receipt. Bulman needed sleep, but Willie Scott was in dire trouble, and if working around the clock would get Willie out of trouble then that was what he had to do.

But why was Willie in trouble if the receipt held the answers? There had to be something else. Or the receipt was only the first leg of a trail that only someone like Willie could pursue. And if that were true then the answers must be well-protected. And that was very ominous. It was very rare indeed for Bulman to feel himself in any form of physical danger, but he felt threatened now, as Moody must have done.

Bulman picked up the protected receipt and put it in the safe. He made a note on his pad and switched off the light. Scotland Yard was open around the clock, but he still felt lonely and exposed as he took an elevator down to ground level. It was warm outside and for a few minutes he watched the slowly gyrating sign. Suddenly he went back inside and arranged for a police car to take him home. Now he knew that he was nervous.

BULMAN WAS ON time for duty the next day, but he was haggard. He had slept badly, his mind too active, and he wanted an answer to the note he had made on his pad. Not trusting even Haldean he took the receipt from the safe, then asked for Inspector Wallis on the intercom.

"Alan," he said heavily, "I want a signature checked. Who's the best man? But really good? The best handwriting expert we've got. It's a nineteen thirty four signature of Sir Oswald Mosley."

"The *very* best is Professor Jenkins. He's red hot."

"I don't want this document to leave the building. Not in any circumstances."

"Okay." Wallis was surprised. "I'll try to get him in. Not easy."

"Tell him it's life or death."

Wallis realized that Bulman was serious. "Right, sir. Presumably you want to know if it's genuine or not. And that means we have to get a genuine sample first. That could take a little time."

"Ring me back when you have it. It won't take the professor long from that point."

He attempted to catch up on some of the work he had neglected. It had to be done, and if it wasn't, Sir Lewis Hope would guess why. In this Detective Sergeant Haldean was a pillar of strength. The sergeant had not seen Bulman quite like this before, and it concerned him because his boss rarely worried about anything. He pulled out the stops, rang his wife to say that he would be late, and then helped get Bulman off the hook.

By four-thirty that day Bulman knew that Oswald Mosley's signature on the receipt was a forgery.

THE CONFINEMENT HAD lasted for two days and was now over. The paper knife had not been found, but keeping the prisoners locked in their cells for a protracted period could lead to even worse trouble than the knife might bring. In the meantime spot-checks of cells had continued.

The hostility around Scott had increased to a point that had the guards worried. They could not miss what was happening to him nor could they discover why. And then the word flashed around the prison that Wally Cooper had hanged himself in his cell. Precise detail was difficult to obtain. The news was later on radio and television, these things always were; but where had Wally found rope? Gradually the answer filtered through, and it came as no surprise to the prisoners. Wally had not used rope or twine at all but electrical cord. He could have obtained that from the cleaners, or taken a piece from a vacuum cleaner. The cleaners, however, claimed no knowledge.

It was cord, all right, that had choked him to death, but had he done it himself? The tragic news added to Scott's melancholy. He felt responsible for Cooper's death. A thirty-year stretch had been deemed sufficient to keep Cooper out of the way. Then Scott had arrived in a futile attempt to contact him. Whatever limited knowledge Cooper had had was enough to have him killed just to keep Scott in ignorance.

The slip of paper under his cell door when he returned from the wood mill confirmed his deep conviction. "One down and one to go." It could mean anything. But Scott well knew what it meant. Wally would not have been expecting to be murdered. The fact that he was killed by hanging suggested at least two people were involved.

Scott reflected that it would need more than two men to kill him in the same way, but the same method would not be used. Ostensibly Wally had grounds for committing suicide; he was not the first to do so, faced with a thirty-year stretch.

With nothing more to lose, Scott asked to see the governor. The guard who passed on this request gave Vernon Healy all the facts of the build-up of venom against Scott. Healey could see what had happened without understanding how. He had not discussed the prisoner Sims with his staff in any loose way. If word had got around that Sims was a police plant, then it must have come from outside. Healey refused the request without explanation to the guard, but for what he himself considered to be a sound reason; if he saw Sims, it would only confirm the rampant belief and it would exacerbate Sims's very unenviable position. But he had to do something or have a murder on his hands. It was bad enough having a suicide. He rang Martin Holmes at the Home Office and explained the situation. Holmes rang back to say that authority for Sims's release should be through in two days—three at most.

A relieved Healey warned his officers to keep an eye on Sims, but he realized the limited protection they would give. The guards could not be expected to watch Sims all the time; it was impossible. The alternative was to place Sims in the isolation block for his own protection. It was a toss-of-the-coin situation, and he decided against it. He might not be sure about Sims but he believed the man had suffered enough. The other prisoners could not know that Sims was to be released in a day or two. Once aware that the guards were keeping an eye on Sims the prisoners would back off, for a while at least. They would wait until the guards eased their vigilance. By then Sims would have gone. The reasoning was sound, but it was based on incomplete knowledge.

The refusal of his request did not surprise Scott. The vicious circle was complete. He was trapped, as he had been from the moment he had entered prison. A chain of machination had led to his present situation, involving innocent people like the governor, who would be held responsible if there was a murder. Men like Collins and Bulman were gagged by the Official Secrets Act, which would still bind them even if they left the force. It was simply a matter of time now before Scott was killed. He knew it. He could not be on guard forever.

THERE WAS A knock on the door and Bulman looked up. Gerrard Sullivan was smiling in the doorway. "Can I come in, sir?"

"Sit down," Bulman said. "Tea? Coffee? Slug of Bush Mills Black Label? Always keep some Irish by me for blokes like you."

"Ah, that's north-of-the-border stuff. Prefer Jamieson's." Sullivan sat in front of the desk.

"It's the best Irish whiskey there is, boyo. Swallow your prejudice."

"I already have. I'd be ostracized by Special Branch if I was caught in here."

"So I'll strike a special medal for you. What have you got?"

"Peter Corrie. He's the guy whose flat your man broke into."

"Peter Corrie? Who's he?"

"Defense ministry. High up. Long term civil servant. It didn't do Wally Cooper any good, did it?"

"So you've heard."

"Hanged himself."

"You still believe in the little people, Gerry."

Sullivan raised a brow. "Really? You think it was murder?"

"I'm bloody sure it was. From what I've heard of Wally, he was quite a placid type. He wouldn't have been over the moon about his sentence, but he would have ridden along with it; bed and three meals a day. Boyfriends on tap."

"Like that, was he? Why would he be murdered?"

"You'll be the first to know after me. Peter Corrie. Would he have been big enough to carry the sort of papers Wally was supposed to have stolen?"

"He must have been. Although it raises the point of why Corrie had them at home."

"And did you find an answer?"

"Not officially. I said before, I was not at the trial. You've heard of top-secret papers being left in taxis. Corrie, apparently, has top security clearance, and, as important, he has a safe. It was the safe Wally Cooper found the papers in."

"Presumably Corrie has to clear and sign for anything he takes out?"

"I should say so. But whatever Wally took was important enough to land him thirty years. It might have been a deterrent, of course. Thou shalt not break into the flats of top dog civil servants and nick their stuff. Particularly if it's in a safe."

"Thanks, Gerry."

Sullivan rose. "You look disappointed."

"It's not what I expected."

"You can't bend facts to fit your case."

Bulman managed a slight grin. "You really do believe in fairies."

"And so do you, sir. Wally was one." And then, "I've done this as a favor."

"No one will know. I'm much obliged." But when Sullivan had gone, Bulman sat back in his chair and let his disappointment show. It was as though someone was laying a trail for him and he was going around all the wrong corners. He called out to Haldean to check on anything he could find on Peter Corrie, well knowing that this might ruffle feathers in the Security Service. Sir Lewis Hope was bound to hear of this one. Bulman was beyond caring.

"THERE'S A VISITOR to see you, Sims."

Scott had wedged the door and had to ease it back for the guard to enter. The guard made no comment; the doors were not supposed to be wedged, but it was clear that the prisoner was under immense strain.

Scott rose to follow the guard giving little thought to who might have called. He was thoroughly numbed by now, his reflexes dulled. It was some distance to the visitors' room, through gates and across yards and then finally through the door leading into the bright room. A few inmates were already seated at tables with their callers. But through the windows at the other end of the room Scott could see a small group of visitors waiting. He saw a face he thought he recognized, and his heartbeat quickened.

Scott looked around. The tables were well spread out and there were plenty vacant. He chose one in the middle of the room. Hashimi Ross was let into the room and came forward to meet Scott, who remained by the table. The Arab was grinning widely, and Scott belatedly realized that so should he be at the sight of an old friend.

"Let's sit over here, man." The Arab indicated a table by one of the windows. As the two men crossed the room, Scott had time to recover from the shock of his visitor's appearance.

Hashimi was dressed in a superbly cut, light gray mohair suit, looking as if he had just stepped out of a male fashion show. His brown shoes appeared to be handmade, his quiet, pale-rust tie, was silk, as was his white shirt. He was clean shaven, but his face was darker and rounder than Scott recalled. He thought Hashimi must have darkened his skin and was wearing cheek pads. The brightness he remembered was still in the deep-brown eyes, but overall, and ignoring the outrageous formality of his clothes, he had barely changed.

"What happened to the jeans and sneakers?" Scott asked unbelievingly. There was little risk of the two groups of guards overhearing the conversation unless they raised their voices. Only the children did that in this room.

"Nobody suspects a well-dressed man in a place like this. It's been a long time, Spider. How've you been? And why is your hair dyed?"

"Never mind that. You're mad to come in here. They've been after you for years."

"This is the safest place on earth. It's outside that they're looking for me."

"But what made you do it? I know I wrote and I know I sent a visiting order, but I didn't expect you to come. I was desperate."

"So was I once. You came good for me."

"That was years ago. You owe me nothing."

"Well, you wrote when the chips were down and you wrote to me. That meant you remembered me. It meant you believed in me. Not what I do, but what I am, right or wrong. How many people do you imagine would contact me like that? Remember me after so long? How many friends do you think I've got? In the circles I move they're shit scared of me. I'm God. Until I'm deposed, and then they won't even remember my name."

"Are you still at it?"

"I'll always be at it. But the jobs are getting fewer. That is to say, my expertise is not so often sought. New people come up, sometimes women. But to many now, I'm an embarrassment. I'm too hot. And I shoot down some of their stupid schemes before I agree to operate. You might despise what I do, and you were never one to hide your feelings, but you know that I'm the best around at doing it."

"Well, Frank, whyever you're here, it's good to see you. I'd like to believe you'll settle down, but I know that you won't."

Hashimi winked. "You slipped into that name nice and easy. But you were always a pro. Had to stain my bloody skin, I ask you. A black going blacker." He laughed, but before he had finished said, "What sort of trouble are you in?"

"I've been set up for a contract killing."

"In here?"

"Where better? Where else can you be sure of a static target? You should know."

"Yes." Memory came back to Hashimi. The stain had given his face a healthy patina. And his white teeth supported the image. "Any idea why?"

"I was put here to make contact with someone who hanged himself yesterday. Only he didn't. I had a note. 'One down and one to go.'"

Hashimi braced himself. "Let's get it straight. You're a police plant?"

"The quick answer to that is yes, but that's too simple. There's no way I could be a police plant as most people would understand it. A mate of mine was killed outside. The bloke who has just been knocked off in here might have had some of the answers. It's not a normal police job. I'm not here to pin anyone. On the contrary, the one who was hanged was on a thirty-year stretch that we might just possibly have got quashed."

"So who *are* you up against?"

Scott did not like the Arab's change of mood. The police had been brought in. He thought quickly. "The Establishment. There's something very bent going on."

The Arab understood that, but suspicion was still there. Scott did not think it mattered much how Hashimi took it. It made no difference, but he would prefer to be understood. "George Bulman handed you my letter?"

"Yes. I almost shot him."

"Why didn't you?"

"That's difficult to answer," Hashimi conceded.

"He's no ordinary copper. You must have seen that."

"I suppose that is the answer. He convinced me he was acting for you and that you were in trouble. Which your letter also explained."

"Just forget about coppers. Suspend your opinion. Can you raise a team to get me out of here? It's urgent. I'm on a day-by-day reprieve. If it's left much longer I'll come out in a box."

Hashimi was quiet for some time, but he did not take his gaze from Scott's face.

Scott said, "I could have spun you a load of bull. I've never done that. It's a take-it-or-leave-it situation. I can raise some cash."

"Cash," Hasimi almost exploded. He quickly lowered his voice. "You think you can *buy* my services?"

Scott cooled it down. "I forgot your rich papa. But I don't want him paying for me."

"You haven't changed, Spider. Thank God, because that's the only thing that reassures me. I don't like this bit about the police."

Scott glanced across the room at the clock over the door of the visitors' exit. He said, "We haven't got all day. I haven't time to explain the police bit. It's too complicated, and you wouldn't want to understand anyway. Do you raise a team or not?"

"No."

Scott sat back and hit the table. Hashimi's refusal was a blow. "Well, that's that. Nice to see you just the same. Really."

Hasimi rose as if to go. "Tea, coffee, or a soft drink? And biscuits?"

"Anything you like."

Hashimi went over to the tea bar and returned with two orangeades and two packets of chocolate biscuits. He set them down and gazed around the room. "Not too many people here today. Less than half full." Hashimi paused.

The visitors' waiting room was now empty. The few groups around the tables were absorbed. Two little girls ran around the room.

"I don't trust teams. There's always a weak link. I'll do it myself."

"You having me on?" Scott undid the cellophane around the biscuits.

"Which is the weakest place in the prison?"

Scott stared at Hashimi. The Arab was serious. "This is top security. There are no weak links. If there has to be one then it's here in this room."

"That's what I thought." Hashimi turned his chair slightly sideways to get comfortable. He looked through the window at an angle. "Free-

176

dom just the other side of this glass. This whole sector sticks out beyond the prison walls and away from the scanners."

"You seem not to have noticed the grids in front of the glass."

"Attractive, aren't they? Nice goldy, bronzy color. And *very* nicely patterned. Good design. Not like the old-fashioned bars. They've gone a long way to make it attractive to visitors. Doesn't remind them too much of what their fathers and husbands and sons are going back to beyond those doors."

"You've become a poet."

"Why not? I went to a good school. Four- or five-foot drop, would you say?"

"Below the windows? I would guess so."

"Take my word for it."

"What's all this about?"

Hashimi took his time. He slowly, and surreptitiously, scanned the room. "It's about blowing the goddamned window out," he said barely loud enough for Scott to hear.

Scott managed to remain dead-pan. He realized with shock that Hashimi meant what he said, but it was a ridiculous idea.

"How are you going to do that?" Scott asked, finding difficulty in speaking.

"Plastic explosive. Command detonated. Radio control, if you like. Usual thing."

"When, for God's sake?"

"Now."

Scott held on to the table. "You're mad."

"I've always been mad."

"Where are you going to conjure up explosive?" Scott was afraid to look around. It was as though he was discussing the crazy idea somewhere else, suspended and isolated.

"It's in my pockets."

Scott kept his gaze fastened on the table, afraid that he might give himself away. The seated guards were talking quietly among themselves, but they were not fools; they were vigilant. Hashimi's hands were on the table, and Scott only now noticed that they, too, had been stained; the fingers were quite steady. Almost hypnotically he saw one hand reach for a biscuit. The Arab was enjoying himself; he had walked into the lions' den as if he had a death wish. And perhaps he had.

177

"I've squeezed the plastic flat, like a wallet. I've got two packs already primed to a miniature radio control. If I fall against this table and hit the button, we'll be splattered all over the place." Hashimi was smiling. He would not be so careless, but he had made the point that he had walked into a prison as a live bomb.

"There are kids here."

"Then you'd better make sure they keep away."

"For God's sake, how can I do that?"

"You'd better make up your mind whether you want to get out."

Scott glanced at his watch. It was three o'clock. There was still an hour left of visiting time. "Why are you so willing to do this?"

Hashimi grimaced. "You don't believe it's to help an old friend?"

"Partly. That's the part I really appreciate. That's not the only reason."

"Okay." Hashimi seemed to go within himself. His voice was low but more passionate. "It's thumbing my nose at authority. Kicking the system in the arse. And it's self-advertisement, once the dust has settled. Nobody can do it like me. It won't be the first prison bust I'll have made. And, Spider, I'm so bored."

Scott took stock of the others in the room. He was shaken, but he was thinking clearly. "People could get killed. And I'm worried about those two kids. Look at them, pretty little things, all of six."

"And without a future worth a mention. Do you want to get out or not?"

Scott had to make a decision. Everything around him had changed its meaning. There was nothing and nobody in the room that could be taken for granted any more. Hashimi was asking the question, and the basic answer was simple, but that answer now affected every man, woman, and child in the visitors' room. Somehow it was not the way he had expected it to be. "What happens after the window's blown out?"

"Can you handle a ultralight?"

"Jesus. I haven't flown one for a while."

"I wasn't sure. I seem to remember you didn't like flying."

"I don't. Not when someone else is piloting. On my own is different. My life's in my own hands. Hanggliding, too. I enjoyed that; no bloody engine to break down and no noise."

Hashimi laughed for no reason at all, and Scott quickly realized that the show was for the guards. He joined in. "This is how it will work," Hashimi said, somehow managing to maintain a grin.

"When I say dive, you hit the deck fast. The people along this wall will be okay, the blast shouldn't touch them, and we've blocked off this window. Those in the middle and across the room are in most danger, but I don't think they'll come to any harm except to be shaken up or knocked off their chairs."

"What about the kids?"

"They're a bloody nuisance. But we could use them as a diversion."

Scott glanced around. "What else?"

"The moment the debris stops falling we dive straight through the hole, race across the grass." Hashimi was speaking casually. "There will be a car with its engine running . . ."

"The guards wouldn't let it stay there," Scott interrupted. "The car park on the left of the main drive up to the prison is staff only. And I've learned they're red hot on that. They wouldn't let any car dally in front of the entrance area."

"There will be a car with its engine running," Hashimi continued, "with a driver who will race up as soon as he hears the blast. Within seconds of that we'll be in that car and away."

Scott considered it. The Arab was thorough, yet this scheme sounded weak and chancey. Hashimi, noticing his doubt, said, "Don't lecture me about roadblocks and alarms and all that. For seconds after the blast, people will be shaken to hell. We need only seconds. The driver knows the island inside out."

"So you have a team?"

"I don't call a driver a team. He's done time in Parkhurst across the street and he's good. Papa doesn't know it yet, but he'll be picking up the tab."

"We can't stay in the same car."

"I know that. Well?"

"There are dog patrols outside. We'd have to reach the car before the dogs got us."

"I know that too. I can see the bloody dog handlers from here. It's a matter of fine timing and good reflexes. The alternative," Hashimi pointed out, "seems to be that you stay inside and wait to be knocked off."

179

"Just try to keep an eye on those kids."

"Is that yes?"

"Go ahead."

"Finish your orange and then nibble a biscuit."

Scott drained his glass. Hashimi rose, took the empty tumblers, and moved over to the tea bar. He brought two bars of chocolate back to the table, well aware that he was being watched. He gave Scott one of the bars and whispered urgently, "Next time around grab one of the kids and tell her to buzz off." He then stood by the table but with his back to the window, while he peeled the foil off the chocolate.

Scott remained seated, fiddling with the chocolate bar; it gave him the opportunity to avoid looking at Hashimi. He heard Hashimi curse and glanced up in spite of himself. Hashimi was licking chocolate off his fingers then wiping them with a handkerchief. Scott knew that there was a limit to the amount of time Hashimi could stand there without attracting comment from the guards. One of the young girls came racing past, and Scott grabbed her by the arm to swing her around.

The girl tried to break loose as Scott whispered to her, "Push off. Stay with your mum." He still held on, and the girl started volubly to struggle.

A man's voice from two tables away asked coldly, "She troubling you? Take your hand off her."

One of the guards, sensing trouble, started to move toward Scott to take the steam out of a potentially tricky situation. The girl's mother, annoyed that the petting with her husband had been interrupted, rose quickly and moved over to grab the girl as Scott released her. "I'm sorry," he said. "I thought she'd hurt herself. Nearly tripped over my foot."

The woman was young and attractive and over made-up. "Keep your bloody hands off her. She was doing no harm." The girl returned with her mother, and the guard went back to his chair. The full focus had been on Scott and the girl. Shakily, Scott turned his attention back to Hashimi, who was just pulling his chair out to sit down.

Scott's gaze drifted beyond Hashimi to the window. The nape of his neck prickled, and he tore his gaze away with the greatest difficulty. Hashimi had planted two packs of plastic, one on the window itself and one on the inset wall just beyond the grid. He could see one of the radio-controlled detonators quite clearly. The whole damned lot was sticking out like a Christmas tree.

180

14

S COTT couldn't speak. Hashimi, who seemed completely relaxed, said in a low tone, "You ready?"

Scott wanted it done before the children started roaming again. He tried to say yes, still keeping a watch for the girls, and finally all he could do was nod an assent.

"Try to face the window when you go down. It will be quicker afterward. Keep your face covered by your arms and your hands over the back of your head."

Scott did not need telling. He moved his chair slightly.

"*Dive.*" Hashimi roared the word as he put his hand in his pocket.

Hardened cons, on seeing Scott and Hashimi throw themselves flat, pushed wives and sweethearts down quickly as they flattened themselves. Guards had half-risen when the almighty explosion occurred. The noise was earsplitting, a cloud of dust and rubble covered fragments of glass and brick and metal, and a great wave of air blasted across the room knocking over people and tables and chairs. There were screams and shouts and cries of pain and, in the middle of this, the dust- and debris-covered figures of Scott and Hashimi rose like phantoms to hurl themselves at the window.

The broken grid was hanging but still fixed at one side. Scott threw himself at it, arms raised to protect his face as he had once done when throwing himself at triple-coiled barbed wire fences. He took the grid out with him as he landed on the glass-strewn narrow path by the wide

181

lawn. He was not sure where Hashimi was, but he rolled as he landed, heard the deep barking of a German shepherd dog, and frantically tried to pick up the sound of a car engine as he climbed to his feet amidst grass, grit, and rubble. Behind him a dust ball was streaming from the shattered window.

Hashimi bawled, "This way." And there was the car in brilliant sunlight, two doors open. Scott and Hashimi flung themselves onto the seats, slamming the doors as the car raced off with tires screaming. A dog leaped at the car but fell back as the vehicle moved.

Scott was sprawling on the rear seat, and Hashimi had jammed himself in beside the driver. The Arab had already produced a bottle of solvent from under the dashboard and was trying to get it open as the car performed a mad half-circle over the lawns, crushed a young sapling, crazily maneuvered between two giant concrete flower pots, swerved onto the outlet road, and then skidded crazily right, the rear end fish-tailing, just missing an oncoming car, swung to the other side of the street, and headed in the general direction of Bembridge. The sirens were wailing before the car had crossed the lawn.

Scott was thrown to the floor and, when he pulled himself up, was amazed to see the Arab wiping streaks of stain from his face with solvent-soaked cotton. He had removed cheek pads, his face was now hollow. He worked quickly and deftly.

Scott looked back through the rear window. There was no sign of the dog, and as yet no one followed them. They now needed luck as well as skill, the sort of luck that would keep chance oncoming police cars out of their way. Before Scott could look back again, they had turned off onto a secondary road and were climbing. They needed to find shelter before a police helicopter got airborne.

Already it seemed to Scott that they had been traveling for hours, but the actual escape had been inside thirty seconds, including reaching the main road. None of them had spoken a word. As Scott struggled up on his seat, he noticed that the driver was built like a jockey, slight, with strong wrists, and he seemed to have total concentration. They turned off again, across rough ground. It was not grassed, which, from the air, would have shown wheel tracks. And then suddenly they stopped.

"Out," Hashimi shouted.

They were in a small gulley with trees overhanging to form good temporary cover. And now Scott saw a small truck and, behind it, a motorbike.

"The truck is yours," Hashimi said. "There's an ultralight in the back. Rogallo-type sail. Control by A frame. Bar forward for up, back for down, left for right and right for left, shifting your weight with it. Okay?"

Scott nodded numbly. Hashimi was already stripping.

Hashimi added, "Get out of those clothes. There's some white overalls in the truck with a company name—Southern Aeronautics. Throw all the old stuff in the car."

Hashimi had removed the stain from his face and now used a small mirror as he reached around the back of his neck. The driver helped Hashimi while Scott climbed into the back of the truck. From every direction now police car sirens wailed, carried on the warm air until the converging cacophony was confusing. The hunt was on. Roadblocks would be set up, and the three men were still near the prison.

They could hear a helicopter now but it was fairly distant, confirming that Hashimi's strategy, so far, was correct. Police would believe the escapees would try to get as far away from the prison as possible.

Scott found the overalls piled beside the dismantled ultralight; he hoped he could still handle one, but this was not the time to reflect. He stripped quickly, aware that his dyed fair hair was now a disadvantage, but Hashimi had thoughtfully provided a white cap with the overalls, with Southern Aeronautics printed on the long peak. He scrambled out and threw his prison clothes into the escape car, an old, tuned up Ford Consul.

Hashimi was now down to his underpants. He had soaked his hands and wrists in the solvent and was now rubbing away the residue of stain from his hands. He appeared more like Scott remembered. All three men had worked frantically. The driver was now wearing a light leather motorcyclist's outfit with a studded back. Hashimi started to climb into something similar. Both had crash helmets. Their gear had been stored in the cab of the truck.

Hashimi said, "We'll meet some time. There is a license and some money in the cab."

They briefly shook hands. "I owe you," Scott said as he climbed into the truck.

"Balls," Hashimi replied. "I've enjoyed it. Still do. Don't tell that bastard Bulman I helped you. It will spoil my image."

Scott waved. The keys were in the ignition, and he switched on. "What about the truck?" he bawled out. It was old but serviceable.

"Leave it where you like. Papa can put it down to expenses."

"And the car?"

"I've time-bombed it. Get moving."

The motorcycle started up behind the truck, and Scott moved slowly forward over the rough ground. He assumed that Hashimi and the driver would go for one of the ferries, something he dared not do. The ferry terminals would already be crawling with police. He gave another wave and headed toward the sound of sirens.

Scott took it slowly as the springs started to creak. He would not be satisfied until he was on the main road; he did not want an airborne copper wondering what a truck was doing on what was little more than a track. He reached the junction and turned right, away from the prison, but before the actual turn he caught a glimpse of it; it was much nearer than he had realized. There were police sirens both behind and in front of him, and the prison alarms were still wailing.

He steadied down to a regular thirty. Something caught his eye on the seat and he saw that it was the driver's license. He picked it up. It was made out to a Mr. Edward Roland Styles. Scott slipped it into the top pocket of his white, but slightly soiled, overalls. The name was easy to remember.

Very shortly the traffic began to thicken, then to pile up. It was increasingly obvious that there was a roadblock ahead. Now he could see the police cars forming an effective blockade through which only one car at a time could filter. Scott raised himself in his seat. The police were waving the traffic down, then examining one vehicle at a time. He could see no sign of a guard, and his spirits rose. A guard who knew him would have little difficulty in recognizing him. He stayed in line.

Scott opened the cab window, for the police would ask him to anyway. Suddenly there was a huge explosion behind and to his right, and palls of smoke and flame pillared shakily into the warm air. He realized at once that the escape car had blown up.

Some drivers climbed out to watch it. The air was so still that the smoke spiral went straight up, orange pierced near its base where the flame was thickest. Then the smoke canopied out on a fickle wind. Scott thought the explosion was uncomfortably near, like the prison. Another siren howled as a police car raced to the scene.

The crawling string of cars was heading south, away from the ferries and the mainland, a direction an escapee might not be expected to take, but Scott well knew that the checks would be just as thorough and that his turn to be checked was not far off. A prison guard emerged from behind a group of policemen, and Scott's heart thumped. It was too late to pull out of line. He was hemmed in. He pulled the peak of his cap down.

He had to sweat it out, car by car. Spot-checks were made of the trunks of cars as a matter of routine. The helicopter hovered over the checkpoint then slowly made its way down the barely moving queue. He gripped the steering wheel to steady his hands. He had been in Albany for eleven days; a lifetime and nightmare combined. They would have to put restraining gear on him to get him back. He sat sweating and worried, and then there was only a taxi and an old brown Vauxhall in front of him. White police cars formed a staggered barrier, and beyond them another lay ready to give chase to anyone foolish enough to attempt to break through.

Now there was only the Vauxhall, and Scott was quick to note that the prison guard was playing an active part. What was more, he recognized the man. There was nothing to do but sweat it out and to try to keep his face shaded.

Suddenly he was signaled forward. Scott eased the truck ahead; the Vauxhall was now speeding beyond the barrier, trying to catch the taxi. A policeman looked up into the cab, and Scott gazed down below the peak of his cap.

"Any passengers, sir?"

"No." Scott used an Australian accent, which came easily to him. But as he spoke, the near side door was wrenched open and another policeman poked his head inside. The door was slammed again.

"What's in the back, sir?"

"An ultralight. I'm taking it to Bembridge airport. What's going on?"

"Escaped prisoner. Will you open up the back please, sir?"

The last thing Scott wanted to do was to climb out. The guard was standing behind the policeman and, at present, was showing more interest in a van behind the truck. That would change if Scott stepped down. "Help yourself, sport. It's open. If he's climbed in there he's all yours."

The policeman moved to the rear. The guard glanced up at the cab, but by now Scott had an elbow on the open window and had cupped his face in his hand. The guard hesitated, then followed the policeman, who had been joined by another colleague at the rear of the truck. After a while he heard them climbing around in the back. There was a worrying silence, then someone banged the side of the truck and he was being waved on. Sweat poured out of him as he drove off.

Across open country the roads were less busy, but on the approaches to the small, attractive coastal resort of Bembridge, the traffic thickened noticeably. When Scott reached the airport he could see that in the distance, small, private planes were strung out along the takeoff strip and others were in the air, some perhaps giving voluntary service to the search for him. Beyond the planes was a low run of hangers and, closer to him, were two commercial helicopters.

History was on Scott's side, even if statistically against him. No man that he had heard of had ever finally escaped off the island. The police knew that, and he prayed that it might work for him.

He continued on until he found a point to turn around. He did not want the airport itself. It was at present too busy and so was the air above it. But it gave him position, and he searched around for a deserted space from which he could use the ultralight.

There was a fair amount of both open and wooded country on the island. The congestions were almost always on the coastline. It was not too long before Scott found a reasonable spot. He had to turn off onto a rough track that might have led to a farm. When he stopped, he decided there was too much traffic on the road below him and he started out again. The sounds of distant car sirens cut the hot air, as police tentacles ever widened.

At last he found a fairly sheltered position, with a pasture in which was a herd of Jersey cows on the far side. He could see no sign of a farmhouse, but it would not be too far away. The truck suddenly lurched, and Scott saved himself from going through the windshield. The offside front wheel had dropped into a pothole. There was no way he could get it out on his own. He would have to take off from here. He climbed out shakily.

He really needed help to get the ultralight out; there were no planks

186

with which to roll down the tricycle. He took the sail off first; a nonrigid delta wing. Then he wheeled the tricycle to the rear of the truck and lowered it as best he could, front wheel forward. When it was all down he wheeled the tricycle around so that it was facing down the slope.

He was actually assembling the machine when the chopper came over, but he took no notice for there was nothing he could do with the truck stranded, and the ultralight had to be in the open for takeoff. Intermittently he picked up the howl of sirens, and twice he caught the distant blue of a police flasher above a hedgerow. As he worked, he wondered about Hashimi and his jockeylike companion and hoped they would get clear off the island.

When the machine was ready he solemnly reflected that it did not matter whether he could fly it or not, he would rather crash it than be confined again. He went to the truck to find the money Hashimi had told him was there. Before he opened the cab door he realized that the chopper was back, circling over the site.

He turned and looked up as anyone would, and he waved to the pilot who seemed to wave back. He opened the cab door and poked around under the dashboard. He found a padded brown envelope full of notes, with some coins, a penknife, and a box of matches. He stuffed them in a pocket. Hashimi had been thorough. Then, with a shock, he remembered that if the truck was dusted for prints the police would come up with a collection of prints for Willie "Spider" Scott.

Scott peered up through the windshield; the chopper had gone again. He dusted everywhere he thought he had touched, inside the cab and out. It took time but it might avoid later complications. Everything from now on would be complicated. He was tempted to put a match to the petrol tank, but that would draw attention and would be easily seen from the air.

He returned to the ultralight, put a foot in front of one of the wheels, reached back, and swung the pusher prop. He climbed in and eased her forward, then opened the motorcycle type hand throttle wide. It was slightly downhill over the pasture, and bumpy all the way. He caught a glimpse of the cow herd, now turned to face him, and he prayed that they would not stampede. There was lift, the wheels less bumpy beneath him, but he gave it a little longer before taking off. He was airborne; it was like sitting in an elevating bucket seat with no support at all.

The warm air currents lifted him like a bird, and he tried to wheel

187

slowly like one, using the bar and his weight. His heart leapt as he saw the chopper again. It dropped down toward him like a grotesque spider on the end of its thread. Scott waved again, relieved that he was wearing crash helmet and goggles. Then, in an act of bravado, he put his right arm out and followed up with a right turn. He believed the chopper's passenger laughed behind the canopy before the pilot took it up again.

Scott headed toward Ventnor, away from the direction he really wanted. Then he turned northwest toward the Needles where hang-gliding often took place, and where he would not be conspicuous. He was as high as the ultralight would go, and he felt a tremendous sense of freedom as hedges and fields and patches of subtropical vegetation opened up below him. Roads crisscrossed the island, and he could spot the occasional congestion of roadblocks.

He realized he was tense and handling the splendid little craft too rigidly. Hashimi had forgotten to mention the range of the machine, but Scott calculated that it should be good for half an hour at thirty knots; it was more than enough. The wound in his stomach began to pulse as he headed for the mainland.

"CLOSE THE DOOR, George." Commander Collins was tense, his features strained. He rubbed his eyes. "Sit down, for God's sake."

Bulman sat, feeling sorry for Collins.

"It's hit the fan, George."

"The commissioner giving you a rough time?"

"Are you kidding? I mean, blowing a bloody great hole in the wall. I ask you!"

"What else could he do? He knew he was due to be killed."

"Did you know about this before?" Collins raised his head aggressively.

"No idea at all," Bulman replied blandly. "But I don't blame him. Speaking as someone who is concerned with justice, of course."

"But who was this character?" Collins glanced at a note on his desk. "Frank Obuti, who took the stuff into Albany? Why wasn't he searched?"

Bulman did not reply; Collins was frustrated and was striking out; he knew perfectly well that prison visitors were not searched.

Collins slammed the desk. "The antiterrorist squad are suggesting that Obuti is actually that bastard Hashimi Ross. He pulled a similar stunt in Frankfurt some years ago for the Baader Meinhof. Almost the same M.O."

"But this bloke was African."

Collins gave him a scathing look. "Straight out of a Cherry Blossom tin. George, if the press finds out that Anthony Sims is really Willie Scott, our heads will roll."

"I'll take full responsibility."

"You can't. I'm the senior officer."

"I'll say I lied to you."

Collins shook his head. "The responsibility is mine. Where did it start to go wrong? Jesus, all we did was put in a plant."

"It started to go wrong when someone saw Willie as a threat. There was no doubt at all that someone was trying to kill him."

"Is the Foreign Office in this? I mean *really* in?"

Bulman spoke carefully. He had not told Collins about the forged Mosley receipt, nor did he want to. "They're certainly involved so far as using the Home Office to retain Scott is concerned. As far as I can see, someone has been giving them a bum steer, to make it appear that both Scott and Moody were somehow tied in with Tuomo, who was sent back home."

Collins said wearily, "There will be an inquiry into the escape. I'll have to come clean. Damn it, I'm not that far off pension."

"There won't be an inquiry," Bulman said quietly.

"There has to be." Collins was looking ruffled as he snapped back.

"Too much will come out. Oh, there'll be an official demand for an inquiry. There might even be a staged version, the verdict written in advance. But neither the Foreign Office nor the Home Office will want one."

Collins stared at Bulman steadily. "All along you've known something I don't. You'd better tell me."

"I'm too scared to tell you. Don't ask me now."

Collins sat back slowly. "What the hell's going on, George?"

"I don't know. And that's the absolute truth. As soon as I do, I'll tell you, because right now you're the only one I trust." Bulman stood up. "You've done nothing wrong. Nor have I. But if I can give a superior officer some advice, Dick, I'd check daily, both here and at home, to make sure your phone isn't tapped."

THEY WENT DOWN to the Thames embankment. Even here, although quieter, they were not free of summer trippers. They avoided the benches and found a deserted area, opposite the Festival Hall across

189

the river. The two men leaned on the parapet, as did so many others on such a nice day. The weather was a little cooler but still fine, the river gray and torpid but given life by the rippling wake of passing boats. It was a scene to be savored, but it was doubtful if the two men were really aware of it.

"It's a bit much when we have to meet like this," Martin Holmes complained.

"Would you rather I spoke directly to the Home Secretary himself?" Sir Roland Powell asked cagily.

Holmes was well aware that Powell outranked him, but he was both annoyed by and somewhat afraid of recent events. Like the prison governor, he felt that he had been used, and he had little to fall back upon by way of excuse. "Yes, I think I would, Sir Roland," he replied testily. "Provided that I am there."

"Come, Martin, these things happen. It's in the nature of the job. We are on the same side, you know."

"I was beginning to wonder. I've been backpedaling to the Home Secretary ever since this damned fellow escaped. It wasn't just the escape but the nature of it. The press and television reporters have seldom had such good copy, particularly in the summer silly season. What exactly is it you want, Sir Roland?"

"The same as you, old boy. We must avoid an inquiry." Powell's eyes had lost all sign of amusement, his features all sense of fun. There was a coldness about him Holmes had not previously seen.

"I don't see how we *can* avoid an inquiry. There has to be one."

"Oh, officially, of course. There must be an inquiry. But it must be comprised of the right people."

"You want a cover-up?"

"Of course I want a cover-up."

"Then you convince the Home Secretary."

Powell turned his head in surprise. "Are you saying you won't help?"

"I've already helped. Look where it's got me."

"Dammit, nobody could foresee this. You must admit that it bears out what Murison was told. Scott *is* dangerous. It's generally thought that the man he co-opted is an international terrorist. What more proof do you need?"

"It's not proof."

"It's enough to justify what we did. He was only held for a few days. Another couple of days would have either seen charges against him or his release. Up to his escape it was a storm in a teacup, stirred by that idiot George Bulman, who almost certainly concocted the whole thing. Bulman played a dangerous game, and he was foolishly backed up by Commander Collins, who should surely have known better. We cannot be responsible for them."

Powell waited for it to sink in. Holmes was pompous, his ego easily appealed to, but other than that he was no fool. "If there is a proper inquiry you must face what will come out. The Home Office held a police plant in Albany Prison illegally." Shrewdly he added, "It would not surprise me if the governor complained, as he would be entitled to do. One senior police officer lied to the Home Office and gave a false name and reason for the man he requested to plant. And on top of this Scott blows his way out. According to some reports there were serious casualties."

Holmes's lips were tight, his face a little pale. He could not exclude his own part, nor that of his subordinate, Toby Russell, from an inquiry. He turned to face Powell directly. "What I did was a favor to you. I accepted what you said."

"Indeed. And nothing has changed in that direction. We are now as convinced as ever about Scott. Believe me, I've never been anything but grateful for what you did. And I have no regrets. Nor should you have. I'm asking another favor. This time for all our sakes. Both ministries are involved and so are the police. It wouldn't look good, Martin. Certain organizations would howl with glee, and public confidence would be badly shaken. Think it over. It's easy enough to arrange."

Holmes had already thought it over, and he knew Powell to be right. That was why he was so inwardly angry. His own position was threatened. He bitterly reflected that it might have been better had the attempt on Scott in prison succeeded. It would have solved their problems.

15

THE weather had been designed for Scott's flight across the narrow sea channel to the mainland. He followed the estuary toward the ferry terminals and then banked right before reaching the wide sprawl of Southampton. It was important to avoid the big port and to reach the open countryside of Hampshire. There was plenty of space between the old-world villages, but he needed to land near a road. He selected his field and brought her down.

Hashimi had told him that there was an address with the money, but when he searched through the notes he could not find one. He checked again and found an address and telephone number on the box of matches. Knowing Hashimi, the matches themselves were a message. Scott peeled back his white dungarees and took off his undershirt. He tore it into strips to make a crude fuse, which he inserted into the fuel tank. He zipped up again, lighted the end of the fuse, then ran across country. When he reached the road he thumbed for a lift. He had still not found one when the ultralight blew up behind him.

He was relieved when a truck driver picked him up. He climbed into the high cab. The driver was a friendly, chunky man with constantly gum chewing jaws. "Andover any good to you?"

Scott was not absolutely sure where Andover was. "That'll be fine. My truck broke down. My mate has gone back with the tow."

Scott did not think the driver had seen the company name on his back,

193

and he steered the conversation carefully into mundane channels. There was no reason at all why the prison break should be connected with the ultralight at this stage, but eventual association was inevitable. Bits and pieces would come together, the roadblock, the stranded truck, and finally the burned out machine in the field. It might take time but it would happen. Meanwhile, it was essential for him to get out of the dungarees, which might be remembered.

The driver dropped Scott at the back of a Waitrose store, from where he could walk through the arcade to the town center. Andover had once been an attractive market town and still carried many of the old features, but a population overspill from London had inevitably changed many of its characteristics. Scott found a telephone booth at the side of the supermarket. He blessed Hashimi for including some coins in the money. He rang the number on the matchbox.

SCOTT HAD A long wait. He felt very conspicuous in the white overalls and cap, and he decided the best thing to do was to get out of sight. He walked down the old High Street, with its cosmopolitan crowd, and felt less conspicuous. At the bottom he leaned on the small bridge and watched the ducks in the sun-cast river. He stayed there until opening time and then searched for an off-the-beat pub.

He found one in St. George's Yard, a Tudor segment of the small town and conveniently off the High Street. As soon as he walked into the oak-beamed atmosphere, he picked up a once-familiar aura. There were troops in here, in civilian clothes but military nevertheless. He ordered a pint of ale, found a space at a table and sat down among the off-duty soldiers.

Time dragged heavily, in spite of good beer and company. He downed a second pint, checked his watch then left the pub and returned to the point where the truck driver had dropped him. There was a bus station to his left, for the single deckers that would call at the surrounding villages.

Scott felt exposed again. The store had closed, the bus queues had considerably lessened, and the taxi rank opposite, outside one of the town's public car parks, had shrunk as drivers had moved off for an evening meal. The evening rush was over, and Scott had been around the spot for some considerable time. He would be remembered, he knew that. The initial all important advantage of the white dungarees was now working against him. He was constantly looking at his watch; the car was almost an hour late.

He went up the steps to the telephone booth. He dialed a London number; the ringing tone had just started when a bright red Jensen coasted uncertainly into the curb. A fine-looking, bare-armed black girl gazed around uncertainly. Scott put the receiver back and ran down the steps. The wide eyed girl looked up at his approach.

"You Sophie?"

"Yes. You Spider Scott?"

He climbed in without invitation. "I was getting desperate there."

Sophie glanced over her shoulder before pulling out. "I've been desperate all the way down here. It took me nearly three hours. I had terrible trouble getting out of London and then got lost on the way down. I don't know this part of the country." Sophie gave Scott a quick glance of remonstrance. "Then you ask me to park on double yellow lines."

"Yes, well I don't know the place either, but I'm really grateful to you. You'll never know how much."

"I can guess." Sophie slipped on some sunglasses. Scott turned to get a better view of her; long legs and the way she held herself, combined with slimness and the style of her flimsy summer dress, prompted the question, "Are you a model?"

"When I'm not helping Hash on one thing or another."

"So you're Hash's steady?"

The smile was wistful. "One of them. I don't fool myself."

There was no answer. Scott could see her bitterness. "Would you like me to drive?"

"Why? Aren't I good enough?" The long legs were working clutch and brake, the bright eyes watching front and mirror.

"You're first class. I thought you might appreciate the break."

"You're considerate. I'll be okay once we reach the M3."

When they were on the London road Scott relaxed. He had taken his cap off. He glanced at Sophie. Her long black hair was held by a multicolored headband. He noticed that she kept to the seventy-mile-an-hour limit, which was difficult in such a high powered car. It was clear that Sophie preferred to concentrate on her driving. Scott sat back. He hated being driven by anyone, but Sophie was handling the car extremely well, and gradually the magnitude of his escape sank in.

There were times, as he sat there being driven by a beautiful woman, that he could not accept what was happening.

It was now over six hours since the breakout and it was dark, the headlights throwing up the shallow undulations of the motorway. But it was still warm. Scott was glad of the darkness. He no longer felt himself to be under scrutiny, and he was better able to think objectively.

He did not know what would happen from this point. It was something to be resolved. Meanwhile he would never be able to thank Hashimi enough; and he could not help but wonder if he would still feel the same when the Arab performed his next act of terrorism.

Sophie took them to Islington. It was one of those streets that had been run-down but had been made fashionable with foresight and hard work. She parked the car outside a terraced house, and Scott followed her through the iron gate and up the short concrete path to the front door. She let them in and said over her shoulder, "Upstairs." They went up, Sophie going first, and she unlocked another door on the landing. "We have this floor and the one above, and someone else has downstairs. All nicely separated."

They entered a tiny hall that led to a small, cozy drawing room. The furniture looked secondhand and comfortable. "You want to get out of those overalls?" Sophie went into a bedroom and returned with a bathrobe which she threw at him. "There's another bedroom where you can change and a bathroom between the two. I think bathrobe'll fit anyone."

He closed the spare bedroom door behind him. It was tiny, but there was a single bed and a narrow, and empty, wardrobe. The bathroom was off the bedroom, and when he entered it he locked the door leading to what he imagined was the main bedroom. There was a bath and shower. He washed off the sweat and grime of the past few hours and tried to swill away the taste and the feel of prison. There were ample towels; when he had dried off he put his underpants back on and then the bathrobe. He returned to the drawing room. Sophie was not there. The main bedroom door was closed, and he assumed she might be changing.

There was a silver-plated tray with some decanters on a small mahogany sideboard. Glasses were in the sideboard and water was in the tap of a small kitchen off a tiny dining room. He was standing at the window drinking when Sophie came back into the room. She wore a

196

dressing gown and high-heeled mules, and separating the two were her shapely black legs.

Scott held up the glass. "I hope you don't mind, but I needed this and I didn't think Hash would mind. Can I get you one?"

"No need." Sophie glided over to the sideboard and poured herself neat whisky. She went into the kitchen, and when she returned she had ice in her glass. "Cheers. Hash never touches the stuff. The Irish side of his family are all boozers and his father's side are strict Muslims. He reckons booze affects his trigger finger."

"That implies that he has nerves. From what I saw today, he hasn't got any."

"Oh, he's got them. I've seen him screwed-up. And while we're talking of screwing, I'm strictly his, okay? Until he throws me out."

"Do you think he'd have let me in if there was a risk to you? I'm the old-fashioned type. A one-girl man."

Sophie crossed the room and sat down, carefully pulling her gown over her crossed legs. "He feels he owes you something, so I don't know how far his mind goes on the subject. He explained something of what you did when you were in prison together."

"It was nothing. I don't really understand the expense and risk he's gone to. It hasn't fully caught up with me."

"The expense is nothing to him. His father is in oil and a close friend of Gaddafi; both crazies. Hash's mother didn't help either. We both know what he is, but I love him and that's all there is to it. I can't win in the end. I know that. But I can enjoy what there is left."

"I still don't really understand why he stuck his neck out for me."

Sophie eyed Scott for a long time, her eyes dark and deep beneath the naturally long lashes. "You gave him something nobody else did. Unqualified friendship, perhaps. Unquestioning help. And trust. Those he works with don't *like* him. If anything, they fear him. And they know he's bloody good at what he does. I'm not even sure that he really supports the causes he helps; not in the same way as the others." Sophie raised her glass, a humorous look in her eyes. "Anyway, I think he was bursting to break out into something. After a while sex is not enough. I don't think he understands a lot about real love."

Scott glanced at the clock on the mantlepiece. "We've missed the late news. I assume you know what happened today."

197

"Oh, yes. You're the man the copper brought the letter from. You have a wide variety of friends, Spider Scott."

"Over the last few days it seemed that I have as many enemies. Did Hash get back okay?"

Sophie tilted her head. "Hash always gets back. But he won't come here while you're here. A matter of splitting the risks, he says."

"He knows I've arrived then?"

"I phoned while you were showering."

"That's another thing. May I use your phone?"

"Only numbers you can dial. No operator calls. It's in the main bedroom."

"Are the directories there too?"

"There're some in the bedside cabinet."

Scott rose. "I don't want you to get into trouble through me. I'll see if I can find a place quickly."

Sophie said resignedly, "I'm doing this for Hash, you understand. I know he thinks a lot of you to do what he's done, but I like you, anyway. Give me your measurements and tomorrow morning I'll go out and buy you some clothes. I'll also bring in some newspapers."

"Hash gave me some money. I'll hand it over to you."

"He seems to think you'll need that for other things. I have enough for the clothes. You'll have to trust my taste. Okay?"

Scott smiled. "Your taste looks pretty good to me. By the way, how do I get my hair back to normal?"

"I thought it was dyed. You either wait for it to grow out or you dye it the color it was before. Do you want me to do it?"

"If you could. It was sort of dark."

"My God, Spider. Go make your telephone call, and I'll have another drink ready."

SCOTT LOOKED UP Bulman's private number and punched it out on the bedside telephone. It was late, not far off midnight, but Bulman's gravel voice was quick to reply. "Bulman." Always the same answer, on or off duty.

Scott dropped into his Australian accent. "*George* Bulman?"

There was a cautious, "Yes."

"Sorry to ring you so late, but I've been meaning to contact you for days. You know how it is, sightseeing and all that. Your Aunt Winnie in

198

Sydney insisted that I gave you a call, just to let you know she's all right."

There was a long silence before Bulman said irritably, "While I appreciate your trouble, couldn't it have waited until tomorrow? Dammit, I was just going to sleep. I mean I haven't seen Aunt Win for over eleven years. We're not close."

Scott knew then that Bulman was aware of who was calling; it couldn't have been easy for him. "I'm off on a tour tomorrow. Windsor Castle, or some place you pommies hang out the flag. I promised her I'd look you up, and I'll try to fit it in before I go back. You all go to bed so bloody early."

"Which hotel are you staying at?"

"I'm staying with friends, but I'm moving out tomorrow. You're a copper, aren't you? Aunt Win said you were a sergeant."

"I've moved up a bit since then. Is there somewhere we can meet? Like you, I'll try to fit it in, but it may not be easy."

"I don't know what time we get back from Windsor. I reckon around six o'clock should be okay. Are the pubs open then?"

"You mean you haven't found out? There's a pub in Charing Cross Road called the Horse's Head, near the intersection to St. Martin's Lane. Try to get there by six-thirty, if you can."

"Horse's Head. Okay. I hope the beer is not as warm as it's been so far. Oh, and bring your wife if you want. Sorry to call so late."

"I'm not married. See you tomorrow." Bulman hung up.

Scott did the same and sat on the edge of the bed. Bulman hated the Horse's Head. He had once quarreled with the manager while Scott was with him and had sworn that he would never go back there. Nor was it all that near to the intersection that led to St. Martin's Lane. On the other hand the Mitre, a pub both Bulman and Scott enjoyed, was actually at the intersection. Was he reading too much into it? Bulman's caution had clearly shown that he did not trust the telephone.

Scott went back into the drawing room. Sophie was at the television set. There were two drinks on top of the set, and she passed one to Scott.

"You want to see the ten o'clock news?" she asked him.

"You video'd it?" He was not sure whether he did want to see it.

"I video'd a film I want to see, but the tape ran on. Well?"

"I suppose I'd better know the worst."

They sat down at opposite ends of a couch, while Sophie juggled with the remote control. She located the news and then fiddled with the control until the prison break was announced. Television South had got some cameras over to the island; their reporter stood in front of Albany Prison to give his report, and behind him police and prison staff could be seen moving about. With dismay Scott noticed an ambulance.

He listened to the trained, stereotype reporting, the words, the deliberate and sometimes overstressed punctuation, but all that registered with him was the number of casualties. Seven people had been taken to the hospital, including a young girl; the seriousness of the injuries was not yet known.

Scott felt sick. Sophie, watching him, switched off. "They always play on that sort of thing," she said. "They exaggerate. It makes you look a dangerous villain."

Scott held his head in his hands. If the TV reporter was playing it up, Sophie was playing it down.

"Nobody's been killed," she insisted.

What was the degree of the injuries? The question drummed through his head.

"Hash told me they were trying to kill you in there. Don't feel so bad about it."

"I've no right to hang onto life at the expense of other people's. Some might be maimed for life."

"You should have thought of that before you gave Hash the nod."

He had thought of it, but her jibe got through. When he reflected on his desperation at the time, he realized he would have done the same thing again.

"Listen," said Sophie rising, "if it will make you feel better you can cry on my shoulder."

The suggestion made him snap from his remorse. He rose beside her. "I needed that kick in the teeth." But his thoughts were still on the injured.

SOPHIE HAD GONE by the time Scott rose in the morning. It was nine o'clock, and he had slept restlessly. He turned on breakfast television, switching channels, but nothing of the escape was mentioned, and he assumed that either he had missed it or it had not been included in the general news.

He ran the video through again and listened more objectively than

200

before. There was no mention of whether he was thought to be still on the island. Both he and Hashimi were referred to as dangerous criminals, with Hashimi being listed as a probable known "terrorist." He learned nothing more and switched off. He showered and made some toast. There was nothing he could do until Sophie returned.

SIR LEWIS HOPE summoned Bulman to his office off Cumberland Avenue. Bulman did not need telling what it would be about. By the time he had been through the security check and had taken the elevator up, he was quietly resigned to it. He knocked on the door and went in.

"Sit down, George."

Bulman saw at a glance that Hope was not happy; the weathered face was rigid and the thin lips compressed. Bulman sat down, feeling rebellious.

"You haven't heard from Scott yet, have you?"

Bulman appeared to be astounded. "I don't really understand your question, Sir Lewis. I'm a policeman. If I had heard from Scott I would have reported the matter."

"I sometimes think that you forget you are a policeman. Your loyalties are not always to the Crown."

"My loyalties have *always* been to the Crown, which does not mean that they always lean toward the Establishment. I would not do anything to harm the Crown, but I speak for myself. I am of the opinion that the illegal holding of Scott could very well harm the Crown and all established justice."

Hope was expressionless. Had he been chief of the Security Service at the time Bulman was taken on, he would never have employed him. Yet, in his more magnanimous moments, he had to admit that Bulman could be extremely useful in certain areas. "You haven't answered my question. Yes or no?"

"Sir Lewis, my home telephone is tapped and probably my office phone. How could Scott possibly contact me without your knowing?"

"Yes or no, George?"

"No, Scott has not contacted me. He would be mad to do so."

"Why on earth did we have to go through that performance to get an answer?"

"Because, Sir Lewis, I object to the question, which was aimed at my integrity." The lie was complete and the penalties could be extreme.

"I don't doubt your integrity. I simply get confused, on occasion, whether it is correctly directed. Priorities, George, and the first one is to this department."

Bulman was warm in the office. He wanted to loosen his tie. "With that very assumption in mind, sir, may I ask whether it is on behalf of this department that you have asked the question, or for some other department of the establishment?"

"That is impertinence."

"That's exactly what I thought of the original question, Sir Lewis." And then, hastily, "Of course, I recognize and accept that you are better placed to use it."

Hope was livid behind his reserved pose. Bulman could try to force an inquiry and that might be embarrassing. He forced a smile. "It's as well you recognize my position, George. You will, of course, notify me the moment Scott makes contact."

"What do you propose to do with him if he is crazy enough to do that?"

"Dammit man, whatever he may or may not have done before, he has now blown his way out of one of Her Majesty's prisons and has seriously injured innocent people in so doing. What do you expect us to do? Just let me know if you hear."

"Of course, Sir Lewis. Is that all?"

"I take it you have finally dropped this nonsense about Moody? It has got you nothing but trouble."

"I haven't the time for it, anyway." Once committed, Bulman decided he might as well lie all the way. Someone was lying elsewhere. He began to rise, but Hope waved him down.

"What about Scott's wife? Isn't she away?"

"She's on a cruise."

"Just as well. Wouldn't do for her to return with this going on."

Bulman looked for a hidden meaning and was disturbed. Hope appeared just as urbane, but why had he raised the subject of Maggie at all?

SIR ROLAND POWELL was in an angry mood and that anger was directed at Norman Murison. "We could be in grave trouble over this. Why the hell didn't you just have the man released?"

Murison, aware that he was treading on hot coals, was equally aware that Powell, when really annoyed, was at his most perceptive. "I was about to. I was giving it another day. The governor had been informed. Nobody could foresee this. Nobody at all."

"What about this source of yours? Had you really got anywhere?"

"The answer is yes, but there is not sufficient real evidence to bring it to court."

"What does that mean, precisely?"

"It means that we are totally convinced of the Moody-Tuomo-Scott links but not entirely sure of Scott's part. He might have been operating, or was about to operate, as Cooper had done; the fellow who got thirty years for stealing defense papers, which we've always believed, but could never prove, was planned by Moody. Moody's accidental death was opportune in some ways, but in others it severed a link we could have followed."

"Then wouldn't Scott have been more use to you *out* of prison? You could have kept an eye on him and perhaps come up with something."

"We were sure he would try to contact Cooper, which would have proved a linkage. While he was in Albany we were able to poke about without his interference, which on past records could have been considerable. The whole thing was unfortunate. We still need to locate him, though."

"So do the police," Powell said dryly. "I've spoken to Martin Holmes at the Home Office. I think he'll smooth things over with the Home Secretary. What we don't want coming out is who, precisely, is the escaped prisoner, because that will raise the interest of every reporter in the country. We don't want it known that we were holding him there with Home Office collusion. This really is a cock-up, Norman. I mean, the bloody man *blew* his way out."

"That only confirms what I've been saying about him. We must find him first."

"And then what will you do?"

"Strike a deal. We'll have to pay out, but we might get back some useful information."

"From what I've heard he's not the kind to do a deal."

"Every man has his price. Not necessarily money. It might be an idea to inform his wife of what's happened. She's on a cruise. It would bring her back, and she might be able to make contact with him. We could bug the place. Her too, if necessary. It's the best chance we have."

"Not too nice for her, though."

Murison shrugged. "She's going to find out anyway. What else can we do? If the police find him first they'll take his prints, check them, and Anthony Sims is suddenly Willie Scott. How will *that* be kept out of the press, and all that it will then lead to? A mass of cover ups, lefties releasing confidential government information on the subject, civil liberties. My God, we could lose the government the next election without even trying."

"I know all that. That's precisely why I saw Holmes. It all looks so messy. And so unnecessary."

"What were we supposed to do? Ignore events? Tell the Security Service without real evidence? They'd have told us, quite rightly, to fly a kite and keep to our own side of the fence. I've no regrets about what we did, only the way it's turned out. There was no other course but neglect."

"Neglect might have got us off the hook."

"It's not in my nature, Sir Roland," Murison replied testily.

"Well, you'd better find Scott before the police do. Tell me," Powell added, eyeing Murison stonily, "What *will* you do if you find Scott and he won't cooperate?"

Murison met Powell's gaze. "I am quite sure that Scott will accept the necessity for cooperation."

"That's an assumption, not an answer. Don't hedge, Norman."

"What we do if he doesn't help will depend entirely on what damage he can do to us."

"That could be considerable, if he has any idea that we were responsible for keeping him in prison. But we both know that. I still want an answer."

Murison was on the end of a hook. "It's not just damage to ourselves. We might have to kill him."

The two men were silent, and the atmosphere between them was uneasy. Eventually Powell said, "This is why you think he will cooperate. You intend to threaten him?"

"Only as a last resort. To let him go public would be disastrous."

"Have you considered that if you threaten him and he refuses to be intimidated, you would have to kill him there and then? You couldn't allow him time to reach a telephone."

"I will draw up contingency plans. No man will throw his life away needlessly."

"Which means that if he does agree to a deal you would have to take his word that he would keep to it."

"Not quite. He would gain financially, but in so doing we could hook him in a way that would negate any trickery."

"You've thought about this a good deal, Norman."

"I've had to. I still have to. From our viewpoint, it has now become a pity that whoever tried to kill him in prison did not succeed."

"Tread carefully, Norman. There is still Bulman, who might well be looking after Scott's interests."

"I've thought of that, too. Bulman's hands are tied. If he steps out of line Sir Lewis Hope will deal with it. We all have an interest. It's a domino effect. If we fall, the Home Office falls, and if they fall the Security Service will fall on this issue. If we all fall, and it would be impossible to keep the press out once it gained momentum, then the government will fall. A full inquiry into the issue could not possibly be avoided. The opposition would love to get hold of this."

"All because of one man?"

"Well, not quite. But Scott's the key. He's trouble. And he has now clearly shown it."

Powell tapped his desk, the noise irritating in the new silence. "Are you sure you can't get solid evidence against him? If you could then we would have no problem."

"We're still trying. All the time. It might be more difficult while he's out. He has underworld contacts."

"Perhaps," Powell said, looking directly at Murison, "it might be better if Scott did not survive." His voice was slightly hoarse.

"It might well be. Am I to action it?"

Powell covered himself as best he could. "The decision must be yours. Only you know whether Scott can be silenced by whatever evidence you might have against him. I will sanction the necessity as a last resort."

"Thank you, Sir Roland." Murison inclined his head and rose, satisfied that he had received the green light.

16

*B*ULMAN continued working with difficulty. It was now so stuffy in the office that both he and Haldean had loosened their ties and removed their jackets. Bulman had checked on the background of Peter Corrie, the ministry of defense man from whose apartment Wally Cooper had presumably taken the forged Mosley receipt, and had come up with nothing. He had checked the positive vetting of Corrie, who was apparently solid. It was true that Bulman had a contempt of the whole vetting system and had proclaimed that those who sat in judgment themselves needed vetting, as they seemed to be making too many errors of judgment. Even so, there was nothing to make him suspicious of Corrie in any possible way. Corrie was not a security risk. But that did not explain why he had a forged receipt in his possession.

Haldean had traced Raymond Langley, and here again all that was revealed was a solid, even brilliant, citizen who, through his financial wizardry had made a lot of money for Britain in hidden exports and a good deal for himself. And, when all said and done, it was his father's name on the receipt, not his. Both men were married with adult children who, in varying degrees, were themselves successful.

There are times when backgrounds can appear too solid. This was not the case with either man. One of Corrie's sons had entered into the drug scene and had finished by committing suicide while still at Oxford.

There was nothing sinister in the tragedy in any security sense. Just one more young man had collapsed under the pressures of modern life. If the son had lacked moral fiber, his father certainly made up for it. And one of Langley's daughters had married badly, her husband being a drifter. Langley had more than sufficient funds to keep the problem from his own doorstep. Nor was Langley involved at any level with national security. He was a money-making machine.

Bulman began to think he was entirely on the wrong track, yet Tom Moody had found a need to hide the Mosley receipt in Dick Avery's home. The receipt had to have some significance.

He went to the safe and for once felt apprehensive. He looked over his shoulder. Haldean's door was open and he was at his desk, but Bulman could not see him from his present angle. What the hell had got into him? He would trust Haldean as much as he would Scott. He opened the safe; the receipt was still there with the Mosley papers. He took the receipt out and went to the copying room. When he returned, he placed the original back in the safe, sealed the copy in an envelope, and put it in his hip pocket.

He glanced at his watch. It was time to go. Haldean, also working late, was clearing up in his office and locking his desk drawers. Bulman slipped on his jacket as Haldean came out of his tiny office. "I could grow tomatoes in there, guv," said Haldean as he locked his office door. "You solved your problems?"

"When have I ever solved my problems?"

"Well, go easy, guv, or you'll crack up. You've looked too worried of late."

"Well, this Scott business stinks."

"Are they after you, guv?"

"They? Who're you on about?"

"There have been some strange faces poking around the door when you've not been here. One came in and knocked your jacket off the stand. Oh, he picked it up and apologized when he saw me. But I was left wondering what he might have done had I not been here."

Bulman checked everything in his jacket, including the contents of his wallet. "Security or coppers?"

"Coppers wouldn't have the nerve to enter your office without a knock."

"Any reasons given?"

"There were two at different times. The last one called just now. He

208

asked for you and said he would call back. Maybe it's routine security to see if we leave the doors open when we're both out."

"And do we?"

"No, sir. No way."

"Well, there's nothing missing from my jacket. Nor anything added."

"Must be me. I sometimes worry about you."

"So you should. Anyway, thanks. Keep your eyes peeled, there's something bloody funny going on."

"As usual," Haldean grinned. The two men left the office, and Bulman turned the double lock. They went down together in the elevator.

The rush hour was in full swing. Bus queues were long, and people were irritable in the heat. Bulman was jostled with the rest but he refused to hurry. There was no chance of getting a cab at this hour, and he had no intention of using a police car. So he walked slowly up toward Trafalgar Square and tried to discover whether he was being followed. There were far too many people about to draw a conclusion. He had a long way to go, but he had left himself plenty of time.

It was clouding up, adding humidity to the heat, and Bulman slowed his already casual pace. A cab stopped near the top of Victoria Street, and Bulman homed in on it with a frantic signal as it disgorged a passenger. He waited impatiently while the cabbie was paid off, then climbed in and asked for Oxford Circus. If he had a tail, they would not be so lucky as he had just been.

He sat back, sweating and hot, and searched for a handkerchief. He patted his pockets and located a small hard lump. He pulled it out to find it was a homing device. His complacency at finding the cab left him. There was bound to be a following car somewhere in the traffic around the cab. Holding the bug in his hand, he guessed that it had been slipped into his pocket soon after he left the Yard.

In a way Bulman was glad it had happened. It clearly showed that Hope did not believe him about Scott. So why should Hope be so interested in Scott that he would have a homing device placed on one of his staff? Bulman pulled out a couple of pound notes and awaited an opportunity to get out. The cab was constantly stopping in traffic jams and at lights.

He bawled through the open glass panel behind the driver. "Take these. I'm going to drop off any minute."

"Okay, guv. Make sure you close the door."

Bulman stuffed the bug down the side of the passenger seat and kept a hand on the door catch. At the next holdup, in Whitehall, he opened the door, kept as low as he could, and sneaked through the stationary traffic.

He cut through under the arch toward the Horse Guards Parade and waited behind one of the pillars. There were plenty of people, even in this relatively quiet quarter, but nobody stopped or hesitated or reappeared. As he made his way toward the Mall, he was nervously attentive to the possibility of a tail. He simply wished he were better at it.

It was about six-fifteen when Bulman approached the Mitre public house from the Covent Garden side. To have come in from the other side would have meant passing the Horse's Head. He was not even sure that Willie Scott had understood his message.

The Mitre was one of their favorite pubs, not far from the Scott Travel Agency. Bulman waited across the street from it. There were ten minutes to go, and Bulman hovered in the doorway of a video shop, keeping to one side as people went in and out.

At precisely half-past six a voice behind Bulman said, "Hey, man. Got the time on you?"

Bulman started. He did not need to look around. "Where the hell did you spring from?"

"In the shop buying tapes. You're a bloody awful copper. Where shall we go?"

"Follow me. And watch my back, it's been prickling all day."

"There's nobody with you. Lead on."

Bulman led the way to the gardens in Leicester Square, again carefully avoiding the route past the Horse's Head. The square was always busy, but the gardens encased within it were an island of peace and floral tranquility. On full public view, it was an unlikely place for a wanted man to go.

Bulman found an empty bench and sat down with his back to the intermittent sun. At first he did not see Scott, who was much farther behind him than he had realized, but when he did he was shocked. Scott was dressed in a well cut, gray lightweight suit, expensive shoes, white shirt with a pale-green tie. And he was carrying a briefcase. Scott sat beside Bulman, his gaze quickly sweeping the gardens.

"What the hell has happened to your hair?" the astonished Bulman asked.

Without turning his head Scott replied, "I couldn't stay blond, so I've had it dyed as it used to be."

210

"As it used to be? Several shades darker, wouldn't you say? And you've had it trimmed. A business executive. Good outfit, Spider. They won't find you from the press mug shots. Nobody could from the fuzzed impressions that have been released, but I don't think it's the police who are meant to find you."

"Who then?"

"I can't get to the bottom of it. Someone is either giving the SIS a very bum steer on you, or it's the SIS itself."

"Before we go on, what about the casualties at Albany? Are they serious?"

"Most have left the hospital. No permanent injuries that I know of. No torn-off limbs. Cuts and bruises and shock."

"Thank God for that."

"Maybe I should never have delivered that letter. We're in trouble, Spider. Both of us. Real, deep trouble up to our hairlines. They planted a bug on me. If they'll do that to one of their own, what will they do to you?"

"I already know what they'll do to me."

"They'll be out hunting. They'll use everything they've got."

Scott was glad that Bulman had chosen to keep the sun behind them; it made it much easier to survey the square and he could see that Bulman, too, was constantly panning. "What the bloody hell have I done?"

"You turned over a stone on Tom Moody's grave."

"As a favor to you. I got nowhere."

"Oh, they'll get me, too, if they get you. Maybe in a different way, but they'll do it. Meanwhile I'm not the same danger to them; I'm harnessed."

"What the hell do you think I am? I'm on the bloody run for chrissake. How can I hurt anyone?"

"You know you were fixed up in stir. And they don't want anyone else to know. Also they can't be quite sure what you might have picked up there. If they had killed you in prison their problems would probably have been solved. They can silence my tongue and Dick Collins's. If we left the force, which would be futile, we'd still be covered by the Official Secrets Act. They can officially discount anything we might say. They can fix us, Spider. Unless we can fix them."

Scott was bewildered. "Are you talking of the Foreign Office?"

"Directly or indirectly. I don't know which. I don't know who might have their ear, but whether for themselves or because of what someone

211

else has produced for them, they certainly kept you inside, by the courtesy of the Home Office."

"But it was the Reverend who ordered the killing."

"I know. But he's just the operator— By the way, whatever you do, don't go home, even through the windows."

"I'm okay. I'm fixed up."

"They might try to tempt you to go home."

Scott eyed Bulman suspiciously. "Spit it out."

"They might try to get Maggie back."

Scott closed his eyes.

"You're showing too much emotion," Bulman warned.

"What do you expect? You know what it would do to her? Please God, no. They wouldn't do that."

"They would if they think it will pull you from your hole."

"Who have I got to get at?" Scott asked aggressively.

"Calm down. I have to tell you so that you don't fall for it."

"She was just recovering." Anguish was twisting Scott's features.

"I know. I'll sort her out. You'll have to trust me." And when Scott did not reply, "It's pressure on me too, you know. How do you think I feel? I started it all."

"No. Whoever killed Tom Moody started it. Fancy stringing up poor old Wally Cooper. He was no danger to anyone."

"It was beginning to look as if he might have been." Bulman watched Scott's passing emotions and chose his moment.

"You'll have to take over where Wally left off."

Scott tore his mind from Maggie. "You're crazy. He got thirty years, which was then upgraded to the death sentence. Tom got killed just for using him."

"They're going to kill you anyway. You can't stay on the run forever. They're not looking for Anthony Sims, only the police have been instructed to do that. They're looking for Spider Scott. The only chance is to find out what Tom knew. Strike back."

While Scott was thinking about it, Bulman produced the copy of the Mosley receipt. "Take a look at that."

Scott studied it. "So?"

"That's what Wally Cooper lifted, when he was supposed to have taken the defense papers from a guy called Peter Corrie. Defense Ministry."

"It doesn't mean anything to me." Before Bulman could reply, Scott added anxiously, "We've been in one spot too long. There might be an accidental sighting."

Bulman agreed. "Should be easier to get a cab now. The rush hour's dying. Stay there, I'll signal you."

Bulman found a cab and waved to Scott from the north side of the square. They climbed in, and in spite of the driver's objections about the heat, Bulman closed the driver's panel. Bulman said, "I've told him to drive to North Kensington." Bulman carefully put the receipt back into his hip pocket. "Mosley's signature is a forgery."

Scott was unimpressed, so Bulman added, "In the mid-thirties some influential British businessmen backed Sir Oswald Mosley, who was head of the British Union of Fascists. Most of them saw the red light and opted out later, but while they were in they gave Mosley financial backing. He was well off himself and very independent, but even so the sums that some of them gave must have helped the party considerably. A lot of it was in cash; the donors didn't want checks going through. Many didn't even want receipts. Most of the support was tacit, though some people did show themselves at functions. I should think they're all dead by now, but sons and daughters live on. Now, what does the forgery suggest to you?"

Scott was sitting well back in the cab, his briefcase on his knees. "Either someone was trying to implicate Robert Langley, or someone took the money and provided a receipt to cover his tracks."

"Which one?" Bulman demanded.

"I don't know. If businessmen were openly giving funds at that time, I can't see the value of implication. What could it have been worth?"

"Some gave openly, some not. It was not then a crime. As the war drew nearer, people changed their minds damned quick."

"Thirty thousand quid," Scott reflected. "A fortune then, I suppose."

"There were some very wealthy people about. So you think it was stolen?"

Scott was fascinated by the passing traffic. Eleven days in jail could seem an eternity. "It's possible. But how? Once it was delivered, or before it got there?"

"Ah! You've pressed the button. If it was after delivery, then it was someone in the Mosley organization. If before, either the person delivering it was mugged and was scared stiff to admit it, in case he wouldn't be believed, or the courier himself took it."

"Wouldn't Langley deliver it himself?"

"Possibly. Or someone he trusted."

"Do I assume his family didn't need the money?"

"They were extremely wealthy. Fortunes changed later."

"So a trusted outsider?" Scott turned sideways to get full sight of Bulman. "If Wally broke in for that, what good would it do if I went in?"

"We need something more than the receipt. We're guessing. There must be something else." Bulman suddenly lowered his voice, as if the driver could hear. "This receipt fingers someone."

"But it's over fifty years ago, George. Who the hell cares now? Nobody will be arrested for it."

"It's more than the theft."

"You think someone in the Foreign Office had something to do with it? Doesn't want the ghost raised?"

"If it was something like that, he'd be retired by now. It can't be that. Break in and see what you can find."

"You mean it can't be any worse for me?"

"Well, can it? For either of us? I'm supposed to be a copper, and I'm riding around with a villain every police force in the country is supposed to be looking for. I'm asking you to break into a top civil servant's flat. How much worse could it be for me?"

"Have you got the address?"

Bulman fiddled in his pocket. "Here, I wrote it down." Seeing that Scott was still hesitant, Bulman said, "They'd be bloody hard pushed to arrest somebody who was knocking off the same flat. They can't pull the defense papers lark again or Corrie will be considered a poor security risk."

"Okay. But I want something from you."

Bulman gave Scott a sideways glance. "Go on."

"I want you to see Rex Reisen. I can't go myself because it's widely known that I know him. With his underworld network it would be a natural for me to approach him."

"I wouldn't get past the front door, Spider. He *really* hates my guts. He knows I'd pull him in twice a day if I could. Anyway, if MI6 is keeping tabs on him to see if you turn up they'll see me. Can't risk it."

"Find a way, George." Scott was angry. "You damn well find a way. I want to know whether Rex was asked to put a contract on me. He knows I'm loose; you'll have to convince him you're speaking for me. If he was asked and turned it down for old times' sake, tell him the Reverend was given it and I want to know why. If he wasn't asked, I still want to know why; he hates the Reverend's guts even more than he hates yours."

17

"**G**UV'NOR, I want a favor."

Collins looked up from his desk as if he could not believe his ears. "I'm on the verge of being suspended and you want another favor? George, you can't be serious."

"I want to make contact with Rex Reisen, and the only way I can do that without the wrong people knowing is for you to pull him in."

"Have you seen Willie Scott?" Collins asked suspiciously.

"No. You should know better."

"You're lying through your teeth, George."

"I'm lying through my teeth to everyone; you're not a special case, sir."

"George, you are playing a very dicey game. You're heading for big trouble."

"I'm already in big trouble. I'm like a gambler who has lost his lot and his only hope is a last throw. What difference can it make to me?"

"You want to take me down with you? All the way?"

"I'm trying to get us both out of a mess. We either throw in the towel and pretend nothing has happened, and in so doing throw Willie Scott into the grave we dug for him, or we strike back. There are no official guidelines we can follow. We're being blocked and pressured by our own people, who are showing far too many signs that they have far too much to hide."

217

"You know how it is with the cloak-and-dagger brigade. They're probably protecting greater issues. This time I really can't help. I'm sorry."

"And Willie?"

"Don't throw him at me, George. I did what you wanted. I'm not responsible for what followed. Anyway, it will all work out in the wash. The Foreign Office might be right about him, but you won't accept it because you're too screwed up."

"And Tom Moody? Godfather to your children?"

"We did our best. Look where it's got us."

Bulman tried to hide his disappointment.

Collins, observing this, added, "George, it's not just a matter of giving in. Reisen is no direct concern of mine. I'd have to fix it with the West End Central Division, and that means involving other coppers. I could use my muscle or, like you, ask a favor, but it wouldn't be right to drag them in. Don't you think two of us in this kind of trouble is enough?"

"Sure. You're right, of course."

BACK IN HIS office, Bulman stared solemnly at Haldean's back. He got a direct line and rang Sir Stuart Halliman. It was almost as though Halliman had been sitting waiting for the call. They arranged to meet at Halliman's club in Pall Mall.

Bulman was dismayed by the further change in the retired intelligence chief. He would have been surprised to learn that Halliman had at once noticed Bulman's own tiredness and suppressed anxiety.

"Have lunch with me," Halliman invited as they sat down in the bar.

"I really haven't the time, Sir Stuart."

"Damn the time." Halliman brushed his mustache. His hair was noticeably grayer, and he appeared to have lost more weight. "I've no doubt you're worried sick about Willie. My God, it's all turned full circle."

"He's in a far worse position now than when he worked for you. It's his life they want, and quickly."

"Who's they?"

"I have an idea you might know that. The attempts are being channeled through a mobster called Phil Deacon, nicknamed the Reverend."

"Well, at least you've come up with that much. You think he killed Tom?"

"Had him killed. Have you still got contacts with the Foreign Office?"

"A specific department?"

"MI6 or the SIS in general?"

"They've been barricaded against me for some time. I can understand; they don't want an old boy poking his nose in."

"But you have a feeling that you don't like what's going on there?"

"That's pretty broad, George. I have no idea what's going on there. I wish I did."

"Does it worry you?"

"Considerably. Tom spoke to me in much the same vein. He did not get too far with it. So very sad."

"Do you think we're being sold down the river?"

"Aren't these questions for Lewis Hope?"

"I've more or less tried them. The old-boy network has closed its ranks, right or wrong."

"I don't think you need worry about moles, or state secrets being passed on, or anything like that. Not in regard to this issue. My feeling is that it's much more serious than that."

"Could you enlighten me?"

"No more than you can enlighten me. It's an instinctive feeling, founded on what happened to Tom and Wally Cooper. It really has a very nasty smell. It worries me a good deal, but I'm completely out of circulation. I no longer have influence and even if I had, to whom would I direct it?"

"You mean whom can you trust?"

Halliman raised his drink with a wintry smile. "Willie's in dire trouble, and you're not getting anywhere, are you?"

Bulman produced the copy of the Mosley receipt. "What do you make of that?"

Halliman studied it. "Why don't you have a word with the present Lord Langley?"

"I considered that. I don't think it would get me anywhere at all. I think the timing is wrong. I need to know something more first. Anyway, I shouldn't think he'd be pleased to be reminded of it, assuming he knows about it."

Halliman handed back the receipt, and Bulman said apologetically, "I should have mentioned that Mosley's signature is a forgery."

Halliman stiffened. "A forgery? A *forgery?* Good Lord."

219

"It means something to you?"

"Half-a-dozen possibilities."

"That's the trouble."

Halliman leaned forward to tap Bulman's knee. "You could be right about the timing, yet it will have to be done. Do you know where Willie is?"

"No. But I've seen him. He's following another line. He wants me to contact Rex Reisen. It's not easy for me. I have a tail. They even planted a bug on me and finished up chasing a taxi around London. They'll expect Willie to go to Reisen for help. Can you arrange a meet between Reisen and me?"

"I hardly know the man."

"But you represent what Reisen always imagines himself to be. He won't know you've retired. If you approach him it will be an enormous coup for him. He'll run up the Union Jack over all his clubs and particularly the one on the gold stand in his office."

"Perhaps, after this meeting, they'll keep an eye on me too, George. But, yes, I can find a way." Halliman was almost his old self. "Let's have that lunch. What a great pity Willie can't join us."

THE SUN REFLECTED off the water in blinding shafts, and the heat was baking. The ship's air conditioning was straining to keep the temperature at an acceptable level. Yachts rocked gently in the Piraeus harbor, and taxis waited on the quay, their metalwork hot to the touch.

Maggie had finished breakfast with her parents and returned to her cabin to freshen up preparatory to going on tour along the coast road to Sounion. There was a knock on the door, and when she called "enter," a well-dressed stranger stood apologetically in the doorway.

"Mrs. Scott?"

"Yes." Maggie had expected the steward or one of her parents.

"I'm Neil Cole from the British embassy in Athens. May I have a word with you?" Cole held out a card for Maggie to see. He was a presentable young man of middle height, with friendly blue eyes, and he wore a fawn linen suit.

"Yes, of course, although I can't imagine what about."

"Are we likely to be disturbed here?"

"I shouldn't think so. I'm meeting my parents in about half an hour."

Maggie, who had put on some needed weight, and was now very brown, was puzzled.

"Oh, that's more than enough. May I close the door? What I have to say is quite private."

Maggie took another look at her caller and decided there was nothing to alarm her. "Please do."

"Good." Cole closed the door and stood by it. He took some papers from his breast pocket and handed a photograph to Maggie. "Is that your husband, Mrs. Scott?"

Maggie took one look at it and said angrily, "Where did you get this? It belongs in our apartment."

Cole was apologetic as he had been throughout. "I believe that's a copy, actually. But it is your husband?"

"Yes, it is." Maggie felt her blood receding. She groped for the edge of the bed.

"I had to be sure." Cole offered a difficult smile of reassurance. "I've received information from London. It would seem that your husband has broken out of prison . . ." Cole's mouth opened silently as Maggie slipped to the floor in a faint.

He did all the right things, and when she started to come around he poured her some water and helped her onto a chair. She was deathly white.

"I'm so sorry," said Cole. "I had no idea . . ."

"Please get on with it, Mr. Cole. I'm all right. Really." Maggie sipped the water, her hands trembling.

"He was in prison under the name of Anthony Sims. He was apparently in prison helping the police to get information from another prisoner. Nobody knows why he broke out. But he's believed to be in grave danger, and it's important that he is quickly found for his own safety. It is hoped that you can help."

Her mind was spinning, she could not grasp what was happening. She felt herself going faint again and quickly put her head between her knees. When she raised it, Cole was fluttering and had lost almost as much color as she.

"You're saying that my husband is still free?"

"That appears to be so."

"But the police know who he really is?"

221

Cole, clearly flustered, quickly referred to some notes. "Only certain senior policemen, who were instrumental in obtaining your husband's cooperation, know who he really is. His real name is being withheld until there is clarification of what precisely is happening."

"But *you* know his real name, Mr. Cole."

"I understand the Foreign Office were informed in order that you might be contacted."

Her mind was still reeling, but Maggie was beginning to think.

"What happens if you find him?"

Cole shrugged. "Mrs. Scott, I'm a messenger boy. There's obviously a grave misunderstanding somewhere, but I am strongly advised that Mr. Scott is in the greatest possible danger and it is important that he is found by the authorities. I would not be here if the danger to your husband was not considered to be real."

Cole's comment seemed reasonable enough. The Foreign Office would not otherwise involve itself. "What is it you want of me?" she asked listlessly.

"We can fly you back to London. It is possible that your husband will try to contact you once you are back. It is then hoped that he will listen to you and understand his danger."

As shattered as she was, Maggie began to see some flaws. "How will my husband know I am back if you don't know where he is?"

"I can't answer you, Mrs. Scott. I can only give you the position as I have been instructed to. Nobody can make you go back if you would rather stay."

Dreading it, Maggie knew quite well that it would be impossible for her to stay. At least in London she would be available should anything suddenly happen. "When do I fly?"

"I can see that you catch this afternoon's flight."

"I can't stay here until this afternoon. I cannot face my parents with this. I'll leave them a note. I can pack a few things now, but you'll have to accommodate me until the plane leaves."

"You can stay at the embassy. I'm sure that can be arranged."

Maggie checked the time. Cole had been there less than ten minutes and in that short time had turned her world on its head. She reached for pen and paper.

WILLIE SCOTT EMPTIED the briefcase of the videotapes he had

222

bought and left them for Sophie. He visited the nearest locksmith and took some leaflets advertising the Chubb Security Systems, which he placed in the case. He then took a cab to Kensington. It was mid-afternoon and the fine weather was bordering on a drought. He was grateful to Sophie for the clothes she had chosen for him; the fit was remarkably good.

Peter Corrie lived in a modern apartment house on the next-to-top floor, one short of the penthouse. The building was behind Kensington High Street, in one of the small tributaries off a small square that had at its center an elongated railing-enclosed garden where residents basked or exercised their dogs. There were two entrances to the building, each with a porter behind a small desk next to an elevator.

Scott was well versed in avoiding porters; they were human with normal needs. He chose his moment and took the elevator to the eighth floor, then walked down to the seventh. Peter Corrie lived in apartment 702, and Scott rang the bell—turning full face to the spy hole in the door. While he waited, he examined the locks. Both appeared to be reasonably straightforward. His skeleton keys and the detachable shank he had made himself were in his own apartment, but he had made a few useful purchases.

Nobody came to the door so he rang again, keeping his thumb on the button. Nobody passed him while he stood there, and only once did he hear the elevator doors clang from the nearby shaft. He rang a third time and could hear the buzzer quite clearly.

Scott took hold of the brass doorknob and pushed the door to assess the pressure. There was resistance, but only from the Yale above the mortise. He produced several sheets of plastic about the size of pocket calendars, which he had got Sophie to buy for him, and placed them in the space between door and jamb, above the Yale. As he pushed the pieces in, the gap widened until he could force no more. He took another strip and inserted it opposite the lock and pushed hard. The catch went, he shouldered the door, and it flew open. He quickly closed the door behind him.

He searched quickly and thoroughly. The drawers of the desk in the small study were unlocked but contained nothing of real interest. He found the safe in the bathroom. A medicine cabinet swung back and there it was; an unusual place. It was covered by a locked wooden door he had little difficulty in opening, but one glance at the safe behind it was

223

enough; he was not equipped to open it. He needed to get his own tools, and that was impossible as things stood. He closed and locked the wooden door covering the safe. As he clicked the cabinet back into position, he reflected that Wally had done well to open it. He reached the hall as a key turned in the front door lock. Scott opened the nearest door and found himself in the stifling closeness of a walk-in clothes closet that he had already searched.

The front door opened and closed. He shrank back as far as he could. After a while he released the door a fraction. It opened the wrong way, so at first he had to use it as a listening post. Water was running in the kitchen. Scott stepped out. The living room door off the hall was wide open, and a woman's crocodile handbag was perched on the back of a sofa.

Scott closed the door quietly and opened the front door as the kitchen tap was turned off. He stepped out and pulled the front door shut very slowly. He stood with his back to the wall, waiting. When he felt ready, he leaned across and rang the bell.

He was standing straight in front of the spy hole when the door was opened. The woman who stood there looked as if she had just returned from a photographic call for *Vogue.* The light, silk, floral, sleeveless dress she wore hung superbly. Her face was coldly beautiful, wide eyes calculating and sweeping. Her mouth was perfectly outlined, her skin too perfect, without laughter or character lines.

"Yes?" It was as chilling as a rapier thrust.

"I'm from Chubbs, madam. Security. I think you will be interested in what I have to offer."

"We have a security system, thank you."

She was about to close the door when Scott said smoothly,

"I'm afraid it's not very good, madam. You forgot to lock the mortise when you went out, and I had no difficulty in getting in."

She stared in disbelief, then her gaze frosted up and she said, "I must say your approach is original. It's also ridiculous. Goodbye."

Scott put his foot in the door and replied easily, "Your crocodile handbag is on the back of your tan-colored leather sofa, and your safe is behind the bathroom cupboard. May we talk, madam?"

There was more than a touch of fear about her now. Her image was still cold, but her manner was less certain. "I'm going to call the police." She tried to close the door, but Scott now wedged the case in the gap.

"If you scream," Scott said quietly, "I'll shoot you as you stand. *Don't move at all.*"

Her frightened eyes gazed down at the hand in his jacket pocket and the bulge that she saw there.

Scott watched the hauteur crumble. This woman was used to treading on people; threats were for others. Until now. A little less coldly he said, "I don't want to harm you in any way, but I do need to talk to you. After that I shall leave, and then you can scream as much as you like and call whom you like. Step back carefully." Scott did not take his eyes off her as he pushed the case inside the door and followed. The first sign of a scream and he would have to stop her.

Once inside, her fear showed more clearly. There were quick thrusts of iciness as she backed into the living room, but overall she was very scared. Vulnerability was almost a new experience in her selfish and pampered life.

"There," Scott said more amiably, "is your handbag where I said it was."

She had her back to the sofa, one hand on its arm to steady herself. "If you were in here," she asked nervously, "why did you leave?"

"I was leaving as you came in. I hid in the clothes closet. Had I crept up you might have screamed before I reached you."

"What do you want?" Jeweled fingers nervously covered a modest cleavage.

"If you are Mrs. Anita Corrie, I want you to open the safe."

Her eyes flickered. "Only my husband has the combination."

Scott smiled. "There is no way any man could keep a combination from someone like you, is there? I would guess you've had your way all your life."

Anita Corrie had pushed herself away from the sofa and had moved slightly along it. Her gaze still drifted to the bulge of Scott's pocket.

"Don't dive for the phone. Don't get suddenly brave and scream, Mrs. Corrie. Your husband is in dire trouble. He has committed perjury in a court case that sent a man to prison for thirty years and who was murdered only recently. So get rid of any notion that the police will help you, or you're going to have your precious face splashed all over the news sheets."

Anita Corrie sank against the sofa again. "I haven't the slightest idea what you mean." Her voice was quivering.

225

"That's more than likely. You will, of course, tell your husband that I've been here. Tell him too, that we have the receipt."

"Receipt?"

"That's right. Just remember it."

"Who are you?"

"He'll know that, too. I'll tell you one thing, Mrs. Corrie; *he* won't ring the police. He can't pull that dodge twice. Who do you think he might ring?"

"I don't understand what you're saying."

"That's possible. So let's get on with it. Open up."

He followed her into the bathroom. "There's nothing in it," she protested. "It's a waste of time."

"Just open it."

When she did, he made her stand between the bath and himself so that she could not dive for the door. He examined the contents. There were several jewel boxes containing precious stones set in gold brooches, exquisite necklaces, and rings. Scott gazed at them appreciatively but there was no time to linger.

In a trembling voice Anita Corrie asked, "Do you intend to take them?"

Scott gazed at her scathingly. "Now you're letting your real interest show." He shook his head and carefully put the boxes back, one by one. "No," he said, "They are far too nice to break down." He closed the safe. "That's a lot of jewelry for a civil servant to buy."

"My husband is next in line as a permanent under secretary. We are not poor."

"That's when he gets knighted, isn't it? I bet you can't wait to be *Lady* Corrie. Where's his address book?"

"He keeps things like that in his office."

"Ministry of Defense?"

"Yes."

"That explains why I couldn't find it. Thank you, Mrs. Corrie. I'm sorry I scared you. Perhaps you have no part in all this except to spend his money." Scott went back to the living room. "Whatever you do, don't ring the police until you've spoken to your husband. He won't thank you for it. And you could miss out on that title." Scott retrieved his case from the hall and left.

MAGGIE SCOTT HAD nothing to do but worry for over four hours on the Athens-London flight. It was impossible for her to imagine what Willie had been up to in her short absence. It put the clock right back to the early days of their association, but he had never broken out of prison before. Neil Cole of the British embassy in Athens had been extremely kind and courteous to her. He had provided her with lunch and tea and a small room to wait in.

At London Airport she was stopped at immigration and politely escorted to a room where a young man, taller than Neil Cole and a little older, introduced himself as Freddie Ashton from the Foreign Office. He had a car waiting for her. She could not understand the fuss.

Ashton did not go through customs; he escorted Maggie to a waiting black Daimler limousine and even carried her solitary suitcase. It was all so organized. In the privacy of the back of the huge car, Maggie asked, "Where are you taking me?"

"I'm so sorry. I thought you realized. To your flat, of course, Mrs. Scott. It's the least we can do."

"My husband breaks jail, and I'm escorted home by a Foreign Office official? Why?"

"We dragged you away from a holiday, what else could we do? You must understand that your husband's jailbreak is something of a complete mystery. Neil Cole, I do hope he looked after you by the way, had only part of the story. It appears that your husband agreed to go to Albany Prison as a police plant to pick up important information from someone there who would not volunteer it to the police. *Very* few people knew of it, otherwise it would have been too risky. The Home Office *had* to be informed, of course. But the police in general had absolutely no idea."

"But *you* knew, Mr. Ashton." Maggie preferred the naturalness of Neil Cole in Athens to this sharp-featured man.

"Yes, indeed. We had an interest in someone there and, through liaison with the Home Office, were instrumental in keeping your husband there a day or two longer once we realized who he was."

Ashton offered a professional smile. "He has quite a reputation, Mrs. Scott. In the best possible way. We were looking for someone in Albany for a quite different reason to the one he went in for and had approached the Home Office for help. They usually refer to the police, of course. So

227

we were delighted to learn that the job was already half done for us. He had to be given time to finish what he went in for before we approached him, and alas, he was attacked during that time."

"Attacked?" Maggie was horrified. What other nightmares had she to prepare for? "Attacked?"

"Oh, nothing serious." Ashton waved away the very notion. "He's perfectly fit, I assure you. But somebody went for him, and he was laid up for a day or two. I'm afraid these sorts of things sometimes happen in prison. Men get frustrated at being incarcerated. But it unfortunately held up our approach to him while he recovered. We could hardly ask a favor while he was laid low, and we decided to keep him there meanwhile. Then, before we could communicate he, with an accomplice, blew his way out." Ashton straightened his creases. "We feel rather guilty about keeping him there a day or two extra. Nobody knows why he escaped."

"He's still missing?"

"Absolutely. I must tell you that there is no danger of scandal to you. The total number of people who know the background to this are few indeed, and they are all top people. The press was given a mock-up sketch from which nobody could identify your husband. Whether the sketch of his accomplice is any better, I'm in no position to judge; that was based on evidence from the Albany Prison staff; it was conflicting as these things invariably are. The man everyone is looking for is Anthony Sims, the name under which your husband entered prison. So don't worry."

"My husband is missing, and you say don't worry?"

"You know what I mean. I'm quite sure he'll turn up."

"I can't see why he found the need to break out in the first place."

Ashton was holding on to the hand-strap, peering through the window. He nodded. "It *is* difficult to understand. Something must have happened in prison to scare him."

"He doesn't scare in that way. He would not panic. If he broke out, then there are solid reasons."

"Oh, I'm sure you're right. It would be useful to know them."

Maggie sat back, thinking. Now she was facing the problem, she was more objective. She was grateful to Ashton for giving her the detail, but she recalled various bits and pieces that she had learned from Willie and Sir Stuart Halliman, who was then code-named Fairfax, and, even more recently, from George Bulman. She said, "What is the Foreign Office's interest in anyone in Albany? Your field is overseas, surely."

Ashton laughed. "Well, of course, that's generally right. But nothing is so simple, Mrs. Scott. If only it were. All sorts of people are in British prisons, some from abroad, some with clandestine connections abroad. As an example, the IRA and the Libyans and the Red Brigade in Italy, and so on. The IRA is ostensibly a domestic issue, but that's a Walter Mitty belief. Naturally, knowledge is shared between departments when appropriate. I don't think I'm giving anything away by telling you that." And then he added teasingly, "I do hope you won't press me for detail."

Maggie sighed. "I don't know yet what Willie went in for. He loathes prison. It had to be serious. Was it about Tom Moody?"

"Moody? I seem to recall . . . wasn't he the retired policeman who collapsed or something? Is that whom you mean?"

"He was supposed to have slipped on a bar of soap."

"Poor fellow. I don't know why your husband went in. That would be beyond my brief. Someone in the Home Office must know, of course."

Maggie was reluctant to mention George Bulman. She had the feeling that to do so might get him into trouble. He was the one person who might be able to help her. When she reached the flat she would ring him. "You've been kind, Mr. Ashton. I appreciate the trouble you have taken, and Mr. Cole in Athens could not have done more for me."

"I'm so glad. This, though, is where we part." The car was pulling up outside the apartment building. "You will let us know if your husband contacts you? I'm sure we can straighten things out in no time at all. Here is my card, Mrs. Scott. If I'm not there you will be given another number. Let me take your suitcase. Please, I insist."

LATER THAT SAME evening Ashton and Murison decided to take a leisurely walk together. This in itself was strange and offered the unspoken inference that both men had taken from the present situation. Four walls no longer seemed safe. It was a sign of nervousness, although each would have denied it and neither gave any sign of it. But Murison voiced the root of it as they strode through the quietening Chelsea streets. "I won't be happy until Scott is stopped."

"Amen," Ashton supplied. The two men were still dressed as if for the office. They stood in front of an antique shop, gazing at the copper pans and Victorian bric-a-brac, and also the passing reflections of other people. It was just after nine and still light.

Ashton glanced apprehensively at Murison, at the moment aware of their disparity of rank. "Do you think it was wise to bring back Mrs. Scott, sir?"

"Don't call me sir because you think I might not like the question, Freddie. Of course I think it was right or I wouldn't have done it. We haven't put a foot wrong where she's concerned. We helped and cosseted her. Even taken a little of the blame for her husband's plight. You've told her enough of the truth to convince her, and the known facts will back up what you said. The prison governor was advised by the Home Office, in consultation with us, that Scott was to be released in two days at the most. Then he broke out. We have already substantially paved the way for a cover-up, if one is ever needed."

"What happens if the telephone and the apartment are found to be bugged?"

Murison chuckled. "Haven't you heard that Scott was tied up with Tuomo and Moody? Anyone could have put them there, including the police under the auspices of the Home Office. Provided there are two or three possibilities there will always be doubt, and it will always be unprovable. Besides, she's not likely to discover them."

"She's an intelligent woman. Well-bred."

"So I understand. I wonder how she became hooked up with someone like Scott." They moved away from the window and continued to walk on. "You know, Freddie, you give the strong impression that there's something you're not happy about."

"Basically, it's the same problem. Scott is loose. We would not want him to do what Moody did. I can't see Scott contacting his wife. He's no fool."

"He'll contact her one way or the other. Directly or indirectly."

"Our resources are limited."

"Indeed they are. But they are in the right places." Murison slowed his pace, as if he had walked enough. "And, of course, we have help when we need it."

They walked on in silence, bareheaded and hot. The light was beginning to go, and the noise of traffic was amplified on the warm air. The smell of petrol and oil clung to the streets.

Murison said, "Remember one thing about Maggie Scott. She has

230

already made it worth our while in bringing her back. She confirmed to you that Scott is looking into the death of Moody. That's valuable confirmation. She's also an insurance, Freddie."

"What about Bulman?"

"He will certainly contact her once he discovers she's back."

"He could well find the bugs. He would expect them."

"Oh, he'll take her somewhere. Come on, Freddie. Cheer up, old boy. You of all people should be looking forward to Bulman's taking Maggie Scott out. We're banking on it. Bulman is the most likely person to make direct contact with Scott. We want them both."

MURISON HAD TALKED himself into a relaxed frame of mind by the time he parted from Ashton. When he found a highly agitated Peter Corrie waiting outside his Chelsea house, his mood changed quickly. "What on earth are you doing here?"

"He held Anita up, damn it. Made her open the safe."

"Keep your voice down, for God's sake."

"I have to tell you." Corrie grasped Murison's arm. *"He has the receipt, man."*

"Let's walk." Murison led the way. By now it was almost entirely dark. "Now calm down. Who the blazes are you talking about?"

"It can only be Scott. Who else could it possibly be?"

"Tell me exactly what happened and stop being damned hysterical."

"It didn't happen to you. My God, he threatened her with a gun."

Murison stopped on a corner. "Evidently she survived to tell the tale. Do get on with it, Peter."

Corrie gazed around, as if he were surrounded. Every protrusion cast shadow, every light a threat. He found the biggest patch of dark shadow and stood in it, as if it would protect him. Then, when Murison followed he related the story his wife had told him. When he had finished, Murison asked, "Did Anita give a description?"

Corrie passed it on.

"*Dark* hair, did you say? Briefcase and business suit? If it's Scott he's dyed his hair again. And he must still have help." Murison shook Corrie by the arm. "Dammit, Peter, this isn't like you. Pull yourself together."

"He went for Anita. Don't you understand?"

"Anita's perfectly capable of looking after herself. Nothing was taken."

"But the receipt. He knows about it. He has it. It doesn't seem to worry you."

"It doesn't much. Its history is too complicated. We already knew it was missing. But if it was Scott who called, it looks as if he has been in touch with Bulman already. It must have been when Bulman dumped the bug. Bulman must have the receipt."

"We must get it back, Norman."

"It would be preferable, I grant you, but he's hardly likely to keep it at home; not Bulman."

"If we got it back there would be no problem."

"Perhaps. We don't know what Scott and Bulman have found out."

"But the receipt is the key. It always has been."

Murison gazed into the thickening darkness. A woman went past with a dog and for a while neither man spoke. When it was safe again, Murison said, "It might be the key for us, but I doubt that it will be for anyone else. It would take one hell of a lot of unraveling."

"So why the drastic measures when it disappeared?" Corrie was thinking logically again.

"Let's go down the street a bit." They walked slowly, window lights spreading a pale haze. "We were right to do what we did. And the same rule still applies. We don't want a situation of 'case not proven.' We want no fingers pointing at us, no suspicion of any kind. We simply can't afford it. There is far too much at stake. And they might strike lucky. We did, after all. No, Peter, we must finish the job. I'll have to step up the search for Scott. He's trying to panic us, don't you see? He certainly succeeded with you. Did Anita see the gun?"

"He kept it in his pocket, pointing at her."

"He would have shown it if he'd had one. But he must be stopped quickly. We can gag Bulman meanwhile, but Scott has to be found and silenced. The attempt in prison proves someone was already after him, don't you see? Go back home and forget all about it. By the way, did you speak to Muriel?"

"I merely rang the bell and asked for you. She asked me in, but I said I'd come back later."

"Good man." Murison turned back toward his house.

"I won't take the receipt again," Corrie asserted. "If it ever turns up."

"If it ever turns up we burn it," Murison replied. "We should have done it a long time ago. You sleep. I'll fix Scott."

232

18

*M*AGGIE felt intolerably lonely in the apartment. She ached for Willie and for knowledge of where he was and what had happened to him. She was surrounded by his presence in the home they had built up together. Yet in spite of her anxiety, her misery at not knowing what was happening, she had regained a resolve that had deserted her after the loss of her baby.

Willie was in danger. She did not know from whom, but she knew that Willie had to be desperate to do what he had. It was no new situation to her. She dreaded it. Yet all her feelings, her considerable determination, her love, went out to the only person who really mattered in her life. Willie needed help. It was enough to shut out any remorse or depression she had suffered before leaving for Greece.

Since being back, she had frequently tried to raise George Bulman, but each time he had been out. She had left a message with Sergeant Haldean.

The shops were shut by the time she had arrived home. Ashton had carried her suitcase up for her and had accepted her invitation to coffee. It was lucky he had preferred it black for there was no fresh milk or cream. While she made the coffee he had used the telephone to advise his office where he was. In the end he had seemed reluctant to go, as if appreciating that when he did she would be left with only her own thoughts. And that was how it had turned out.

She was afraid to leave the flat in the event of the telephone ringing, yet in the morning she would have to do some shopping. The thought of going to bed alarmed her. There were apartments all around, yet she felt vulnerable. She started when the doorbell rang. Opening the front door, she was just about to call out with relief at the sight of Bulman, when he stepped forward and clamped a hand over her mouth. He still held her as he said in a cultivated voice, "Good evening. I'm so sorry to disturb you at this time, but I'm looking for Mrs. Grealish?"

Bulman took his hand from Maggie's mouth, and she said as steadily as she could, "She's the next floor up. Directly above this one."

"Thank you so much." Bulman stepped in with his finger to his lips and closed the door. He whispered in Maggie's ear, "We're leaving the flat."

She nodded silently and, misunderstanding him, went back into the living room to get a handbag and jacket. Bulman was still standing by the door but his appearance startled her. In that short time he had donned a gray wig and matching mustache. He held his finger up again to caution her. He opened the door silently, and when she had preceded him into the corridor he closed the door carefully. Still he warned her not to speak. And then, to her amazement, he began to search her, starting with the pockets of her jacket.

It probably would be impossible for her to have a bug on her person without her knowledge, but, even so, he checked her small emerald earrings that went so well with her auburn hair and then turned out her handbag. The bug had been forced into one corner. Only an inspection like Bulman's would have found it, unless Maggie had lost something and turned the bag out herself.

He held it up for her to see, placed the bug back in the handbag, unlocked the door with her keys, then pushed the bag in the apartment hall and quietly closed the door again. He gave her a peck on the cheek, embarrassed yet pleased. "Not used to it," he explained in a normal voice. "Good to see you, Maggie."

"Oh, George." She was on the point of tears. "What's going on? Is Willie all right?"

"Willie's fine. Look, I can't take you out. They'll see us. I had to wear this stupid disguise to get in. The damned mustache is tricky. We'd better go down to the basement."

They took the elevator down. At the bottom two bare electric bulbs cast light and shadow over pipes and empty cases. They went around the corner of the elevator shaft, and there was Willie's bicycle propped against a chipped plaster wall. Maggie's hands went slowly to her mouth.

"Steady, Mag." Bulman put an arm around her shoulders. "I saw him. Never looked so well."

"What about the attack on him?"

"Oh, I believe it's a bit sore. But he's solid. You know Willie. Fit as a flea. It hasn't slowed him down."

"Are you going to tell me what happened?"

"Bloke took a skewer to him. But Willie was too quick. I saw him down there afterward. Now sit on that empty box, I'll sit on this one and I'll tell you what I know."

And Bulman did; he told her everything he knew because he did not consider she could be in any more danger than she was already. They would use her if they had to, in order to get at Willie. It was better that she knew this and the actual extent of the danger. It was no use trying to fool her because Willie was on the run. Nor was it any use asking her to go away again; she had been away and had chosen to return, and here she would stay until Willie was straightened out.

They sat opposite each other in the poor light, hearing the rumbles of the hot water pipes, while Bulman explained what he knew. When he had finished, she sat quietly for some time. "How can you possibly win if every official hand is turned against you? Wouldn't it be better to give up?"

"I've considered giving up. It goes against the grain, but in any event it's too late now, Maggie. They would always be wondering. If they'll kill Tom Moody and Wally Cooper and who knows who else, they won't suddenly start trusting people. I don't know what they have to hide, but they're willing to bend the rules and to kill for it. But not every hand is against us."

"That's what it seems like, George."

"It's the old-boy network. One ministry asks another a favor, which seems perfectly reasonable at the time. They put up a plausible case and who will doubt colleagues, even if in another department? They've known each other for years. Some went to school together. It works for me with Special Branch. The old pals' act. And I get information far quicker than going through normal channels, where I might be blocked.

235

Normally, there's nothing wrong with it. If there is a sinister reason, then at some point cooperation begins to crack. The trouble is that department chiefs are too apt to protect their own against others. It's both a strength and a weakness, but it protects the bad guys for a while."

"They seem to be all bad guys."

"To me too, but it's not the case. A bad boss who has made a gaff will keep it to himself, and sometimes that means continuing the gaff. He certainly won't want his staff to expose it. Someone who's really on top of his job doesn't give a damn. He can and will cope, regardless. Right now Dick Collins and I are under extreme pressure and are not too well trusted because someone, somewhere, is putting up a much more plausible case than we are. A detached look at what Dick and I did doesn't come out too well. How do you say to your boss, we did it this way because we don't trust you? I disobeyed orders because I think you're a bloody idiot, sir? In my game, Maggie, this sort of thing can happen. Eyes swivel at the slightest suspicion."

"You're only confirming what I said, George. Whatever the reasons, you can't beat the system."

Bulman reached out and took her hands. "If I thought that, Maggie, if part of the system is corrupt, then I'd have quit long ago. Willie would agree with me."

"Where is he, George?"

"I don't know and I don't want to know."

"But you've seen him."

"We met. It's up to him to contact me again. But he's well set up, well dressed. Fit. The police sketch is useless; apart from Dick Collins and myself and a deputy commissioner, maybe the commissioner himself, they are all looking for the wrong fellow. It's the Home and Foreign Offices we have to worry about. I think the Home Office is clean, so that narrows it down to the Foreign Office. Someone there has a lot to protect. Both Willie and I are working on it."

"Are you saying that Neil Cole in Athens and Mr. Ashton here, are involved against Willie?"

Bulman grimaced. "I shouldn't think the Athens people have the slightest idea of what's going on. They merely acted for London. They would have been genuine. But Ashton is another matter. He showed his hand quite early." Bulman was apologetic. "I've nothing on him, Maggie. Your flat will be bugged and so will your phone. It would be impossible to prove who did it. Your handbag could have been fixed at

236

any time. Even as early as a steward on the boat. Did Ashton have an opportunity?"

Maggie considered it. "While I was making the coffee."

"Okay. Well, the one thing we know is that they are worried. They are showing their desperation."

"Why don't you explain all this to your boss?"

Bulman laughed quietly. "Do you think he'd listen to me against the heavyweights of the Foreign Office? I went to the wrong school for a start, and he doesn't like me anyway. Eventually it will catch up with him, when the evidence is there. Meanwhile he's doing everything he can to stop me. He's been convinced that Tom Moody's death was accidental and that I'm a stirrer. Most men who are basically unsure of themselves, invariably check advice from their colleagues with outside sources. They can't trust their own judgment and are therefore reluctant to trust that of their subordinates. The bloody man should never have had the job. Stuart Halliman wouldn't have used him as an office boy."

"How do we keep in touch?"

"You'll have to rely on me to find a way. Just as Willie must with me. Both you and I are being watched in the hope that we'll squeeze out Willie between us. He's the one they fear most. Willie has a formidable history against stiff-necked hypocritical bastards. I'm sorry, Mag. I've rambled on."

"I'm frightened, George. Terrified."

"It was no use my kidding you. Just be on your guard. I'll be in touch." Bulman helped her up. "It's stupid to say don't worry, we're all worried, but we're beginning to shake the tree, Mag. Believe me. Keep your chin up."

BULMAN WAS NOT sure whether his disguise was sufficient. It was dark, of course, but there was little he could do about the silhouette of his stocky frame. He had never worn a disguise in his life, and he resented the necessity and felt ridiculous.

He caught a cab and tried to determine whether or not he was still being followed. He had left his home by the back way and had taken precautions from there. It seemed to be clear behind him. The cab took him into Soho, which was just coming to life for the late-nighters. Shaftesbury Avenue was alive with light and people, couples mainly, or groups of youngsters hoping to pair off.

He paid the cab driver and joined the loose throng along Dean Street.

The strip clubs were active. The good old days of straightforward prostitution and thuggery were gone. Now it was sex shops, strippers, and porn on open view.

Bulman took note of the life-size photographs of busty nudes. They looked different at night, lighted up and three dimensional. He turned to a plain door beside one of the clubs, rang the bell, and announced himself into the voice box. The door was released and he went in.

He climbed well-carpeted stairs and was stopped on the half-landing by two of Reisen's minders. He flashed his card, but there were no exceptions to being searched. He was shown into a fair-sized waiting room; expensive chairs, low tables, and numerous copies of the *Tatler, Punch, Country Life, The Times,* and *Financial Times.* He found it difficult to believe that Reisen ever read them.

Bulman was kept waiting a long time, and he accepted that this was part of being humiliated by probably the most powerful villain in the country. It was half-past eleven by the time he was shown into Reisen's office.

As the door closed behind him, Bulman recognized how accurate Willie's descriptions had been. The expensive but gaudy carpeting, the massive desk, the painting of the queen behind it, and the Union Jack on its eighteen-karat gold stand on a corner of the desk.

The small, pinch-faced figure behind the desk did not rise, nor did Bulman expect him to. The narrow chin rested on cupped hands. The desk lamp caught the very dark, piercing eyes and reflected on their jet hardness.

"Bulman?"

"Detective Superintendent George Bulman. You Reisen?"

"You're the first copper to come in here without a warrant."

"You must feel privileged. May I sit down? It's been a hard day."

Reisen indicated an armchair by the desk. Bulman was having difficulty in coming to terms with the color scheme; hearing about it had somehow failed to prepare him for its bad taste. He sat down, removed his wig and mustache to Reisen's astonishment, and said, "Have you got a drink? I need one badly."

Reisen, taken by surprise, pressed a buzzer and when a minder came in ordered two large Remy Martins. Neither man spoke another word until the drinks arrived. Bulman cupped a hand around his brandy balloon, "Cheers." It tasted good.

"You're a funny bloody copper," Reisen said bluntly. "I was dead against meeting any copper, but Fairfax said it was of national importance, and he's a man I respect. But don't take too long. The nightly takings reports are due in soon."

"Did Fairfax tell you it was about Spider Scott?"

"Spider. No. I haven't seen Fairfax for years. Only met him briefly, but I've done jobs for him. For the country. I bet that surprises you."

"Not at all. Why do you think I approached Fairfax to arrange a meet?" In fact, Bulman knew that Reisen had *never* worked for Fairfax, but there had been a couple of times when Willie had convinced him that he had.

"Cards on the table," Bulman said. "My visit is not official. Whatever is said between these walls remains between them. Nothing you say accidentally or deliberately will ever be used against you. You have my word and you can check the value of that with Fairfax. Tape it if you want."

"I already have, Bulman." Reisen opened and closed a drawer, as if Bulman could see into it. "Okay. What's wrong with Spider?"

"He's on the run. I need your trust on this. I believe you rate Spider highly."

"I like him. He's a good creeper. He's never ratted. And I guess I trust him. He's different. But that does not mean we haven't had our differences. There have been some dodgy moments with him. But, like me, he's done undercover work for Her Majesty, and we have that in common."

"Would you help him if he's in trouble?"

"Depends. If he's on a government job and he's in trouble, I'll help if I can."

"Right. He's on a job." Bulman held up his spare hand. "Don't ask me about it. Not yet. You read about the two characters who blew their way out of Albany? Spider's one of them."

"Spider? That's not the name in the papers. Nor the mug shot."

"Anthony Sims. It's Spider. Someone fingered him in prison, and someone's fingering him now."

Reisen was pensive. His sharp, unpredictable mind was working fast. "What was Spider doing in prison? I've heard nothing on the vine."

Bulman had to be careful. To mention a police plant would be the end with Reisen. "I'll have to ask you to switch off the tape if I'm to tell you."

Reisen, satisfied now about the general drift, pulled the recorder from

239

the drawer and switched it off in front of Bulman. He then removed the microphone, rewound the tape, and switched to record. "I'm wiping it out. We don't want state secrets hanging around."

Bulman knew then that he had made considerable ground.

"He was in there sniffing out an IRA man who was working with a Libyan, inside. They were doing an explosives and arms deal, and the word was that they had a mad scheme to blow up Princess Diana. There must have been something in it, for a contract went out on Spider while he was inside. He got out quick."

"The papers say the other guy's a terrorist."

"That's rubbish. Have you ever been approached by anyone to kill Willie?"

Bulman could feel the chill from where he sat. The atmosphere, at no point friendly, had now changed for the worst. Reisen opened his middle drawer, eyes blazing at Bulman, who hoped the gangster would not be foolish enough to draw a gun. All the many things he had heard about Reisen came to mind. The man could be highly unpredictable, but Willie had handled him and Bulman recognized that so must he. "Don't misunderstand my question," he said slowly. "I know that you would not hurt Spider without good cause. But has anyone asked you to do it?"

Reisen seemed to disappear into the folds of his director's chair, and the steam slowly left him. "No one has approached me. Don't ever suggest it."

"I didn't think they had, or I wouldn't have asked. I had to be sure. Have you heard of anyone else being approached?"

"No. It's not my line. I don't do contract killings. What would I need them for? I'm one of the richest men in the country. Only hoods do that sort of thing."

Bulman resisted asking how Reisen had become so rich. He said, "The Reverend had a contract on Spider."

"Phil Deacon?" Reisen's contempt was clear. "Who gave it to him?"

"I don't know. In a way I'm sorry you weren't asked, for we would then know who."

"Deacon is rubbish. He tried it on me, and I drove him south of the Thames."

"Does it strike you," Bulman asked blandly, "that you might not have been asked because of your special relationship with Spider?"

"It crossed my mind just before you said it. That means the bleeder who put Deacon up knows of that little thing. No one with any sense at all would go to the Reverend if I'm available. Nobody who knows anything."

Bulman did not point out the contradiction of Reisen's remark about contract killings. Instead he submitted mildly, "It would be useful for me to know who hired Deacon."

"You sure it's him?"

"Spider found out in stir."

"Are you asking me to start a gang war?"

"Would it mean that?" Bulman asked innocently. "I should have thought that with your stature a few threats might go a long way."

"Like I said when you came in, you're a funny bloody copper. I don't dig you at all."

"I'm a copper and you're a villain, Reisen. Nothing will change either of those things. But we do have one thing in common —well being and mutual respect for one Willie 'Spider' Scott. That's why I'm here, and that's why you're listening."

"I'll see what I can do." Reisen checked the time. "Pity. You're too late for a show, or I'd have taken you down."

Bulman said nothing. They could not bring themselves to shake hands, but they parted with a peculiar sense of rapport.

19

"YOU made a cock-up of Albany." The man had a northern accent, probably Liverpudlian slightly watered down.

Deacon had already realized this. He still did not know the man's real name and knew him only as Salter. Even during the first contact, now some years ago, Salter was the only name given. Deacon had always seen him as being of similar background to himself. He was well-dressed, in his mid-forties, hard-faced with a generally blank look about him, and was neither tall nor short, big nor thin. But for the uncompromising features there was nothing distinguishing about him. His dark hair always appeared the same, and Deacon suspected that the sideburns were touched up to cover the gray. He never felt quite comfortable in his presence.

"What do you expect?" Deacon retaliated. "No notice and a killing in stir? I was lucky to get somebody to get a poke in and it nearly came off. After that I'd got the pot boiling nicely, which increased the number of candidates, when the bastard broke out."

"But you're still looking for him?"

"Of course I'm still looking for him. The whole bloody country's looking for him."

"You'd better find him first, Deacon. If the police get to him you're in trouble."

"Are you threatening me, Salter?"

"Bank on it. This one is much more important than all the others put together. If this goes down, you go down."

"You use language like that and you'll leave here as pig swill in one of those speaker containers." He pointed to one of the big corner speakers.

Salter came near to smiling; it made Deacon realize that he had never seen Salter smile. "You can take me here if you want. It won't make any difference to what happens to you." Salter opened a briefcase and produced a small parcel. "Thirty grand. Count it. It's in fifties. Six hundred notes. All clean. That's much more than you could ever expect and it's without asking for a refund on the job you didn't do. Tax free."

Deacon was fascinated by the money. Sight of any money always made him react like this. He glanced up. "But it's conditional?"

"You catch on, Deacon. That's the price of success. Failure is the end of you. One way or another."

"Don't keep threatening me. I can take care of myself."

"Can you put up the sort of money I've been giving you over the years? Think about it." Salter pointed to the envelope. "I won't even miss it."

"We'll find him."

"Try the terrorist angle. Some of the crappier papers are saying that the bomber was the Arab. They could be right. Find one and you'll find the other. The Arab has a reputation for pulling the birds. See if you can find any of them. It's easy for you. You don't even have to make it look like an accident. It's now a matter of prison record that someone tried to get him while he was inside."

"Okay. I've always finished the job. And they've been good."

"They have," Salter conceded. "But we don't want a first time. Or you're on a last time."

NORMAN MURISON RANG through to make an appointment with Sir Roland Powell and saw him in his office later that morning. Murison was quick to detect that Powell was not in a good mood, so he stood in front of the desk, more formal than usual.

"Yes," Powell snapped. "Make it quick, Norman."

"Our bird has flown. She did contact me before she went and I gather it's a normal change of duties."

Powell looked up. "Am I supposed to know what you're talking about?"

"Our contact with Maria Wolfstholme worked for Aeroflot in London. She'll be useful elsewhere, of course. In a small way. But I was hoping she could put the final nail in Scott's coffin. Now we'll never be absolutely certain. It's a pity."

"For you or for Scott?"

"I was never in doubt myself."

"Am I to understand that the whole business has been a waste of time and that there is a man out there on the run who can do us considerable damage because of it?"

"He's out there because he's guilty. I will let you have the file. I'm only saying that, unless something else crops up, we'll not be able to prove it. The girl was not high ranked; she could only get bits and pieces after Maria died, but they were adding up nicely."

"It's a pity you ever started this. I said at the outset that it should have gone to MI5."

"I'm sorry, sir, but it's not that bad. We smoked him out after all. Scott had some contacts in high places. It's possible that our 'friends,' the Russians, are also looking for him. If they find him before we do, we'll then have the truth of it."

"You sound as though you hope they get to him first."

"It would solve our problem. And it would close the file on him."

Powell took more interest, "This whole business is messy. These things happen, of course, but here we've used other departments. That's all right if it works, but it hasn't. It's hanging over us, Norman. And from where I'm sitting it feels like a guillotine. I suppose we have to assume that Bulman found out that it was us who kept Scott in Albany."

"I'm sure he did. And he would have told Scott. When this is over, Bulman should be sacked. He's broken every police confidence. It's really not good enough."

"I understand he handed his resignation in, anyway. Anything else?"

"No. I thought you should be told the position."

"Then you'd better find him before anyone else does," said Powell dryly.

THEY MET DURING the early performance at the Pavilion Cinema in Leicester Square; at this time of day it was not difficult to get rear seats in the balcony. The screen flickered way below them. Scott had sent a letter to Bulman at home. He had posted it first class; had Bulman not

245

received it the following day, Scott would have visited the cinema until he had. Bulman had read the note and burned it at once.

"What have you done with your hair?" Scott whispered.

Bulman was tired of trying to shake off his tail and of diving into toilets to put on his basic disguise. He was not sure that he had arrived at the cinema alone, he only knew that he had done his best. They would leave separately. "Maggie's back," he whispered softly. He thought Scott was going to jump from his seat, and he clamped a hand on his arm quickly. *"It's okay. It's okay.* She's fine."

Scott shook his head in despair. Bulman said swiftly, "She knows everything and she's taken it really well. She's rooting for you. It's taken her mind off herself."

Bulman took his hand away as he felt Scott's muscles relax.

"Have you seen her?" Scott demanded.

"Of course, I've seen her."

"What happened? How did she . . ."

"Not now, for God's sake. Some other time. She's fine. Now, what is it you want?"

"I called on Corrie. Met his wife. Scared her half to death. Then I staked out the place until the old man came home—it was a bloody long wait—and followed him when he pushed off. Here's the address he went to." Scott handed Bulman a slip of paper and gave a fair description of Murison. "It was dark. Corrie got there first and decided to wait outside, for some reason. He actually saw me when I passed him, but he was too knotted up to notice."

"Good work, Willie. I'll trace the address. It was lucky Corrie didn't phone."

"He might have. I still think Murison and Corrie have met somewhere. I did a good job of frightening. His wife's a beauty. As cold as charity."

"Is that it?"

"I have another move to make, but I could do with help."

"Who?"

"Knocker Roberts."

"Jesus. I don't want to know what you've got in mind. I got in touch with Reisen. He's going to try to shake down Deacon. Be careful, Spider. You've put out the frighteners. They'll go like hell to find you."

"I won't use the post again. We'd better decide on a rough code over the phone. They'll break it down if you're bugged, but by the time they do it should be too late."

Ten minutes later Scott said, "See you," and worked his way down the line of seats.

KNOCKER ROBERTS SAT in the old Ford and weighed the situation. The body had been sprayed to cover the stripes and numbers that might reveal it as an outdated stock-racing car. The reinforcing done by the previous driver remained.

Roberts gave the impression of being an insensitive machine. He was solid bone and muscle but would never win a Mr. Universe competition. His body was shaped like a concrete block. He was not particularly tall, but there was no apparent physical weakness. Bull-necked and square-chinned, he frightened most people with whom he came in contact. Roberts was insensitive to pain, whether causing or receiving it. One side of his face was mashed up from a long forgotten battle, and he had recently had some skin grafting done on it. It was generally agreed that the result was no better, if not worse, than before, but nobody was reckless enough to tell him. He was a psychopath, sometimes as gentle as a mongrel dog and sometimes murderous. He had served several prison sentences, but as his reputation for excessive violence grew it had become increasingly difficult to find anyone who would testify against him. These days, mere mention of him was enough to scare most others in the underworld.

But he was efficient as well as violent and could be relied upon. He had already traversed the streets close to where Phil Deacon lived. A Mercedes and a Jaguar were still outside the house. It was well known that Deacon liked to keep them on show when not in use during the day, as a sign of affluence and power. Nobody would dare touch them. At night they were taken to a garage a block away.

Roberts knew all this. He had played a large part in driving Deacon south of the river. His concern now was to establish that the general area was clear of police. It was a matter of timing, and dusk would be the ideal moment.

He started the engine again, pulled out, and went around the block once more. There were cars parked all along the street where Deacon lived, and there was still a fair amount of activity, but most of the kids had gone indoors. As he went past Deacon's house again there were

247

three men at the top of the steps, but not Deacon himself. Roberts accepted that he could not reconnoiter again without being noticed. As he turned the corner into Deacon's street for the last time, he accelerated fast. Heads turned. Just before he drew level with the house he swung over in a calculated move and tore along the side of the Mercedes and Jaguar. With a terrible screaming of metal, a door was torn off and a wheel casing rolled in the street. He pulled out at the last moment, looked in the mirror, and saw men racing down the steps of Deacon's house.

Roberts turned the corner in a controlled skid and smiled to himself; he had managed it without ripping his door off. The dusk should protect the damage to his own car, and, with this in mind, he kept to the back streets. The registration number he carried was meaningless, but he doubted that Deacon would call the police.

"IS THAT YOU, Phil? It's Rex. Rex Reisen. Ringing up to say how sorry I am."

"Sorry about what?" Deacon sounded shaken.

"About the accident. I know what that Mercedes meant to you."

"It's only just happened, you bastard. It was your boy Knocker who did it. What have I done to you?"

"Knocker? Can't be Knocker. He's been with me."

"How long's he been with you?"

"As long as you like, Phil. Whenever it happened." Reisen chuckled.

"You bastard," Deacon repeated. "I'll get back at you for this."

"No you won't," Reisen replied reasonably. "You'll try. You've one or two good boys. But not good enough. I'm sorry you're so uptight. These things happen. Look, if it makes you feel any better, come over and have a drink tomorrow. I'll give you lunch. Guarantee your safety. Anyway, the insurance will cough up on the cars. Lot of damage, was it?" Reisen did not laugh outright until he had cradled the receiver.

THERE WAS NO real reason why Scott suddenly had doubts about the safety of the apartment. He took a can of beer from the refrigerator and poured it into a chilled glass. He went to the nearest window in the living room and peered out carefully. There was nobody who aroused suspicion, but the feeling of menace was strong.

Sophie returned at five o'clock, and he made her a dry martini. She looked tired and said she had been chasing around London in taxis from one photocall to another. As she flopped down in a chair, long legs stretched out, she gazed up at Scott quizzically. "Something wrong, Spider boy?"

Scott was still gazing down into the street. "Anyone follow you back?"

Sophie's dark eyes widened. "I don't look for that sort of thing."

"Not when you're with Hash?"

"Baby, he does the looking, not me. Besides," she added with an impish smile. "I'm used to being looked at."

"There's looking and there's ogling." Scott changed his position to get a better view of the street.

"You worried, honey?"

"Someone walked over my grave."

"Look," Sophie said, not moving. "Let me finish this drink. I'll take a shower, and then I'll go out again. I've been meaning to look up a friend. Another model. I'll keep a lookout, okay?"

"Don't make it obvious. How long will you be?"

"About an hour and a half. I'll be back to eat here."

"I'll get something out of the freezer and have it ready."

She spread her legs, relaxing, her head against the back of the chair. "You're getting restless."

"That's possible."

She turned her head to study him, her drink held high. "You sometimes remind me of Hash. You depend a lot on feelings."

"That's because we've both been on the run. Like now."

Sophie rose gracefully. She drained her drink. "I'll have that shower. No peeping." It had become a joke between them.

It was almost six when Sophie emerged, now wearing a silk blouse and skirt. Whatever she wore would look good on her.

"Give me a latest time back," Scott requested. "A time I can rely on."

She checked her watch. "You *are* edgy. Not like you."

"You don't really know me. Give me the phone number of your friend."

"You're beginning to frighten me."

"I hope so. You're not taking this seriously enough."

She stood by the door, mocking him a little. "How can I not take it seriously after living with Hash? You know how many times we've moved? Don't worry, Spider. I'll look out and I won't be late. Get some wine out. You never know, Hash might drop in."

Scott stepped forward and gave her a peck on the cheek. "Watch out," he warned; Hash was supposed to be out of the country.

"After that I can hardly wait to get back," she rejoined. "Such passion."

He went back to the window to watch her going out, but she evidently remained on the same side of the street—and he was not certain which way she went. He was certain though that nobody on the other side of the street made a suspicious move. He poured himself another beer and sat down to watch television.

After a while he realized that he could not concentrate. His mind kept drifting to Maggie. Why had she come back? Someone must have told her what had happened. He gazed over to the telephone, very tempted to ring her. The fact that her phone would be bugged did not matter at the moment. He could make a quick call to make sure she was all right and then hang up before a trace could be made.

He left the chair and picked up the phone and then, with difficulty, put it down again. A quick call could upset her, remind her too much of the caution he must take. Scott went back to the chair, aware that to call her would be more to satisfy himself than to help her. He must rely on Bulman to sort things out. He again tried to concentrate on the television and eventually got caught up in the seven o'clock news. During the half hour that followed there was no mention of his escape. Suddenly he realized that Sophie was due home.

He switched off the set and went to the window. Nothing had changed. He checked the time again; Sophie was definitely overdue. He told himself that women were invariably late, but Sophie was different; she was used to living with someone on the run and knew the importance of time, something she would, in any event, have learned in her job.

At ten to eight, twenty minutes after her promised return, Scott rang the number of her friend. "Is that Marie? I'm a friend of Sophie's. Has she left you yet?"

"Sophie? I haven't seen her for some time. What makes you think she was here?"

Scott's heart sank. "I've obviously got it wrong. So sorry." He hung up. There was nothing he could do for Sophie unless he rang the police. He did not believe that they would take action anyway, not after so short an absence to report a person as missing when she was twenty minutes late would appear ridiculous.

There was one man who would believe him, but it would be dangerous to telephone. There was little Scott could do until it was dark. He was now satisfied that his original feeling had been right. If someone had Sophie, they would now know where he was.

Scott was sure that the house was being watched. It was too light to leave, yet he had to get out somehow. He went into every room to check through the windows, but whoever might be waiting for him was on the house side of the street. He put the chain on the front door.

The passing of time had slowed intolerably. He was worried sick about Sophie; then he began to worry about Maggie. Again he resisted the need to phone her; they could be waiting for just that. There was nobody he could safely contact; he was now in his own prison.

Scott grew impatient and his concern deepened. As the first signs of darkness approached, he calmed a little. He always did when action was imminent. He switched the hall and living room lights on and left the television on with the sound turned down.

At nine-thirty the door buzzer sounded. He went into the hall and called through the door. "Who is it?"

"Sam Woolley. I've a message from Sophie, man."

He sounded like a West Indian.

"If it's verbal say it now, if it's written slip it under the door."

"Aw, come on, man. Open up. This is Sophie's pad."

Scott knew that he was only prolonging the problem. He had to know for certain. "Okay," he called close to the door. He stepped behind the door as he opened it as far as the chair would allow. Immediately a gun with a silencer came through the gap, and Scott hurled himself at the door as the gun swung toward him.

The man yelled out in pain as his arm was trapped, and the gun fell to the floor. Keeping his weight against the door, Scott hooked the gun toward him with his foot.

"Jesus, you're cutting my arm off."

But Scott, guessing what would happen next, kept firmly where he was. There was a terrific crash against the door that almost dislodged him, but Scott held on desperately while he bent down for the gun. There were two men straining to get the door open, but the man with his arm trapped was now whimpering.

Scott could not hold out. With the arm still in the gap, the door could

251

not be closed. The weight against him became too much. The door was pushed open sufficiently for the man to pull his arm back. Scott scooped up the gun and ran through to the bathroom, quickly locking the door behind him.

He heard the crack of the door chain breaking from its moorings just as he opened the bathroom window. He climbed through, the gun in his waistband. He knew where the drain pipe was and fell sideways toward it. Once he had a steady grip, he went up the pipe toward the roof.

Reaching the gutter he hooked a leg over, then the other, and crab-crawled up the slates to the apex. He straddled the roof and recovered his breath. Someone pounded down the steps below him and called out, "He must 'ave come down that side. From the bathroom."

Scott did not hear the reply. Stage by stage, he worked his way along, pausing now and then to pick up what was happening below. Suddenly a flashlight swung up to probe along the edge of the roof. Scott swung over the other side and held on to the apex, his body flat against the tiles. He edged his way along slowly, the beam traversing above his head. When his arms ached, he allowed himself to slide down the tiles until he suctioned a halt with flat hands. He turned over, pulled his legs up so that his feet were flat on the slates, then sat up. In this position, using hands and feet, he eased his way along. Below him were faint pocket-sized gardens.

When he reached the end of the long terrace, Scott waited. It was almost eleven o'clock. Street noises had diminished and had subtly changed. Footsteps were often in pairs and slower than before. Giggles and whispered protests floated up to him.

Eventually Scott went down the roof in a sitting position. He located the nearest pipe, which he descended. He was in a small, overgrown garden with a rough path bisecting it and a shed on one side. He followed the path, reached a rickety fence at the bottom, climbed over, concerned at the creaking of weak palings, and dropped into a yard.

He wasted no time in approaching the rear of the house on the next street. As he had hoped there was no alley. He listened closely before climbing the side fence, and he lowered himself carefully. He was in a short street at right angles with the one where Sophie lived. There might be a man on the corner.

Scott stood against the fence, certain that he could not be seen. He waited until satisfied that his presence was undected, then walked down the remaining section of the street, past the house without an alley. He kept close to the fence and he moved quite silently.

At the corner he waited again, peered around, and crossed the street, heading away from Sophie's place. He breathed a little easier when he reached a main street, well lighted and active. He looked for a cab.

THE TAXI WENT slowly along the street where Bulman lived. It was not easy to trace a stakeout from the confines of a cab, but Scott located one dark figure in a doorway and an occupied parked car. He told the cab driver to go around the block; he then located a second occupied car. He wondered whether Bulman had fooled anyone with the wig and mustache, but in any event, whoever had planned the surveillance would by now have had time to sort out the weak links. He tapped on the glass. "Pull up."

Scott went around to the driver's side. "What's the fare?"

"Three fifty."

Scott handed over five pounds. "Keep the change, but I still need you."

"Okay, mate, get back in. You could have settled the fare when you've finished."

"I want an extra service. I want to call at a certain house, but I don't want anyone to know. The only way I can do that is for me to drive the cab and for you to call at the house."

"What's your game, mate? I can't let you drive. I'd lose my license."

"What's it worth?"

"Forget it, mate. It's too dodgy and it's outside the law."

"The bloke I want to see is a detective chief superintendent at Scotland Yard. But there are certain people who don't want me to get to him. A hundred quid do it? Plus the normal fare?"

"A hundred?" The driver put his gear back into neutral. "What exactly do you want me to do?"

"Ring the bell. Hand over a note once you're inside. Then come back. All I need to do is drive the cab around the corner to the house and drive back around the corner when you've done. It's dead easy money."

"You might pinch the cab."

"I could have done that any time, I'm twice your size."

"A hundred you say? Let's see it."

Scott showed him. "Have you got anything to write on?"

"The margin of a newspaper do?"

"It'll have to." Scott climbed back inside, and the cabbie turned the light on as Scott took a newspaper from him. He scribbled around the white margin and tore off the strips, then folded them. He passed them through the sliding glass partition. "When he answers the door, tell him you're from Willie, and tell him you have a message that must be delivered inside. Let him read it, in case he sends a message back. Then climb back into the passenger's seat."

"What's his name? I mean, how will I know it's him?"

"Bulman. Detective Superintendent Bulman." Scott saw no way around giving the name, but the whole scene would be witnessed so it really made no difference.

"Okay, I'll do it."

"Count the money."

Scott slipped off his jacket and threw it on the rear seat. He took off his tie and climbed into the driver's seat, waited for the cabbie to settle in, then drove off. He turned the corner, slowed right down as if peering at the street numbers, then coasted into a double-parking position outside Bulman's place. "That's the one."

The cabbie climbed out and opened the gate before the short path. Scott was tempted to switch off the engine, but he left it running as a sign that he would soon be leaving. On the opposite side of the street, in doorway and car, observers would be wondering if Bulman would get into the cab.

Scott saw the door open and Bulman's stocky frame; after a few words he invited the cabbie in. Nothing happened around Scott, and he believed his ploy would work.

The cabbie emerged, and now, feeling braver, waved at Bulman as he left, and climbed back into the passenger section of the cab. Scott drove off. "He said he'd see to it," the cabbie called out.

BULMAN RE-READ THE note on the strips of newspaper margins. He learned that Sophie was probably in dire trouble and the address of the house that was blown. There was no mention of where Scott would go now. He called upon his upstairs neighbor, apologized for the lateness, said his phone was out of order and asked to use theirs. He instigated a search for Sophie, giving the description that Scott had supplied. Bulman had only the one name, as Scott had, but a beautiful black model could not be so common, and the model agencies would come up with the rest.

Bulman admired Scott's nerve. The surveillance team would rave if they realized that Scott had been right under their noses. But it meant that Scott's options had shortened. Small hotels and boardinghouses would have long since been contacted.

20

"SIT down, Phil. And take your time." Rex Reisen signaled the waiter and ordered champagne; since he owned the restaurant he knew he would get the best.

Phil Deacon gazed around the plush surroundings with deep suspicion and envy, much to Reisen's amusement.

"Have the chair with your back to the wall, if it makes you feel happier. You can see everyone from there." And when Deacon had seated himself, added, "Relax. I wouldn't do it on my own doorstep. You must know that, or you wouldn't be here."

"What's happened to my boys?" Deacon demanded, still not satisfied.

"They're next door in the strip club. They'll be fed with anything they want. *Anything.* You shouldn't have brought them. I told you, this is business."

Deacon was noticeably bigger than Reisen, who would appear small in almost any company. Deacon was trying to find his way through a menu he did not understand and would have been happier in the knowledge that neither did Reisen, when his host said, "Try a prawn cocktail. King-sized. And the steak. If it's no good, we'll castrate the chef together." Reisen laughed and Deacon chose to join in.

The champagne arrived, and the waiter filled the flutes and put the wrapped bottle in the ice bucket. "I never try it," Reisen asserted. "If the temperature and taste ain't right the wine waiter will be looking for social security. He knows that. Now, who told you to knock off a geezer called Tony Sims?"

Deacon's hand froze on his glass, then he withdrew it and started to rise.

"Sit down, Phil. You'll reach the first door, but you'll disappear somewhere between there and the lobby, or the cloakroom and the front door. Be your age."

"You've no right to ask that."

"I see you don't deny it. I only want to know who's paying. The champagne is vintage, sod you, try it."

Deacon drank slowly, wondering why he had come and at the same time worried about what might have happened if he had not. He was fully aware that his organization was no match for Reisen's. But he had been building up nicely these past few years and he did not want anything to go wrong. "For God's sake, Rex, you know I can't tell you. I'd lose the contract and a lot more."

"You're gonna lose anyway, Phil." Reisen leaned back as the prawns arrived. When the waiter had gone he said, "You're under pressure. From the geezer who hired you and from me who's going to stop you."

"What can it mean to you? A lousy killing of a bloke I've never heard of. Small-time stuff."

"He's a friend of mine," Reisen said, after chewing.

"Oh, shit, I didn't know that. If I don't go through with it, I'm in trouble."

"If you do go through with it, you're in worse trouble. I'll cover your fee. How much are you being paid?"

"Thirty grand."

"*What?*" Reisen almost choked. When he recovered he was about to call Deacon a liar, but he saw that he had been given a simple truth. *"Thirty grand for one killing?"*

Deacon nodded. "I don't ask why. I just take the money."

"I'm not matching *that*. So I'll settle for who's paying."

Deacon was pleased with Reisen's reaction. He felt he had scored one. He continued to eat his prawns, ignoring Reisen's demand.

Reisen pushed his plate away. "I'm gonna find out one way or the other, Phil. If I have to give Vi a new face, I will, but you won't want to take her to bed again."

Deacon scowled. "Leave her out of it. Vi has nothing to do with this."

258

"Balls. Who's going to spend the thirty grand? I mean it, Phil. You want your steak medium or rare?"

"You can stuff your steak."

"And you'll know where I'll stuff it. How's your drink? Prawns okay?"

Deacon was suspicious and uncertain again. He stared at his empty dish and at his glass.

"That's right," Reisen said, reading his thoughts. "You'll never be sure. Not ever again. I'm asking a small enough favor. A bloke who pays that much has got to be special. He won't know because all I want is the information. You scared of him?"

"It's ethics."

Reisen roared with laughter. "You're knocking off a friend of mine and you're talking about ethics?" After the steak arrived Reisen said, "You're not taking me seriously. You'd better check on your fire and health insurance, Phil. Those medical bills on Vi will be hefty. For God's sake, I'm not kidding. I'm giving you a chance. You'd better take it."

Deacon cut his steak to gain time. He did not want a gang war he could not win; he had already learned that bitter lesson. Only Reisen could smash his cars and get away with it. He weighed Salter against Reisen. He knew nothing about Salter except that he always paid big money. Over the years it had been a very lucrative arrangement. There had always been ample time for proper planning. Some contracts had taken months, and not one had gone down as murder in police files.

There was pressure now, though, and he could not understand why Sims was so important. He had never been sure of Salter, but he had suffered practical experience with Reisen, who he knew did not make empty threats. The threat to his wife really worried him. She, along with the Mercedes and Jaguar, was his outward sign of affluence. And in his strange way he loved her. "Just the name?" he asked.

"Well, I take it for granted that you won't have the address."

"I don't think it's his real name."

"Give me what you've got."

"He calls himself Salter. I think he comes from Liverpool but has lived south for a bit." Deacon gave a physical description.

"How does he contact you?"

"You asked for a name."

Reisen mulled over the rebuttal. "Okay. It's not much, is it?"

"It never has been. But it's all I've ever had."

LATER THAT AFTERNOON, when Bulman played back the tape that Reisen had sent him by personal courier, he paid great attention to Deacon's words. He might be reading too much into them, but they suggested to him that Tony Sims was not the first request for a killing by Deacon. He burned the tape in his ashtray because Reisen was too implicated, then went down to Commander Collins's office.

Dick Collins seemed not too pleased to see Bulman. The possibility of an inquiry was still hanging over his head. Bulman sat down thoughtfully. "I'm beginning to make a little progress," he said cautiously. "Can you get someone to contact the Liverpool police to see if they've got anything on a bloke who calls himself Salter. Presumed Liverpool accent. There's a physical description." He handed over a typed sheet he had made out.

"You can do this yourself."

"Everything I do is being monitored."

"Well, it's more in line than before," Collins commented. "What's he done?"

"Paid Phil Deacon thirty thousand to knock off Willie Scott."

"Jesus. Are you sure?"

"Completely. This is no trick. We're on the edge of something. If it all comes right you'll be a deputy commissioner, Dick."

"Or on the beat, if it doesn't. I'll find out what I can. Anything else?"

"No, thanks." Bulman kept to himself that he had tracked down the address to which Willie had followed Peter Corrie as belonging to one Norman Murison. A powerful figure in MI6, second only to Sir Roland Powell who one day he was expected to succeed.

SCOTT CAMPED OUT, under the arches at Charing Cross. It had been a long time since he had slept like that, and in the morning he felt drained. He went to the toilets at Charing Cross underground station and washed there, then found a nearby barber to have a shave. He was finding the gun a nuisance and was constantly worried that its bulk would be seen. He did not want it, yet he was reluctant to get rid of it.

All he could do until evening was to fill in time in cafés and clubs and cinemas, when they opened. There he caught up on a little sleep when he wasn't worrying about Maggie.

BULMAN MADE AN appointment to see Lord Raymond Langley at the Langley & Cognum Merchant Bank in Threadneedle Street. This golden square mile of high finance of inner London was watched over, perhaps cynically, by the mass of St. Paul's Cathedral.

At three-thirty that day he presented himself, and the uniformed commissionaire directed him through the pillared hall to a reception area. He was shown into the wood-paneled office some ten minutes later.

The office was richly and tastefully furnished, and the Chippendale desk governed the room, in spite of challenge from oil portraits hanging on the walls in gilded frames. It was a little dark in here, but it was cool and possessed an aura of wealth, as did the man behind the desk.

"Detective Superintendent, do come in." Lord Langley was soberly dressed and gray haired. He indicated a chair, his eyes amused at the prospect of a visit from someone from Scotland Yard. The face was florid from good living but still firm, and, by and large, Langley gave the impression of a man who had looked after himself.

"I think this is the first time I have ever had a visit from the police. Certainly not from someone of so exalted a rank and from Scotland Yard, no less. What can I do for you?"

Bulman produced the copy of the receipt and passed it across the wide desk, between a battery of telephones. Well-manicured fingers took the receipt, and Langley put on glasses as he read it. Bulman watched the eyes and the hands and learned nothing from either; Langley was a poker player.

"Where on earth did you get this?" Langley asked, slightly amused. "It's rather ancient."

"I can't tell you where I found it. It came into my possession, and, as it bore your father's name, I thought it might interest you, sir."

"It interests me very much. Are you sure it was made out to my father? I mean, weren't there any other Robert Langleys?"

"Not to our knowledge, not who had a connection with Sir Oswald Mosley."

"Ah! I take your point. Long time ago, Mr. Bulman. So what do you want of me?"

Bulman noticed that the eyes had cooled considerably, but the fingers that held the receipt were quite steady. "Well, it's part of your family history. I wondered if you knew anything about it."

Langley laid the receipt on the desk and took off his glasses, still holding them. "Well, I suppose it is family history." He smiled. "Perhaps a part I would prefer to forget."

"You haven't seen it before, sir?"

"Good Lord. It's over fifty years old. I was seventeen or eighteen. In fairness to you, I suppose I would have remembered something like this, so I must assume I have not seen it before. You are aware that this is a copy?"

"Of course."

"Do you know what happened to the original? And why would someone make a copy?"

"I made the copy, Lord Langley. And I know where the original is."

"Now you are fencing with me, Mr. Bulman. Of what possible importance can it be?"

"That's what I'm investigating."

"Why?"

"Mosley's signature is a forgery."

"Really? Is there a point to all this?"

"I don't yet know."

"You've lost me. I simply can't see the importance of a fifty-year-old receipt with a forged signature."

"It probably means that the money never reached Sir Oswald. Someone else had it."

"Are you about to make an arrest, Mr. Bulman? It would surely be a record for time lapse?"

Bulman looked sheepish. "I've wasted your time, Lord Langley. But I had to show it to you. There was just a chance that you might have come up with something useful." Bulman rose, thinking that the timing of confrontation with this man would always be a toss of the coin.

"May I keep this?" Langley asked, holding up the receipt as he rose.

"I'd rather you didn't, sir. Not if it means nothing to you."

"What about the original? It is a family heirloom, so to speak."

"When I've finished with it, I'll be happy to pass it on to you; if, by then, you would still like to have it, sir."

Langley came around the desk, a handsome figure, if slightly overweight. "Mr. Bulman, I don't think you are being quite honest with me. A man of your rank does not call by appointment with apparent trivia. Now what's on your mind?"

"I did not say it was trivia, sir. It could be of vital importance right now. It's unfortunate you are unable to help; it might have hastened the inquiry. There's nothing more I can say. Thank you for your time."

"But you did say you have the original, did you not?"

Bulman saw the first trace of a haircrack in Langley's urbane image, the first suggestion of concern. "No, sir. I did not. I said, I know where the original is."

When Bulman had gone, Lord Langley returned thoughtfully to his desk. He sat down, his features giving nothing away until a hint of a smile touched the corners of his mouth. He pressed the intercom switch. "Miss Palmer, hold all calls for another five minutes." His smile widened. He picked up a direct line and punched out a number.

"Raymond Langley," he announced. "You might be surprised to hear from me. And I might be speaking to the wrong person. But I don't think so. I believe you are the end of a fifty-year chain. You've all had a good run. I thought you should know that I've just been shown the Mosley receipt. The police have it, although I can't imagine what they hope to gain from it or how they got it. Anyway, there it is. You won't expect further donations." About to put down the receiver, he caught the tail end of a question and answered it. "A fellow called Bulman. Scotland Yard. Detective superintendent." He then hung up; his smile turned into a loud chuckle and finally a full-bodied laugh. He had deliberately not mentioned that the receipt was a copy.

BULMAN WAS NOT sure whether he had gained or not. Men like Lord Langley were exceedingly hard to break down. He returned to Scotland Yard to find a dossier on Salter, which was, as he suspected, an alias. He was always surprised to find that men who used aliases invariably used the same names time and again. They may have had half a dozen, but they stuck to them, seldom, if ever, using a different name for every crooked occasion. Con men were the worst.

Salter was not a con man. His real name was Walter Janeski, British by birth but the son of a Polish airman who had escaped from Nazi occupation during World War II and who had fought for Britain in the RAF; a brilliant pilot with a brilliant record. He had died two years ago. His son, Walter, Jr., had been many things, including a mercenary soldier in Africa and, at one time, a gunrunner. Junior had a conviction for armed robbery in a bank holdup and had somehow obtained a reduced sentence after serving five years of a twelve-year stretch.

263

That was his only conviction but he was suspected of many other crimes, including post-office raids. The names of Halter, Retlaw, Tawler, as well as Salter had appeared with physical descriptions that fitted, but never with sufficient evidence for conviction. He had clearly stuck to names similar to Walter, or had used anagrams of it. Bulman asked Commander Collins to put out a call for Salter to be picked up. Someone would know where he was.

What puzzled Bulman was how Salter could have the funds to use someone like Deacon. Salter's record showed him to be a hard man. He sat down and wondered if he would ever break down the barriers that were now becoming evident. He called out to Haldean, "Anyone been after me?"

"Nobody, guv. Not even Sir Lewis."

Bulman wasn't sure whether it was his own crowd, allied to MI5, who was shadowing him, or the Foreign Office who nurtured MI6. It made little difference except to motive. Officially, he accepted that he had asked for it.

Salter was traced quickly, and a report came through that he was being held at Amersham Police Station in Buckinghamshire, some twenty-seven miles out of London. Bulman took a train, which was considerably faster than going by road. The Amersham police sent a car to meet him at the station, and he was taken to the modern building that was only a stone's throw away, next to the magistrates' court.

Salter, under his real name of Janeski, was in a basement cell but was brought up to an interrogation room that was placed at Bulman's disposal. Bulman dismissed the policeman standing inside the door and sat opposite Salter across the small table.

"Walter Janeski," he said, "born in Croydon, Surrey, moved to Birkenhead at the age of five and lived most of your life in the Liverpool area until a few years ago." Bulman had memorized the detail on the train journey. "Right so far?"

Salter made no reply so Bulman continued, "You are now living at Little Chalfont and are quite well known as a local antique dealer. Big shop, is it? Profitable?"

Salter kept quiet.

"It had better be, because I am told that your house is on two acres of splendid land and is of considerable value." Bulman gazed around the almost bare room. "Pricey around here, they tell me. Near to London.

264

On the edge of the Chiltern Hills. Nice, when someone succeeds like that. Particularly when he's got a prison record."

Salter did not change expression.

Bulman went on, "Why are you paying the Reverend all this money to have people knocked off? What have they done to you?"

Salter sat still, with a trace of an insolent smile around his lips.

Bulman said, "Interesting that you don't deny it. You're going to talk sometime, cocker, so why not now? I don't like to see anyone get life without trying to defend themselves."

Salter decided to break his silence. "I was just listening to what you had to say. I don't deny a prison history; it's a matter of record, but the rest of what you've said is rubbish. In which diocese is this reverend?"

"The diocese of South London or, squeezing it tighter, the Wandsworth area. Phil Deacon received thirty grand from you to knock off one Anthony Sims, who has just moved out of Albany Prison in a hurry. That's a lot of money for any killing, but Sims is a nothing. So why?"

"I don't know why, because I don't know Sims and I don't know Deacon."

"If you're not paying out yourself, who is paying you?"

"I've listened to your crap. I've been falsely arrested, and I'm going to cause trouble."

"You won't cause trouble, Salter. That's the name Deacon gave us, by the way. Said it was the only one he knew you by, even after all these years. You have used it before, of course. Deacon is now a material witness. Oh, and nobody has arrested you. You know that. You've been pulled in for questioning. I haven't given you a caution, have I? This is just between the two of us."

"Right, then, I'm off." But Salter did not move. Bulman had not said so much, but had given the impression that he knew a lot more.

"I'm not stopping you," Bulman said. "We can pick you up again, anytime. Why did you get Deacon to knock off Tom Moody?" Bulman was gambling.

"Who?"

Bulman smiled. "That was the wrong answer, Salter. Where's your indignation at the suggestion of killing anyone? You put the finger on Moody. And Sims. And Wally Cooper. And Michael Rossi. And James McLaren, and Bertrand Hill. And others I'm still working on. You're not going to see freedom again in your natural lifetime. And once you're inside, if not before, someone is going to put the finger on *you*. You'll probably get the electric cord treatment like poor old Wally, who choked to death from the bars of his cell."

"Bullshit."

"Don't kid yourself, matey. You're not kidding me."

"Arrest me then, if you're so bloody sure of yourself. And if you do, I'll sue you for wrongful arrest."

Bulman appeared shocked. "I'm not going to arrest you. That takes time and money and lawyers and judges and courts; God, it's tedious. There's nothing wrong with a little natural justice now and then. I *want* you to go *free*." Bulman stood up. "So I'll arrange it with the locals. By the way my name is Detective Superintendent Bulman. B-U-L-M-A-N. I'll be at Scotland Yard if you feel at any time that you would like to save your neck."

Bulman left the room to arrange certain details and was escorted upstairs to the superintendent's office. He had a beer in the recreation room before leaving, then caught a train back to London. He was not satisfied with his interview with Salter; he had certainly not expected a confession—people like Salter never confessed—but he had gained the impression that while the names he had mentioned might be familiar to Salter, the people themselves were not. And that could only mean that Salter was part of a chain. Bulman was a realist; he knew that if the chain was a long one he might never reach the end. Someone was very effectively covering their tracks, and it was more than possible that whoever it was had never heard of Salter under any of his aliases. And that in turn meant that the thirty thousand Salter had paid had started out as a much larger sum with each link skimming off a fat commission as risk money. Someone had a lot of money to spare.

On arrival at Baker Street, Bulman hailed a cab to take him to Deacon's territory. He made an open approach after the hot, traffic-thick, journey. At once he noticed that the Mercedes and the Jaguar were missing but the spaces were unoccupied; Deacon still ruled. Tired and feeling in need of a bath, he trudged up the steps of Deacon's house and rang the bell.

The door opened almost immediately and Vi faced him, a hand on jutting hip, lashes over-black around the hard but beautiful eyes.

"I saw you coming," she said. "You'd better come in quick before we get a bad name."

"Is he at home?" Bulman asked, as he stepped into the hall.

"'Es just gone around to the betting shop. Be back in a minute. He owns it," Vi added, with a glance over her bare shoulder as Bulman followed her swaying hips down the passageway; she was wearing an off-the-shoulder Grecian blouse and a tight skirt.

"You're friendlier," Bulman commented, as Vi showed him into the music room.

She winked at him. "I'm never friendly with coppers. I just wanted you off the bleeding doorstep. Don't touch anything in here, he'll go off his nut."

"What's happened to the cars?" Bulman asked innocently. The door slammed and Bulman smiled quietly; it was the only light relief he had received that day.

He crossed over to a rack of tapes. Deacon had a strangely catholic taste in light classics and old pop songs, now called ballads. Crosby, Sinatra, Ella Fitzgerald, and Peggy Lee. He was still looking at them when Deacon came in.

"Take your 'ands off those, you'll leave grease marks."

"I found Walter Janeski," Bulman said without turning. "Uses other names like Retlaw and Halter. *And Salter.* He admitted paying you thirty grand to kill Tony Sims in a hurry." Bulman turned then. "Tough nut. I wouldn't have got a thing out of him except that someone near and dear to him is in grave trouble, and we are in a position to help. Lives in Little Chalfont in Bucks. Nice area."

Deacon's mouth was still half-open when Bulman added casually, "Thought you should know, Phil. I haven't quite wrapped it up yet. You know that, because I'm not going to take you in. Well, not yet. But I wanted you to know that I know. Give me the names of the boys you use."

"You're off your rocker," Deacon exploded at last. "You're talking rubbish."

"I'm always talking garbage. It's better than knocking people off." Bulman removed one of the tapes to examine its label. "He also mentioned that he'd paid you for knocking off an ex-Yard man called Moody, a backroom Commie named Michael Rossi, a powerful trade unionist, James McLaren. And there was a bloke called Bertrand Hill. Did you know Hill was in MI5? You've been on very dangerous ground, Phil. You still are." Bulman put the tape back. "Pity your Mercedes and Jag are missing; I was going to ask for a lift."

Deacon was shaken to his roots, his face drained. He said hoarsely, "You haven't got a thing on me. You're setting me up."

"You might be right," Bulman replied, gazing noncommittally around the room with its array of acoustics. "But you can prove me right by finishing the job on Sims. Then I'll have it complete. You do realize, of course, that Salter is not the brains behind the killing? He's the last link in the chain before the executioner, which is you. If you knew who was really pulling your strings, Phil, you'd get Vi away damned quick, and you should follow as fast as you can. Unfortunately, I can't let either of you leave the country. That's official. I want your passports."

"Get stuffed. Anyway, I never keep them in the house. You can search it. When you've got a warrant."

"In the bank, are they? Afraid of their being pinched? Or is it that you have several under different names? I want them handed in to the local police station tomorrow. I'll check that you've done it. See you in court."

Bulman opened the door himself and almost bumped into an agitated Vi, who glared hatred at him. As he squeezed past her Bulman said, "With all that gear he's got, you'd have thought he'd have put a wire through to save you listening at keyholes."

"Piss off, you bastard. And leave my Phil alone. 'E wouldn't hurt a pussycat."

"Cheers, Vi. It's not the pussycats I'm worried about. Take good care of him. I shall need him."

21

SCOTT waited outside Dr. Habise's office and did precisely what he had done before when a late patient arrived. He joined the patient under the portico and partly hid his face behind the three empty boxes he was carrying. He made the same excuse to the nurse when she opened the door, and even reminded her of the first occasion when he had arrived too late for the upstairs printers. She vaguely remembered and let him in, and he told her he would leave his delivery outside the printers' reception-office door. He climbed the stairs as she closed the front door.

The wait turned out to be longer than before, but the procedure was the same. The last patient was shown out and a little later the nurse left, after saying good night to Habise.

Scott ran silently down the remaining stairs. Habise's office door was open, and Scott went in. Habise was sitting at his desk, filling out a medical card. He put the card in the index, generally tidied his desk, and rubbed his eyes before he was aware of Scott standing there. He visibly started, "Who the devil are you?"

"I'm the bloke you invited to break in by leaving your alarms off about four weeks ago. It was a wasted effort actually, I was already in the building. Like now."

"I'm calling the police." Habise reached out for the telephone and Scott drew his gun. The plop from the silencer and the sound of the shattered telephone as it crashed off the desk were impossible to separate.

"My God. You're mad." Habise gazed at the receiver still in his hand, the cord snaking to the floor. Scott came around the desk and ripped the cord from the wall socket.

"Open the index box and pull out the card for T. Moody."

Habise sat quite still. He was hanging onto the receiver as if he did not know how to let go. He watched Scott warily; the shot had impressed and frightened him.

Scott stood at the side of Habise so that he could watch both feet and hands. Habise said, "If anybody rings and gets no answer they will send someone around to investigate."

"Why? Don't doctors go home? But you're not talking of patients, are you, doc? You're talking of your extra-medical activities. It would give me great pleasure to put a bullet straight through your scheming head. You helped cover up the murder of an old mate of mine, so be very, very careful. Are you listening?" Scott spoke with intense feeling.

"I'm listening."

"Drop that phone."

It was doubtful if Habise was aware that he was holding the receiver. He glanced at it in surprise, then dropped it to join the ruptured remains of the cradle.

"Now pull out the index tray."

"What do you intend to do with it? That's a list of my patients."

"It's more than that. I'm going to burn the lot."

"You're mad. There are very sick people listed there."

"And some foreigners among them? Foreign embassy staff, maybe?"

Habise did not reply so Scott said, "Keep your hands away from the desk. It's important that you know what's going on, so to save time I'll ask you the important question first. Who instructed you to add Tom Moody to your list of patients?"

"Don't be ridiculous; he came himself."

"Right, doctor. Get this through your head. I'm the bloke who broke out of Albany Prison. The police are after me. So is a bunch of villains run by a bloke called Phil Deacon. He is most likely hired by whoever told you to add Tom Moody to your list. The Foreign Office, or one of its sections, is also after me. They tried to kill me in prison, and now they are trying again. Just what the hell do you think I've got to lose by putting a bullet through your mouth? And I can easily make it look like suicide. You're an accessory to murder. It will look as if you couldn't stand the thought of all the future publicity."

"Murder? I know nothing about murder."

"You're about to. And it won't be nice. Are you one of MI6's tame doctors? Turn one or two foreign diplomats before they go back?"

"I know nothing at all about a murder. Nothing."

"It won't sound like that in court. You or your nurse made out the card. Somebody else entered your name and telephone number in Tom's phone index. You've been taken, old son. But your greatest danger is me. I've got only a few rounds. Just one magazine. I can't afford to waste any more on demonstrations. My life is on the line. So is yours, now. How does it feel?"

Habise was about to raise his hands when Scott shouted, "Don't move." The hands came down slowly.

"Don't let's go through the old pulling-the-fingernails-out routine. You're a doctor. You must know your breaking point. You're not the heroic type." Scott came around the front of the desk and held the gun across it. Still pointing it at Habise, he removed the silencer.

"You wouldn't blow your head out with a silencer on, would you? Anyway, the building is empty but for us, and walls aren't made as solid as these anymore. It's your last chance, doc."

Scott leaned forward. "Now put your hands on the desk," he said. "Come nearer."

Habise was petrified. He could not move; the hole in the barrel of the gun appeared enormous and was growing by the second.

"Norman Murison," he croaked.

"Who?"

"Norman Murison." Habise slumped as if now resigned to whatever happened next.

"On your feet," Scott instructed, not lowering the gun.

Habise had to cling to the desk to rise. He staggered around the side of the desk, using fingertips to steady himself.

Scott positioned himself behind the doctor. "Go to the receptionist's room." He followed Habise through and, once inside the tidy office, told Habise to sit down in front of the desk. Scott picked up the telephone. He did not take his gaze from Habise while he pressed the buttons and kept the gun pointing.

"Is Detective Superintendent Bulman still there? Special Duties."

Bulman came on with a terse, "Yes?"

"Spider. I don't think it matters anymore if you're being monitored. Does the name Norman Murison mean anything to you?"

271

"Bang on, Spider. That's where Corrie went. I've since checked. They were at school together. Close buddies all their lives. Where are you now?"

"Where nobody can find me. I tried to get hold of Habise, but he'd left. I'll be in touch." Scott hung up. "Now we wait," he said.

BULMAN OBTAINED A car with driver; the siren and flasher were used all the way to Harley Street, dissecting the rush hour traffic as if it was life or death. And it could be if he did not reach Harley Street first. On arrival he told the driver to wait directly outside, even though double-parked, and to keep the flasher going; it might act as a deterrent. He ran up the steps and rang the bell. The door was opened by Habise, but Scott was just behind him. They all went into Habise's office.

Bulman said without preamble, "You probably don't realize what you're into, doctor. This isn't a game of turning people or of encouraging defection. It is common murder. There have been several and, innocently or not, you are involved in one of them."

"For God's sake, man, you talk like that when I've been held up at gunpoint by this man who is wanted for breaking out of prison and God knows what else. Arrest him, dammit."

Bulman looked at Scott. "You're under arrest."

"Okay."

Habise was standing near the desk, with Scott to one side and Bulman blocking the door. Habise burst out, "He threatened to shoot me. He's armed."

Bulman turned to Scott again, who had put the gun back in his waistband. "You armed?"

"No."

"He says he's not armed, sir. I'll have him searched back at the Yard. Now, doctor, you are in a very hot seat. Real trouble. I know who Mr. Murison is, and I know the nature of his work. If you inform him of what has happened here I think you realize that he will ditch you. He will disclaim all knowledge of instructions to you. Will you please produce Thomas Moody's medical card for me?"

Habise flipped through the index, partly reassured by Bulman's presence, but disturbed by the strange rapport a top policeman had with a gunman. Bulman took the card and slipped it in his jacket pocket. "Just in case you decided to destroy it, sir."

Bulman stared down at the smashed telephone, which still lay on the
272

floor. "It's time for you to appraise your future, doctor. Does it lie in medicine or intelligence? I have acquired a great deal of evidence that could put you away for some time. A part of it is in my pocket. That, I imagine, would kill off your career. If you inform Mr. Murison of what has taken place here, I shall be unable to protect you. Nobody could. So I'll strike a bargain with you. I won't tell him if you won't. And you'll be off the hook."

"That's easy to say. What about this—this . . ." Habise indicated Scott, who was standing easily.

"We will both give our word. And let me tell you that the word of this man here is absolute. Think it over very carefully, but do not underestimate the problems that surround you."

"All right. I give my word."

"Thank you, sir." Bulman held out a hand. "That is probably the wisest decision you have ever made. Good night to you."

When Scott and Bulman were out on the steps, Scott said, "Do you think he'll keep to it?"

"It's to his advantage. That's all I can say."

Scott noticed the flasher beyond the line of parked cars. "You reckon that will make them hesitate?"

"It will confuse them. You waved a gun at Habise."

"I'd have handed it over to you, but you wouldn't have returned it."

"Don't do anything foolish, Spider. It worries me, but I know what you're up against. Now listen. Deacon gets paid for knocking off certain people. There's a chain of approach and we've been lucky to top and tail it. A fellow known as Salter contacts Deacon, but I don't know who contacts him. I'm now sure it starts from Murison. I don't know the motive; it could be extreme right-wing nationalism. I have no hard evidence, but I'll have to present what I've got to Sir Lewis Hope. If that doesn't work, I have another source."

They had gone down two steps when Habise came out and passed them as if they had never met. They watched him disappear, then Bulman said, "In order to get Deacon off your back, I've told him that I know, which means he'll probably leave the country. You're still too vulnerable, Spider. And so is Maggie. If Murison feels the pincers closing, he'll strike out any way he can. As he did with Tom. We don't know the half. And where does the money come from? Huge sums. It can't come out of normal Treasury finances."

"I'll call on him."

"Think it through."

"I can't hang about thinking. Tonight worked."

"Tonight was not Murison, but a very frightened doctor."

"You shouldn't have let Deacon go. He did Tom and Wally."

"He did far more than that. But I've taken him off your back. We'll catch up with him some other time. Dick Collins is already working on the men Deacon uses. Sooner or later we'll get the actual killers, but that's a matter of routine. Murison is not. I'd better drop you off somewhere."

"I've got nowhere to go. Can you get Maggie out of the flat? If Murison gets desperate, he'll go at her to get me."

"I'll go around there. Put her up at my place."

"You're sticking your neck out too far."

"My neck's already out all the way. Standing here talking to you is enough. Murison's crowd might be watching us right now. They won't try anything with the car there and while I'm here."

"If they're that close I don't fancy Habise's chances."

"No. You sure you'll be all right?"

"I'll take a lift as far as the Strand. Always wanted a ride in a squad car without the cuffs on. Any news of Sophie?"

"None." Bulman shook his head sadly. "Don't be hopeful. She'll turn up one day, but she won't be alive."

They went down the remaining steps and stood at the bottom.

"I'd better bring you completely up to date before we get in the car. I don't want the driver's ears flapping." Bulman talked concisely. When he had finished, Scott asked, "Where does Lord Langley live?"

"He has a spread in Chorley Wood, in Hertfordshire."

"Can you let me have that copy of the receipt?"

"If you give me the gun."

"I can't do that, George. I'm up against the wall."

"I know that better than anyone. But if it got out that I let you keep a gun it could kill our case. It would be damning in court. I've got to act like a copper some time."

"Compromise. I'll keep the gun and give you the ammunition. I need a frightener."

"If it all goes wrong, that will reduce your sentence from twenty-three years to eighteen."

"I'll chance it."

274

Scott slipped the magazine out in the back of the police car.

Taking it, Bulman said, "Now the one in the breech."

Scott cursed quietly, then slowly pulled back the breech so that the driver would not hear. He put the silencer back on; it would look more authentic if he needed it. "Drop me near a phone booth," he asked.

SCOTT RISKED RINGING Rex Reisen and realized what a good job Bulman had done on him when Reisen agreed to loan out Knocker Roberts on short notice. Scott made a big issue of thanking Reisen over his handling of Deacon and of the importance of it. Reisen thrived on gratitude relating to jobs he believed to be for the Crown.

Roberts collected Scott in his blood-red Aston Martin outside Victoria Rail Station. As he climbed in he wondered why Knocker always chose such conspicuous cars, as though he were tempting the police to stop him so that he could prove ownership.

Knocker grinned as he pulled out, the masked side of his face wrinkling like a pickled brain. "How are you, Spider, old cock? Nice to see you. But why are you dressed like a bleeding bank manager, and what the bloody hell have you done to your hair?"

"It's a long story, Knock. Keep your eye on the road."

Roberts bridled. "I'm as good a driver as you, mate."

"Sorry, Knock. I'm tired. I'm on the run and it's wearing me down and my stomach hurts."

"Chorley Wood, ain't it?"

"Straight down the M40."

BOTH MEN KEPT an eye on the possibility of a tail on the short journey north. It would be difficult to find two men more practiced at the art. Both were satisfied that they had not been followed.

But as they sat in the car, the cooling wind cutting through the open windows, Scott considered what Murison might do. With the possible loss of Deacon and his men, Murison would have limited forces. He would be reluctant to use his own men, but he would have to unless he had an alternative to Deacon. And he would group his limited force around the considered danger areas. Langley's house might be one of them.

Brook Park House was an address that needed no street name. It was a local estate of some note and on the south fringe of the scattered, small

Hertfordshire town of Chorley Wood. Asking the way could not be avoided as the shops were closed and they had no local map. Knocker stopped at a filling station, topped up, and received directions from there.

The town was too near for the estate to be considered remote, but it was well tucked away in its own grounds on a country lane. Knocker drove past to establish the position. The drive gates between modern brick pillars were open. Scott caught only a glimpse of a large modern house at the end of a curving drive that bordered a huge front lawn. Knocker drove on a hundred yards and pulled into a recess.

"What's the plan?" he asked.

"The place might be staked out. We'd better see." He calculated that there was little more than half an hour of daylight left.

They climbed out and walked slowly back. They jumped over a farm gate and followed a hedgerow to a long line of laurels that flanked the grounds of the house, occasionally peering through gaps in the greenery. When they were opposite the side of the house they could see a Rolls Royce being sponged down by a shirt-sleeved man.

"There's nowhere to effectively hide in front of the house," Scott commented.

"Would the geezer know if his pad is staked out?" Knocker asked.

"I shouldn't think so. They wouldn't want him to know."

"Then it's got to be the other side of the lane, behind the hedgerows there. There's nowhere else. It's some dump he's got, Spider. Sort of place you used to rob."

Scott did not want to be reminded. "I think we'll try it openly. Turn around and drive up to the front door. You stay in the car and keep your eyes peeled. I'll give a shout if I need you."

"Right." Knocker looked pleased. He pressed his scarred knuckles together and Scott winced.

They went back to the car, and Knocker reversed to face the house. He drove off and entered the gates, the gravel drive crunching under the tires. As they approached the house the Rolls was moving toward a garage, away from them. On the side they approached were tennis courts lying well back. Scott noticed the alarm high on the wall before Knocker swung around in front of the arched porch to pull up.

Scott climbed out and rang the bell. A maid opened the door. Very politely, Scott said, "I would like to see Lord Langley. My name is Scott."

276

"Does he know you're coming, sir?"

"No. Tell him it's about the receipt Mr. Bulman showed him."

The maid, not sure, asked Scott to wait, but closed the door on him. She returned quickly and asked him to step in. Scott followed her through a spacious hall to a book-lined library-cum-study. There was a large desk and a smaller one on which sat a television set with share prices flickering on the screen. Langley, as tall as Scott himself, switched the set off and went behind his desk, as if he needed something between his visitor and himself.

"We haven't met before, have we?" Langley asked.

"No." Scott produced the receipt, much as Bulman had done. "This is not the copy the fuzz showed you. It's another. They're becoming common. I don't know what you fed the copper, but I want the true story."

Langley's hand went to the desk drawer he had already opened. He pulled out an old army Webley, but when he looked up he found Scott was already pointing a gun at him. Scott said, "You can chance your arm if you like. It's in your hand. Fire it. You'll have to get me first shot because you'll never get another one in."

Langley hesitated. The Webley was barely clear of the drawer. "What do you want from me?"

"I certainly don't want to harm you in any way. But I will protect myself." Scott held the receipt up. "For some reason, partly because of this, I'm on the run. I've nowhere to sleep, and I've nothing to lose if I plug you. All I want from you is the history of this thing. If it incriminates you, it won't matter to me. Can we save a lot of time? Put down the gun and get on with it?"

Langley had not used the gun for many years, and he had never been proficient with it. He was quite cool while he appraised Scott, who was clearly a man with nerve. He let the Webley drop back into the drawer, which he closed.

"That was sensible," Scott said. "Are we likely to be disturbed?"

"I don't live the life of a monk."

Scott crossed over and turned the door key. "Just in case. What does the receipt mean, Lord Langley?"

"I don't intend to tell you. You can take it from there."

"Do you mind if I open the window? It's warm in here."

"You have the gun. How can I stop you?"

"Come around the front of the desk. Stand there and don't move."

277

Scott backed to the windows, unlatched one, pushed it open and called out, "I need you." He could see the Aston Martin a short distance away. He did not let his gaze drift from Langley. He stepped away from the window, and a few seconds later Knocker climbed through. Scott closed the window again.

"This man," Scott said, "is going to get the truth from you. He'll do it brutally because he finds it effective. And he enjoys it." As Langley's mouth opened, Scott aimed the gun at his head and snapped, "Don't do it. If you bring anyone in, I'll shoot them."

Knocker circled behind Langley. Langley tried to watch both men and found it impossible. He still showed no fear.

"You've got guts, sir," Scott said appreciatively. "It's sad that we'll have to spread them around on open view."

Langley swung around as Knocker came up behind him. Knocker jabbed him under the heart and rammed a gag in his mouth as Langley doubled in agony. He then held him by the hair to prevent his falling all the way. Langley retched behind the pad. Scott nodded, anxious now because Langley had gone so pale. Knocker tore the pad out of Langley's mouth and looked to Scott for further instructions.

Scott crossed the room and helped Langley to rest against the desk edge. Langley was rasping. "Another blow like that could kill you at your age," Scott pointed out. "And that's the gentle stuff."

"All right." Langley held up a hand in surrender. "All right." He peered sideways at Knocker.

"I know," Scott said. "He's like granite. You could hit him with your Webley and it would make no impression."

Langley was holding his ribs. "My God. It's come to this."

"Tell us about it."

Langley nodded slowly. His face was gray, which worried Scott. "Whatever you tell us will not be made public," Scott promised.

"There's some brandy in the bureau over there." Langley pointed. "Could you get it?"

Knocker brought a bottle and a glass, which he half-filled and handed to Langley. "I only tapped you, mate," he said aggrieved. He did not pour Scott or himself a drink.

Langley sipped and a little color came back to his face. "May I sit down?"

Knocker pulled a chair out for him. Langley said, "It's a ridiculous story really. Utterly ridiculous. The signature on the receipt was done by me." He laughed a little light-headedly. "Do you know, that's only the second time I've ever actually admitted that." He paused to suck in air.

"Quite simply, I wanted to be independent of my father. Even as a youth I had a head for finance. I could see that it was only a question of time before the family business collapsed. The war gave it a temporary reprieve, but the inevitable finally happened." Langley pushed himself up from the chair after putting his glass down on the desk. "It's all right," he said as Knocker moved toward him. He took in a great gulp of air. "It's even good to talk about it after all this time."

"So your old man gave you thirty grand to give to Mosley and you decided to set yourself up with it," Scott said tersely.

"That wasn't the sole reason. My father saw himself as something of a philanthropist. He gave freely to keep his image. His accountants warned him. The money I took was a salvage job. And, later, after the war I made it work."

"But someone knew about it and put the screws on?"

"Oh, it was ridiculous. My best friend, Dickie Urquin, and I were going through some of my father's papers. Father was terribly untidy. Dickie actually found the receipt, and I foolishly told him about it. It was a huge joke between us at the time. We roared our heads off. Much later I discovered he had not put the receipt back, and then, when things were going quite well, he openly blackmailed me."

Langley picked up the brandy. "I couldn't believe it. I certainly did not want anyone else to know that I had founded my business on stolen money, least of all my father. He would not have prosecuted, of course, but the shock might have killed him. And I did not want my reputation as a banker to be stillborn. It could have finished me before I was wholly under way. So I paid sums I could afford."

Langley rubbed his ribs and gazed reproachfully at Knocker.

"The odd thing was that Dickie told me that the money was not for him but for a good cause in the national interest. At that time I did not know whether to believe him, but eventually I accepted it. Subsequently, as my business grew so did the demands, but they were never outrageous. They were paid into an account in Jersey."

"What's the name?"

"It's never changed. Union Holdings."

"Do you still pay?"

"Oh, for many years now it's been routed through a Bahamaian company. It would be very difficult to trace."

"That hasn't answered my question."

Langley smiled as he looked at Scott. "There will be no further payments. Once I knew the receipt had come to light, I decided to stop."

"So you told Norman Murison."

Langley jerked visibly. Scott added, "We know what he does. I wondered if you knew. Among other things, he pays out vast sums to have certain people killed. You could be one of them if you've stopped payments."

Langley was shaken. "It can make little difference. So much has been paid over the years that if the money has been properly invested it will be self-perpetuating. It hasn't always been Norman Murison. There have been many others down the years. I sometimes thought it was a case of natural selection. A continuing coterie of identical interests. Reason, and knowledge of him, suggested to me that he was currently in control."

"But Murison is the one who has turned rogue. Whatever the money was used for before, it would seem that the purpose has changed. Is it your impression that there is an elite section within an organization?"

"I have often considered so."

"You could have stopped paying a long time ago, Lord Langley, when perhaps more reasonable people controlled the funds."

"Oh, I know as time passed the receipt was less damning. Publication still wouldn't have done me any good, of course. But it wasn't that so much. I had been paying all those years. A vindictive person could have pointed the tax authorities toward me and gone deeply into the figures. Union Holdings could have moved away from obvious detection, meanwhile."

Scott put his gun away. "I'm sorry we had to clout you. Weren't you worried all those years?"

"Not at all. I was never extended financially. And after a while I really did believe that the money was being used sensibly."

"Perhaps. But it must have been used for purposes that could not be met from normal Treasury funds. A slush fund the government didn't know about. Who's died because of it? There might have been other

Murisons down the years. More subtle. Not so stupidly over the top. If it is run by a coterie, why not be openly part of the organization? Murison has to be stopped, Lord Langley."

"I have only your word for it that he's using the funds in the way you say that he is."

"Well, I just hope you don't find out the hard way. Do you know a Doctor Habise in Harley Street?

"No."

"Have you heard of an ex-Yard detective called Tom Moody?"

"Should I have?"

"I'm satisfied Murison had Moody killed for lifting the receipt. Perhaps not because of that alone, nor even for finding out what you've just told us, but for fear of his discovering what he was doing with the money. And he's still after me. I've still got to negotiate bomb alley. And Murison well knows it."

"He's a clever man."

"I know he is. We'll get out of your hair. I'm obliged to you."

"What are you going to do with what I've told you?"

Scott smiled. "It'll never go public," he assured. "Bank on it. Did you ever pay your old man back?"

Langley returned the smile. He was thoughtful. "Not directly. He would have squandered it. You're a strange man, Mr. Scott. I feel I can trust you."

"Fine. But don't trust Murison."

Knocker Roberts, who had struggled to understand the entirety of what had passed between Scott and Langley, followed them to the front door. He climbed into the driver's seat of the Aston Martin, and Scott jumped in the other side. Langley stood on the porch, eyes reflective, not quite certain of what he should do. Then he went in. Scott knew that there was no risk of Langley ringing the police.

Knocker drove off, disappointed at not being extended. He drove toward the gates and braked as a motorcyclist pulled up in front of him.

"Duck," Scott yelled, flinging himself to the floor. A burst of sub-machine gun fire rent the summer silence and scattered birds from the hedgerows. The windshield smashed into fragments as it blew out over the inside seats. Shots hit the car, and the metal screamed in agony. There was a roar of the motorcycle revving and, as it drew away, Scott and Knocker raised their heads carefully. Once they realized the motorcycle had gone, Knocker let out a tremendous roar, thumped the accelerator, and shot between the gates in a wild skid.

Blood was flowing down Knocker's face in wide runnels, and, as Scott noticed it, he felt it trickling down his own. The blood must have been caused by the shattered glass for he was sure he had not been hit, but Knocker had a rent at the shoulder of his jacket where the padding now puffed out.

The light was poor but they could see the faint dust trail of the disappearing motorcycle. The Aston Martin was accelerating fast. The expression on Knocker's blood-streaked face was terrible to see; Scott guessed what he had in mind, and he was not sure that he wanted to stop him. In this mood nobody could stop Knocker. As he gained on the motorcycle he bawled out, "See what he's done to my car? I'll get that bastard."

Scott sat back; there was nothing he could do but shout back, "He still has the gun." But the warning had no impact on Knocker.

When a brief throb of gunfire sounded above the engine, both men barely ducked. Nobody traveling at that speed could turn on his seat to fire accurately. The cycle started to weave as Knocker gained ground, but the car was held on a straight course. Whatever Knocker had in mind would have to happen before they reached Chorley Wood. Knocker increased speed and was now on the tail of the motorcyclist, who turned with the gun but could not find an angle to fire; the car was too close.

"Now, you bastard." Knocker edged the bike, and it flew up the small embankment and into the hedgerow. Knocker pulled up with a scream of brakes and burning tires, jumped out, and ran back, with Scott following. Knocker went through the gap where the motorcycle had torn through. The driver was moving when Knocker reached him. The crash helmet was still on but the goggles were broken. Knocker twisted the man's neck as if he were a chicken, and Scott heard the break as he came panting up.

"He's dead," Scott said breathlessly, when Knocker refused to let go. "We've got to get away from here."

The message finally got through. The cycle was some feet away, the wheels still spinning. Near the corpse was a Stirling submachine gun.

"Leave it as it is," Scott instructed. "Let's get away before it's too late."

They ran back to the car. Knocker bandaged his hand with an oil rag and punched out the jagged remains of the windshield. Scott managed to stop his taking a more critical look at the damage. "Chelsea," he said as they moved off. "But first turn off into one of these narrow lanes. We must wipe the blood off or we'll be stopped. After that I must ring Bulman."

"IT'S GOOD OF you to see me so late, Sir Lewis."

"I've had to come back here for this, George. I left a dinner party at your insistence. It had better be good." Hope was still wearing a dinner jacket.

Bulman thought the Thames was more alluring at night, the lights from the opposite bank twinkling across the water, and the meager night river traffic passing like leisurely stars against the dark background.

"I don't think it could be more important," Bulman replied. "The integrity of this department is at stake, and, if I may say so, sir, your personal reputation could be on the line."

"Be careful, George. You're being insolent again."

"To a point where I say that you've been blind, Sir Lewis. I've made a detailed report, and I have a copy put away."

"Don't dare threaten me, George. Get to the point or get out."

"I'll get to the point, but the threat is real. There's a friend of mine out there, on the run, his life at stake, because of a series of bureaucratic blunders kindled on the old boy network. Norman Murison and his clique are using a private slush fund to hire killers to knock off those who they consider to be enemies of the state. And, to some extent, you have unwittingly helped them."

Hope sat quite still. Then he said, "I've never in my life heard anything so monstrous."

"That's the reply I expected and that's why I've hidden a copy of my report. Insolent or not, Sir Lewis, it is in your best interest to hear what I have to say." Bulman was too restless to sit down, but now he had to curb his impatience while he carefully outlined what Scott had been told by Lord Raymond Langley. He then listed those killings he believed to be attributed to Murison, and he related the role of Dr. Habise and the false medical card. He named Salter and his connection with Deacon and the weight of circumstantial evidence that pointed to Murison.

Hope listened nervously, but in silence. When Bulman had finished he said, "You've put up an impressive case. But it still remains circumstantial."

"Lord Langley's statement is not circumstantial. I have the original receipt safely tucked away. We have the name of the account and the bank. It will be easy to check out payments. My guess is that a large withdrawal will be found prior to each murder. Scott was fired at on leaving Lord Langley. The man who tried to murder him is dead, lying in a field outside Chorley Wood. The local police were notified just before I came here. Would you like a bet that the corpse was one of Murison's wild men? For some reason, Deacon had decided to opt out. The last I heard was that he'd gone to Brazil. But Commander Collins is working on what remains of Deacon's organization. He'll break them down in time. We'll have to wait for Deacon himself."

Lewis peered at Bulman a little awkwardly. "Who are the people you think were murdered?"

Bulman listed them. "There may be far more. He killed anyone who came close to finding out what he was up to. The one that puzzles me is Bertrand Hill. He was one of our lot, wasn't he? Ostensibly committed suicide."

Lewis's long fingers massaged his temples.

"Odd, as it may seem, he is one man who lends conviction to your argument. He was rather like Bettaney, currently serving thirty years for treachery. He was unstable, but one had to be sure. We were still deciding what to do about him when he killed himself."

Bulman said cynically, "Murison obviously thought you were taking too long. He did your job for you."

Lewis did not reply. He sat there gazing at the desk, face drawn with a haunted look in his eyes. Eventually, he said, "There was always a small hard core in SIS who wanted sterner action against men like Burgess and McLean and Philby."

"It looks as though they finally got together on it. When Murison took over he became judge, jury, and executioner. Like all such men who operate like that—in the patriotic conviction that they are ridding the country of political disease—they create a bigger one themselves and bring down the very people they claim to protect. What do we do about him?"

"We don't want a public trial."

"We can't bring him to one until we have the hard evidence. It will come, but slowly. I agree, though, it's best under the carpet. But something has to be done about him *now*, Sir Lewis."

Hope had difficulty in meeting Bulman's eye. Bulman added, in a more conciliatory tone, "I mentioned the old-boy network. Well, it's true. The Foreign Office asks the Home Office a favor, which seems reasonable enough. I'm quite sure Murison had an impressive file on Willie Scott to convince his boss, who convinced you. I'm equally sure I can tear it apart. But I used the network, too. I obtained part of the information I needed by using old friends. Most times it works for us, until someone like Murison abuses the system. I know Ashton is involved. We've got to winkle out the others."

"I'll speak to Sir Roland Powell." Lewis glanced up. "You don't think . . . ?"

Bulman shook his head. "I think Norman Murison was nearer the top of the heat than anyone before him. The slush fund was an enormous temptation. Strangely enough, I have the feeling that it has not been abused on a personal basis. It was used for his beliefs. The loyalty was grossly warped, but the personal integrity was there. Like so many of those they oppose, they have political tunnel vision and a vast amount of money to indulge it."

KNOCKER FOUND A space not far from Murison's Chelsea house. It had been dark for some time. "You want me to go in with you?" Knocker asked hopefully.

"I want you to watch my back. There might be someone keeping an eye on the house. If you hear a shot while I'm in there, ring Bulman at one of these numbers." Scott passed over a slip. "If you can't get him, ring the nearest police station."

"But you've got a silencer," Knocker pointed out, misunderstanding Scott.

"I've got no bloody rounds. The gun's empty. So it won't be this one you'll hear, but someone plugging me. Okay?"

"Empty? Now he tells me. Okay. I'll be around. I hope you know what you're doing."

Scott climbed out and crossed the road. He rang the bell, and the door was opened by a pleasant-looking woman in her forties.

"Is Mr. Murison in?"

"He is, but it's rather late. Is he expecting you?"

"My name is Scott. I can arrange another time if he can't see me now."
Scott could judge by the position of her hand that she was covering a
panic button.

"You don't mind if I close the door while I ask him. One hears so
many things."

"Not at all." Scott felt sorry for her. If she was Mrs. Murison, then
one way or the other her life was about to be ruined. She came back,
asked him in, and showed him into a small, comfortable sitting room.

Murison was standing by the draped bay windows; as soon as his wife
had closed the door to leave them alone he produced a Colt, with
silencer, from behind his back. Scott sat down in the nearest chair.

"Keep your hands on the arms, Mr. Scott. My word, you've caused
me some trouble. It was good of you to solve my problems by calling."

"Don't kid yourself, I have help outside."

"And that is where it will stay. It's too late for a deal, if that's your
idea. The time for that was when you were still in prison."

"I wouldn't do a deal with someone like you, Murison. I wouldn't
have the time to watch my back. I called because I know you're having
labor problems. You must have wondered why the lines of communication have broken down. Well, Deacon has pushed off to Brazil with Vi.
And Salter, whom you probably don't know but who was the final link
to Deacon, was pulled in and is now under surveillance, so he can't make
a move."

Scott weighed up Murison and decided he well knew how to use the
gun. "That left you with problems. There can't be many in your own
happy band in this country who'll drop someone just like that. You had
one, for sure. The last I saw of him, he was lying in a field outside
Chorley Wood, with a broken neck."

"Am I to make some sense of this?"

"We have proved Tom Moody's medical card at Habise's to be
phony. Oh, yes, and we have the original Mosley receipt. You left it
with Peter Corrie for safekeeping. Old school friend, was he? Don't
trust deposit boxes? We haven't all the names of the people you knocked
off, but we have Michael Rossi, James McLaren, Bertrand Hill, Wally
Cooper, and, of course, the one man responsible for bringing George
Bulman and myself into it, Tom Moody. So cut out the crap, Murison.
Sir Roland Powell is being informed. You're cooked."

Murison stood with a faint smile toying along the line of his thin lips.

286

"Do you know why this has happened? Don't you understand the importance?"

"Oh, sure. Wally Cooper lifted the receipt for Tom Moody, and they were getting too close."

"I don't mean those two."

"I do. I just wanted you to know from me because Tom was a mate of mine."

"There won't be a trial."

"I suppose not. You'll just have to sit around waiting for someone to kill you. Your turn will come." Scott got up.

"Don't be so fast, Scott. Perhaps we *can* still do a deal. You can refuse to give evidence. After all, it will all be in private."

"No chance."

"Ring your wife. You might change your mind."

Scott went cold. He followed Murison's gaze to the telephone table and crossed to it. Before he picked up the receiver he said,

"You're dead if anything's happened to her."

"Nothing has. And nothing will if you are sensible. If you are not, I have nothing to lose by destroying her. And you, too. Phone her."

Scott dialed. He kept his features rigid, not wanting to show his feeling of desperation. "This is Willie Scott." He listened and glanced across at Murison who was smiling cynically, aware that Scott was not speaking to Maggie. Scott listened for some time then he said, "Put her on." When Maggie came on the line he said, "Keep it cool, Mag. I can't say much now. Everything's okay. I'll be home in a minute. Put the bodyguard back on." Scott waited, then passed the receiver to Murison. "He wants to speak to you."

Murison, sure of himself again, took the receiver. His face changed as Scott said, "It's the police. They're keeping an eye on her." He pointed to the gun. "You know what to do with that, don't you?" He was through the door while a pale-faced Murison was still holding the telephone.

THEY MET AT the Connaught. Bulman assured the others that Sir Lewis Hope was picking up the tab, a fact he described as conscience money. Scott and Maggie had been reunited for a week, and Maggie was blooming. She felt sorry for Betty Moorcroft, the fourth member of the party; Maggie had liked Tom Moody a great deal.

They ate well, but Betty had never doubted what it was all about. She waited until the liqueurs arrived before she asked, "Well?" directing this at Bulman.

"You were right," said Bulman. "Tom didn't slip on a bar of soap."

"So who killed him? And what will happen to him?"

"That's more difficult to answer," Bulman replied, glancing at Scott and Maggie. "You know the sort of work he did."

Betty closed her eyes. She appeared to be tired, as if the events of the last few weeks had happened to her and not the others.

"So he goes free," she said listlessly.

"Oh, no. No way. It's been dealt with, Betty. Believe me. Justice has been done."

"So I'll have to settle for that?"

"Do you want a cock-and-bull?"

"No. Thank you for what you've done."

"It was nothing," Scott said, taking Maggie's hand under the table. "Just plodding routine."

Bulman agreed and called for more drinks. When Betty resisted he said, "Listen. Someone else is paying the bill. He can afford it, okay? And he's fixed the fuzz for breatheralyser."

They laughed quietly. Scott and Bulman exchanged glances. How could they tell her that Murison had left his house just after Scott. He had not shot himself. He had tossed the gun over Westminster Bridge and, a little later, had thrown himself in front of a train at Charing Cross Underground. Ashton and three others had since been suspended and were awaiting their subsequent fate. And the long toll of deaths, many overseas, were still filtering in and had changed nothing.

288